ONE NIGHT
MORE

ONE NIGHT
MORE

Mandy Baxter

ZEBRA BOOKS
KENSINGTON PUBLISHING CORP.
http://www.kensingtonbooks.com

ZEBRA BOOKS are published by

Kensington Publishing Corp.
119 West 40th Street
New York, NY 10018

All Kensington titles, imprints and distributed lines are available at special quantity discounts for bulk purchases for sales promotion, premiums, fund-raising, educational or institutional use.

Special book excerpts or customized printings can also be created to fit specific needs. For details, write or phone the office of the Kensington Special Sales Manager. Attn.: Special Sales Department. Kensington Publishing Corp., 119 West 40th Street, New York, NY 10018. Phone: 1-800-221-2647.

Zebra and the Z logo Reg. U.S. Pat. & TM Off.

First Printing: September 2014
ISBN-13: 978-1-4201-3479-7
ISBN-10: 1-4201-3479-5

First Electronic Edition: September 2014
eISBN-13: 978-1-4201-3480-3
eISBN-10: 1-4201-3480-9

10 9 8 7 6 5 4 3 2 1

Printed in the United States of America

For Niki. May you find the perfect grilled cheese.

ACKNOWLEDGMENTS

A huge thanks to my family for the ridiculous amount of patience they have with me when I'm writing like a fiend and under deadline. I love you guys! I especially have to thank my husband, Juan, who got me out of many a sticky plot point with this book. I don't know what I'd do without your help.

Special thanks goes to Delhia Alby, who was indispensable in helping me with my French translations. When you have someone translating dirty talk to another language for you, you know you've found a true friend. Also, to Shawntelle Madison for helping me to hone my tech speak. Anyone who knows me can tell you that my tech jargon doesn't expand past "Internet" and "e-mail." Thanks for making me sound smart!

This book wouldn't have been possible, though, without my amazing editor, Esi Sogah, who truly whipped the story into shape and helped me find my way in uncharted waters and my agent of awesomeness, Natanya Wheeler. I'd need an entire book to thank you properly. Your support, hard work, and your belief in me and what we're doing kept me going when I was ready to throw in the towel. Thank you! And also . . . tenacity!

As always, I take full responsibility for any and all mistakes. And to those I might have forgotten to thank in my writer's brain haze, you know who you are and what you mean to me.

Chapter One

"I can't believe you snagged this detail, you lucky son of a bitch."

Galen Kelly quirked a brow and raised his glass in a silent salute. "Luck has nothing to do with it, Landon. I *earned* this detail."

"After a couple of months in Louisiana, you think a few weeks back in Portland is enough to keep me from being pissy over you ditching me for greener pastures? I think the elevation is getting to you," Landon scoffed. "You're the luckiest bastard I've ever met. Handpicked by Monroe for the SOG program, and don't even get me started on how you breezed through the training."

Granted, a couple of weeks back home weren't long enough. And despite his attitude, Galen knew Landon had missed the shit out of him. They were as close as brothers, and he'd lost track of how many nights they'd sat in this very booth at Score, the local sports pub that had been like a second home to them in their rookie days. Now, at twenty-nine, Galen already felt like a seasoned member of the U.S. Marshals Service, though he knew a superior officer or ten who might disagree with him.

Landon was only giving him shit, but in truth, Galen had never wanted anything more than to prove himself the best man for the job. For the past month and a half he'd trained at Camp Beauregard in Louisiana for the U.S. Marshals Service's elite Special Operations Group. The number of applicants accepted into the program was small, but the number of marshals who came through the program with credentials was even smaller. Serving as the head of personal security for the U.S. ambassador to France for the next year would elevate his career to the next level.

"Yeah, yeah," Landon remarked, tossing back what was left of his Jack and Coke. "You get to go play in France for a year, while I'm stuck here doing prisoner transfers."

Landon liked to bitch, but he lived for the job. They'd gone through basic training together at Glynco. It was Landon who'd pushed Galen to go ahead with the application for the SOG program after their supervisory deputy, Curt Monroe, suggested him as a potential candidate.

"You could apply for the program, you know," Galen replied. "Live the glamorous life of a moving target for foreign dignitaries. Or wait around on call twenty-four-seven to be flown halfway across the country or God knows where and throw yourself into dangerous situations at a moment's notice. Good times."

"No way, man," Landon said with a laugh. "I hate fancy foreign food almost as much as I hate being on call. One day without ribs or a cheeseburger and I'd go out of my mind. You play the part of human shield and eat escargot. My ass is staying here. I'm going for another Jack. You want anything?"

Galen swished what was left of his beer around in the mug. "Nah. I'm good." He had a 10 AM flight to Louisiana, where he had another stack of paperwork to fill out before he headed on to Paris. As it was, he'd be lucky to drag his ass out of bed in time to make the flight.

As he watched Landon weave his way through the crowd, his gaze settled on a trio of women at the back end of the pub. Two blondes leaned against the bar, facing a third woman with long, chestnut-colored hair, her back angled toward Galen. They raised their shot glasses in a toast, laughing before they tossed back some neon, fruity-looking drink. His attention began to wander until he caught a guy from the corner of his eye. Tall, a little on the grungy side, too lanky—not to mention his shifty eyes and uptight, twitchy stance— he had suspicious creeper or strung-out tweaker written all over him. Galen's instincts were sharp. He had years of experience dealing with the criminal set. And this guy was trouble. Chatting up the group of women with a smarmy grin plastered on his face, Galen watched as the guy reached out and took the hand of the brunette and tried to bring it to his lips.

Everything about his behavior indicated this guy was a skilled predator. After months of classes in human behavior, Galen had learned to read body language well. From their demonstrative actions— wide, sweeping hand gestures, the way they tossed back their heads as they laughed, and loud voices— Galen surmised the blondes to be more outgoing. The brunette, on the other hand, stood relatively still, her drink clutched in her hand as if it grounded her. The creeper passed up the blondes, presumably to hit on the one who looked like the easiest mark. Galen's spine stiffened, his hand instinctively reaching for where his shoulder holster usually hung—a habit he'd developed over the years—only to remember he wasn't carrying his gun. Though, by the way Creeper's target jerked her hand out of his grasp and laid into him with a string of words that Galen could only guess translated to "fuck off," he decided that her shy appearance had been deceiving.

Unfortunately, the SOB didn't give up easily. Round two ended much as round one, with a cool rebuff. Galen smiled, impressed with her spirit. She turned on the creeper, putting the bar to her back. Smart girl. With her friends at either side of her and the bar behind her, she'd taken a defensive stance. She brushed a wavy lock of dark chestnut hair away from her face, her hazel eyes narrowed in a silent threat. Galen forgot all about Landon or anything else as he studied her. He couldn't tell from this far away, but it looked like her nose was dotted with freckles, which were also scattered haphazardly across her cheeks. Her mouth was drawn into a hard line, but even so, Galen could tell her lips were full and lusciously dark pink. He smiled as he watched her poke a finger at Creeper's face before turning her back to him, all but dismissing his failed attempts at being marginally charming.

Intuition tugged at his senses, a tingle that dribbled from the crown of his head and trickled down his back in an icy shiver. Point apparently made, she turned back toward the bar and set her drink beside her, but Galen sensed this guy wasn't done with her yet. He kept his eyes glued to the woman. Even with her back turned to him, he was intrigued by the waves of hair that reached her shoulder blades, down the curve of her back to where her fingers fiddled with the cell phone clutched in her grasp at her side. Creeper sidled back down the bar, all but ignored by the woman he'd try to win over. He tucked a hand in his pocket and produced a cellophane baggie containing a few tiny white pills. Slipping one from the baggie, his arm jutted out as if he was stretching and he dropped it into her unattended drink. As stealthily as he'd moved in, Creeper slunk away, watching with sick anticipation as the woman who'd so effectively shot him down, turned to retrieve the glass and brought it to her lips.

Galen shot out of the booth, none too graciously nudging people out of his way as he raced toward the bar. He scooped the drink out of the woman's hand, sloshing half of it on his own shirtsleeve and set it down forcefully on the bar. "Don't drink that," he said.

She looked from Galen's face to the bar and back, her jaw slightly slack. "Huh?"

A smile tugged at Galen's lips. That one dumbfounded sound was cute as hell. "Hold that thought." He turned and headed after the creeper, who'd taken Galen's interference as his cue to get the hell out of Dodge.

He might not have caught the bastard if Landon hadn't been paying attention and abandoned his trek to the bar to see what was up. They'd worked together for years, and he'd obviously slipped back into old patterns, noticed that shit was going down and jumped in to help, cutting off the back exit. The asshole had no choice but to double back the way he came. Galen rammed his shoulder into Creeper's gut, taking him down in a tackle that sent the weaker man sprawling to the floor. In one fluid motion, he flipped the guy onto his stomach and wrenched his hands behind his back while holding him firmly in place with one knee. He reached down and whispered in the asshole's ear, "You fucked up big-time, buddy."

Galen relaxed his leg, letting his full weight down on the guy and ignoring Creeper's grunt of pain and labored breath as he waited for Landon to pick his way back through the crowd, all eyes turned to the excitement near the back exit. "Cuffs?" he asked when Landon was in earshot.

He made a show of patting his pockets. "You know, I must have left my spare set in the truck. Jesus, Galen, can't you even go out for a drink without going all Wyatt Earp on the place?"

The bartender and a couple of bouncers joined them, and Landon instructed the bartender to call the Portland Police Bureau while Galen turned Creeper over to the bouncers, who'd keep him in one of the back offices until the cops could show up to take over. He exchanged a few details with the bouncers, instructing them to search the guy's pockets for drugs. And if that wasn't enough for PPB to make an arrest, there was a drink on the bar they might want to save for forensics. "You're a show-off, you know that?" Landon asked, clapping Galen on the back. "I'm glad you're leaving town. I forgot what a glory hound you are."

Galen chuckled, only half-listening to what Landon said. Bright hazel eyes studied him from several feet away, that same dumbfounded look puckering her brow. Landon followed Galen's gaze and gave an amused snort. "Yeah, you're the luckiest son of a bitch I've ever met," he said. He grabbed Galen's hand and pulled him close in a half-hug. "I've got an early shift in the morning, so I'm outta here. Have fun in Paris, brother, and keep your ass safe."

Harper Allen's eyes were glued to the spot on the floor where, seconds before, the nasty asshole who'd hit on her had been knocked on his ass, flipped on his face like a human pancake, and pinned to the floor. All she'd wanted was a fun night to celebrate her recent graduation from the University of Portland and the journalism degree she'd worked four hard years to get. She hadn't expected to be thrown into a scenario right out of an episode of *Southland*.

"Holy crap, Harper, did you see him take that guy out? I mean, shit, that's one way to make an introduction," her friend Sophie shouted. Put a few drinks in that girl and her voice amplified from fifteen to about fifty. Harper averted her gaze, suddenly conscious of the fact that she must look like a fish out of water with her mouth hanging open and her eyes bulging out of her head. "Boy is *fine*, too," Sophie added, as if Harper needed someone to point out that fact. "It must be your lucky night, girl."

Lucky? Not quite how she'd describe what just happened. She stole a glance toward the bar at her discarded bourbon and Coke. What in the hell was in that drink that had warranted something so drastic? Either the mystery man had saved her ass, or this was officially the strangest way she'd ever been hit on.

Like, ever. "What do you think it's all about?" she asked, turning back to Sophie.

"Who cares?" Harper's cousin, Addison, chimed in. "I wonder if we took up a collection, if we could get him to do that again!"

Harper gave Addison a wry smile as she pictured her offering up a wad of one-dollar bills for a repeat performance. She focused her attention on her would-be savior and wondered if he was the sort of guy who enjoyed being the center of attention. From the way he ignored the murmurings and pointed fingers of the people around him, she doubted he needed the validation. He stood not ten feet from where he'd performed the graceful football tackle, talking to another guy. They leaned in to each other in one of those typical tough-guy bro hugs, knocking their shoulders together. His friend gave him one last clap on the back and left. Alone, with everyone around him giving him plenty of space, he looked up and fixed his gaze directly on her.

The intensity of his stare sent a riot of butterflies adrift in Harper's stomach. Sophie said something low and Addison broke out into a fit of laughter, but their conversation was white noise in the back of Harper's mind. The rhythmic thrum of her heart rushed in her ears as her mystery hero started toward her, his rolling gait reminding Harper of a sleek lion with the night's dinner in its sights.

"Oh, yum!" Sophie exclaimed, again, *way* too loud, her eyes stuck to him like Velcro. "I want to lick him right—" Harper's leg jutted out as if on its own, her heel catching Sophie in the shin. "Ow! What the hell, Harp?"

"Oh my God," Harper hissed in Sophie's ear. "Shut up. He's coming over here."

Before Sophie could get a word in edgewise, he stepped up to her. "Sorry about that," he said, jutting his chin toward the bar.

"It's okay," Harper replied with a nervous laugh. "Do you always tackle strangers after stealing drinks from women? Or do you really have an aversion to bourbon and Coke?"

He flashed her a wicked grin that made Harper's bones go soft. "I'm not usually so grabby."

"He can grab me any day," Sophie whispered in Harper's ear, and she swung out with a hip, knocking her friend back a few steps.

"Oh, so you made an exception for me?" she teased.

"He slipped something into your drink."

"I knew that guy was nasty!" Addison said from somewhere behind her.

As if she couldn't help herself, Harper's voice dropped to a husky murmur. "I guess that sort of makes you my hero, doesn't it?"

He smiled and Harper flushed with warmth. She hoped to hell she wasn't blushing, because this guy had clearly stepped right out of the pages of a Marvel comic. All he was missing was a cape. Her inner damsel in distress was totally swooning.

"How about I buy you a drink?" he suggested. "One that hasn't been tampered with."

"No way," Harper said with a shake of her head. "I'm buying *you* a drink."

Harper chanced a sideways glance at Sophie, who mouthed, *Oh my God!* as her knees buckled in a mock swoon. Harper smiled, her eyes widening in silent agreement. Guys this gorgeous—or charming—never paid much attention to her. They usually zeroed in on girls like Sophie or Addison who had bigger personalities. It wasn't like Harper was a wallflower. She didn't suffer from a lack of self-confidence, but she didn't exactly stand out, either.

"Hey, man, thanks for taking that guy down," the bartender said as they approached the bar. He reached out to shake Harper's hero's hand. "Several bars in the area have had complaints about someone slipping roofies into drinks. I'd be willing to bet he's the guy. What'll you have? This round is on the house."

"Looks like you'll have to buy me the next round," Harper's mystery man leaned in and murmured close to her ear. She shivered at the near contact and couldn't help but find it exciting that she didn't know his name yet. An anonymous hero who stepped in to save the day. She wondered if this was how Mary Jane Watson felt the first time Spider-Man came to her rescue.

Like the good friends they were, Addison and Sophie melted into the scenery, striking up a conversation with a small group of people farther down the bar and leaving Harper alone with her hero. The bartender slid a fresh bourbon and Coke toward her and popped the cap off a bottle of Stella Artois for her hero. Should she ask for his name? It seemed silly to keep referring to him like he was some sort of Superman. But no guy had ever tackled another man on her behalf before, and it was the most chivalrous thing anyone had ever done for her.

"So," she began, taking a sip of her drink for a little liquid courage. "I know you enjoy tackling would-be sex offenders and you like imported beer. How about a name to go with your superhero persona?"

He brought the bottle to his lips and drank deeply, as if needing a moment to consider her request. When he turned to face her, his navy-blue eyes sparked with mischief. "No self-respecting superhero spills his secret identity. I mean, as soon as the hero's alter ego is revealed, his heroine inevitably finds herself in danger. You've already had a brush with evil once, tonight. If I want to protect you, I really don't have a choice, do I?"

Holy crap, Harper didn't think this guy could be any hotter. She was on the verge of a full-on nerdgasm. *Don't scare him off yet, Harper. Try to rein it in a little.* Her stomach performed a three-sixty as she brought her glass to her lips and took a moment to study him. She'd compared him to Peter Parker, but that wasn't quite right. He didn't have that boy-next-door quality. His personality wasn't dark enough to be Bruce Wayne, though his navy-blue eyes possessed a depth and hardness that told her he'd been through his fair share of rough times. Definitely not bumbling enough for Clark Kent, though his dark hair was precisely trimmed and he was clean-shaven. From the way he'd wrenched that guy's arms behind his back, he could be a cop. Maybe even military? Though she doubted he had ever been as weak and scrawny as Steve Rogers, she could totally picture him as his alter ego, Captain America. Whoever this guy was, he definitely had the body of a superhero. There wasn't a square inch of him that didn't look to be chiseled from marble. And even through his button-down dress shirt, she could make out the hills and valleys of sculpted muscle.

Without thinking, Harper reached out and traced her fingers down his forearm. Yep. Just like marble.

"Far be it from me to ask you to reveal your true identity." She couldn't believe her brazen behavior. Since when had she become the sly seductress? "But if I can't have your name, maybe I won't give you mine."

Chapter Two

Jesus. What in the hell are you doing, Galen? He was leaving in less than twelve hours yet the thought of walking out the door and ending whatever this was before it had a chance to begin was the last thing he wanted to do. It had been a long damned time since he'd felt any kind of spark with a woman, and the electricity he felt when she put her hand on his arm was more than a simple spark. It was a full-blown current.

"Okay," he said, more than willing to play her game, "no names. We'll be two strangers having a conversation over drinks."

"And protecting our alter egos." She laughed.

"I thought that was a given."

Her smile brightened, and Galen couldn't help but stare. High cheekbones, delicate, straight nose. And her hazel eyes were intriguing in their oddness. The green blending into the lighter brown to fuse into a bright coppery tone. Her freckles were adorable, making her look almost too young to be in a bar. He wouldn't call her beautiful in a traditional sense, more exotic. Her eyes were a little too large and wide, lending her a shy, innocent appearance, and her lips were a bit too full. But damn, the combination was intoxicating.

"So we've established that names are off-limits." She traced her finger along the edge of her glass. "Anything else? I mean, I'd like to know what it is you do when you're not on superhero duty."

"Law enforcement," he said, knowing there was a fifty-fifty chance she'd buy it. Not that it was a lie, but Galen wasn't in the habit of flashing his U.S. Marshals credentials to impress women. He was more than just his job and he'd dealt with his fair share of vapid badge bunnies over the years. "You?"

Her brow furrowed and she cringed as if embarrassed to say. "Unemployed," she answered with a sigh. "Fresh out of college with a journalism degree waiting to be put to good use."

Galen couldn't help but laugh, and she gave him a look. "Sorry, but you have to admit, your alter ego is a news reporter? Sort of fitting, don't you think?"

She laughed too, a light, trilling sound that shot through Galen's blood like liquid fire. "You're right," she said. "It's perfect. And totally not made up."

"Of course not." Galen didn't trust easily. Deception was unforgivable and honesty was his number-one ground rule. But something about this girl made him feel at ease. "Let's agree, just because we're not using names doesn't mean we can't be totally honest. No bullshit."

"No bullshit," she agreed with a nod. "Hometown?"

"Coos Bay," he said.

"I love it there," she said. "My dad's cousin has a house in Seal Rock, we used to drive down to Coos Bay when I was a kid. I bet my small town beats yours, though. I grew up in Cascade, Idaho."

"Never heard of it," Galen said with a laugh. "But it can't be that much smaller."

"Oh, it is," she said. "Maybe a thousand people. I'm pretty sure there are more bodies packed into the Lloyd Center on a busy weekend."

"What do people do to pass the time in Cascade, Idaho?" Galen asked. "Churn butter and mend fences?"

"I said it was a small town, not a pioneer town." She screwed her face up into a cute grimace. "There's plenty to do. Ski, hike, camp, swim. Fish and hunt if you're into it. Soak up the summer sun. There are a couple of lakes, a ski resort, and trailheads everywhere. Hot springs, hidden places that only the locals know about. Lots of tourist traffic in the summer. It's not so bad."

"Sounds great," Galen said. Really, it didn't seem too different from Coos Bay. Though the economy focused more on balance between commercial fishing and tourism, the town saw its fair share of summer visitors. "I used to fish from the jetty all the time when I was a kid. I still hike when I get the chance, and honestly, I'd rather rough it in a tent than order room service any day." He'd spent almost every summer in the lush rain forests surrounding Coos Bay camping with his family before his parents had separated. "Siblings?"

"Only child," she said.

"One older sister," he countered. "She's getting ready to open a bakery not far from here."

"I always wished I had a sister." Her mouth turned up into a soft smile that melted something inside Galen's chest. "Do you guys look alike?"

He shrugged. "If I said yes, she'd probably take it as an insult."

She gave him an appraising look. "If you share the same gene pool, I doubt that."

Galen smiled at the compliment and took a small step toward her. He didn't want to come on too strong, but damn, his body all but urged him to get closer. She took a deep breath and slowly raised her eyes to his until their gazes were locked. "Girlfriend?" she ventured, her voice cracking in an adorable show of nervousness.

He chuckled. "Single."

She must be way drunker than she'd thought. Sure, Harper was a lightweight, but never in a million years would she be so brazen with a guy, which forced her to conclude that she'd wandered past being a little tipsy. Still, she wasn't so drunk that she couldn't think straight or make logical decisions. Her stomach had been in a constant state of acrobatics for the past hour, and every time their eyes met, Harper broke out into delicious chills. And if their physical chemistry wasn't enough to have her acting like a smitten high school girl, the easy flow of their conversation was sure doing the trick.

Maybe Sophie was right. Luck was definitely on her side tonight. Not only was her mysterious hero drop-dead gorgeous, he was easygoing, charming, and funny, and had a raw, sexy edge that turned her insides to Jell-O. Add to that the fact that they shared similar interests . . . he was almost too good to be true. Harper knew that she should cut him loose now before he did something to shatter the illusion. In the past, the men she dated had always had a way of disappointing her down the line. She could leave now and chalk it up as a win. The problem was, she didn't want to leave with nothing more than some flirty touches and witty conversation for the night. She wanted *more*.

"Okay." Harper cleared her throat and closed the distance between them until her arm brushed his. His muscles stiffened from the contact and his expression burned with an intensity that stole her breath. She drained her glass in a couple of swallows and leaned in toward him, ready to take a leap. "I know where you grew up, that you failed sophomore geometry, and that you love fish tacos. How about your type?" she asked, trying not to sound too breathy. "What sort of woman are you attracted to?"

He pulled back and dragged his eyes from her toes to the top of her head in a way that made her skin tingle as though it were his hands and not his eyes touching her. Then he leaned in and put his mouth close to her ear, causing Harper to shudder with excitement. "Oh, about five-five, long dark hair, killer hazel eyes. I'm particularly fond of journalism majors."

"Oh." The word escaped her lips in a whisper.

His hand caught hers, his fingers fluttering against her palm in a way that made her wonder what those talented digits would feel like moving against a softer, more sensitive part of her body. Harper bit the inside of her cheek, worried that she'd give her desire away with some sort of desperate whimper that would send her superhero running at Mach 10 in the opposite direction. This wasn't like her. She was the cautious one, the logical thinker, the girl who didn't even go to second base until the fifth or sixth date. She wasn't a one-night-stand sort of girl, and she'd never gone home with a guy she'd met in a bar. Still, what would it hurt to sow her oats a bit? She was twenty-two years old, for crying out loud. Young enough to be reckless and old enough to know her opportunities to act this way were coming to an end. She didn't want to look back on this night months from now and regret that she hadn't lived a little. Screw it. Tonight she was going for it.

For a few moments, they stood there, her hand in his while he swirled a sensual pattern across her palm. Harper's heart fluttered in her chest, anticipation of what might happen next igniting all of her nerve endings into hyper-awareness. Her breath came in quick little bursts of air as she built up the courage to tell him what was on her mind.

Her hero reached up with his free hand and swept her hair away from her face, tucking it behind her ear as he leaned in close. "Let's get out of here," he murmured, his lips brushing her ear as he uttered the exact words she'd been dying to say.

"My apartment's five blocks from here," she suggested.

He leaned back and smiled, his navy-blue eyes smoldering in their heat. "Perfect."

After a quick good-bye to Addison and a not-so-gentle let-down for Sophie—who'd requested a few naughty pics as soon as she got him good and naked—Harper was more than ready to get out of there.

"Text or call if you need me," Addison said one last time. "He's sexy as sin, but even good-looking guys can be scumbags, Harp."

"I know, I'll be careful," she said. "I've got you on speed dial."

"Good girl," Addison said with a grin. Out of the three of them, Addison was the most motherly. "Don't have too much fun!" she called after her.

"Have I taught the two of you nothing?" Sophie

shouted at them, her voice still amplified by the amount of liquor in her system. "Wreck that shit, Harp!"

"Right," she said, giving Addison a look. "Talk to you tomorrow."

"Bye!" they called in unison, waving Harper out the door.

When she stepped out of the bar into the cool night air, Harper half expected her mystery man to be gone. Maybe nothing more than a drunken figment of her imagination or perhaps he'd sobered up enough to hightail it out of there before he had to explain that he'd changed his mind. So when she saw him waiting for her at the curb, the door of a taxi open in invitation, a smile broke out on her face. She knew too much about Tolkien, *Star Wars*, and the personal histories of way too many comic book characters to score a guy like that. And likewise, a gorgeous stranger had never swept her off her feet. Yet, here she was. Too. Freaking. Awesome.

"I take it you're not much of a walker?" Five blocks wasn't that far, and he looked fit enough to walk ten times that. Still, she couldn't resist the urge to tease him.

His lips curved up in a seductive smile. "No. Just impatient."

She walked to the cab, a silly smile plastered on her face. Hoping she didn't look too eager—or desperate for that matter—she ducked into the cab and said to the driver, "1410 Southwest Broadway, please."

Harper's hero climbed in behind her and closed the door. The quiet was deafening, the air almost too thick. She gathered her courage and turned in the seat so she could face him. Before her eyes could adjust enough to the dark for her to focus, he took her face in his hands and put his mouth to hers.

His kiss was like a deep sigh. The kind of slow, measured release of breath that clears your mind and relaxes you from head to toe. His lips caressed hers, featherlight, almost a tease, pulling back a little when she pressed forward to deepen the kiss. He was maddeningly deliberate in his tactics as his hands slid down from her face, his thumbs stroking upward along her jaw as his fingers wound around her throat. His grip was gentle and for some crazy-ass reason, Harper trusted him to hold her this way. He eased her head to one side and left a searing trail with his mouth as he kissed across her jawline, his nose nuzzling below her earlobe as he nipped lightly at the flesh near her pulse point.

Harper gasped, the light sting of his teeth replaced by the soothing heat of his tongue on her skin. She'd never made out with a guy in a cab before, but the driver could have turned around and recorded the entire thing with his phone and she wouldn't have noticed or cared. With her eyes closed, there was nothing but this moment, the sensations dancing across her flesh as this unknown man kissed, licked, and nipped at her throat. Her pulse raced in her ears and a deep throb settled between her thighs, her body awakening in a way that she'd never thought possible. Oh sure, she'd had boyfriends, and she wasn't some giggling virgin, but she'd never come alive with desire like this from something as simple as a kiss.

Upping the ante, he wrapped his arms around Harper's waist and twisted her around until she straddled his lap. Harper ducked her head in the enclosed space, their position forcing her to lean over him in a way that pressed their bodies even closer together. His erection strained against his fly, pressing against

Harper's core in a way that made her shudder with need. Her lips found his again and this time, she was the one to tease, flicking out with her tongue at his lips. He groaned into her mouth, grinding his hips against her. How the hell long did it take to drive a few blocks, anyway? Because if they didn't get to her building soon, she'd be naked in the back of this cab and not giving a single shit who happened to see.

This was a night of firsts. Her first time to be roofied—or almost roofied—at a bar. First time to make out in a cab. And her first sexual encounter with a total stranger. As Harper slanted her mouth against his, finally allowing her to deepen the kiss, she knew she'd remember this night for the rest of her life.

The cab pulled to a stop and the driver cleared his throat. When that wasn't enough to break them apart, he said, "That'll be five eighty-two."

Harper was bucked in the air as he dug in his pocket. She broke their kiss only long enough to see him hand the driver a wad of bills that could have been six bucks or sixty for all she knew or cared. And apparently, he wasn't too concerned either. He pulled her out of the car and took her in his arms, kissing her like he was starved for her. She barely had time to kick the car door shut as the cab pulled out into traffic, and if she hadn't needed to see where she was walking, she would have kept her lips locked onto his the entire way up to her apartment.

He pulled away, his expression pinched as if it pained him to put distance between them. Twining her fingers with his, he walked toward the entrance of Harper's building as calm and collected in appearance as Harper was wound-up and shaky. It wasn't nerves that affected her, but rather the need to resume where they'd left off. She'd never wanted to give over control like she did right now. The consummate control freak, Harper had made the rules in all of her previous relationships. She'd said when. She'd dictated how. Maybe it was because of the anonymity of the situation that she was so ready to relinquish control. And despite that need, it terrified the shit out of her.

They walked without saying a word through the lobby to the elevators. And just as silently waited for an available car. Harper moved toward the first set of doors to glide open, but when he noticed someone was already inside, he held her back. "Go ahead," Harper said with a nervous laugh as she urged the woman to go on without them. She must have been on her way up from the underground parking garage. Cutting an annoyed look Harper's way, she jammed her finger onto the control panel and the door glided shut.

As they waited for another car to get to the lobby floor, his warm breath caressed her ear. "Sorry, but I want you all to myself."

Chapter Three

Was she crazy to trust a perfect stranger? A second set of doors slid quietly open to reveal an empty car and he pulled Harper inside. She pressed the number four on the panel and when the doors shut, he brought their clasped hands to his mouth and kissed each one of her knuckles.

"If I asked, would you tell me your name?" Harper whispered as he abandoned her hand for that sweet spot on her neck that made her break out into delicious chills.

He didn't pull away, but kept his mouth on her, the words vibrating against her skin when he said, "Would it matter? Would you trust me more? Less? If you knew my name, would it change what's happening right now?"

"No," she breathed, knowing that it wouldn't change a thing. He was still her knight, the guy who'd taken down the slimeball who'd tried to drug her. Knowing his name wouldn't change anything they'd talked about in the bar, the stories they'd shared about their lives and childhoods. What did his name matter?

Harper already knew everything she needed to know about him.

He brought his face up to hers, his eyes boring through her as if searching for some hidden truth in her expression. And then his mouth descended in a ravenous kiss, urgent as he backed her against the wall, lifting her up until Harper had no choice but to wrap her legs around his waist. He reached under the hem of her T-shirt, his touch like a brand as he grazed his fingers against her bare skin. Harper gripped his shoulders, arching into him, as he twined his tongue with hers in a sensual dance that left her breathless and aching for more.

Too soon, the elevator doors opened to the fourth floor. He set her down on her feet and Harper led the way as she dug her keys out of her purse. His footsteps were a steady cadence beside hers, a dull thud on the industrial carpeting, as she walked to the end of the hall and her studio apartment. When she got to the door, she fumbled with the key, suddenly nervous as she realized she'd come to the point of no return. Once on the other side of that door, she was one hundred percent committed to whatever was going to happen. And of course, this was the perfect time to realize that she couldn't remember if she was wearing a nice bra/underwear combo. *Crap.*

As though sensing each and every one of her fluttering nerves, he reached out and eased her key from her grasp. Harper turned, her back plastered to the door, breath speeding in her chest. His arms were braced on either side of her, caging her in, and Harper's eyes locked on the navy-blue ones gazing back at her with that same openness and intensity that made her knees go weak. "Are you sure you want this?"

he asked, low. "I won't go in unless you're positive this is okay."

Harper reached out and laid the flat of her palm against the hard planes of his chest. His warmth penetrated the fabric, heart beating in a steady rhythm. She closed her eyes, reveling in that reassuring thrum for a moment. "I want this," she murmured without opening her eyes. "I'm sure."

At those words, he slid the key into the lock and turned it. The door eased open and Harper took his hand as she backed inside, the layout of the tiny six-hundred-square-foot apartment leaving her nowhere to go but toward the bed. Through a narrow hallway, she backed her way past the cramped closet and bathroom and into the kitchen. He set her keys down on the counter and took her other hand in his. The apartment was dark, the only illumination coming from the streetlights outside. Harper wanted it this way, not because she was embarrassed or worried, but because she wanted her senses to be heightened like they were in the cab. Only the sound of his breath, the sensation of his touch.

When the backs of her legs hit the bed, she stopped and quickly deposited her purse and cell phone on the bedside table. The streetlight cast shadows on the lines of his jaw and nose, morphing his features into sharper angles, adding to her superhero fantasy. She disengaged her hand from his grasp and reached up to thread her fingers through the silky-soft strands of his hair. He lowered his mouth to hers in a gentle kiss, the same teasing flutter that had driven her mad when he'd kissed her in the taxi. Her hands moved to his shirt, and one by one she released each button, spreading the halves of his shirt apart. In the low light and play of shadow, every defined ridge of his chest and torso stood out. She passed her palms up from his washboard abs up and over his pecs and flat nipples, across his collarbone to his shoulders, where she eased his shirt the rest of the way off. It hit the floor in a whisper of fabric and his breath seemed to hitch as she tucked her fingers inside his waistband.

He took her wrists in an iron grip, stopping her before she could unbutton his pants. Harper's heart beat wildly as he held her, the thought of giving him total control causing her body to clench with lust. She stood perfectly still, no longer on the offensive, waiting for him to act. After several moments, he raised her arms above her head and released her wrists. Harper didn't dare move as his fingers traced down her sides, eliciting chills and a flush of heat all at once. The pads of his rough fingers skimmed her skin as he grasped the hem of her T-shirt and pulled it up her body and off. Still, she didn't put her arms down. Harper refused to make a move until bidden. He rested his palms flat against hers and stepped close until his bare chest touched hers. Slowly, he caressed down her arms, his fingers brushing the outsides of her breasts downward to her torso and then around to her back. Then, he traced his way up her spine and she couldn't help but arch into him as he unclasped her bra.

"Put your arms down," he commanded in a husky growl.

Harper obeyed, and he pulled the straps over her shoulders, discarding the garment somewhere behind him. Her breasts became heavy, her nipples tightening, exposed to the air. Eyes closed, she waited for him to kiss her, touch her, anything to end the desperate need throbbing low in her belly. Breath stalled, anticipation unfurled within her like a length of ribbon.

He cupped her breasts, his thumbs flicking across her nipples, and Harper let out a whimper, a surge of sensation clenching between her thighs.

When his hands left her body, she wanted to guide him back. Or better yet, bring his mouth to where his thumbs had just been. But she resisted the urge to take control of the situation, giving herself over to him completely. He lowered his hands to her hips and spun her around until her back was flush with his chest. Harper let her head fall back against his shoulder, and he cupped her breasts again, this time pinching her nipples with enough pressure to cause a sudden rush of wetness between her legs. She'd never been so ready, so damned wound up. If he didn't take her soon, she'd come before they even got started.

As he continued to tease her nipples with maddening precision, he lowered his mouth to her throat, kissing, biting, licking. She tilted her head up and his mouth seized hers, desperate, hungry, his tongue thrusting into her mouth, his lips hard and demanding. His hands traveled from her breasts down her belly to her jeans. He popped the button and slid the zipper down, pushing her jeans and underwear over her hips to the floor, where Harper kicked them free of her ankles in a rush. Then he brought his mouth to her ear and whispered, "Get on the bed."

Harper hesitated. Did he want her to turn around? Lie flat on her stomach? Uncertainty filled her with anxiety that she might do the wrong thing and ruin the moment. Again he took control, easing her forward until she was on all fours, arms stretched out on the bed, her ass jutting up in the air. Never had she allowed herself to be so vulnerable, yet with this stranger, she could let go in a way she'd been too guarded to do with anyone else. Her body stilled, heart hammering in her rib cage as if it were looking for a way out. She heard him shift behind her and then the silky strands of his hair brushed her thighs as he positioned himself beneath her. Harper took a deep breath and held it, her heart hammering with anticipation. His tongue flicked out at her clit and Harper let out a low, drawn-out moan.

Like his kisses, each pass of his tongue was a tease, the contact deliberate and too soft for her to find release. She pushed against him, desperate for him to increase the pressure, but he gripped her hips to keep her still and continued his unhurried assault, wringing desperate moans and near sobs from her throat with each pass of his tongue. A rasp of stubble brushed her inner thigh. *Oh, God.* That coarse contact with her flesh made her crazy. Harper buried her face in the coverlet of her bed, winding the fabric in her fists as he began to alternate between tentative licks and deep, hungry sucks that brought her to the edge.

"I'm so close," she gasped, not caring if she sounded desperate. She was. "Don't stop."

But at her words, he stilled and Harper groaned in frustration. This was his show, not hers. He stood, and the rustle of fabric as he shucked his jeans caused her to shiver with delicious anticipation. Harper didn't move, didn't turn around to see what he was doing. Completely at his mercy, she waited, her body humming with pent-up energy that ached for release. Large hands gripped her thighs, sliding up and over her ass, his thumbs pressing into her spine as he caressed his way up her back. He leaned over her and she stiffened as the hard, velvet smooth length of his erection brushed against her. "I don't want you to come until I'm inside of you." He paused before asking, his tone almost embarrassed, "Do you have condoms?" The tense laughter that followed made Harper smile.

"You didn't leave the house prepared tonight?" she teased.

His body stiffened as individual muscles rippled against Harper's sensitive skin. When his erection brushed her ass once more, Harper rocked into him. He groaned, and pulled back. "I might be a superhero for the night, but apparently I'm no Boy Scout."

"Top drawer, bedside table," Harper said on a breath, thankful she'd kept the condoms left over from her previous relationship.

His sigh of relief brushed the back of her neck. "Thank God," he said, and she laughed.

It should have been awkward, Harper sprawled out on all fours, waiting as he retrieved the condom and ripped the package open. But it wasn't. She thought back to all of the clumsy sexual encounters she'd had—truth be told, they'd all been a mess in one way or another—and weighed them all against this one moment that was more perfect than all of her previous ones combined.

When his strong fingers gripped her hips, Harper started, and his deep, rumbling laugh made her smile. He eased her over until she lay on her back. With the streetlight casting its glow on his body, he looked all the more commanding—too perfect to be real. She drank him in, committing every shadowed detail of his body to memory. A grin of pure male satisfaction curved his lips as her gaze roamed over him, and when it lingered on the thick, hard length of his erection, his fists clenched at his sides as if it took a conscious effort not to pounce on her.

Harper kept her eyes glued to him as she eased her way up higher on the bed until her head rested on the pillows. She let her knees fall open and his gaze followed the path of her legs, settling on the spot where his mouth had been, sending a rush of excitement through Harper's body. He crawled up the bed, reminding her once again of an animal on the prowl, and settled himself between her legs. A stab of apprehension twisted her stomach. His size was enough to make a girl's breath hitch.

He lowered himself on top of her, his arms bracing him up. Harper arched up to meet him, tasting herself on his lips as he opened his mouth to her. Seized by lust, she lapped at him, twisting her tongue against his, her teeth scraping against his bottom lip as she took it into her mouth and sucked. He trembled above her as though fighting for control and eased himself slowly inside of her, not completely, just enough to get her body used to his size, and then just as slowly pulling out. For long, agonizing minutes he taunted her this way, making sure her body was ready for him. She trembled with the need to have him fully inside of her and thrust her hips up to meet his, biting the inside of her cheek as a slight sting of pain shot through her.

He drew his breath in a long hiss, and stilled, waiting a moment for them both to adjust. But then he began to rock slowly and the discomfort melted away into a warm, throbbing sensation as her inner walls clenched around him. He kissed her again, his control finally slipping as he slanted his mouth furiously across hers. Harper gasped against his mouth as he pulled almost completely out of her and then drove hard and deep, his shaft grinding against her clit in a way that stole her breath—and her ability to form a coherent thought. Swept up in passion, she arched into every frantic thrust, his pace increasing with his labored breath. Harper dug her nails into his shoulders, clinging to his body like a lifeline, her teeth gnashed together as her body coiled tight, constricting until she felt as tiny and inconsequential as a speck of dust floating in a vast universe. Then, bliss crested over her, an explosion that broke her apart, sending wave after wave of sensation coursing through her body, the orgasm so intense that she sobbed her pleasure in tight little moans until her throat felt raw and her limbs limp and heavy. His body stiffened as hers yielded, and he thrust deep inside of her, his own voice strained and primal as he came.

For a moment they lay still, the only sound that of their racing breaths. Harper enjoyed the weight of his body, the way his arms encircled her as he planted featherlight kisses on her brow, cheeks, and lips. She twined her fingers through his hair, slick with sweat, down the back of his neck and he shuddered. She suppressed the laughter that threatened, wondering at his sensitivity. Where else was he ticklish? Did he have to work tomorrow? What was his favorite breakfast food? TV show? Was he a reader or did he always wait for the movie? Questions assaulted Harper's mind, details that she wanted to know, little inconsequential facts she was dying to learn about him. Her chest swelled with emotion as he held her. She marveled at the intimacy she'd shared with him, a total stranger. And yet, in this moment, she felt as though she'd known him all her life.

When he pulled away and withdrew from her body, Harper felt empty. Cold. He kissed her forehead and she listened to the sound of his steps as he padded across the floor and then shielded her eyes as the bathroom light flicked on and was then blocked out as he pulled the sliding door closed. Panic infused the blissful moment. What would happen now? Would the inevitable awkwardness rear its ugly head? Watching from the bed as he threw on his clothes and beat a hasty retreat out of there. The sound of the door sliding open filled her with dread as she waited for him. He walked to the side of the bed, his features illuminated in the dark so she could barely make out the shadow of his grin.

"Do you want to sleep on top of the covers?"

Harper relaxed in an instant. She scooted the coverlet and sheets out from underneath her and he slid into bed beside her, taking her in his arms and tucking her body against his. "That was—" she began to say, but he shushed her.

"I know," he said. "Shhh."

Harper smiled in the dark and nestled closer. She allowed her eyes to drift shut and her body relaxed. *Perfect*, she thought as her breathing became deep and even. *That was perfect*. And tomorrow she was going to let him know how perfect tonight was. No more games—she'd give him her name and demand his in return. When she wanted something, Harper went after it, and she wanted *him*.

Chapter Four

The sound of a bell invaded Galen's consciousness. Maybe not quite a bell, but like a triangle in an orchestra, a *ting! ting! ting!* that made him think of an elevator chime just before the doors slide open. He smiled to himself as a barrage of images from the night before blew up in his mind. The softness of her lips as he kissed her in the taxi, her legs wrapped around his waist in the elevator, her taste as he licked her swollen bud, her nipples teasing his chest as he moved above her. The way she clenched tightly around him as she came, and then his own orgasm . . . His body responded to his thoughts, more than ready to resume where they'd left off last night. Galen wanted to take his time with her, go slow, coax those sensual mewling sounds from her again and again. Learn every inch of her body, committing the details to memory.

Galen was surprised at himself. Intimacy was a word that he'd erased from his personal lexicon a long time ago. His dad had shattered any illusions he'd had about relationships, family, love. He'd lost all respect for his father when he'd gotten old enough to understand what it was his mom and dad fought about all the time. And when his dad had finally grown the balls to own up to his many affairs and leave them, the pain had driven his mom over the edge, leaving his nineteen-year-old sister as his appointed guardian—because he refused to go within ten miles of his dad—and Galen a sixteen-year-old kid who already had a jaded outlook on life and love. He never opened up to anyone. Refused to put his trust in anyone except for his sister and maybe Landon. But last night, he'd trusted. Opened up. To *her*.

She stirred beside him, seeking out his body's warmth as she cuddled closer. Galen pulled her against his chest, absently stroking her arm in the gray morning light. The sun wasn't up yet; he guessed the time was about 6 AM. He could reschedule his flight, maybe fly out tomorrow or the next day. The chief deputy would cut him some slack if he came up with a good enough excuse to postpone. All he knew was that the thought of leaving the woman sleeping soundly beside him made his gut twist up with an anxiety he'd never felt before.

Was it possible to feel so connected to someone he barely knew? As soon as she woke, he was laying it out on the table. His name, his job, the position he'd taken in France. He was already committed to the SOG assignment, and he couldn't turn back now, but maybe they could work something out. He'd pay to fly her over to visit. They could talk on the phone, Skype, whatever. It could work. His stint overseas was only a year. Twelve measly months and he could come home if he wanted to. All he knew was one night with her wasn't enough.

Galen's thoughts were interrupted again by the *ting! ting! ting!* of a bell. He rolled toward the sound and the nightstand where she'd left her cell. The screen lit up as another text message came in, followed by a vibrating buzz, and yet another message. He hadn't meant to look, but the screen was stacked with conversation bubbles labeled "Chris." Against his better judgment, Galen tipped the phone up and glanced over the messages, each one more frantic than the last.

Where r u?
Babe, answer ur phone!
I need to see you.
Call me!
Coming over.

Galen's heart dropped into his gut like a stone pitched off a thousand-foot cliff and he clenched his teeth hard enough to grind the enamel. Shock turned quickly to bitter anger, burning his throat as if he'd guzzled acid. Even though they'd agreed to no names, they'd likewise agreed to total honesty in all other things. She'd asked him last night if he was single, but it had never occurred to him to ask her if she was seeing anyone. A lie by omission was still a damned lie. Christ, what an idiot he was, acting like some sort of lovesick puppy. He'd saved her ass from being drugged last night and she'd given him the thank-you of a lifetime. End of story. He was nothing but a fling. A one-night stand she could talk to her girlfriends about the next day. Awesome.

This was the reason why Galen didn't do relationships. There was no such thing as a grand connection between two souls, no deep respect to be treasured and nurtured. People lied, end of story. He'd let his own hero complex paint the events of last night in some ridiculous romantic light. What a joke. He didn't have the time or patience to play games—he had a flight to catch. He'd busted his ass for his position on the SOG team, and it was time to cut bait and get back to Louisiana.

Galen flipped the switch on the side of her cell to vibrate, lest the asshole in desperate need of a visit from the grammar police wake her up before he could make a stealthy retreat. Yeah, it was a total dick move to sneak out before she woke up, but as far as Galen was concerned she was reaping what she'd sown. In fact, she was lucky he didn't wake her up now and tell her exactly how he felt about being played. She wasn't worth his time or the effort it would take to tell her off, though. Shit, she probably wouldn't even care. She hadn't cared enough last night to be honest with him. Fuck her and every cheater in the world like her. He didn't appreciate being made a fool of and there was no way in hell he was going to waste another minute of his time in this apartment.

Slipping his arm out from underneath her, Galen slid off the bed without even jostling her. She sighed, the sound a caress in Galen's ears that he forced himself to ignore as he threw on his clothes. He was missing a shoe, and dropped to the floor to look under the bed, finding it buried under a pile of her clothes. He'd come here with nothing but the clothes on his back. A quick pat-down confirmed that his own phone was still tucked in the back pocket of his jeans. Unlocking the screen, he noticed he had a text from Landon and a missed call from his supervisor at Camp Beauregard. He'd call everyone back in the cab on his way to his apartment. After that, he'd grab his shit and head for the airport with plenty of time to spare to make it through security checkpoints.

As he headed for the door, Galen chanced one last

look back at the bed. Even in the innocence of sleep, her face bore a soft, seductive quality that made his stomach clench tight with lust, longing, and most of all, loss. He knew he had no right to feel that way. Was it even possible to lose something that he'd never truly had? The doorknob turned under his hand and the door whispered open as if aiding in his quiet retreat. When the elevator doors slid open at the end of the hall, he ran to catch the car before it went on without him. Once inside, he closed his eyes, unwilling to remember anything that had happened in this exact elevator the night before. His trek through the lobby was equally quick, and he hailed a cab as soon as he shot through the door. He chanced a quick look back at the awning with REGENCY APARTMENTS scrawled across it, but he fought the urge to gaze higher toward the fourth-story window. Only minutes before, he'd been ready to take a chance. To open up for this first time in his life. What a joke. Now he was reminded why he needed to keep his mind on the job and stay on track. Forcing his gaze away, Galen jumped in the cab and gave the driver the address to his place.

The sound of someone banging on her door caused Harper to bolt upright in her bed. She rubbed the sleep from her eyes, and gathered the tangled mass of her hair and twisted it up in a bun, tucking the end of her hair into the knot to keep it secure. The details of the previous night came rushing back to her, and she looked to her side to find the bed empty where there should have been a naked male body that would have made Adonis feel self-conscious.

Another round of frantic knocks came on the heels of the first and Harper's brow furrowed. Maybe he'd gone out for coffee and locked himself out? His clothes were gone. She quickly wrapped the sheet around her body like a toga, tripping as she made her way toward the door. Her pulse quickened at the thought of opening the door to see his face on the other side and her body warmed at the prospect of a repeat of last night's performance.

"Hey . . ." The word died on her tongue as she threw the door open only to see her ex, Chris, standing on the other side. Harper's heart jumped into her throat and she swallowed down the lump of disappointment that nearly choked the air out of her lungs. "What are you doing here?"

"I've been texting you since last night, Harper. What the hell?" Chris pushed his way past her into the apartment, looking ready to come unglued.

Thoughts raced through Harper's mind, too fast for her to grasp onto a single one. She'd broken it off with Chris over three months ago, yet he still insisted on inserting himself into her life as though nothing had changed. He craned his neck as he entered the apartment as if looking for something—or someone— then poked his head in the closet. "I can't find my running shoes and I'm pretty sure I left them here."

"Bullshit, Chris. You didn't leave *anything* here. This place is marginally larger than a shoe box, and the chance of me overlooking any of your things is slim. What do you want?"

Chris leaned against the kitchen counter, looking her over from head to toe. "I just want to talk, Harp."

The contrast between Chris and the man she'd been with last night was almost laughable. Chris gave the impression of a skinny child in comparison: a little too short, dirty, and unkempt. His hipster vibe was a big hit with the college set. It had been what attracted her to him in the first place. But the thick black-rimmed glasses that framed his dark brown eyes were where the measure of Chris's ambition and intelligence ended. Chris didn't even have his own place; he camped out wherever he ended up after the sun went down. He was a vampiric hipster mooch, leeching off anyone he could talk into giving him a free ride. Harper was done with him and boys like him. Running shoes, her ass. He didn't run anywhere. Ever. What a loser.

"There's a reason why I haven't been returning your calls or texts," Harper said, standing at the door still held wide open. "*We broke up.* Three months ago. I don't want to see you, talk to you. We're through."

"Harp. Come on."

"Leave, Chris," she said, indicating the door. "I'll be sure to let you know if I find your shoes."

He pushed himself off the counter, his lip curled in a sneer. Brushing past her, he walked through the doorway and then turned to face her. "I talked to Sophie this morning. She said you had a good time out at Score last night. But it still looks like you woke up alone. See you around."

Harper slammed the door in his face, the bite of Chris's words slicing through her like myriad razor blades. Had she imagined everything that had happened last night? Maybe her mystery man had been a drunken fantasy come to life. Because the guy she'd brought back here never would have walked out without even saying good-bye.

Oh no? A niggling voice mocked in her mind. *You asked for it, Harp. Played the whole secret-identity angle, refusing to give him your name. And then you jumped into bed with him like you made a habit of hooking up with strangers. He probably ran out of here this morning, thankful you hadn't killed him in his sleep.*

No. There was no way she'd imagined the connection between them. He'd felt it, too. He had to have. He'd treated her with such gentleness that she'd never once felt like what happened between them was simply sex. They'd made love last night. And it was the most intense, most intimate experience of her life.

Then why did he walk out on you?

Harper shuffled through the apartment like a zombie and flopped down on the bed. She closed her eyes, but it did nothing to block out the memories of the previous night that buffeted her subconscious like a spring hailstorm. His touch, his mouth on hers, the way he'd wrung pleasure from her body with just the flick of his tongue. The intensity of his navy-blue eyes as he looked down at her. The heat of his body as he entered her.

Tears stung at Harper's eyes as a chasm of grief opened up inside of her. If she'd done something differently, told him her name, taken things more slowly . . . would it have changed the outcome of this morning? Maybe he would have stuck around for breakfast, hung out with her for the rest of the day. Or maybe he simply would have left with an awkward kiss to her cheek and an empty promise of "I'll give you a call" spilling effortlessly from his lips.

Or maybe he still would have snuck out in the middle of the night, just like he did.

Her cell vibrated several times and Harper rolled over to retrieve it from the nightstand. Funny, she didn't remember turning the ringer off last night. It always bugged the crap out of her mom if she turned the sound off so she made it a habit to always keep the volume up. She checked the caller ID to see Addison's picture pop up on the screen. Harper grinned. No doubt Addison was checking in to make sure she hadn't been chopped into bits, her body disposed of in the Columbia River.

Rather than answer, she fired off a text letting her cousin know everything was good and she'd give her a call later. Addison's response came a few seconds later in the form of a colon and capital D, the wide smiley face an obvious assumption as to why Harper was too occupied to answer the phone.

Harper lay in bed staring at the ceiling for what felt like forever. The sun crested higher in the sky and she sighed. She had too much to do to mope around her apartment all day. She needed to follow up on the résumé she'd dropped off at *The Oregonian* last week. If she didn't find a job pretty soon, she'd be moving home whether she wanted to or not. At least a busy day would take her mind off of her heartbreak. Heartbreak she had no right to feel for a perfect stranger.

But he hadn't been a stranger to her last night. *He hadn't.*

Her phone vibrated again in her palm and she brought it up to check the ID. Sophie. Unlike Addison, Sophie wouldn't quit calling until she answered. Text messages or not. With a sigh, she slid her finger across the screen and brought the phone to her ear.

"Oh. My. God," Sophie said without even waiting for Harper to say hello. "Tell me *everything.*"

Chapter Five

One year later

"Are you sure I can't convince you to stay? The food's great, the pay's better than all right, and if you'd go out every once in a while you'd know that working personal security makes the girls go weak in the knees. That's got to count for something."

A corner of Galen's mouth hitched into a half smile, but Corrine had a point. The personal secretary to Ambassador Wallace had been trying for months to get him out and socializing, her argument being that if he made friends—or found a girlfriend—in Paris, he'd be more inclined to stick around.

"Who needs a complicated relationship when I've got you? You're all the woman I need."

"Oh, stop." Corrine swatted her hand in his direction as she gazed at Galen over the rim of her glasses. "I'm old enough to be your mother. I just hope they don't send us some cocky little upstart with something to prove, because that will seriously ruin my year."

Galen looked up from his computer screen. "It

doesn't matter who they send. You'll have him whipped into shape before the first week is over."

"You're probably right." Corrine let out an exaggerated sigh. "My hard-ass nature is why they keep me around. Sign here and here," she said, pointing to the appropriate lines of the release papers she'd placed on his desk. "I'm going to miss you, kiddo, but I bet you're excited to see your sister."

"She's the only thing that could tear me away from you, Corrine." Twelve months wasn't all that long, but with the time difference and Michelle's busy schedule, Galen hadn't talked to his sister much over the past year save an exchange of e-mails and a few short phone calls. Her bakery was up and running, and pulling in some great reviews from the local food critics. "I'm excited to be going back to Portland. I've missed it."

Corrine snatched up the stack of papers from Galen's desk and returned them to the file folder she held in her hand. "You be sure to stay out of trouble," she teased as she headed for the door. "And please, promise me you'll go out every once in a while. You're too good a man not to have a sweet girl to come home to."

"I'll see what I can do, Corrine."

She gave him a wink in response. *"Fais bon voyage et prends soin de toi."*

He smiled at her formal departing words—"Have a safe trip and take care of yourself"—because they were spoken with motherly affection.

"Tu me manqueras aussi," he replied as she closed the door behind her. And he really would miss her, too.

It had been one hell of a year. Not disappointing by any means. In fact, the ambassador had been so pleased with Galen's job performance, he'd put in a special request to his supervisors that he stay on another year. When Galen respectfully declined the offer, the ambassador had offered him a private gig working personal security for his family, along with a hefty pay raise. Though he'd been tempted to take the offer, there was so much more he wanted to do with his life. In his career. And he wasn't going to get any of it accomplished staying here.

The e-mail alert went off on his laptop and Galen glanced over at the preview window to see a message from Michelle. He opened the e-mail and skimmed over the text:

> *Less than forty-eight hours to go! Can't wait to see you. Woohoo! I attached another awesome review for* A Slice of Heaven. *Bet my beignets would give the ones you've eaten over there a run for their money. So. Excited!*
>
> Shel

Galen had a feeling that if he agreed to stay on for another year, Michelle would have flown over here and dragged him home herself. All they had was each other, and it saddened Galen that he hadn't been there for her when A Slice of Heaven opened. She never let him forget, though, flooding his inbox with copies of the menu, pictures of the dining area, and the many reviews that had started to come in. He clicked the link and a page from the "Life and Leisure" section of *The Oregonian* popped up in his browser window.

A SLICE OF HEAVEN DELIVERS THE GOODS: STOP FOR THE PASTRIES, STAY FOR THE AMBIANCE AND SERVICE.

He skimmed over the article, smiling. It looked like the business was taking off and he knew it wouldn't be long before Michelle's little bakery was the talk of Portland. Two days and then he could tell her in person how proud he was of her. Galen was about to close the window and get back to work when a link to the next article caught his eye. From life and leisure to politics, the next feature focused on an up-and-coming super PAC that had thrown their substantial money behind an emerging GOP senate candidate. But what caught Galen's eye wasn't the story. No, what made his heart rate kick into high gear was the photo and byline of the reporter.

Harper Allen.

How many times over the past year had he dreamt about her? How many days had he spent imagining her soft lips, warm body, and sweet voice? How often had his mood turned sour when he thought of how she'd played him, deceived him, used him?

As if getting her out of his head wasn't hard enough, now he had a name to go with the face that haunted him. *Great.* Maybe reassignment wasn't such a great idea. No chance of running into her on the streets of Paris, but once he got home . . . *Fuck.* Would he approach her if he saw her? Would he say anything if they passed on the sidewalk? Like it mattered. As far as he knew, she still had a boyfriend. What was the jackass's name? Cameron? Carson?

Not that he cared. She was his past. A meaningless one-night stand to remind him that relationships brought nothing but heartache. Galen didn't have room in his life for that kind of bullshit. Corrine wanted him to find a nice girl to settle down with? He let out a derisive snort. Nice girls were as rare and elusive as the Loch Ness Monster. The nice girl he thought he'd met a year ago . . . nothing more than a reminder that besides Michelle, there wasn't a woman on this planet Galen could trust.

Still, he couldn't help but stare at her picture for a second longer before closing the link and exiting from his e-mail. "Harper Allen." He liked the way it sounded, the ease of how her name rolled off his tongue. A couple of days and he'd be home, and then what? *Then you go back to your job, and your old life, and your family. Nothing changes.* Instead of making him feel better, the thought left him feeling just a little too goddamned hollow.

"Harper, do you have that story on the IRS scandal ready to roll?" her editor, Sam Yates, asked as he approached her desk.

"E-mailed it yesterday." She shot him a disappointed look. "Seriously, Sam, you should check your inbox more often."

Sam's gray eyes sparkled with humor as he rapped his knuckles on Harper's laminate desktop. "You know, just for that smartass remark, I don't think I'm going to tell you that I heard Senator Mark Ellis is in town this week before he heads back to DC. Rumor has it that he's finally meeting with the Oregon League of Conservation Voters this evening."

Harper shot out of her chair, pulling a drawer open to retrieve her purse. She threw a new notebook and a couple of pens in the large hobo bag even though she was pretty sure she already had a few notebooks and several pens somewhere in the bottom along with her digital voice recorder.

"You've been holding out on me, Sam," she admonished. "Just for that, I'm telling Maggie you've been dumping out the herbal tea you're supposed to be drinking." Sam's wife was trying to wean him off of caffeine, but Sam wasn't having it. He liked to say that no self-respecting newspaper man drank Earl Grey.

"I'm fifty-two; I work in an industry that's slowly being choked out by bloggers, iPads, and the Internet. I don't smoke, or drink, though God knows I deserve to. I love my wife, but I'm keeping my coffee, damn it. I just told you about Ellis so I'm not, in fact, holding out on you. And before you run out of here hell bent for leather, I said *this evening*. Not this second. So cool your jets."

"All right, fine." Harper returned her purse to the deep desk drawer and tossed her cell back on her desk. "Since you gave me the heads-up about Ellis, your secret is safe with me. I'm gonna go stake out his office and see if I can snag a few minutes with him this evening, though. I've been trying to get my hands on him for months."

As far as politicians went, Mark Ellis was an anomaly. He'd run a campaign based on shameless full disclosure. It had thrown the GOP for a loop because they had no idea how to retaliate against the Democrat's tactics. Dirty pool and smear campaigns didn't work when the candidate in question beat you to the punch. He'd laid his life bare to the public, owning up to everything and professing that his constituents deserved a forthright representative in Washington. He'd won by a landslide, despite his indiscretions.

Sam leaned a hip on her desk. "You know, Harper, Ellis might be the real deal."

"Senators don't own *all* of their misdeeds. It goes against nature. Deception is in their DNA. If he's the real deal, then I'm Super Girl."

"You manage to find something that Ellis hasn't

already admitted to, you will be. Not to mention the fact that if you break a story like that, I won't be able to afford to keep you here. On second thought, forget what I said about Ellis. I'm pretty sure he's already left town."

Harper opened a Word document on her computer and started jotting down a list of notes and questions, in case she lucked out and managed to corner Ellis. "You have nothing to worry about, Sam," Harper said as she typed. "When I'm famous and being courted by the *Washington Post,* I'll remember who gave me my start."

"Cheeky," Sam quipped. "While I've got you here, my nephew's coming to town this weekend. Maggie wants you to come over for dinner on Saturday."

"I'll think about it."

"You know, Harper, there's this little thing called life. It's what the rest of the world does when they're not working. You might want to look into it."

"Ha ha, Sam." Harper shot him a stern glare before turning her attention back to her screen. "Like I said, I'll think about it."

"All right, all right." He pushed himself away from Harper's desk and started to walk away. "Good luck with Ellis. Let me know if it pans out."

"Will do."

Harper was in the zone, typing out notes as fast as her fingers could move. Sam was the reason she had a job at all, and he'd suffered some backlash from a few of the more seasoned reporters when he'd given her a weekly feature a couple of months ago. She'd proven herself, put in the time, the hours, and the hard work over the past year. Sam might have given her the feature, but he hadn't done her any favors. She'd earned it.

As she jotted down a question about Ellis's past as a county clerk, she had a vague recollection of Sam inviting her somewhere. Oh, right. Dinner. He'd been trying to fix her up with his nephew for a few months now, but Harper wasn't interested. Honestly, dating didn't hold any allure for her. Why bother? Her fingers hovered over the keyboard, her concentration shot, mind blank. Well, not entirely blank. There was a reason Harper wasn't interested in dating anyone, and it had nothing to do with her ambition or work ethic. She was such a hopeless romantic. Strike that. She was such a hopeless *idiot*.

Seriously. Who in their right mind spent an entire year daydreaming about a one-night stand? Granted, it had been one hell of a night, but still. Despite the fact that he'd ditched her without so much as a good-bye, Harper couldn't get him out of her head. The slow, methodical way he kissed her, his strong hands caressing her skin, the way his tongue slid across her flesh . . . Harper sat up a little straighter in her chair, looked around to see if anyone was watching her. Just thinking about that night caused her skin to flush with warmth. Whenever her mind wandered back to that night, Harper racked her brain, wondering what she could have done, said differently to change the outcome. She couldn't help but feel as though she'd done something to scare him off. Why else would he have snuck out before she woke up? Was she that bad in bed?

He'd ruined any other man for her and she didn't even know his name.

Of course, Sophie had argued for months that Harper hadn't given any other guys the chance to prove they could give her nights of intense passion and mind-blowing orgasms. "You're young and your body's still tight in all the right places, Harp. Don't let those boobs go to waste!" Eventually, she'd dip a toe back in the dating pool. Just not now. It was silly and foolish to hold every guy up to a standard that might as well be a figment of her imagination, but Harper didn't care. She wasn't ready to let go of the memory of that night. Not yet.

Harper gave her head a shake, as if to dislodge the thoughts that settled there. In a few short hours, she might be face-to-face with the most candid—and therefore the most suspicious—U.S. senator on record. Distractions weren't an option if she wanted to get under his skin. By the end of the night, Senator Mark Ellis would be cursing her tenacity. If there was one thing Harper wasn't, it was a quitter. And she was getting that interview.

Chapter Six

What was it about parking garages that made them so damned creepy? Then again, who was Harper to judge what was creepy? She was the one lurking in the shadows, waiting to jump Senator Ellis after his meeting. Yeah, this *might* get her arrested. If she got Ellis to go on the record and answer any of her questions, it would be one hundred percent worth the criminal record.

Good Lord, how much longer was she going to have to wait? These garages had closed-circuit surveillance, didn't they? Someone was bound to notice her camped out by the senator's Audi. And if they didn't, they really needed to think about putting a few cameras in here. You never knew what kind of weirdo might be hiding out behind your car. Harper checked the time on her cell and groaned. Why hadn't she thought to pack a snack? Voodoo Donut was just down the street. She'd give her left arm for an apple fritter right about now. The sound of voices echoing in the garage distracted her from her growling stomach and Harper peeked over the trunk of Senator Ellis's Audi.

If she weren't trying to be stealthy, she would have jumped up and down with excitement.

Senator Mark Ellis, in the flesh, strode toward his car, his aide, Jason Meader trailing behind him. Harper scowled at Meader, hoping his skin burned from the heat of her glare. Meader was a damned good employee, especially at running interference for the senator. He'd thwarted her attempts at nailing him down for an interview time and again, which made him a thorn in Harper's side, not to mention a raging pain in the butt. *You're too late, Meader!* The thought took root in Harper's best impersonation of a super villain. *You can't protect the senator now. Bwahahaha!*

Afraid she might scare him off, Harper stayed tucked down low behind the senator's car, waiting for the right moment to approach him. She paused, legs bent, shoulders hunched. *Oh God.* She was *so* the parking garage creeper! Now she felt just a little skeevy. Not to mention dirty. As she dug through her bag for her notes and voice recorder, Harper made a mental note to take a nice hot shower when she got home. Parking garage stalker or not, she wasn't leaving here without getting a quote from Ellis.

Their approaching footsteps quieted, and Harper peeked around the rear bumper to see what the holdup was. Senator Ellis patted his suit jacket pockets and checked inside. "Damn it. I left my phone back at the office."

Crap! Thanks to the holdup, "forgetful" was going on the top of Harper's list of the senator's faults. How long would it take for him to backtrack for his damned phone? She was starting to lose feeling in her legs!

"Jason, run over and grab it for me." Senator Ellis

instructed rather than asked, but Harper wondered at the way his voice quavered, almost nervous. "And since you're going, can you bring the file on Prop Fifteen while you're at it? I, uh, I should probably review it before tomorrow's meeting."

Yeah, Jason. Go! Get out of here! With the possibility of getting the senator's bulldog out of the way, Harper amended her list and made "forgetful" one of the senator's attributes.

"Sure. Is there anything else you need while I'm over there?" Meader's tone was polite, but Harper couldn't ignore the edge of annoyance.

"No, that's all. Thanks, Jason."

Meader's footsteps retreated, while Ellis's came closer. Adrenaline spiked in Harper's limbs, the fact that she was about to land a potential story filling her with a euphoric excitement. As soon as Meader was out of sight, Harper emerged from behind the car, her voice recorder held at the ready. Senator Ellis caught sight of her, and he started, looking behind him and to either side before swiping his palm across his brow.

Wow. Nervous, much? Harper's journalist impulse took over; she was like a shark scenting blood in the water. He was hiding something. She *knew* it. "Senator Ellis," she greeted him as she walked around the front of the car. "I'm Harper Allen, with *The Oregonian*. I was wondering if I could ask you a few questions."

"All press inquiries are handled by my office," Ellis said, his eyes darting from one end of the parking garage to the next. What was up with this guy? Nervous over being hijacked was one thing. He was as twitchy as an informant in a crack house.

"I've tried, several times I might add, to schedule an appointment through your office. I have to say,

Senator, the fact that Mr. Meader has kept the press at bay makes me wonder what the most above-board politician in recent U.S. history might have to hide."

Ellis loosened his tie, looked everywhere but straight at her. "Young lady—"

"Senator," Harper interrupted. "This is the sixth time in two months you've met with someone from the state fire marshal's office. Yet, there's nothing on the books, no upcoming votes that pertain to fire code mitigation. Meanwhile, the Oregon League of Conservation Voters has been trying to get your attention since last year. What's so important to warrant a meeting almost every week with the fire marshals and yet you continue to turn your back on OLCV? You claim to ignore the lobbyists, but from the looks of it, someone within the union or maybe even the state is courting you. Care to comment on why that might be?"

Ellis's head snapped around and he fixed Harper with an appraising stare. "Who did you say you are?"

"Harper Allen. From *The Oregonian*."

A horn honked as someone in the garage disengaged their car alarm, and Senator Ellis damned near jumped out of his shoes. A bead of sweat trickled down his forehead and he released a shuddering breath before taking a handkerchief from his suit pocket and dabbing at his face. Either he was on the verge of a heart attack or something had him genuinely spooked. Though Harper's journalistic Spidey sense was tingling all over the place, she couldn't help but be a little concerned.

"Are you all right, Senator? You look like you should sit down."

As though he expected someone else to jump out from behind a car at any second, Ellis grabbed Harper by the arm and dragged her behind his car, his back to the concrete wall. He let her go and jammed his fists into his pockets before leaning in, way too close to Harper's face. The scent of alcohol lingered on his breath and Harper quirked a brow. *Drinking on the job, eh, Senator?*

"When I ran for office, I meant everything I said in my campaign." His words were rushed, urgent. "I don't like secrets, never have. They're too much work. Sure, I made mistakes. So does everyone. It's called being human. But rather than go through the trouble and backlash of covering up my imperfections, I embraced them. Voters appreciated that." He ducked his head closer to hers, and Harper got another nasty whiff of alcohol. A few more minutes and she'd have a contact buzz. "But the truth is, no one wants to fix the system. They like things the way they are. The more broken the better. The more secrets someone keeps, the easier they are to control. I did the best I could with what I had to work with, but . . ." His voice broke, "I'm not as strong as I thought I was."

Harper clutched the voice recorder in her palm, and tried to keep from getting too excited. She'd come here tonight, prepared to browbeat the senator into some kind of shocking confession, but here he was, confiding in her without so much as a nudge. *Awesome.* Sam was going to shit a solid-gold brick when she told him. "Senator Ellis, maybe we could go somewhere. Sit down and talk."

"You look young enough to still hold onto some of your convictions," Ellis said absently. "Wide-eyed, determined, out to make a name for yourself and change the world. Am I right?" Well, yeah. Of course she was, but this wasn't about her. Harper opened her mouth to speak, and Ellis cut her off before she could redirect the conversation. "Maybe that's the problem. Maybe there are too many selfish, outdated, under-handed assholes like me trying to run this country. You're still young enough to have convictions. Mine died long before I swore my oath of office. So, you want to change the world? You want to make a point? Show everyone just how broken the machine is? I'll give you a story that'll make your career, Miss Allen."

"Does this have anything to do with the OLCV?"

"Not even close," Ellis said with a snort. "Listen to me—"

A resounding crack echoed through the parking garage like a clap of thunder. Harper jumped, but the echoing of sound was nothing compared to her shock when Ellis gripped onto the strap of her bag and pulled her down on top of him as he crumpled to the ground. The voice recorder flew from her grip, skidding to a stop several feet away, but Harper didn't have time to worry about the damage it might have sustained. "Mobile hazard assessment. Bl—L-Lake. Swa—Lake," he murmured in a thick, strangled voice. Mobile what? And was he trying to say Blake? Or maybe Blue Lake? What was he talking about? He sounded like he was talking through a mouthful of sludge. She looked down to find a deep red stain blossoming over his white dress shirt slowly spreading across his chest. Harper scrambled away, his fist catching on her bag, and Ellis's arms went limp at his sides, his eyes staring blankly ahead. A last shuddering breath gurgled in his chest and a panic so intense washed over Harper that she couldn't form a coherent thought.

"H-he-lp." It took a physical effort to push her voice from between her lips and even then it was barely louder than a whisper. "H-help." Louder this time, the sound clearing some of the confusion from Harper's mind. "Someone help!" she shouted at the top of her lungs, her throat aching from the effort. "Senator Ellis has been shot! Can anyone hear me? We need an ambulance!"

Footsteps tapped on the concrete, growing louder the closer they approached. A knot of dread congealed in Harper's stomach. From across the garage, a dark figure emerged, tall, features shrouded by the shadows. Anyone coming to help would have been running at full speed. The measured cadence of whoever walked toward them now made her realize that she was alone, in a dark parking garage, with a murderer. Harper was a witness and the killer wouldn't be too happy about any potential witnesses. As she hurried to slide her body underneath Ellis's car, she couldn't help but wonder who Sam would assign to write the story of her death.

Harper tried to control her breathing, but her heart was beating so fast, she couldn't slow the intake of air. A pair of black combat boots stopped beside Ellis's Audi. A gloved hand swept down to retrieve her voice recorder before continuing a slow stroll around the car. Harper swallowed down the sob that worked its way up her throat. She was too young to die, damn it. She hadn't accomplished anything in her career. And how sick was it that her last thought as death stared her in the eye was of a man whose name she'd never know. Pathetic.

"Did someone call for help?" A shout in the distance filled Harper with relief. The booted feet in front of her paused.

"Hey!" Another voice joined the first, closer this time. Tears of relief flooded Harper's eyes as the sound of a siren joined the mingled voices. "What are you doing over there?"

The senator's murderer turned around, his boots pounding on the concrete as he fled. The sound of the siren grew louder, scurrying footsteps turned to loud claps, and two pairs of shiny, patent leather shoes stopped near the front tires of the car. Harper looked to her left, at Senator Mark Ellis's lifeless body, and the helpless sobs she'd held in her chest finally broke loose, the tears spilling over her cheeks. At the sound, two security guards bent down and grabbed Harper's hands, pulling her out from underneath the car.

"What's your name?"

"Have you been hurt?"

"Are you the one calling for help?"

Past the wracking sobs, Harper forced the words from her mouth, "Behind the car. Senator Ellis. He's dead. Someone shot him. Oh my God."

One of the guards spoke into a radio attached to his shoulder while the other guided Harper away from the car. "It's okay, you're going to be okay. Try to calm down. The police are on the way and we're calling an ambulance."

Harper's knees buckled and the security guard wrapped his arm around her waist to support her. No need for an ambulance. Ellis was dead.

"There's nothing else? No other details you remember about the shooter?"

Harper stared at FBI Special Agent—something-or-other . . . Davis, maybe—the questions slow to process. He studied her, his nearly black eyes glinting with suspicion. She wondered if they brought in guys like him—tall, imposing, deep voice and rough exterior—when they wanted to shake a witness up. For the record, it was sort of working. Strike that. It was totally working. Even seated, he towered over her, and his dark brows accented his mocha skin and impenetrable eyes in a way that made him look like he could see right through her.

"I don't think so." She stared into the paper cup she held in her hand as though the answer might be floating in the coffee. "I don't really remember. It happened so fast."

Portland police had already questioned her, and she'd given them the same answers. But this homicide was high profile, a United States freaking senator, and once the local news outlets had gotten a hold of the story, the FBI swooped in and moved Harper to a more secure facility, away from the press. Bitter laughter threatened as she realized that if she weren't sitting here as a witness to the actual crime, she'd be covering it for the paper. Doing everything in her power to get just one word with the woman who'd witnessed the senator's death.

"Did the senator say anything to you that would have indicated who might have killed him?" Harper looked at Davis and she was pretty sure her eyes were bugging out of her head. "Maybe a name? A person or an organization that had a grudge against him."

Like, *Oh, hey, Miss Allen, just want to give you a heads-up that the League of Women Voters hired a hit out on me, so you should probably keep your distance*? "No," she replied. "Tonight was the first time I've ever spoken with him and our conversation was very short."

Agent Davis leaned forward in his chair. "What did you talk about?"

Oh, the usual. The weather, our favorite bands. And he hinted about the fact that he'd been wandering the path of immoral political slimeball. "Like I said, our conversation was very short. I've been trying to get face time with him for months. I sort of waited in the garage for him." No use hiding that shameful little tidbit. "When he showed up I pressed him about why he hadn't met with the OLCV yet."

Davis nodded his head as though he was following along, but Harper had the feeling he was giving her the rope he expected her to hang herself with. "Was Jason Meader with him when you approached him?"

She supposed Jason could be considered a suspect. Though anyone in the senator's office surely would have vouched for the fact that he'd returned for Ellis's phone. "No. I overheard the senator mention that he forgot his phone in his office. He sent Mr. Meader back for it."

Davis nodded as though she'd passed his little test. What a douche. "And there's nothing else you can think of? Every little detail matters, Miss Allen."

"No." Even now, the details blurred in her memory. Everything seemed to happen in double-time. "Wait. He did say something about a hazard. And maybe a blue lake?" Blue lake, was that right? Crap, her brain was *mush.*

"What do you think he meant by that?"

How was she supposed to know? Without a clear memory of what he'd said, not to mention any other information to link it to, Harper had nothing useful to offer. It could have been a string of nonsense words said in the throes of death for all she knew, which was a totally morbid thought. And without her voice re-corder, she couldn't even be sure that she'd heard him correctly, let alone offer anything that would have much bearing on their investigation. "I'm just really shaken up. Maybe if I get a good night's sleep—"

A sharp knock at the door interrupted them, and a man with graying hair and bright green eyes poked his head in. "Hey, Curt, come on in," Davis said, pushing out his chair and standing to shake the older man's hand. "Miss Allen, this is Curt Monroe from the U.S. Marshals Service."

Oh, super. All she wanted to do was go home and try to forget what she'd seen tonight and now she had to endure another round of questioning from yet another branch of law enforcement. What was next? CIA? NSA? DHS? There weren't many more acronyms to get through.

"Hi, Harper," Curt Monroe said as he took a seat at the table. Whereas Davis was severe, Curt seemed easygoing and friendly with a comforting, fatherly vibe. He sat back in the chair, seeming very relaxed, only his sharp gaze told her another story. Easygoing or not, he was still a seasoned pro. "Can I call you Harper?"

Anything was better than Miss Allen. It made her feel old. "Sure. But I've already told the PPB and the FBI everything I know. I doubt I'm going to magically remember something for the U.S. Marshals that I haven't for anyone else."

Curt chuckled and the sound put Harper at ease. He wasn't trying to assert dominance over his territory like the Portland Police guys and he didn't possess the crisp, intimidating manner of Davis. Rather, he came across as genuine and concerned. "I'm actually not here to question you, Harper. I think you've been through enough for one night." He raised his brows, his gaze directed toward Davis, and Harper fought back a smile.

"Chief Deputy Monroe is in charge of protective services, Miss Allen."

Curt rolled his eyes at Davis's interjection. Davis was a real killjoy. Harper bet he was the type who ruined surprise parties and told people what was inside a box before they had an opportunity to open the present. *Here you go, happy birthday. It's a watch.* "Well, there you have it." Curt shifted in his seat, turned his back to Davis. "What the FBI lacks in subtlety, they make up for in the quality of their suits." He winked at Harper and shot over his shoulder, "Hey, Davis, you mind grabbing me a cup of coffee? Black."

Davis scowled and headed for the door. When he closed it behind him, Curt said, "So, Harper, this has been some hell of a night, huh?"

Understatement of the century. "I've never seen anyone die before." Harper's voice sounded foreign in her ears. Quiet and unsure.

"It's an awful thing for anyone to have to go through. But, Harper, I'm sorry to tell you that this is going to get a lot worse before it gets better."

Worse? A lump formed in Harper's throat and she swallowed it down. That did not sound good. "Worse how?"

"Here's the thing. If you got any kind of glimpse of Ellis's murderer, chances are he got a decent look at you, too. This puts you at risk. Especially since we don't have a motive. Whoever killed Ellis might think you know something. He might think you're able to identify him. And that puts you in danger."

Like a puzzle piece snapping into place, Harper made the connection as to why Curt Monroe had been brought in to talk to her. "Protective services." She rolled her head back on her shoulders. Yep, things had just gotten worse. "You're here because the feds are putting me in the witness protection program, right?" No. Hell, no. "They can't do that. I've got a job. And a life. And friends and family and—"

"Calm down, Harper." Curt's expression reflected enough sympathy that she knew she wasn't going to get much choice in the matter. Tears sprang to her eyes, but Harper willed them to stay put. No way was she going to cry. "Not witness protection. We're not to that point yet. While you won't technically be in the Witness Security Program, we are going to assign a twenty-four-hour protective detail to you. Just until the FBI concludes their investigation."

Harper nodded. Allowed herself to breathe. "And then what?"

"After that, we'll reevaluate."

Okay. She could live with that. For now. "So, when does it start?"

"Immediately. You'll be keeping me and a few deputies company for the next few days, then we'll assign you a more permanent protective detail."

Harper quirked a brow. "Permanent?"

"Well." Curt smiled. "Semi-permanent. For now."

"Okay, Curt," Harper said on a sigh. "First things first, can we get out of here? Davis gives me the creeps."

"FBI," Curt agreed. "They're all creepy. Come on, Harper. I'll buy you dinner."

Chapter Seven

"Did you even get any sleep before they put you to work? Or was Monroe too anxious to have Galen Kelly, marshal golden boy and SOG hotshot back in the field?"

Galen looked up from his desk, feeling a little like he'd stepped into a time warp. Landon hovered over him, a sarcastic smile plastered on his smart-assed face. This exact scenario could have taken place a year ago. It was almost too easy to slip back into the familiarity of his old life.

"*Va te faire foutre.*"

Landon snorted. "Fancy. What the hell does that mean?"

"Basically?" Galen shrugged. "Fuck off."

Landon rocked back on his heels and gave a low whistle, clearly impressed. "You really learned how to utilize the local dialect while you were over there."

"Yeah, well, I tried." Galen couldn't help the yawn that crept up on him. Damn, he was seriously jet-lagged.

"Monroe should have let you get adjusted before calling you in," Landon remarked. "But we're sort of understaffed right now and he's been covering. Did he brief you yet?"

Galen stretched, eyed his empty Starbucks cup. It didn't hold a candle to Corrine's coffee. He'd need a caffeine IV before he'd be awake enough to think in a straight line. "Protective detail. What else?"

It was too early in the morning for Landon's mocking laughter. "Well, after tagging along with dignitaries for a year, you probably consider babysitting a civilian a piece of cake."

"Not necessarily. Though to tell you the truth, my protective detail in Paris wasn't exactly action-packed."

"Well, PR-wise, Monroe knew what he was doing when he assigned this detail to you." Landon parked his ass on Galen's desk. "This is a high-profile case. The witness was standing about six inches from Senator Ellis when he was shot. According to the security guards who found her, she was hiding under a car, scared half to death, with the shooter about to tie up his loose ends. It's been plastered all over the local news for the past two days. A total media shit storm."

Besides feeling like he was in a time warp, Galen was also way out of the loop with local—or national—news. Since touching down two days ago he'd done two things: first, check in on Michelle. Second, sleep. Followed up with more sleep. And he still felt like a goddamned zombie this morning. Transatlantic travel sucked. "I'm supposed to be meeting Monroe and the witness at nine. Hopefully the FBI won't trip on their own feet trying to wrap this investigation up."

The FBI/U.S. Marshals rivalry was legendary and not relegated to the Oregon District. The Marshals had been *the* elite government law enforcement agency before the FBI took the reins away. Needless to say, the bitter feelings had been passed down through the generations.

"Sean Davis is running point," Landon said. "So you know it's going to be a total cluster fuck."

Galen rolled his eyes and leaned back in his chair. Special Agent Sean Davis was an ex-Army Ranger and had all the people skills of a rabid dog. He didn't work well with others, and likewise, never considered any theories or options but his own. Galen had met a few brick walls less stubborn than Davis. No doubt the investigation would drag out forever. People didn't often respond well to dickish attitudes. Which didn't bode well for their witness. "Great."

"Hey." Landon bucked his chin toward the wall clock on the far side of the room. "Didn't you say you were meeting Monroe at nine? It's almost nine thirty."

"Shit!" Galen shot up out of his chair and took off toward Monroe's office.

"Good luck, golden boy!" Landon called after him.

Galen didn't look back, but he did give Landon the finger.

Nothing like making your boss wait on the first day back to work. Jesus, he was exhausted. And his brain didn't seem to want to get with the program. If it wouldn't have drawn attention, he would've given himself a good, hard slap across the face. Sure, ass hats like Davis made jokes about witness protection and the marshals being nothing more than glorified babysitters, but truth be told, Galen considered it the single most important duty the USMS had. The responsibility of having someone's life and safety in his care was something he took very seriously. And he wasn't about to step into that office less than one hundred percent.

When he got to the chief deputy's office, Galen

paused for a moment to collect himself so he wouldn't appear rushed or out of control. Witnesses generally liked to know the people protecting them had their shit together. Muted voices permeated the door: Monroe and the soft laughter of a woman. Well, he'd known the witness was female, but something about her laughter struck him as familiar. And why did that cause his gut to curl up into a tight knot? Had to be the jet lag. Considering the circumstances, the witness sounded cheery this morning, but Galen was willing to bet Monroe wasn't quite as jovial. The man was obsessed with punctuality.

Galen rapped his knuckles twice on the door before letting himself in. "'Morning, everyone. Sorry I'm late. My internal clock is a little . . ." The words choked and died somewhere between his sternum and tongue. When he first walked through the threshold, all he could see of her was her slim back and lush auburn hair. But then she turned around to face him, and all logical thought took a permanent vacation from Galen's mind. He'd died. It was the only explanation. His plane had gone down somewhere over the Atlantic and for some reason he'd gone straight to hell.

Because only hell could have devised such a sweet, beautiful torment.

Monroe stepped from behind his desk. "Harper Allen, I'd like you to meet Deputy Marshal Galen Kelly. He'll be the deputy in charge of your protective detail for the remainder of the FBI's investigation."

The look of shock that settled on her face couldn't have mirrored his own reaction to the situation any better. She stared for a moment too long, her jaw slack. After the initial shock passed, a smile lit her face, and the sun couldn't have been brighter in its brilliance. She took a step forward, the recognition obvious in her expression. Son of a bitch. Snap decisions were part of his job, essential to his training. And yet, this decision was one of the hardest Galen had ever had to make. Too much rested on his reaction. He forced his expression into a passive representation of professionalism.

"Nice to meet you, Miss Allen."

She stopped dead in her tracks and Galen's stomach bottomed out. His lungs seized up. The hurt that marred her soft features was enough to make him want to kick himself in the ass. And at the same time, with the way they'd parted, how did she expect him to react? He didn't have time to process what he was thinking or feeling right now. If Monroe had even an inkling that Galen knew Harper, he'd be jerked off this detail faster than he could say desk jockey. No way was he going to spend his first weeks back on the job shuffling papers.

Harper's gaze hardened and her lips thinned. The fire in those hazel eyes was enough to make Galen sweat. She bucked her chin up, squared her shoulders, and said, her tone detached and formal, "Nice to meet you, Deputy."

Monroe motioned to one of the empty chairs in front of his desk. "Well, now that you're introduced, let's get you up to speed, Galen. Sean Davis is going to want to talk to you, as will the Portland Police Bureau. But as far as I'm concerned, you don't need to meet with them. A phone call ought to do fine."

Galen's steps were mechanical, each one precisely placed as he moved to the empty chair and sat his ass down. He was pretty sure Monroe was saying something important, but he couldn't seem to focus on the words. Perched not two feet away from him—within touching distance—was the woman he'd spent an entire year trying to forget. Life sure had a way of kicking a guy in the nuts.

". . . doesn't have any leads, but it's only been a couple of days . . ."

God, his memory of her hadn't done her beauty justice, the thumbnail of her image on his computer screen a pale representation of her exotic features.

". . . I expect you to cooperate with their investigation . . ."

She'd recognized him right away and damn, if that didn't make him feel like crowing.

". . . Harper knows what's expected of her in this situation, and though we understand the inconvenience this is causing her, she's agreed to work from home for the time being . . ."

Don't forget, as far as you know, she still has a boyfriend, dumbass. Aaaaand, just like that, the spell was broken. Jesus, what was wrong with him? He needed to speak up, right now. Tell Monroe that he couldn't work this detail because he knew the witness. Get his ass out of this office and the hell away from her.

Despite the fact that he tried to keep his eyes forward, they seemed to move on their own and he caught a glimpse of her from the corner of his eye. The past year melted away, rocketing him back to that night. Her wit, her smile, her scent, her warmth. He should say something. Do something. Put as much distance between them as possible. But when he thought about walking out the door, walking away from her, something inside of him locked down. Maybe it was curiosity. Or maybe, deep down, he was a sadist. Either way, he knew that there was no fucking way he was going to tuck tail and run out like he was guilty of anything. She'd used him. Not the other way around.

This was his assignment. Period. And if she had a problem with that, then too damn bad.

"Excuse me, Curt." Galen leaned back, crossed his arms over his chest. "But, with the high-profile nature of this investigation, and Miss Allen's visibility, wouldn't it be better to move her to a safe house outside of Portland. Temporarily, of course." Harper stiffened beside him and took a deep breath. He had a feeling she was about to object so he cut her off before she could speak. "We're dealing with a highly sensitive case. One that's going to be in the media spotlight for a while. Not to mention the fact that the FBI will be under pressure to produce a suspect. If Senator Ellis's murderer has an ounce of sense, he'll want to eliminate the witness sooner rather than later. Don't you agree?" Damn, he'd pulled that out of his ass. As it was, Galen found it too damned hard to focus with Harper so close. But seriously, since when did protocol allow for a witness to remain in her home? Especially when her face was plastered all over the evening news.

"First of all," Harper jumped in, "I have a name. It's not Miss Allen, and it sure as hell isn't 'the witness.' I'm not a cup you guys can pass around from one location to the next. I have a job, responsibilities. I've already told Curt and I'll tell you, Deputy Kelly. I'm not going *anywhere*."

Funny, she forgot to mention the boyfriend in that short list of excuses.

"Harper, I think what Galen is trying to say—"

"Is that you have no choice in the matter," Galen spoke over Monroe. Jesus, had no one explained to her the danger she was in? "It's my job to protect you in any way I see fit. If that means moving you out of the city, that's what I'm going to do."

"Curt, did you or did you not tell me that until the FBI concluded its investigation, witness protection was off the table?" Though the question was directed at his superior officer, Harper's gaze landed on Galen, challenging him to disagree.

Monroe cleared his throat. "Well, yes—"

"And Chief Deputy Monroe has put me in charge of your protective detail, making you *my* responsibility now. By all rights, you should have been relocated the night of Senator Ellis's murder. Curt, she should be placed in WITSEC and we should be in the process of assigning her a new identity, setting her up in a new town. Since when do we let witnesses make the rules?"

"I told you, my name is not '*the witness*.' And I didn't ask for the Marshals Service to insert itself into my life. I don't need a babysitter."

Galen snorted. *Debatable.* "Why don't you let me decide—"

"Okay, okay. I think everyone needs to settle down." Monroe looked from Galen to Harper as though they'd both lost their minds. "Deputy Kelly is coming off a long flight home, and I know that this situation isn't ideal for you either, Harper." He eyed Galen and frowned. "But like we discussed, your situation has become a little more complicated over the past few days and we have to be more cautious than I'd originally assumed."

Galen's ears perked at Monroe's words. "Complicated how?"

Harper sighed and Monroe shot her a chiding look before he continued. "Harper was using a digital recorder to interview Senator Ellis before he was shot and his murderer managed to get his hands on it before he took off. In the past couple of days, we've been tracking a potential threat."

Was Monroe purposely trying to drive him crazy? "What do you mean by 'potential'? It's either a threat or it's not."

Harper opened her mouth to speak, but Monroe pointed a finger at her and she slumped back in her seat. "A couple of days ago, someone left a voice mail on Miss Allen's office phone. It was a playback of Harper calling for help after Ellis was shot. The FBI is looking into it."

Potential, his ass. "Sounds like a threat to me."

"We don't know that it's Ellis's killer," Harper argued. Why was she arguing? "For all we know, the guy could have chucked my recorder into a Dumpster and some kid is playing a prank on me. Nothing else has happened, and you promised—"

Dear God, was he the only person left in the world with an ounce of common sense? "She should be moved. Period. Her identity is compromised and she's at risk."

A series of spluttering sounds escaped Harper's lips, and Curt made a calming motion with his hands as though he sensed Harper was about to go off the deep end. "I know, I know, Harper. So far, we don't think Ellis's murderer knows anything about Harper other than where she works. But we also discussed that that could change at any moment and we won't hesitate to move her if we need to. For now, we're letting her stay in her apartment. Our office has assured her that our intrusion into her life will be minimal unless we deem it necessary to change that fact. Is that going to be a problem for you, Deputy?"

Intrusion into her life? What about her intrusion into his? "No, sir."

* * *

Once, in the third grade, Harper had accidentally tucked the back of her dress into her tights and everyone on the playground had gotten a nice, long look at her Wonder Woman underwear. That was marginally less humiliating than how she felt right now.

Days wasted daydreaming about him. Potential relationships shunned. Nights alone in bed with nothing but a memory to keep her warm. The romantic in her had imagined this moment so much differently. They'd cross paths. He'd smile and rush over to her. Offer up a perfectly acceptable explanation as to why he'd run out that morning. He'd confess that he thought about her. And she'd do the same. A quick cup of coffee would turn into dinner and from there . . . *Gah!* What an idiot. She was pathetic. Worse than pathetic. She might as well go to the SPCA, adopt twenty cats, and call it a day.

He had no idea who she was. Zero recognition. Not even a *glimmer.* The cool, collected deputy marshal, he'd strode in as though the entire world waited to do his bidding and then plopped down in the chair beside her, her safety nothing more than another day at the office for him. The potential uprooting of her life as inconsequential to him as the choice over what shirt to wear or what to eat for breakfast. He'd completely trivialized her. Who knew he was so bossy? Pushy, even. Total turn-off. Her mortification evaporated under the anger that began to burn through her veins. Obviously the night they'd spent together had been nothing more than a random booty call. And how awesome was it that she'd been stupid enough to think there was more to her mystery man? A decent guy that she'd been eager to get to know. Yeah, right. Harper swallowed down the bitter snort that threatened to surface. Nothing like a healthy dose of disillusionment to start off your day. She'd rather tuck her dress into her underwear and walk through downtown Portland any day than spend another minute with the man seated beside her. Nothing was more humiliating than knowing she was just that forgettable.

"Do you have any questions for Deputy Kelly before I hand over the reins, Harper?" Curt looked at her expectantly.

Yeah, do you have a lot of one-night stands with anonymous women, or was I the lucky exception? "No, Curt, I think you've laid it all out pretty clearly. Thank you."

Curt's brow furrowed at her icy tone and he leaned back in his chair, studied Harper as if trying to crawl into her thoughts. Maybe he should ask his deputy if there was anything about her that he found even remotely familiar. She'd love to hear the answer to that one. Or maybe he'd only recognize her with her clothes off. No doubt he'd forgotten everything from her neck up. *Galen.* She fought the urge to say his name out loud, try it out. Ugh. Why worry about a murderer on the loose? Harper was pretty sure she'd die of embarrassment long before some unidentified killer got a hold of her. No freaking way was she going to be able to stand weeks on end with him. If the FBI didn't get it together and solve this case—fast—she was going to go out of her mind.

"All right, then," Curt said as though he was reluctant to turn them loose. "Since we're all caught up to speed, I'll let you two get on with it. But Harper"— he fixed her with a stern yet affectionate stare—"you be sure to stay out of trouble and let Deputy Kelly do his job. Understand?"

Jeez. You'd think she was a flight risk or something. Or two years old. Okay, so once in the past four days she snuck out for donuts. But in her defense she'd had a serious craving for an apple fritter. "Are you saying I'm difficult, Curt?"

"I would never say that." Curt paused. "Out loud."

Heh. "Don't worry." Harper stood from her chair and slung her purse over her shoulder. "I'll behave."

"Don't forget to give Davis a call," Curt said to Gal—uh—Deputy Kelly. No use getting too familiar with him. After all, she was his job; they weren't on a date.

"Will do."

Harper kept her gaze straight forward, all but ignoring him as he rose from his chair. She was not looking. At all.

"After you, Harper." He swept his hand in front of him and it was all Harper could do not to kick him in the shin. Curt thought she was a pain in the butt for going out for donuts? He hadn't seen anything yet.

"I'm sure Chief Deputy Monroe has already told you this, but no matter what you think to the contrary, we'll try to make this situation as stress-free as possible for you. The upheaval in your life will more than likely be temporary."

As they made their way toward the elevator, Harper wondered if the "We're here to help" speech was Deputy U.S. Marshal Galen Kelly's usual spiel, or if he saved this particular one for women he'd slept with.

"Temporary?" Harper's gaze met his and she quirked a brow. "I bet Senator Ellis's family doesn't consider this a temporary upheaval." The elevator doors opened and she stepped inside.

He stood on the other side of the door, unmoving, his brow furrowed. Harper shot her hand out to keep the doors from closing, a sigh building in her chest. Why? Out of all of the marshals in the entire country, why him? "Look, Deputy Kelly, let's just serve our time together as peacefully as possible. If you agree to give me plenty of space and stay out of my hair, I'm sure we'll get along fine."

His frown transformed into an arrogant smirk and Harper's stomach did a backflip. Amusement lit his blue eyes as he stepped inside of the car.

"See, that's where we're going to have a problem." He hit the button for the garage and faced her head-on. "I can't guarantee to stay out of your hair because it's sort of my job. You're just going to have to get used to having me as your shadow." The smirk widened into a smile that under different circumstances would have blasted the clothes right off Harper's body. "At least for a while." He turned away as if disinterested and folded his arms across his chest. "Oh, and by the way, Harper, you might as well call me Galen. We're going to be spending a lot of quality time with one another from here on out."

Chapter Eight

No way would I have slept with you if I'd known you were such an arrogant pain in the ass. Harper glared at Galen's back, wishing she had laser vision and could burn her thoughts there as a warning to any of his future conquests. She followed him out of the elevator and into the parking garage, a plan of attack already forming in her mind. It didn't take a rocket scientist to figure out that there was some bad blood between the feds and Marshals. And likewise, that they didn't put a lot of stock in Special Agent Sean Davis getting the job done.

"I need to stop by my office."

Galen's stride didn't even falter. "No, you don't. You're working from home."

Please. If he thought the detached, tough-guy routine would spook her, he had another think coming. "True, but Curt and I had an agreement that my day-to-day life wouldn't be disrupted. I have a story due on Thursday and I need to stop by the paper and pick up a couple of notebooks that have information I need in them."

"I hate to break it to you, Harper," Galen said

without a break in his steps, "but your life has already been disrupted. You're a witness to a high-profile murder. Your face is all over the news. And obviously, Senator Ellis's murderer is trying to send you a message by dangling the fact that he knows who you are in your face."

"That's only a theory at this point," Harper quipped. Okay, so maybe the voice mail had spooked her more than she wanted to admit, but she didn't want him to know that. "I'm not too concerned."

"You should be," Galen said. "I'm sorry to tell you this, but whatever you thought of as a normal life is long gone."

Wow, wasn't he a ray of sunshine. "This will blow over." She wasn't about to subscribe to his doom-and-gloom outlook. "And when it does, I don't want to have to rebuild the life I've put on hold."

"This isn't going to blow over until Senator Ellis's murderer is found. That could take months. Years. You're going to have to come to terms with that fact."

The hell she would. If the FBI couldn't get the job done, she'd take matters into her own hands. Harper considered herself a decent investigative reporter. She'd been researching Ellis for months. Since his death, she'd been racking her brain, trying to remember exactly what Ellis's dying words to her had been. She was pretty sure he'd mentioned something about a mobile hazard. The other part, blue . . . something . . . was still a little hazy in her mind. Still, she figured she had enough of a lead to find something of use. And when she uncovered whatever it was Ellis was talking about, she'd make sure to share with the FBI. She refused to sit back and simply allow the Marshals Service to create a new life, a new identity, for her while they searched aimlessly for the bad guy. Curt had made a promise to her and she'd make sure Deputy Kelly upheld that promise.

Her office wasn't more than a few blocks from the U.S. Courthouse building. She had to get away from her newly appointed guardian for a while. His foreboding words and stern attitude was seriously bringing her down. Harper wasn't stupid; she knew the severity of her situation. She wasn't about to run too far away from safety. But at the same time, she wanted Galen Kelly to know, without a doubt, that he couldn't bully her or control her. Plus, she did need the notebooks. The first thing she planned to do once she caught up on work was try to find a lead on Ellis's murder. Harper had a couple of informants on the political scene who might be able to help point her in the right direction.

"I need to stop by the paper," she repeated. Better to press her previous point than allow him to worry her with the prospect of leaving her life behind. "Curt and I have an agreement."

"Agreement or not, I doubt that *Chief Deputy Monroe* let you run all over the city." Harper wondered at the way he stressed Curt's official title, as though she wasn't allowed to call him anything else. "Whatever you need can be picked up and delivered by someone from our office. End of discussion."

Had Curt been easier to sweet-talk? Or was Galen just trying his best to be an asshole? Maybe it was time to switch tactics. "You're right." Harper made sure her tone was complacent, her voice, soft. "And I'd take you up on the offer, but my desk is a bit of a war zone." She gave a little laugh. Too over the top? Maybe. Crap. "I've got this sort of organized chaos thing going on. I'm worried that the wrong notebooks will be delivered and we'll have to start all over again.

I mean, I don't want to inconvenience anyone any more than I already have."

Harper led the way through the maze of cars, Galen close behind her, just to her right. She stuffed her annoyance down to her toes, worried she might explode at any minute. Seriously, did he expect to follow her like a deranged guard dog for the next few weeks—or longer—while basically pretending she wasn't even there? He stopped and pulled a key fob out of his pocket. The lights flashed on a newer Ford Taurus. Must have been government issue. For some reason Harper had always imagined him as a truck sort of guy.

"First it's a notebook," Galen said as he opened the driver's-side door. "Then, it's a file." He motioned for Harper to get in as he settled into his seat. "After that, it's a staff meeting that you can't miss, or some other work function you forgot about. I've been through this hundreds of times with hundreds of witnesses. Protective custody isn't fun, Harper, but you're going to have to stick it out."

Galen turned the key and the engine roared to life. Since they'd left Curt's office, he'd barely made eye contact. Was she just that inconsequential? At least with Curt, she'd felt like someone was truly concerned for her safety. With Galen, she felt like a burden.

As they exited the parking garage, Harper pulled down her visor to block the too bright morning sunlight. It was a perfect representation of her life right now: blinded by something she couldn't see past with nothing but the unknown stretched out in front of her. A heavy sigh escaped her lips, one she hadn't meant to free. But she needed to release some of the tension that stretched her body taut or she'd snap.

"Harper—"

Without thinking, she pushed open her door and jumped out of the car before he could pull out into traffic. Without a look back, she darted across SW Third, barely missing the light change. The traffic signal gods were definitely smiling down on her today, giving her a chance to duck her babysitter while covering her tracks. He was dead in the water until the lights changed again.

As Harper blended in with a group of pedestrians, the sound of her phone ringing cut off the frantic string of thoughts assaulting her mind. Thank God. The last thing she needed right now was an attack of conscience over ditching her protective detail yet again. But seriously, if she'd had to listen to any more of his I'm-in-charge assertions, she would've cracked. She checked the caller ID and said a silent thanks for best friends with good timing. "Hey, Sophie."

"Hey. I thought I'd check in and see how you're holding up."

For the most part, Sophie was the go-to friend when you needed a wild night out, or someone to cheer you up. She'd treaded lightly with Harper for the past few days, though, and it was a nice change. No matter how practical Harper tried to be or how tough she wanted to act, Senator Ellis's murder had really shaken her up.

"Eh, I'm hanging in there," she said, careful to keep her eyes forward and her pace steady. No use drawing attention to herself by running down the street like a madwoman. She didn't dare look back as she walked down the sidewalk. No doubt Gal—*Deputy Kelly*—was hot on her tail. "Well, I got my new babysitter today, so there's that. And apparently, I'm not allowed to even stop by the paper to pick up what I need to work at home."

"Seriously? Not gonna lie, Harp. I'm on their side on this one. These guys have you on a super tight leash for a reason. Or do you not remember the lovely voice mail someone left for you at work?"

Harper stopped at the crosswalk, toe tapping with impatience. *Hurry up, you stupid streetlight.* "Okay, I'll give you that one. I'm still a little freaked out about it, but I'm not going to let some asshole scare me into hiding. Plus, you'd think I was the criminal the way I'm being treated. I guess it could be worse, though. I could be locked up in a room somewhere."

"You and solitary confinement?" Sophie remarked. "Probably not the best match. God, I hope they find the asshole soon."

"You and me both." The little man on the crosswalk sign lit up and Harper took off across SW Main. "Anyway, my day's going to be a total wash until I can get my notes. I guess I'll just hang out at the apartment. Stop by if you want. It's not like I'll be going anywhere any time soon."

Sophie laughed. "I'm working the late shift today, but maybe tomorrow or Wednesday I'll swing by and we can watch a movie or something. So"—her voice took on the conspiratorial tone that signaled trouble—"tell me about the new bodyguard? Cute? I need the lowdown. You know, I'm not opposed to sexy older men."

The anxious knot unfurled in Harper's stomach and fluttered as though blown by a strong wind. Curt hadn't been Sophie's type, but the guy they'd brought in to replace him sure as hell was. "Sophie, you wouldn't believe me if I told you."

"Well, in that case, I'm definitely coming over tomorrow night. I'll text you. Let me know if you need anything, okay?"

"I will."

"Um, Harper? Why do I hear the sound of traffic in the background?" Harper smiled at Sophie's suspicious tone. "You didn't ditch again, did you?"

Sophie knew her all too well. "No one comes between me and my notes," Harper replied, admitting to nothing.

"Harper, I hate to be the responsible one in this situation, but you really shouldn't be running around the city without an escort. Get your notes and get your ass home. See you tomorrow."

"Bye." As Harper disconnected the call, she hit SW Broadway and jogged down the sidewalk toward *The Oregonian*'s offices. That had to have been the fastest seven blocks she'd ever walked. Knowing she was being pursued by an annoying deputy U.S. marshal probably had something to do with her new land-speed record, though.

As she headed into the building, she couldn't help but worry about what would happen once Galen managed to catch up to her. Would he drag her off against her will to a safe house somewhere or would he actually take her home? A day trapped in her apartment with the star of her sexual fantasies for the past twelve months. What could be better? Dental surgery. Filling out a twelve-page marketing questionnaire. A visit from pushy missionaries. Door-to-door encyclopedia salesmen.

She could only hope that whatever happened, he'd go light on her. After all, spending time alone with him would be punishment enough.

* * *

Galen's car idled at the stoplight while he stared across the street, mouth agape. He watched as Harper blended in with the pedestrians scattered on the sidewalk. She appeared to be well-practiced at stealthy getaways. Her pace wasn't quick enough to draw attention but wasn't slow enough for him to keep an eye on her. She made sure to stay away from the street side of the sidewalk and remained close enough to the person walking near her that she appeared not to be alone. Smart. Of course, he'd known that about her. Not that ducking her protective detail was currently an accurate representation of her intelligence. Galen cursed as he pulled his cell from his pocket. What was she thinking, taking off like that?

Guess he'd asked for a rough go of it, what with his presenting her zero options in her situation and all. More oftentimes than not, intimidation tactics made it easier for him to do his job. He had plenty of practice at behaving like a disconnected dick. Sort of came with the badge. If you pushed hard enough, most people wouldn't push back. It was how he controlled a situation. Apparently, he hadn't pushed her hard enough because she was one of the rare witnesses who hadn't responded to his tactics. Damn it, he was not in the mood for playing games. Add to that the fact that he'd painted himself into a corner with Harper by pretending not to know her and subsequently treating her *exactly* like a cup being passed around, and his day—hell, maybe even his entire year—was basically shot to shit. Too late to worry about it now, he supposed. He pulled his cell from his pocket and dialed the office. Not even five minutes out of the building and he was already calling his supervisor for help. Awesome.

"Monroe."

Christ. As if this weren't humiliating as hell. "What's

The Oregonian's address?" Only a year gone and he had to reacquaint himself with the city. Lord. "And when I get there, what floor is her office on?"

"You lost her already, Galen?" Monroe all but blurted. "I figured it would be at least a few hours before she managed to dodge you."

Galen cringed. By tomorrow he'd be the office joke. "Yeah, well, she's . . ."

"Feisty?" Monroe ventured.

"Something like that." This detail was going to be the death of him.

"1320 South West Broadway. Second floor," Monroe said through a bout of laughter. *Ha. Ha. Ha.*

"Thanks."

"Keep an eye on that one, she's trouble when she gets a donut craving."

Okay, that was new. Witnesses had tried to give him the slip for various reasons but never for pastries. "Noted."

Galen ended the call and pulled out into traffic. He could drive the seven blocks to the newspaper's offices faster than she could walk if the traffic lights changed in his favor. His fists gripped the steering wheel tight, his knuckles turning almost white. Was the tangled knot forming in his stomach one of anger or worry? Nothing pissed him off more than a difficult witness. But was that all there was to it? Or did the underlying sense of dread that caused his death grip on the steering wheel have more to do with his concern for Harper's safety?

Seven blocks felt more like seventy as he kept his eyes peeled for any sign of her. The morning rush of traffic didn't do much for his uptight attitude and the commute of pedestrians made it impossible for him

to spot her. He reminded himself that Harper wasn't
stupid. She knew the seriousness of her predicament. Her running probably had more to do with as-
serting control over her situation than a disregard for
her safety. That didn't mean it didn't rile the shit out
of him, though.

Galen turned onto SW Broadway and pulled up in
front of *The Oregonian*. As he cut the engine and got
out of the car, he caught sight of her, beelining it to
the entrance, head down, arms swinging with purpose. A smile threatened and Galen tucked it away.
Her comical stride was *not* amusing.

"Harper, hold up!" Galen called after her, but she
headed into the building without even a glance back.
He hit the key fob and locked the car, sprinting to
keep up. Once through the entrance, he got a glimpse
of her auburn hair as she ducked into an elevator,
the doors sliding behind her and shutting him out.
Damn, she was fast. "Goddamn it," Galen ground
from between clenched teeth.

More times than not, the ones who ran always took
the stairs. If she was hoping to ride the elevator up
and take the stairs down, he'd cut her off. Plus, by
taking the long way up, he'd give himself a few minutes to cool off. If he came face-to-face with Harper
right now, he'd be tempted to cuff her to him. And
that probably wouldn't go over too well.

The second floor was separated into several large
rooms for the various departments. He found a set of
double doors marked newsroom and went inside.
The wide-open space was pretty much what Galen
had expected: lots of cubicles. A maze of desks and
partitions designed to aggravate him to the point of
spontaneous combustion. Flat-screen TVs hung high

on the walls, dialed in to regional and national news outlets. The clicking of computer keys mingled with murmured voices and the ringing of phones. He'd go bat-shit crazy in this anthill environment day in and day out. There was too much hustle and bustle. And that was saying a lot considering what he did for a living.

A woman with her face plastered to the screen of her smartphone approached, and Galen reached out to tap her on the shoulder. She looked up and around as if she had no idea where she was, and gave him a bright smile.

"I'm looking for Harper Allen. Have you seen her this morning?"

"Yeah." She put a hand on her hip and canted her head to the side. "She's in Sam's office. Can I help you with something?"

"No," Galen said, looking around. "Sam is . . . ?"

"Editorial." She pointed to the back of the building toward a set of enclosed offices. Her expression grew wary, and Galen had the impression he was being inspected and logged into the woman's personal memory bank. "Is Harper expecting you?"

Right. Of course everyone here knew what had happened. And likewise, it was nice to know her coworkers were looking out for her. He swept his jacket aside to show her the badge affixed to his belt and she relaxed. "I'm with the U.S. Marshals Service." He held out his hand. "Galen Kelly."

"Tiffany." She shook his hand. "If you head straight back to the far wall, Sam's office is on the left."

"Thanks." Funny how accommodating people became when they found out you had the power to arrest them.

Galen took off toward Sam's office. Monroe's mocking laughter echoed in his mind as he realized that keeping track of Harper might be a little tougher than he'd thought. Dignitaries expected you to be close. Welcomed the human shield who was ready to take a bullet for them. He'd thought the high-profile assignment would keep him on his toes. But nothing could have prepared him for what he'd come home to. *Hey, Galen. Welcome back! How 'bout you spend the next few months with the best sex of your life while you try not to think about the fact that she cheated on her boyfriend with you. Sounds like fun, right?* Woo-fucking-hoo.

He knocked twice and entered Sam's office without being invited. If Harper was prone to wander, as Monroe had indicated, he could fix that particular problem in two little words: tracking anklet. Sam looked up and Harper turned around as Galen closed the door behind him. Her expression fell, and her shoulders slumped. Nice to see her deflate like an old balloon the second she laid eyes on him.

"You know, you'd think since I'm doing you a favor by not setting you up in a safe house, you'd do one for me and stay close like I asked. I don't know what you thought you were doing, Harper, but taking off like that isn't going to fly with me. This place is *off-limits*."

Harper cocked a brow and settled back into her chair. "You call that taking off? It took you, what, ten minutes to catch up to me. I guess I better be careful when we get back to my place. Don't want you to think I'm *taking off* when I slip into the bathroom for a few seconds."

Galen gnashed his teeth together until he thought his jaw might break. He fixed a pleasant expression on his face, and reminded himself that witnesses under protection, like errant teens, had a tendency to test the waters with their appointed guardians. Sometimes witness security was a lot like parenting. In some ways, Galen felt like a temporary foster parent for troubled adults.

"Sam?" He looked past Harper to the older man seated at the desk. "I'm Deputy Marshal Galen Kelly. I'm in charge of Harper's protective detail. I wonder if I might have a moment alone with her."

Chapter Nine

Great. Now what? He was going to take her to task for ditching him, lecture her on the merits of playing it safe, and remind her once again how he was so freaking magnanimous for not carting her off to a hotel somewhere and tagging her with a new name and Social Security number before setting her loose in the wild? Sam gave her a questioning look and she nodded. Might as well get it over with now. Harper sat in the chair, staring at the wall behind Sam's desk and the framed IRE, Polk, and Northwest Journalism awards, milestones of a career decades in the making. Would she ever get to hang anything like that on her own wall? For that matter, would she even live long enough to be something more than a hot news story herself?

What's the real issue here, Harper? Are you tired of your every move being followed and cataloged? Are you scared? Or are you simply that pissed he doesn't seem to remember anything at all about that night?

Yes, yes, and yes.

She could be upfront with him. Galen might not remember anything about her, but she remembered everything about him. No lies. No bullshit. They were mere hours into what could be a weeks'—maybe months'—long relationship. Strike that. Whatever this was, it wasn't a relationship. It wasn't even a partnership. She could safely call this a *whatevership*. She was a responsibility. A work assignment. The equivalent of a professional shrug. Whatever. And when it was all said and done, she'd return to her life and he'd return to his. Everything would go back to normal. It was what she wanted. So why did she already feel such a profound sense of loss? She released the sigh that had built up in her chest. Damn, she was tired of this game and it had barely begun.

"I didn't know it was a gunshot at first," she said before Galen could lay into her. She sat facing Sam's desk, Galen behind her. It was easier to talk to him if she didn't have to see his face. "It sort of sounded like a car backfiring. A loud pop. And then he just . . . fell. He pulled me down on top of him and I noticed he was bleeding." She hadn't talked about what had happened since the night the FBI had questioned her. Her chest constricted and Harper found it hard to breathe. "I—I shouted for help, but I knew that he wasn't going to make it. Not with the way he was bleeding. And then I realized that whoever shot him had to be close and all I could think was how stupid I was for calling out. I should have run, but I crawled under his car like an idiot, waiting to be killed."

The carpeting in Sam's office muted Galen's footsteps, but Harper knew the second he was within touching distance. The charge in the air sparked along her skin, and her pulse quickened.

"I have to know. I *need* to know why my life's been uprooted, why someone is trying to scare me." She'd never said the words out loud. It sounded so callous, as though she were more concerned with the whys than the man himself, but that wasn't the case. "Ellis's family deserves to know why he died."

"The best way to get that, Harper, is to keep a low profile and let the FBI do their job."

His voice tingled through her, sending a shiver down her spine. If she closed her eyes and focused on the warm timbre, she could almost pretend she was standing in her dark apartment again, his breath warm in her ear. "My parents are freaking out over this. They want me to come home. Ever since I got that crazy voice mail, Sam ordered me away from the office and threatened to fire me if I came back before the investigation is complete. My own peers have smeared my face across every news outlet in the country. I suppose it's poetic justice. A determined political reporter finds herself at the center of a political scandal." She scoffed. "Hell, I'd report on it."

Galen came from behind her and settled on the edge of Sam's desk. Funny, but she sort of liked having him at her back. Despite the fact that she was nothing more than another day at the office for him, she felt safe. He studied her with those intense blue eyes, his dark brows furrowed. If she'd ever wanted to crawl into someone's thoughts it was right now.

"I know this is new and uncomfortable for you. But it's not for me," Galen reassured her. "I've done the high-profile thing. I've worked details that lasted a week and others that have lasted months or longer. The point is, we're here to make sure not only that you're protected, but that you're not overwhelmed. You don't have to take on more than you can handle, Harper."

She'd never been good at asking for help. Asking

for help meant you were weak. That you couldn't hack it. From the time she was a kid, her dad had drilled that philosophy into her brain. His side of the family was huge: brothers, sisters, cousins all coming out of the woodwork to stand in line with their hands out. They were constantly asking for loans, favors, a helping hand. And Tom Allen didn't want his daughter to be the type of person who couldn't stand on her own two feet. He wanted her to know the satisfaction of being independent, of not having to owe anyone for anything. Harper had depended on herself for so long, she didn't know if she could allow herself to depend on anyone else. Once she opened that door even a little, would everything she'd worked for come crashing down?

Galen's words were so sincere, his gaze so clear and focused. If only she could let go. Allow herself to give up control. If only there weren't history between them. She averted her eyes and stood, unwilling to see the honesty in his. "I got what I came here for. Let's go."

The trek back through the office didn't do anything for Harper's dour mood. Pitiful glances and commiserating half smiles followed her out the door and into the hallway. Poor, sad, pathetic Harper. Was ten in the morning too early to start drinking? She hated the pity that wafted off of everyone she passed. She didn't need Galen's concern. Didn't want his softly spoken words to comfort or warm her. It was easier to hold on to her anger when he acted like the hotshot arrogant deputy marshal, and it helped to lessen the sting of his . . . what? Rejection? You had to remember the person you'd slept with in order to reject them.

"Curt always left after eight and another deputy took over the evening shift, along with a second deputy who's usually posted outside of my building for the night. Is that going to change now that you've been assigned to my detail?" God, if Galen had to spend the night in her apartment, she'd crack for sure.

Galen pushed the button to call the elevator and took a step back. "Nothing changes. I'm the deputy in charge of your detail, so everyone else on shift reports to me. We want you to feel comfortable, and let's face it, no one sleeps well with a stranger camped out on the couch."

Harper's lips spread into a reluctant smile. Nothing like waking up to an armed man on your sofa to start off the day. "Curt assigned a female marshal to stay in the apartment over nights."

"That's not going to change. Everyone who's been assigned to your security will remain on your detail." The elevator doors slid open and Galen stepped inside. Harper followed and tucked herself in the opposite corner of the tiny car. Last year's elevator ride with Galen had been decidedly steamier, and she needed to put a little distance between them. "If you're uncomfortable with anyone or have any questions, just say the word. A lot of witnesses get nervous."

"I'll be fine."

Galen's brow furrowed. He looked like he wanted to say more, but thankfully he kept his thoughts to himself.

"Do you really think whoever shot Ellis is a threat to me?" It was a stupid question. One she'd asked the FBI, the police, and Curt the first night she'd met him. Harper didn't really need any more confirmation, but for some reason, she wanted to hear him say it. "He didn't confide anything to me"—*except for a bunch of gibberish I barely remember*—"but Curt says the shooter can't afford to take any chances."

"If it was me," Galen said, thoughtful, "I'd take you out in a heartbeat. No questions asked."

The mere two-story elevator ride was one of the longest of Harper's life. Despite the fact that Galen had assured her that her life was in danger, all she could think about were her legs wrapped around his waist and the hard length of his erection as it brushed against her core.

"Are you okay, Harper?" Galen asked as the elevator doors opened. "You look a little flushed."

Oh, God. Not at all embarrassing that he noticed the blush her memories evoked. Harper Allen, wanton slut right here, folks! "I'm fine." *Mind out of the gutter, Harp. Keep it clean.* She needed to get that night out of her head once and for all. He certainly didn't remember it, so why should she? *Um, how about because it was the best sex of your life?* Okay, so maybe it would take longer than a day to quit thinking about that night. At least she had work to occupy her in the meantime.

Galen made a silent vow to avoid elevators for a while. The second the doors slid closed, all he could think about was his hands on Harper's body and how damned good it had felt to kiss her. And wasn't he a king-sized asshole for fantasizing about their passionate elevator ride together while she was obviously upset over the situation she was in. *Nice, dude. You earned your dickhead-of-the-month membership today.*

While he was trying not to picture Harper without her clothes, a thought did cross Galen's mind. With the high-profile nature of this case and the yet-to-be-determined motive of Senator Ellis's murder, chances were good that the bastard responsible was holed up somewhere, doing his research on the sole witness. He already knew where she worked. It wouldn't be long before he knew everything about her. Where had Harper said she'd grown up? Iowa? No. *Shit.* Where the hell was it? He'd have to check in with Monroe, find out if he'd sent anyone to keep an eye on Harper's family. More times than not, suspects took the backdoor approach, using the witness's loved ones to get to the witness.

Once free of the torturous elevator, the rest of the morning took a nosedive from there. Harper didn't speak and her pensive mood was starting to rub off on Galen. He climbed into the car—from one enclosed space to another, it seemed—and he gave himself a mental pep talk as he pulled out into traffic and headed south down SW Broadway.

"You're going the wrong way."

Galen kept his eyes on traffic. Had Harper moved? She said he was going the wrong direction, but the Regency Apartments were on Broadway, not far from the newspaper. *Wow, dude, how pathetic is it that you remember where she lived?* Maybe they weren't headed to her apartment. The thought that he might have to deal with being stationed at her boyfriend's place made Galen want to turn the fuck around and head back to the office.

Harper pointed behind them and said, "My condo's off of Burnside, on Northwest Uptown Terrace."

"Gotcha. Thanks." Galen switched lanes and circled the block, backtracking to SW Jefferson. Monroe had sent all of Harper's pertinent information—work info, home address, apartment number, cell number, etc.—to his phone, but he hadn't thought to look at it yet. The fact that she might have moved was a sore reminder that a hell of a lot had changed over the course of a year and he had no business living in the past.

The twenty-minute drive to Harper's condo passed in silence. It was clear she wanted him to give her a little space, and to be honest, he wasn't interested in trying to make small talk. When they pulled up to her building, a cold lump of dread settled in the pit of Galen's gut. The last things he wanted to see were pictures of Harper and her boyfriend, his clothes scattered around the house, or worse yet, the guy in the flesh. That would be the cherry on top of a *stellar* day. Yeah, he'd been played. A fucking *year* ago. So why did it feel like it just happened yesterday? Fair didn't work into the whole life equation. Was it fair that his dad had cheated on his mom more times than he could count? *No.* Was it fair that she'd abandoned him and Michelle because she couldn't snap out of her depression? *Nope.* So what good would it do him now to be angry over something he had no control of whatsoever? *Nada.*

If he hadn't killed the engine, Galen doubted Harper would have even noticed they'd stopped. She looked up at her building, and then at him. God, he wanted to comb his fingers through her hair, take her face in his hands, put his mouth to hers, and make the past year disappear. Her face was drawn, her usually sparkling hazel eyes dull. She looked exhausted. Knowing that she wasn't his to comfort, to touch, sliced through him like a knife to the chest. She belonged to someone else.

There was no use sitting out here in the car like some sort of pussy. Life wasn't fair. Suck it up. If the boyfriend was there—fine. If he had to endure the sight of them together—fine. He was a professional, damn it. He would not let this get under his skin.

"Ready?"

Harper sighed and got out of the car. "I'm on the sixth floor." She'd devolved from snarky smart-ass with a comeback for everything into a passive, nonverbal passenger who seemed to be just along for the ride. Galen liked the smart-ass side of her personality much better than the quiet brooder. At least the snark kept him on his toes. Hell, at this point he'd settle for passive aggressive.

Harper looked up at her building, almost as though she were preparing herself for the arduous journey to the sixth floor. Maybe she wasn't any more excited to have her boyfriend meet the guy she'd had a one-night stand with than Galen was to be meeting the ass hat who'd managed to snag her. What was his name again? Camden? Carl?

"Curt brought his laptop so he could work," Harper remarked as she stepped up onto the sidewalk and headed for the building. "You're probably going to be pretty bored. I don't have anything but basic cable and a weak DVD collection."

Galen stepped up beside her and cocked a brow. Whereas Monroe's administrative duties usually kept him chained to his desk, Galen spent a lot of his time in the field. "I'll be fine." He motioned Harper up ahead of him while he scanned the building and surrounding area, gathering a mental cache of information he would later use to develop a risk assessment. Already, he spotted several areas—the parking garage next door, an alley across from her building, not to mention an abandoned storefront fifty yards down the street—that made perfect cover for a shooter with even marginal aim. The fire escape was a huge risk as well. Funny that something put in place as a safety measure could actually put Harper closer to danger.

Though he wasn't thrilled about the neighborhood—honestly, her tiny studio on Broadway would have been safer—Galen felt a little better about Harper's living situation once they made it past the lobby. The condo complex was older, but it did have twenty-four-hour front-desk staff. He made Harper wait for him at the elevators, well within his line of vision, while he checked the interior stairwells. All equipped with emergency exits that led to the fire escapes and sturdy doors that opened up onto each floor.

"Curt and his team did the whole marshal treatment on the building a couple of days ago." She stepped into the empty elevator car and raised a brow as if daring Galen to step inside. Holy hell, that one look was enough to stir his blood. He took a deep breath and forbade himself from thinking of two things on the ride to the sixth floor: Harper's naked body, and well, Harper's naked body on his naked body.

"There are deputies positioned around the block." Talking about work was sort of like taking a cold shower. Harper's eyes wandered to his mouth and his gut clenched. Shit, it was going to take a hell of a lot more than office banter to cool him down. "And, um"—he cleared his throat—"of course, the FBI have personnel in the area as well. If I have to evacuate you—"

"Why would you have to do that?" Her voice dropped an octave, the low, seductive quality sending an electric jolt through Galen's body.

Soccer. His grandma. Gunshot wounds. Damn it,

he needed to get his mind off the thick locks of her auburn hair. A tangle of curls he wanted to bury his face in . . . Landon in a bikini. Okay, that would be straight-up hilarious. "We'd do our best to intercept any potential threats before anyone could make their way to your apartment, but I like to hope for the best and plan for the worst."

"Do you really think he'd be stupid enough to come after me in my own home?" She worried her bottom lip between her teeth, and Galen swallowed a groan. Was she doing this to him on purpose?

"I think a desperate man is capable of anything."

The elevator deposited them on Harper's floor. Never had Galen been so thankful to be free of an enclosed space. In fact, he might swear off elevators from here on out. Taking the stairs everywhere they went couldn't be too bad. He could use a little more cardio in his workout routine.

"I didn't see anything. And if there is anything incriminating on my voice recorder, it's not like I have it anymore. Why not just disappear and leave me alone?"

While Harper led the way to her unit, Galen acquainted himself with the layout of her floor, the exits, and closest neighbors. Surely Curt already had names and pertinent information.

"I think he had a plan. And you weren't part of it. He doesn't have room for liabilities and you're a loose end that needs to be tied up."

Harper stopped in front of the door marked F6. Keys in hand, she put her back to the door and faced him. Galen's heart hammered in his chest and he stuffed his hands into his pockets to keep them from balling into fists at his side. Just like on that amazing night a year ago, her expression became unsure. As though letting him into her condo would change everything.

"So now I'm a loose end?" she murmured.

What are you doing here? You should not *be working this assignment.* He reached out and took the keys from her hand. Her hazel eyes shined with emotion, something almost hopeful that damn near choked him.

"A threat. Unfinished business. In this case it's all the same." Galen reached around her waist and slid the key in the lock. His arm brushed her torso and she shifted away. Hopeful? More like uncomfortable. *Way to go, dickhead.* Where was a brick wall to bash your head against when you needed one?

Harper turned, the action abrupt. Yeah, definitely uncomfortable. She opened the door and retrieved her key, heading deep into her apartment in a nervous rush. One of the most important aspects of protective detail was to make sure the witness felt safe. So when she acted like she was afraid to be alone with you, it sort of hit high on the epic-fail-o-meter.

Galen gave her some space—God knew he needed a little—and did a mini sweep of the condo. The sixth floor was safer than the ground level at any rate, but that didn't do much to put Galen at ease. The fire escape provided easy access to Harper's apartment, and if Ellis's shooter was as determined as Galen suspected him to be, it would be no great feat to get to Harper. The sliding patio doors that led out to her terrace were cheap and flimsy, the lock easy enough to break given the proper motivation. Likewise, the blinds in every window were pulled up to expose Harper's movements to anyone who cared to look. And while the thought of Peeping Toms watching her undress made him want to break something, he was more concerned with how easy it would be to take her out with a single shot from a sniper rifle.

Christ, he felt unprepared. Monroe had basically thrown him into this assignment. Off the plane and back to work. He had a lot of catching up to do before he'd be confident in his ability to protect Harper. Galen didn't like going out half-cocked and he wouldn't feel completely ready until he had every detail on his assignment down to Harper's shoe size.

To the left of the living room was a galley kitchen, a much bigger space in comparison to her previous place. Then again, her last apartment had been the size of a saltine cracker. Harper stood in front of the sink, her eyes unfocused, her expression lost. Her beauty sucked the oxygen right out of Galen's lungs. He'd been so sure when he met her that she was someone he could trust. The hard truth of her betrayal burned like a hot cinder in Galen's throat.

Honesty was his number-one rule. As he lost sight of everything but her, he reminded himself that a lie by omission was still a goddamned lie.

Chapter Ten

What was it about Galen that made Harper break out into a full-body sweat? Three hours. After an entire year apart, one hundred and eighty measly minutes together had her undone. Two elevator rides in one day had prompted fantasies about him stripped naked with her wrapped around him like a second skin. And when he had her back to the door, caged in by his arm as he unlocked it . . . the memory of what his hands had felt like on her bare skin was enough to send her blood racing through her veins. She pulled away when his hand brushed her side, but only because she was afraid he'd sense the tension in her body. Or worse, the low thrum of desire that pulsed between her thighs. If she hadn't put a little distance between them, she would have pounced and ridden him right there in her hallway with all the abandon of a cowgirl at the county rodeo.

Sooooo ladylike.

Where was her pride? This was a guy who'd slept with her and disappeared the next morning without even a "Thanks for the good time!" He couldn't have known what that night meant to her. She wasn't a one-night-stand sort of girl. But apparently, Galen Kelly was well-practiced at the one-nighter. So practiced, in fact, he couldn't even remember Harper. She suppressed a disdainful snort. He'd probably picked dozens of women up in bars. And there were probably many more he couldn't bother himself to remember.

The kitchen seemed like the safest place to hide. At this point, she was vacillating between wanting to kiss him and wanting to kick him. A low countertop separated the kitchen from the living room, and unless Harper wanted to vault it like an Olympic gymnast to get to him, she was marginally safe from making a fool out of herself either way.

"You want a grilled cheese?"

Galen's brow furrowed at the question and Harper stood there, jaw slack, brain cranking to keep up with her mouth. *Really, Harp? "You want a grilled cheese?" You couldn't think of anything else to say?* Did she even have cheese? Or bread? Argh!

Galen's lips quirked in a half smile, and his eyes lit with amusement. "I love grilled cheese."

You'd think after one brief encounter almost a year ago, he would have diminished in her memory somehow. But he was just as perfect as she remembered. It was totally unfair that in addition to being under house arrest for who knew how long, she was forced to endure the torture of his nearness and suffer the constant sting of his rejection. Oh, not to mention the fact that she had to pretend as though they'd never met before today. Hell might be a nice place to vacation once this ordeal was over. "Is Gruyere okay or are you a traditionalist?"

Galen took a seat on a stool at the bar and leaned his arms on the surface. Harper caught herself wishing he'd take off that ridiculous sport jacket. And while he was at it, his shirt too. *Focus, Harp!*

"I'm good with anything. Cheddar, Swiss, provolone and yes, even Gruyere. I don't discriminate against any cheese."

His body was permanently etched in her mind, and his wit had remained firmly anchored in her memory. She was glad that aspect of his personality hadn't changed. But, damn, fate was certainly turning the screws on her. "Lightly toasted or darker?"

He smiled. "A little on the burned side."

"Really?" Harper grabbed a pan from the rack hanging above the bar and went to the pantry in search of bread. More than two slices would be preferable. Not moldy, even better. She grabbed half a loaf out of the cupboard and checked it for freshness. Score! "Burned grilled cheese is sort of gross, you know."

"Blasphemy. You just say that because you've never tried it. How do you like your grilled cheese, then? Soft and soggy?"

"Golden brown," she said defensively. "Just crunchy enough."

"Ah." His voice became solemn. "So you're one of *those.*"

Harper tried to remain aloof, but a burst of laughter put the kibosh on that plan. "One of those what?"

"A grilled cheese snob."

"I am not."

He stretched his arms out on the counter, and Harper forced her gaze from wandering to his hands, fingers splayed out on the surface. Man, did she want those hands on her.

"I bet if the bread is toasted even a shade darker than gold you won't eat it." Harper gave him a look as he continued to tease her. She slapped some cheese on the bread and grabbed a plastic container with butter. "I like mine with a lot of butter," Galen added.

She slathered the bread with a generous slice of butter. "Me too. Guess I'm not the only grilled cheese snob here."

"I admit to nothing."

While they ate their grilled cheese, Harper kept the conversation light. It didn't do anything for the lump of regret that congealed in her stomach, however. Galen was so easy to talk to once he let down his I'm-in-charge-here attitude. This had to be the real him. The guy she'd met at the bar that night. Not the guy who'd left without saying a word. And not the bossy know-it-all.

"I should probably get some work done." At this point, her only other option was to offer him a full-body massage and she didn't think that fell under his marshal duties. If only. Yeah, if Harper didn't get to work, she'd have no pride left to speak of.

"Me too," Galen said in a way that made her think work was the last thing on his mind. Of course, she'd misinterpreted him before, so she tried not to read too much into his tone. "I need to call Agent Davis and check in with Chief Deputy Monroe."

"Right," Harper said, the easygoing air of their previous conversation devolving into something stilted and awkward. *Damn.* "I'm on deadline, so, yeah . . ."

"I really need to check in with the rest of the team . . ."

And then it floundered and died.

Silence descended like an impenetrable fog that Harper couldn't seem to find her way out of. The moment had passed, that instant connection, so like the night they'd first met, lost. She gathered their plates and put them in the sink, and searched for something, anything to salvage the moment. That was pathetic, though, right? Her inner voice chimed in to remind her that she'd wanted something more with this man a year ago. And he'd left her apartment before she'd woken up without a word in parting. It sent a pretty clear message. So why try to force something between them that was never meant to be? A good reporter knew when a lead was about to dead-end, and this one was running out of road.

"Harper? I asked if you'd mind if I use the balcony to make a couple of phone calls."

Harper looked up from the sink. How long had she been standing there, staring into the stainless-steel basin like some kind of freak? She suppressed a groan of embarrassment and turned toward Galen, who was studying her again with that perplexed expression. *Great.*

"Sure. Let me know if you need anything."

He gave her a wan smile and opened the sliding glass door. A frown creased his forehead and his expression darkened. "Monroe should have mentioned this, Harper, but you need to be sure to keep all of your doors locked at all times. Even this one. Okay?"

"Oh. Okay. Right, Curt did mention that. I must have forgotten. Sorry."

He gave her a nod and slid the door closed behind him.

Hadn't she locked that door? She could have sworn she'd checked it twice before heading to Curt's office with him this morning. Huh. Maybe she was losing it. From now on, she'd triple check. Even though she doubted anyone would climb up to a sixth-floor balcony, Curt said it was a security precaution, so she'd keep it locked. Period.

Galen had his phone to his ear as he paced back and forth, back and forth across her balcony. She could have watched him all day, the way his body rolled with an easy grace, each step precisely placed as though he'd transformed the act of walking into art. She knew from memory the shape of his body, his strong thighs, rippled abs, sculpted shoulders, and if she closed her eyes, she could picture the muscles bunching and releasing as he walked. Harper gave herself a mental shake. *Snap out of it and get your head on straight!* Nothing but heartache would come from dwelling on something that was never going to happen again.

While Galen did his thing out on her balcony, Harper set up camp at her dining room table. Okay, so calling it a "room" was a bit of a reach; the space was a little square of tile to the right of the living room only big enough to accommodate a tiny table. Still, this condo was a palace compared to her former studio apartment. With her notes spread to one side of her laptop, she hunkered down and got to work. Her story on the long-term effects of abolishing collective bargaining in certain unions was an easy piece. Really, all it needed was a quick polish and it would be ready to send to Sam. Harper stared at the cursor as it blinked beside her byline. No way would she be able to focus on reading and revising this story right now.

She opened a Web browser and typed Blue Lake into the search engine. The first result was a farm in southeast Minnesota that grew nothing but the blue lake variety of green beans. She doubted Senator Ellis wanted her to look into organic beans. *Crap.* Wisconsin, Colorado, organic farms, geothermal farms, farms for sale, back country lakes in Washington and Michi-

gan, a school district in Pennsylvania . . . Page after
page failed to produce anything related to Oregon,
Senator Mark Ellis or his wife, or anything political
in nature. Obviously, the senator had intended to tell
her more, but unfortunately, the bullet in his chest
had put an end to any conversation—or revelation—
that would have done Harper any good.

Down but not out. If Harper was anything, it was
persistent. On an exhale of breath, she let her eyes
drift shut as she thought back to that night, but the
images were garbled and confused. One minute she
was standing in front of Ellis. The next, a loud pop
and he was dragging her to the ground, his voice
strained in her ears. He'd mentioned a hazard of
some kind. Mobile hazard? Hazard assessment? Could
he have been referring to a threat? She might not
have much to go on, but Harper was far from throwing in the towel. While Davis and the FBI were con-
ducting their investigation, she was going to conduct
one of her own. Being proactive would help her feel
a little less out of control and who knows, maybe she'd
find something useful she could pass on to Agent
Davis. Harper had a friend or two at the state capitol
who might be able to help her out. She did a precur-
sory check to make sure Galen was still preoccupied—
yep, pacing away—and grabbed her phone. Scrolling
through her contacts list, she selected the entry
named Liz, and dialed.

A not-so-chipper voice answered. "Did we or did we
not agree that calls during business hours are prohib-
ited?"

"I know, and I'm sorry." She valued her contacts on
the "inside," and *Liz*, as she'd requested Harper refer
to her, was very strict about phone calls while she was

at the office. "I wouldn't call you during the day if it wasn't important."

"Well, what's done is done. Besides, you should be taking it easy. You've been through the wringer, sweet cheeks. The last thing you need to worry about is work."

"If I don't work I'll go crazy." Especially with Galen ever present.

"I get that. Sometimes work is a good distraction. Considering what you've been through the past week, I suppose I can let you off the hook this once. What do you need, cupcake?"

Liz was a sixtysomething secretary for the lieutenant governor and had the inside scoop on a lot of the goings-on around the state. Aside from having a penchant for using silly nicknames—cupcake, lamb chop, sweet potato, and Harper's personal favorite, baby butter bean—she was the person to talk to if you wanted dirt, gossip, the inside scoop, or in this case, a phone number.

"I'm after two things, Liz, and if you can get even one of them for me, I'll . . ." What? What perk could she possibly offer in exchange for a little info? "I'll hook you up with a sexy U.S. marshal." Okay, so she wasn't positive that Curt was single, but he looked about Liz's age and didn't wear a ring. And he was pretty good-looking for an older man. Whether or not he'd be up for a blind date was another matter, but if it came down to it, Harper would work her charm.

"Cute?" Glad to see Liz had her priorities straight.

"Would I offer otherwise?"

"All right, pumpkin. What can I do ya for?"

Harper craned her neck toward the balcony. Thank God Galen was long-winded. "First, I need you to check out anything that contains the words 'blue lake' and let me know if you get any hits. I'm looking for whatever you can dig up, really. Local, related to Ellis, his family, his campaign, or any of his staff."

She responded, "Hmm," which in Liz speak translated to, *Oh reeeaaally. Is that all?* "And second?"

"Can you snag me Jason Meader's personal cell phone number?"

"Your marshal better be *really* cute," Liz warned.

And in classic Liz fashion, she hung up without even saying good-bye.

Galen pulled the phone away from his ear and stared at the screen. On a good day most of the words out of Davis's mouth translated to, "Blah, blah, blah." But today, he'd hit an entirely new level of stupid.

"You're telling me that after four days of investigation, you're leaning toward a robbery gone wrong? Ellis was a United States senator, Sean. Not some random guy leaving work for the day."

Davis took a while to answer, and Galen wondered if the FBI special agent was too busy practicing his golf swing to respond. "I'm sure you think you're better equipped to handle this situation, Galen, what with coming off an international assignment, but maybe you should leave the heavy lifting to the grown-ups. Your job is to babysit the witness and that's *all*."

Dickhead. "See, here's where we're going to have a problem." Galen's blood was rising, his temper close to the surface. "What you fail to consider in this situation is the fact that you're gambling with someone's safety on your hunch. Let's say this is a robbery gone south—why would a random mugger with no ties to the senator threaten Harper by letting her know that he had her digital recorder in his possession? If the suspect hadn't reached out, I'd agree that Harper might not have much to worry about."

"We don't know it's the suspect reaching out," Davis stated in the smug tone that drove Galen insane. "It could be someone playing a prank."

"Did you trace the call?"

"Yeah, traced it back to a pay phone downtown."

Great. Nothing like a dead end to add to an already difficult case. "Look, Davis, I'm not saying that our guy isn't a freaked-out mugger. I just think that by making that sort of assumption, and not exploring every possibility, we could be risking Harper's safety. If your theory is wrong"—Galen took a deep breath— "it's her ass, not yours."

"Last time I checked, *Deputy*, you're not my supervisor. In fact, you're nothing more than a grunt working for me. So I'd advise you to watch the accusations. I don't answer to you, and I'll do my job however I damn well please. Ellis wasn't exactly squeaky clean. The man was a total fuck-up in his personal life. He cheated on his wife, he couldn't keep his kids in line, pissed away most of his money, and as far as I'm concerned, he bumbled through his job. But he came clean to the press, his wife, his constituents, time and again without even blinking. And his record over the past couple of years is pretty damn clean. No scandals. We can't find a concrete motive for anyone to kill him, ergo, there's no lead."

Galen was going to take Davis's *ergo* and shove it right up his overconfident ass. "Honestly, I can't believe I wasted my time with this phone call. I was told I'd be brought up to speed on your investigation, but the only thing I know for sure is that the FBI doesn't have a fucking clue how to do their job and you've got your head shoved so far up your—"

"I'd watch the next thing you say," Davis warned. "All it takes is a phone call and you'll be off this detail and writing reports for the next six months."

Bullshit. Davis couldn't do anything and he knew it. Monroe would laugh in his face if Davis tried to throw his weight around like that. The Marshals Service and the FBI worked together when they had to, but neither had power or jurisdiction over the other.

"Maybe you ought to ask the reporter what she knows about Ellis's death." Galen didn't like the sneer in Davis's voice. He clenched his hand into a fist so tight, the circulation cut off. "Maybe she's got motive. The shooter left her alone—maybe they were working together. I interviewed her. She might be hiding something."

"What in the hell are you talking about?" Galen squeezed his fist tighter, imagining Davis's neck in his grip. "The security guards who found her said she was scared shitless. If they hadn't interrupted the shooter, she'd be dead."

"That's what she says. The parking garage security staff said they saw a man standing by Ellis's car. The garage was dark and they didn't get a good look at him. What if he was coming to collect his partner, but rather than take any chances, they split up. She pretends to be a hapless victim, he escapes without being identified."

Galen had heard some far-fetched theories before, but this one took the cake. "And what would her motive be?"

"That's what I'm trying to find out. Like I said, I

think she's hiding something. Maybe she and the senator had a fling on the side and he wanted to end it. Maybe she was stalking him. His office has logged frequent phone calls and interview requests from her."

Jesus. Davis was certifiably stupid. "She's a political reporter, Sean. I'd say interviews come with the territory. Did his office know why she made so many requests?"

"His assistant said he turned down every single one of her requests. Why? Ellis has been known to be pretty friendly with the press. And the more he turned her down, the more she persisted."

Galen couldn't help but smile. It fit Harper's personality to a tee. Tenacious. It didn't make her a target for suspicion, however. "How do you explain the missing voice recorder and the voice mail at her office, then?"

Davis scoffed, "We have nothing to go by but her word that the shooter took off with her digital recorder. For all we know, she left that message herself to throw us off."

Was Galen hearing Davis correctly? The guy was clueless. "You're off base. She's not a person of interest in this case."

"She's a person of interest until I say she isn't. This is my investigation."

Great. So not only would Galen have to protect Harper from being a loose end that needed tying up, he was going to have to protect her from the FBI as well?

"This is the wrong move, Davis."

"I think you need to do your job, and stick with

the witness. Don't worry about *my* job or how I'm doing it."

Galen disconnected the call before he said something that he wouldn't regret, but that might get him fired. He leaned back and looked through the glass door at Harper, typing away on her laptop. She had no idea she was a suspect. And why should she? No doubt Monroe had kept that little fact to himself.

Damn it, Harper. You got yourself into one hell of a mess.

Chapter Eleven

"I don't believe it. I mean, seriously? What are the odds?"

Sophie sat curled up in a chair on Harper's balcony, a glass of Moscato in her hand. She'd been perched in her seat for the past hour and her eyes were still bugging out of her head. Which under any other circumstance would be pretty hilarious.

"I know, right?" Harper took a sip from her glass and followed Sophie's gaze to where Galen sat in the living room. "I'm pretty sure fate wants to see me suffer."

"If this is what suffering is like, sign me up. Maybe I ought to go out and throw myself in the middle of a crime in progress. I need a hot deputy marshal for a babysitter, too."

"Funny," Harper remarked. "If you think I'm enjoying this, think again. He has no idea who I am, Sophie. Do you know how humiliating that is?"

Sophie arched a sinister brow. "You could always strip naked and remind him."

"Yeah, I don't think so. One rejection from him is enough, thank you very much." Harper leaned in toward her friend. "And can you please stop staring? He's going to know we're talking about him."

"I can't help it." Sophie reached across the patio table for the bottle of wine. She dragged her gaze away from Galen long enough to refill her glass. "Boy is fine, Harp. Like, *fine*, fine. I don't know how you can focus enough to put one foot in front of the other, let alone make conversation."

"Yeah, well, conversation isn't the problem." Her initial plan to be a pain in Galen's ass had sort of dissolved after the first day. Once you extolled the merits of a perfect grilled cheese to a guy, it was sort of difficult to play the tough girl. "He's almost too easy to talk to."

Sophie flashed her a knowing smile. "I take it you're not going out of your way to be a royal pain in his ass anymore?"

"Not so much. Honestly, this situation is stressful enough without adding another layer. I thought it would make me feel better to put him through his paces, but really, it's not worth the effort." Over the past couple of days, her whatevership with Galen had settled into companionable professionalism. It wasn't too bad, until her thoughts drifted to memories she was better off not focusing on. Then she found herself envying Galen's lack of recollection.

"Did it ever occur to you that he might be pretending not to know you?" Sophie pointed her glass at Harper as though to drive her point home.

"I doubt it." Why play games? The night they'd met, he'd proclaimed himself to be a straight shooter, and even now he didn't pull any punches. Harper imagined someone like Galen wouldn't be able to downplay the situation. "When he saw me in that office, his face was totally blank. Not even a hint that he recognized me."

"So, what, you just exchange small talk all day while you try to avoid mentioning that you've seen him naked?"

"Pretty much," Harper said with a shrug. "He texted me last night to check in after his shift was over, though."

"Oh, really?" Sophie said in an arch tone. "Sounds promising."

"I think we've reached the stage of our whatevership that he's just trying to put me at ease. The U.S. Marshals' version of customer service."

"Whatevership?"

"Yeah, it's what I've dubbed our arrangement. How else would I describe my situation? Holed up in witness protection with the guy I slept with who doesn't seem to remember the event."

"Whatevership is right." Sophie laughed. "I can't think of a better way to put it. So, what does he say in his texts? Anything naughty?"

"You wish," Harper replied. "Mostly small talk. Checks up on the other deputies, makes sure I don't need anything."

"For a guy who doesn't remember sleeping with you, he seems pretty concerned," Sophie said. "I bet I'm right and he's pretending. Maybe tomorrow, he'll say good morning by visiting you in your shower."

Harper's gaze shifted to Galen. His feet were propped up on her coffee table, his laptop resting on his thighs. Whatever he was working on had his full attention, and Harper had never been so jealous of a piece of technology. "It's been a few days, Sophie, and I've yet to have company in the shower. Don't get your hopes up."

"Hey, I've got zero prospects at the moment. Until I can find a sexy marshal of my very own, I've got to live vicariously through you."

Harper lifted her wineglass in a toast. "Let's hope when you find him, he remembers you."

"Amen to that." Sophie clinked her glass against Harper's.

By the time Harper's friend left, Galen had only an hour of his shift left to go. Was it wrong to be annoyed that the other woman had monopolized Harper's time, leaving him nothing to do but catch up on reports? He had a vague recollection of the vivacious blonde as one of the women who'd been with Harper that night at the bar. He'd barely noticed her, though. Hell, the entire sports pub could have burned down around them and he wouldn't have noticed anything but Harper. *Seriously, dude, time to let it go.*

While she busied herself in the kitchen, Galen closed his laptop, no longer interested in work. "You're lucky that Curt's allowing you visitors." He'd meant the comment to be good-natured, but suspected it came off sounding too harsh. She looked up from the sink, her expression sullen. Yep. Too harsh. "I just mean that your situation is unusual for such a high-profile case. That's all."

Harper rolled her eyes, and though she seemed dismissive, there was still a trace of concern in the hazel depths. "The only good thing about my work connections at the moment is the fact that the media has backed off. No droves of reporters or news vans parked out on the street. Don't think Curt didn't give me the riot act about reaching out to friends and family, though. I had to bitch up a storm for permission to see Sophie."

"We're good at what we do, Harper. We wouldn't put these restrictions on you if we didn't think they were necessary."

"Yeah, I know." She left the dishes she'd rinsed in the sink and turned away from him as she rifled through the refrigerator. "You know what I miss the most, though? Takeout. I'm seriously jonesing for some sushi. There's a great place a mile or so from here on Burnside. It's funny how something as simple as grabbing food at a restaurant can become so important."

An opportunity presented itself and Galen wasn't about to pass it up. Though they were civil now, he couldn't deny that their current relationship had gotten off to a rocky start. Mostly because he'd been an insensitive dick who'd treated Harper like a piece of luggage to cart around. And though he still hadn't forgiven Harper for lying to him all those months ago, he knew that what she was going through right now wasn't easy. He had to start thinking of her as he would any other witness under his protection. She deserved any scrap of normalcy he could offer.

"Do you have a menu?" he asked.

Harper straightened and shut the refrigerator door. The smile she gave him almost made him forget why professional detachment was a good idea. "Are you serious? We can get takeout?" She fished a menu from a stack in a basket on the counter and handed it to him.

"Yep," Galen replied. "I have the perfect delivery boy for the job."

* * *

"Dude, you owe me big-time for this," Landon said as he handed over the cardboard box of sushi takeout. "I had to drive across town to pick this up, you know."

"Quit whining," Galen said as he crossed to place the box on Harper's dining room table. "You have to be over here in an hour for your shift anyway."

"Yeah, sixty whole minutes. Just because you don't have a life doesn't mean that I don't. Last time I checked, this badge I'm wearing doesn't cover food delivery. Since you've ruined my evening, you might as well feed me."

Galen hurried to the door, blocking his friend from entering. "Sorry, Deputy, but I only ordered for two."

"You suck," Landon griped as Galen moved to close the door. "I won't forget about this. I'm so gonna make you my bitch when I run a witness security detail."

"*If*," Galen stressed. "If you ever run a security detail, you can pay me back. See ya." He closed the door in Landon's face, but that didn't shut out the string of snarky comebacks Landon left in his wake.

"That was quick," Harper replied as she emerged from her bedroom. She'd changed into a pair of yoga pants that hugged every soft curve of her ass and a little thin-strapped top that revealed the muscle definition of her slender arms. *Namaste.* "I thought it was against the rules for strangers to drop by."

Galen smiled as he laid the food out on the table. "See, that's where having a staff of trained professionals comes in handy."

Harper's mouth quirked in a half smile as she walked to the dining room and sat down. "You didn't seriously have one of the deputies deliver us food, did you?"

"Landon's on shift in an hour. He had nothing better to do."

She eyed him suspiciously, her mouth still puckered in that not-quite smile. "Do you mean Deputy McCabe? I met him a few days ago. He's a nice guy."

Any woman with a pulse got a healthy dose of Landon McCabe charm, and Galen suspected his friend had doubled up with Harper. The detached professionalism Galen was trying so hard to exhibit took a backseat to a flare of annoyance at Harper's affectionate tone. Annoyance because jealousy would indicate that his feelings toward the woman sitting across from him were something more than casual. *Which is why you were checking out her ass before she sat down? Real casual.*

"He's all right."

Harper quirked a brow at Galen's stilted response. Sure, Landon was the closest thing he had to a brother, but that didn't mean he wouldn't pop the guy in the nose if the situation called for it. Galen's brain conjured up an image of Landon flirting with Harper in Monroe's office. Definitely an offense worthy of a shot to the face.

"Well, if he brings me sushi once a week, he's more than all right in my book." She grabbed one of the spicy tuna rolls with her chopsticks and took a bite. "Oh my God," she moaned. "So. Good. I amend my previous statement. He officially has my undying love and devotion."

Holy shit. He had no idea that watching a woman eat sushi could be so damned *erotic.* That not-jealousy burned in Galen's gut. Food delivery services earned Harper's devotion? Galen was here twelve hours a day, six days a week ensuring her safety and protecting her life, but Landon gets her undying love? What a crock of shit. *Says the idiot who let her play him like a fiddle.* For all he knew, she still had a boyfriend somewhere. *Yeah, one she cheated on with you.*

Harper abandoned any conversation in exchange for an intimate moment with her dinner, which was fine by Galen. He didn't feel much like making polite conversation at this point. Why did it seem like he had to constantly remind himself that Harper was the type of woman he shouldn't get involved with? Lying and cheating were his top two deal-breakers. But the Harper he'd spent the past few days with didn't strike him as the kind of person to practice deceit. Could it be that his assumptions were just that?

Too late to contemplate that now. What was done was done. He was on this assignment and that meant he had to put the past behind him. Acknowledging a previous relationship with her would be career suicide, and that was something Galen couldn't afford.

Maybe he should have stayed in Paris.

"Galen?"

He met Harper's concerned expression, her chopsticks hovering in midair. "Sorry, did you say something?"

"Yeah." She laughed. "I asked if you wanted the last spring roll."

"Oh, no. Go ahead."

"Are you okay?" Harper canted her head to the side as she examined him. "You seem a little . . ."

Broody? Pissed off? Flaky? Unprofessional? Childish?

". . . pensive."

Oh, great. Pensive. The polite way of saying your mood is a total downer right now. "I'm fine. Just tired."

Harper poked at her spring roll with the chopsticks.

Now who was pensive? "I know this can't be the most exciting job in the world. Sorry."

The soft side of Harper was not what he needed right now. He'd spent the past few days in a constant state of reflection, digging up the past, reminding himself why Harper was bad news, and then making up excuses as to why he should text to check up on her at eleven o'clock at night. The more he convinced himself to stay away, the closer to Harper he wanted to be. He'd never felt so conflicted, so utterly unfocused. And he didn't know how much more of this he could take. A few days with someone shouldn't have such an impact, but it did.

"I told you, this is my job. It's not about the excitement or whether or not this is a waste of my time. Because it isn't. You didn't ask to be a witness to a murder, and you sure as hell didn't ask to be in the kind of danger you're in. The upheaval in your life is real and it sucks a hell of a lot worse than the time we spend making sure you're safe. So don't be sorry, okay? You have nothing to be sorry for."

The soft expression on Harper's face caused Galen's chest to tighten. She averted her gaze and pushed the plastic container with the spring roll toward him. "Well, if I can't be sorry for the fact that you have to babysit me, you can take this spring roll as a token of my gratitude."

Galen smiled as he accepted the proffered roll. "Gratitude for what?"

"For not throwing me in solitary as punishment for ditching you the other day. You have to admit, I've been pretty good lately."

"True," he conceded. "Though I've been warned to beware of sudden donut cravings."

Harper nodded solemnly. "Oh, dude. When it comes to donuts, all bets are off."

Keep it professional. This is a job and she's a witness. The mantra was becoming harder to enforce with each new day. How could he possibly keep his distance from her when she smiled at him like that?

Chapter Twelve

"They want me to come in for another interview."

Harper stood in the doorway, eyes wide, brow furrowed. Anxiety permeated the air around her, causing all of Galen's five flights of self-coached detachment to take a tumble back down to the ground floor. The past week had been smooth sailing. He should have known something—or someone—would topple the balance Galen had strived to achieve. "Okay, before you get too upset, let's sit down so you can tell me what's going on."

Peggy Murphy, the deputy assigned nights with Harper, was already headed out the door, her bleary-eyed zombie shuffle a pretty clear indicator that she was getting tired of sleeping on Harper's couch. "Harper, try not to worry," she said at the threshold. "It's standard operating procedure. I'll see you tonight, and you can tell me all about it, okay?"

Harper nodded, and Peggy cast Galen a knowing glance before she closed the door behind her. They were trying to keep Harper level, but even Peggy realized a second interview wasn't a good sign. As if he weren't even there, Harper turned and paced the confines of her condo, circling through the galley kitchen, into the dinette area, and back through the living room. She paused only long enough to snatch a mug from the counter before she continued on her track, round and round until Galen started to feel a little dizzy.

He intercepted Harper on her fifth lap and planted his hands on her shoulders as he bent down to get to eye level with her. "First things first, sit down. You're making me motion sick."

Harper plopped down on the couch. She seemed to be making a meal of her thumbnail, biting away as her face screwed up into something that looked a lot like pent-up anger. If she didn't hit the release valve soon, Galen was pretty sure she'd explode.

"Since day one, that FBI agent has been up my ass. Why? I told him what happened, regurgitated everything I could remember. Now, he wants me to come in and tell it all to him again. And do you know why?" Her hazel eyes locked on Galen's. "Because he's trying to rattle me, that's why. I'm not stupid. I'm aware that he thinks I'm involved in Ellis's death. Why else would he call me in for another interview? He thinks I've gotten comfortable and let my guard down. And he's going to use the opportunity to try and shake me up. He'll lay into me, play the asshole FBI agent and try to push me into faltering, changing my story, admitting to something. Seriously, the guy is a total douche. If he thinks for even a second that I'll—"

"I think you need to take a couple of breaths, Harper." One more sentence without air and he was pretty sure her face would turn blue. "Don't jump to any conclusions. Like Deputy Murphy said, follow-up interviews are standard. Especially in an investigation of this magnitude." Galen didn't like lies. Or lying. But softening the edge for Harper seemed like the best thing to do right now. Truth of the matter was, she had Davis spot-on. That son of a bitch was absolutely trying to shake her down. He didn't have any leads, and so, the next best thing was to pin Ellis's murder on the person who'd been standing next to him when it happened. "What time are you supposed to go in?"

Harper looked at Galen as though she was having trouble processing his question. Not great. She needed to be sharp as a tack to thwart Davis's browbeating. She needed to get her head in the game. "What? Oh, he said to come in around ten."

That gave him two hours to coach her for the interview. Totally doable. "Okay, good. I'll go in with you and you won't be alone with him for the interview. But I don't think either of us will be worth a shit on an empty stomach. Go get ready to go."

Harper frowned. "Where are we going?"

"Rumor has it you have a thing for donuts. So, I'm going to take you out for the best pastries you've ever eaten."

"You said eating out was against the rules."

Galen grabbed her hand and pulled her up from the couch. "Today, we're going to disregard the rules. Now, hurry up. I don't have all morning."

What are you doing, Galen? When he'd suggested taking Harper out before her interview it had seemed like the most logical thing in the world to do. But now, as he parked in front of A Slice of Heaven, Galen was starting to doubt his own sanity.

"The paper did a write-up on this place a few weeks

ago," Harper remarked as she unbuckled her seat belt. "I've been meaning to drop by, but then things got a little crazy."

"I guarantee you, you won't find better scones anywhere in the city. Maybe even the entire state."

Harper laughed. "Do they have apple fritters?"

Galen opened his door and Harper followed suit. "Absolutely. But they're probably not what you're used to."

"A food challenge." Harper headed for the entrance and ducked under Galen's arm as he held the door wide for her. "I'm intrigued."

So was he. And that was the fucking problem.

Michelle waved from behind the counter. "Hey, Galen! Sit anywhere. You guys want some coffee?" Her knowing smile as her gaze lit on Harper was enough to solidify the fact that bringing her here was, in fact, a monumentally bad idea. Why had he told his sister about Harper? Christ, Michelle had a hard time keeping her enthusiasm to a minimum when there was nothing to be excited about. He'd given her more than enough ammo to go all uber-cheerful and nudge-nudge, wink-wink with him. Great.

The bakery was busy, but not so busy that Michelle couldn't tear herself away from manning the counter for a few minutes to hand-deliver their coffee. Damn it. She plunked two wide, white porcelain mugs in front of Harper and Galen and poured coffee from a French press into each. "So, brother, what prompted you to darken my door this morning?" She turned to Harper and gave her a way too wide and way too cheery smile. "And who's your friend?"

You damn well know who she is. Michelle would pay for her treachery. "Harper," Galen said as he tried to unclench his jaw. "This is my sister, Michelle. Michelle, this is Harper Allen."

"Harper's an interesting name," Michelle said as she reached out to shake Harper's hand.

Harper settled back into her chair and cast a suspicious glance Galen's way before responding. "My mom's a high school English teacher. She reads a lot."

"Harper Lee," Michelle said with a snap of her fingers. "Cute."

"Um, thanks."

"So . . ." Galen caught Michelle's eye and gave her a look that he hoped conveyed her need to make a speedy exit. "Harper has a meeting in an hour, so we're sort of in a hurry." Translation: *Leave us alone and don't ask her a bunch of embarrassing personal questions.* "Do you have any apple fritters today?"

Michelle puffed up her chest and Galen couldn't help but smile at the pride his sister had in her little bakery. "I took a batch out of the oven this morning. Prepare yourself for pastry bliss, Harper. No lie, my apple fritters are orgasmic."

Harper's amused laughter caused Galen's chest to swell for an entirely different reason. Damn it. Detachment was a hell of a lot easier when the other person didn't draw you to them like a magnet.

"I consider myself an apple fritter connoisseur. Hit me!"

"Oh, I like you," Michelle said with a wink. "Next time ditch the suit"—she jutted her chin toward Galen—"and we'll drink some coffee, eat until we pop, and I'll dish all the dirt you want on my baby brother."

Harper looked at Galen from the corner of her eye, and a mischievous smile curved her full lips. "I might have to take you up on that offer."

* * *

The apple fritter was better than orgasmic. More like I've-died-and-gone-to-heaven good. A slice of heaven? Um, yeah it was. Never in a million years would Harper have thought her undying loyalty to Voodoo Donut would be called into question, but after eating Michelle's masterpiece, infidelity to her beloved donut shop was more than just a possibility.

Puff pastry surrounded an entire baked apple, the core removed and the negative space filled with brown sugar, honey, cinnamon, pecans, and all sorts of delicious flavors Harper couldn't identify. The entire culinary masterpiece sat in a shallow pool of warm vanilla bean custard and the plate rimmed with fresh Marion berries. Her eyes rolled back in her head and she groaned as she took yet another bite. Would it look weird if she chewed *reeaally* slowly, just so she could savor the taste for a while longer?

"I told you," Michelle said with pride. "Is it not the best apple fritter ever?"

"Oh my God," Harper all but moaned. "So good. I could live on these."

Michelle was a spitting image of Galen: dark hair, intense blue eyes, a quick smile, and charm in excess. She had an easygoing personality that put you instantly at ease and a fun sense of humor that made Harper think she'd be up for all sorts of shenanigans. This morning's pit stop was the perfect remedy for Harper's anxiety over her impending interview with Special Agent Doucheba—uh, Davis. Too bad Galen wasn't feeling the happy-go-lucky vibe this morning.

Harper had to admit, there were times during their conversation that Michelle treated Harper more like

Galen's girlfriend than simply another case assignment. Although, to be fair, she doubted Galen brought many of his charges to his sister's bakery for breakfast. At least, she hoped not.

"Galen hasn't dated in almost a year, you know."

"Michelle, there's a customer at your counter. Don't you think you should go see what she wants?"

"Did you know that Galen is a member of the Marshals' SOG team? They only take a certain number of deputies for the program."

"Michelle, I think I heard your phone. You better go check."

"Did you know he speaks French? French!"

"Shel—"

On and on it went, volley after volley, like a verbal tennis match. With every compliment or fact about Galen's skills, childhood, or hygiene, his scowl grew darker. After this morning, Harper was willing to bet this would be the first and last time they visited A Slice of Heaven. Together, anyway.

When Michelle finally seemed to run out of steam, Galen pushed his chair away from the table and stood. "Harper's interview is across town and we don't want to be late. I'll call you later." That last little bit sounded too much like a threat for Harper's peace of mind and her heart took a nosedive into her gut. No doubt he was none too happy about his sister treating Harper like she was more than a work acquaintance. Was there a better way to start the day? A harsh reminder that the guy you wanted didn't want you back followed up by a grilling from an FBI agent who'd apparently watched too many FBI movies. Awesome.

"Can I get a fritter for the road?" Harper asked as Galen ushered her toward the door. If anything, she could bury her sorrow in puff pastry and baked apple goodness when she got home.

Galen's scowl seemed permanently etched into his face as he let out a deep, burdened sigh. That's what she was, wasn't it? A burden. An assignment he probably hadn't wanted in the first place. Galen's sour mood had managed to rub off on her. She could officially consider today a total wash.

"Here you go, Harper." Michelle handed her a beautiful pink and white decorated pastry box tied with a black bow that was in itself a work of art. "Come back soon, okay?"

Harper gave her a wan smile. "I'll try. Thanks." She motioned for Galen to go ahead of her out the door, no longer interested in any mock shows of gallantry.

Once in the car, Harper turned her attention out the window, watching the traffic pass them by as they traveled down Cascades Parkway toward the FBI building. Past a scattering of hotels, an ITT Tech, and a Target, the friendly retail façade melted away to be replaced by the well-manicured, orderly presentation of federal buildings, jutting straight and tall like giant soldiers. Harper suppressed a shudder. She was more nervous about meeting with Davis than she cared to admit. Maybe they could take a detour at Target. She could stand for a little retail therapy.

Galen hadn't made a sound since they'd left A Slice of Heaven. His hands planted firmly on the wheel at two and ten, his gaze straight ahead, he was the epitome of U.S. marshal professionalism.

They pulled up to the building and Harper let out a deep sigh. So far, she hadn't heard anything from Liz on Blue Lake or Jason Meader. Today's visit with Agent Davis would have been better if she could've brought something useful to the table. Now, she had nothing to offer the cocky FBI interrogator. And if he was going to start treating her like a suspect, she wasn't sure she'd want to offer him anything without an attorney present.

"Should I have gotten a lawyer?" The question was redundant. She didn't expect Marshal Cranky Pants to actually offer up an opinion. Harper's dad had suggested it, but of course, she'd brushed off his concern. Now, she wasn't so sure.

"Honestly, when a person of interest comes to an interview lawyered up, it sends up a red flag."

Huh. He speaks. In a tone nominally more friendly than a growl. "So, I'm a person of interest now? You said I wasn't a suspect. That this was standard in a high-profile case." Too bad Harper couldn't control the escalation of her own voice.

Galen turned in his seat. His expression, serious and stern, should have been a total turn-off, but it wasn't. Likewise, the angry fire in his blue eyes was more alluring than it was frightening. The straight line of his jaw, the tiny crook in his nose just below the bridge, the way his brows drew down and his forehead crinkled when he frowned. All of it should have pushed Harper away, but instead, she found herself wanting to reach out and brush his dark locks from his brow, smooth those furrows, trace the stern line of his clenched jaw, and the hard line of his lips. What was she really upset about? The fact that she had to endure another pummeling from Davis, or the fact that she'd once again been the victim of Galen's hot/cold treatment. Did it really matter which one?

"Harper."

"Never mind," she snapped, reaching for the door handle. "Let's get this over with so I can go back home and sit in solitary for the rest of the day."

They checked in at the front desk, Harper turning over her ID while Galen flashed his credentials and handed over his gun at the security checkpoint. Once through the metal detectors, they took the stairs—what was it with Galen and stairs?—to Davis's office on the fifth floor.

After yet another check-in at yet another reception desk, not to mention a lengthy stay in the waiting room that went on for just shy of *forever*, Agent Davis stepped out of a long hallway. Harper looked him over from his military-precise haircut, to the black, emotionless depths of his eyes, over the flawless mocha skin and down to his suit and polished loafers that seemed totally out of place on him. The color of his ensemble, gray, fit him to a tee, though. Blank and emotionless. Just like him. His eyes narrowed when he noticed Galen and he motioned for Harper. "Follow me, Miss Allen."

Chapter Thirteen

Not a suspect, my ass.

"Could you tell me why blah, blah, blah, blah, Miss Allen?" Harper had quit focusing on anything coming out of Agent Davis's mouth about a half hour ago. "And when did blah, blah?" What a jerk. "What about blah? Did you blahblahblahblahblah?"

"You can ask me the same questions, a million different ways, in whatever order you want, Agent, and you're still going to get the exact same answers I gave you a couple of weeks ago. I was in the parking garage because Senator Ellis refused to grant me an interview and so I went after one. I'd only been talking to him for about five minutes when I heard the gunshot. No, he did not give me any indicator as to who might have shot him or for what reason because as far as I know, he wasn't a psychic and had no idea he was about to be murdered. Yes, I called for help. Did you not read the police report? And no, I didn't get a good look at the shooter as I was hiding under a car at the time. Anything else I can answer for you, *Agent*?"

Smoke should have been billowing from Agent Davis's ears by now. His frustration stifled the air in the tiny interview room until it sucked up all of the breathable oxygen. Beside her, Galen sat relaxed, one ankle resting on his knee, arms folded across his chest. But Harper knew it was all an act. He might have looked calm and disinterested, but his eyes were hard and focused, his jaw clenched so tight a muscle twitched at his cheek.

Apparently, he didn't like the FBI agent any more than she did.

From her insistence on interviewing the senator, to her knowledge of his schedule, Davis laid into her, one ridiculous question after another. *Why do you think Ellis refused to meet with you?* She had no idea. That's why she'd had to stalk him in a parking garage and corner him into an interview in the first place. Didn't his refusal to speak to the press come off as a bit suspicious? *Had you ever met the senator before the night he was shot?* Nope. *Do you have any knowledge of the senator's personal life?* Nothing that he hadn't already made public, hence the interview. *Did you ever fantasize about being with the senator in a sexual way?* Ew! He was older than her dad. Big no. *What about your finances? Any reason you might have wanted to blackmail the senator? Maybe a piece of information you'd dug up on him?* What kind of a person did he think she was? As a reporter on the political beat, her responsibility was to report the facts to Ellis's constituents and the truth was, he'd slacked off on the job in the past few months. He'd been dodging the OLCV for months, and that was out of character for him. *Any idea why that might be?* And . . . they were back at square one. No, she didn't have any idea. That was why she'd wanted to put Ellis on the spot. On and on it went for another hour, round and round until Harper's head began to throb and a knot the size of a goose egg welled up in her throat.

She looked to Galen, hoping that he could see she needed a lifeline. Tears stung at her eyes and her mouth was almost too dry to speak. Falling apart right now would make her look guiltier than ever in Davis's eyes, but damn it, she was stressed out. And when she was stressed, she cried.

Galen straightened in his chair, his expression, fierce. His blue eyes seemed to darken and spoke of a brewing storm. "Sean, can I see you out in the hall for a second."

It wasn't a question. Not even a polite request. Galen's tone meant business, and Agent Davis stood there, staring. Eyes wide as though he couldn't believe Galen would actually have the balls to order him around. Rather than wait for a response, Galen opened the door and stepped out into the hallway. Davis looked from Harper to the hallway and back at Harper, his lip curling as he stormed out with Galen, slamming the door behind him. The walls practically rattled with the force, and Harper cringed, knowing all too well that Galen was about to get a major ass chewing if not worse.

A fresh round of tears threatened and Harper dug through her bag for a tissue because, damn it, she did not want either Agent Davis or Galen to see her with mascara running down her face. The large hobo bag was great for carrying all the things Harper needed, but not so great when she actually needed to find something. Most people cried when they were sad or distraught. Not Harper. She cried when she was overwhelmed or just plain pissed. Right now, she was both. She mined her way to the bottom of the bag, through notebooks, pens, her wallet, her backup digital recorder, several tubes of lip gloss and lip balm, a hair brush, sunscreen, a paperback copy of *Full Blooded* (because who doesn't love a good werewolf book?), and a pair of ballet flats—oops, those were Addison's, better give 'em back—until she found a wadded-up tissue.

And one more thing that didn't belong to her.

Harper rolled the silver thumb drive in her palm. Where had it come from? She was obsessive about backing up her work. She had a mental catalog of every single one of her backup drives and she was absolutely freaking positive this one wasn't hers. She'd been to the paper a total of two times since the night Ellis had been shot, and the rest of the days had been spent in her condo, or riding around in a car chauffeured by a marshal. She doubted the flash drive belonged to Curt, or Peggy, or even Galen. Which really only left one option in her mind: the drive belonged to Senator Mark Ellis.

If Harper had actual Spidey senses, they'd be tingling like mad right about now. Would it look suspicious if she bolted? Because she wanted to go back home so badly she was practically vibrating with excitement. A mystery awaited her. The story she'd been digging for months to get, perhaps. Some answers as to why she was wrapped up in this nightmarish situation. Or possibly all the drive contained was a long lost sci-fi manuscript Ellis had been dying to publish. *Heh.* Either way, she was damned antsy to get back to her laptop and find out.

The door to the interview room swung open, and Harper buried the thumb drive in the bottom of her bag. As with the wardrobe leading to Narnia, she had to hope that the bag would still contain the flash drive when she dove back in.

"Let's go, Harper." Galen held open the door, his expression even darker than it had been before he'd stepped out into the hall. Ugh. The ride home should be loads of fun.

Agent Davis stood right outside the doorway, making her exit more than a little uncomfortable. She had to sidle past him to get out of the room, which had obviously been his plan. A little alpha-male chicanery to make her nervous. Well, it worked. Frankly, Davis scared the ever-loving shit out of her even when he wasn't playing the big-bad FBI guy. And after today's interrogation—because no way was this an interview—she had even more reason to watch out for him.

As she walked down the hallway toward the staircase, she felt Galen at her back, his footsteps nothing more than a whisper on the industrial carpeting. She picked up her pace, worried that she wasn't moving fast enough for him, or worse, that he'd step on her heels if she didn't get her butt in gear. But instead of backing off, he matched her pace, so close now that the heat from his body engulfed her.

Harper took a right where two hallways met, toward the stairs, but Galen stopped her. "Take the elevator." His tone was harsh as though harnessing a barely restrained rage. Harper shuddered at his commanding words as she veered left, uncertain if fear or excitement had caused the tremor. And how sick was that?

She hit the down button on the wall of elevators and waited. She didn't need to turn around to know that Galen stood to her right, close enough to touch. If she simply reached her hand back, she'd surely brush his arm. Why was he suddenly crowding her? Was he angry with her, too? Taking a page from Agent Davis's intimidation tactics manual?

When the doors slid open, a jolt of anxiety seeped into her bloodstream. What would Galen do once they were locked up inside that stupid metal box? Had Davis convinced him of her guilt as well? Would he confront her? She had nothing to hide and she'd always been straight with Galen. The question was, would he believe her?

As the elevator began its descent, Harper's stomach did the same. The silence in the car was deafening. The air, stagnant.

"Don't push Davis's buttons, Harper." Galen's voice sliced the quiet like a swath of shadow through sunlight. "He'll go after you for no other reason than to cut you down, do you understand me?"

Harper was playing with fire and she had no idea how close to the flame she was. If the evidence against her weren't circumstantial at best, Davis would have had Harper locked up in a super-max by now. *Davis. What a cocksucker.* Harper's quick responses and witty, biting retorts had done nothing to cool the FBI agent's jets. If anything, he'd be more up Harper's ass than ever. A fact that clouded Galen's vision with a haze of red.

"I won't." Harper's voice sounded tiny in the enclosed space. "I—I think maybe I'd better get an attorney."

Unfortunately, Galen agreed. "Do you know anyone you can trust?"

"My friend, Sophie, her dad's a lawyer. I'll see if he can recommend someone."

Galen's hands clenched into tight fists at his side, more to keep them from shaking than anything. He'd never been so close to slamming a colleague into a wall, but Davis's head would have made a great dent. Rage still burned through Galen's bloodstream, his inability to control the situation making his anger that much worse. No doubt he'd get a call from Monroe after what had happened in that hallway. Namely, him backing Davis against the wall as he'd warned him to stay the hell away from Harper and lay off her as a suspect.

Way to keep it classy, man. No doubt that move would advance his career. *Yeah, right. Desk duty, here I come.*

"Harper, can I ask you a question?" Not that it mattered. He didn't believe for a second she had anything to do with Ellis's death.

She answered slowly, "Sure."

"Why were you so obsessed with Ellis?"

"I wasn't *obsessed,*" she said with disdain. Great, he'd pissed her off and managed to put her on the defensive. "I was curious."

Cryptic. Looked like he'd have to coax it out of her. "Curious about what?"

The doors slid open and Harper made her way to the reception desk to turn in her guest badge. She waited by the door as Galen did the same, her expression thoughtful. His firearm was returned to him and he slipped it in the shoulder holster before heading for the exit. Harper stayed a few steps ahead of him all the way to the car, and even after he unlocked the doors, she stood there, staring at him over the hood.

"Have you ever had an itch you couldn't scratch?" she asked. "You know, one that's just under the skin and no matter how you try, you can't make it go away?"

Galen nodded. He opened his door, but Harper stayed where she was.

"Ellis was that itch. I mean, he copped to *everything.* Shamelessly. Most politicians try to hide their misdeeds or hang their heads and grovel when they've been caught. They cast blame. They lie, try to cover up the truth, or follow the old *deny, deny, deny* tactic.

He ran this huge campaign based on honesty. He stood in front of the cameras and laid his life bare for the people, admitting to everything and denying nothing. He was apologetic, but so human in his admissions. 'I'm not perfect. I make mistakes. So does everyone.' Of course he'd win the election. People are tired of being lied to by their lawmakers. They wanted to believe that even though Ellis had a laundry list of faults, there was at least one honest man in Washington. In the course of the election, he'd duped everyone into believing that he had nothing more to hide."

"But you didn't believe it?" Galen ventured.

Harper leveled her gaze. "Not for a second. I think he used his honest proclamations as a distraction. He was meeting with someone at the state fire marshal's office almost every week for the past couple of months. Yet, the Oregon League of Conservation Voters can't get him to meet even once. Ellis was a staunch Democrat and preached a green lifestyle. He made everyone on his staff convert to hybrid cars, for Christ's sake. Why would he dodge a group like the OLCV? The fire service has nothing on the books right now. No legislation pending and I recently did a story on collective bargaining. The state's firefighters were in no danger of losing their bargaining rights anytime soon."

Galen marveled at Harper's emphatic tone. Her eyes lit with excitement, and when she got worked up, she talked so fast he had a hard time keeping up. His smile grew as she went on and on, point after point, the consummate journalist hot on the trail of a story.

I'm particularly fond of journalism majors.

He'd been teasing when he'd said it to her that night, but he'd be damned if it wasn't true. "Don't take this the wrong way, but did you ever mention any of this to Davis?"

Harper cocked a brow. "I tried," she said with disdain. "But you saw how he treated me today. He doesn't care what I have to say."

True. Davis had settled on Harper as a suspect from day one for some crazy damned reason. And until Galen could find a way to go over Davis's head on this one, Harper would remain in his sights. "Fair enough. But promise me, Harper, that when your friend's dad gets you hooked up with an attorney, you tell him *everything.* Okay?"

She sighed as though the weight of her ordeal had settled heavily upon her. "I will."

"Good. Now, get in the car. Davis is probably watching us with binoculars from the fifth-floor window."

She smiled and opened the car door. Galen responded in kind, his earlier annoyance over Michelle's overzealous behavior and Davis's utter dickishness melting under the warmth of Harper's brilliant expression.

Galen spent the drive back to her condo doing his best to keep her mind off her predicament. He fired off questions in rapid succession, giving her no choice but to come up with quick responses. It was a win-win for him. Each answer told him more about her, and it managed to lighten the mood. Mac and cheese was her go-to comfort food. She'd do just about anything for a donut (good to know), she refused to drink soda without ice, and she wanted the *New York Times* or *Washington Post* to offer her a job just so she could turn them down, though she wouldn't be opposed to a freelance gig. She loved the Pacific Northwest, and though she was ambitious and wanted to advance her career, she didn't think she'd ever move east of the Rockies.

The flow of conversation was easy. Comfortable. It reminded him so much of the night they'd met. He remembered wanting one more hour of time with her. One more question answered. Harper fascinated him, and very few women had ever managed to do so. Galen found himself wishing the drive would go on forever. Too bad her condo wasn't farther away. Say, in Montana, maybe?

"Favorite movie?"

Harper cocked her head to the side and puckered her mouth as she contemplated her answer. "It's hard to pick just one. Plus, I watch all kinds of movies. If I have to pick . . ."

Galen waited for her response. Probably *The Notebook*. Or some other chick flick.

". . . I guess *The Avengers*."

That's right. She had a thing for superheroes. "It was all right, I guess. Superman is the only true superhero in my opinion. The rest are poseurs."

Harper stared at Galen, her jaw slack. After a couple of weeks together, he still couldn't get enough of that scandalized expression. It was so easy to push her into a spluttering state of shock. "You're kidding, right? I mean, you have to be." You'd think he'd called her mother fat or insulted her grandma's cooking. Galen laughed and if anything, she grew even more indignant. "Batman? Spider-Man? Wolverine? They're not true superheroes?"

"I'm just saying. Those guys are cool and everything, but they're still only human. Bruce Wayne has no super powers at all, just a jaded attitude, a lot of money, and shit ton of gadgets. Spider-Man would still be a hapless high school kid if not for the spider bite. Wolverine? Mutant. But still human. Superman is so awesome that he has to *pretend* to be human. And the only way he thinks he can blend in with the rest of us is to make his alter ego a clumsy, awkward, working-stiff doofus."

Harper's answering laughter exploded out of her, the sound a relaxing balm to Galen's foul mood. "So what you're saying is that Superman is so amazing, he actually has to dumb himself down to interact with the lowly humans he protects."

"Something like that."

"Why protect them at all, then? I mean, if he thinks he's so much better than the rest of us, why bother?"

Galen thought for a moment. "Because he feels sorry for us. We're weaker, we can't fly, and we're not bulletproof. Plus, we're obviously no match for the super villains, otherwise we wouldn't need him at all."

"Pity protection?" Harper responded with incredulity.

"Yeah," Galen said, smug. "Totally."

She rolled her eyes, but a smile still curved her lips. "Whatever."

As they pulled up to her building, Galen reflected on the events of last year. What he'd wanted, the way he'd felt, the experience they'd shared, and of course, the text messages he'd read on her phone and his assumption that she'd used him and played him for a fool. An unspoken accusation she hadn't even been given a chance to defend herself from.

Harper turned to him and smiled. "I think I'll make us grilled cheese for lunch."

Maybe those assumptions didn't matter to him so much anymore.

Chapter Fourteen

Harper didn't know what was better: the little silver nugget she'd found in her bag, or the way the dark cloud of Galen's mood had lifted. Once again she found herself feeling optimistic, and that was a very dangerous thing. Their superhero conversation was so reminiscent of the first time they'd met. Had it jogged anything in his memory? God, was it totally stupid of her to hope that it had?

She led the way to her condo as she had so many times over the past week with Galen not far behind her. His protective instinct overwhelmed Harper in its intensity. As though reassuring her on a subconscious level that he'd never let anything happen to her. Her hand shook as she retrieved her key from her pocket and slid it into the lock. She knew if she leaned her head back, it would find his shoulder. And if she did, would his strong arms encircle her like they had that night? Would he reach up and cup her breasts? Tease her nipples into aching peaks? His mouth hot against her skin?

"Harper? Are you all right?"

Galen's voice rumbled in his chest and the vibration traveled the length of Harper's spine. No matter how many times she told herself to let it—*him*—go, she couldn't do it. Why? Why him? Why now? "I'm fine." She let out a deep sigh, hoping he couldn't hear the tremor in her voice. "Just taking a little breather."

He put his hands on her shoulders, and Harper started, not because he'd caught her off guard, but because the physical contact was something that she'd wanted for so long. A year was a long damned time to be without a man's touch. Not that she'd had a whole hell of a lot of it before her one-night stand with Galen.

"It's going to be okay." Every syllable rippled through her, each word drilling into her stomach with the force of a jackhammer. How was it possible to want someone so badly?

"I know." The words were hollow as she spoke them. No matter the outcome, nothing was going to be okay. Not if, when it was all said and done, Galen turned his back and left her again. Forgotten.

He reached over her and his hand covered hers. Harper's eyes drifted shut as she reveled in the sensation of his skin on hers. The warmth of his touch. He turned her fist, and the key, in the lock and pushed the door open. His breath sent chills down Harper's spine as he said close to her ear, "Come on. I'll make you a grilled cheese."

Harper's appetite rarely failed her. Until today.

She stared at the perfectly golden-brown grilled cheese cooling on her plate. Was it wrong to hope that Davis, in all his ineptitude, never found Ellis's killer? And then Galen would have to stay with her indefinitely. Wouldn't that be nice? Her own captive U.S. Marshal. Surely Galen would jump at the chance to spend the rest of his life hanging around her apartment. *Ugh.*

"I really like Michelle." She picked at the crust of her sandwich. "And her apple fritters are the best thing I've ever eaten."

"Everything Michelle makes is the best," Galen said as he slid a second grilled cheese onto his plate. "Her beignets are absolutely killer."

The pride in his voice caused Harper's chest to swell with emotion. She'd always wanted a brother or sister. Being an only child could be so lonely. "Are you guys close?"

Galen demolished almost half of his grilled cheese in a single bite. After a pause, he said, "Yeah. She pretty much raised me. I lived with her full-time from sixteen on."

For some reason, Harper had always pictured Galen as having a super well-adjusted childhood with a storybook life. Maybe her fantasies of the man she'd imagined him to be had bled over into her perception of the man he really was. Imperfect. With trials, bad memories, hang-ups, and baggage just like everyone else.

"Oh." She didn't really know what to say. Maybe she didn't need to say anything.

"My parents fought a lot." He gave a rueful laugh. "More to the point, my dad yelled and browbeat my mom a lot. She tried to keep him level, but he was just a son of a bitch who thought the entire universe revolved around him."

Harper took a bite of her grilled cheese. More to

give her mouth something to do than anything. She didn't want to interrupt Galen or make him feel like he was obligated to continue. Up until now, their conversations had been light. This took their *whatever-ship* to a deeper level, and she didn't want to ruin the moment by asking a nosy question or saying something that might put him in retreat.

"My dad sort of demanded attention, you know? To the point that my mom put Michelle and me on the back burner to deal with him." Galen stared at some far-off spot and Harper wondered what unpleasant memories he'd dredged up. "He acted like an entitled kid all the time so we really didn't have a choice but to become the adults."

"That's awful." Oops. There went her mouth, screwing everything up.

Galen gave her a lopsided, albeit sad grin. "I'm probably making it sound a lot worse than it really was. It's not like we were chained in the basement with no food or water. We had good times, too. When everything went smoothly and my parents were relaxed. I didn't know for a long time exactly what it was they fought about all the time. It was only after my dad finally got sick of us and left that Michelle told me about his affairs. She knew because my mom didn't have anyone else to talk to about it. I think Michelle told me because she didn't want to have to bear the burden of it alone. She was the only thing keeping Mom together."

"That must have been a lot for her to deal with," Harper said. She wrapped her fingers around the bar stool to keep herself seated so she wouldn't succumb to the urge to go into the kitchen and wrap her arms around Galen. "How old was she?"

"Nineteen," Galen said. "She didn't go to college

because she didn't want to leave me home alone with our mom. She sort of shut down. Couldn't cope with the divorce." He snorted as though the idea were ridiculous. "In the long run, I guess it wasn't such a bad idea, though."

"We don't have to talk about this, you know. I didn't mean to pry."

Galen quirked a brow. "You call that prying? I thought you were a journalist. Aren't you supposed to peel back my layers, inch by painful inch, digging your way in until I tell you what you want to hear?"

"If you were up for reelection, maybe." In one sarcastic sentence, Galen had managed to lighten the mood, but Harper couldn't help but wonder if he was merely deflecting. Had they crossed a professional line? And what would it mean if they had? Harper suppressed a groan. Her journalistic mouth might have kept quiet, but her damned overactive brain made up for it. Why couldn't she quit analyzing every last detail and simply live in the moment? "Is it true that you speak French?"

"Michelle's got a big mouth." The words were scolding, but laced with affection. "Yeah. I spent all of last year in Paris working a personal security detail for the U.S. ambassador to France. A group of extremists had made some threats and as a part of my SOG duty, I was sent to oversee his security."

France? Wow. Could that explain why he'd walked out on her last year?

"SOG?" Harper's curiosity got the best of her. There wasn't a single detail about Galen Kelly that she didn't want to know.

"Special Operations Group," Galen said. His face lit up with the words, as though he couldn't wait to talk about it. "It's an elite division of the Marshals Service.

We're on call twenty-four-seven and take certain special assignments. They don't take many deputies for the program. I got lucky."

Right. As if luck had anything to do with it. His modesty was part of his charm, but Harper knew that Galen had to have earned the appointment. She smiled. "Will you say something in French?"

Galen reached around and rubbed the back of his neck, his expression almost sheepish. Good God, that simple act had Harper's toes curling. Now she had to hold on to her chair for a completely different reason. Want swelled within her like storm clouds boiling in a summer sky. Her stomach clenched tight, and she realized her lips had parted as though in anticipation of a kiss. *Keep it together, Harp.*

"*Tu es la femme la plus belle que j'ai jamais vu et je déteste avoir autant envie de toi. Je pense à toi chaque nuit et je compte les secondes jusqu'au petit matin.*"

Oh. Holy. Shit. Was it possible to have an orgasm without touching? Because if he said one more thing, Harper was pretty sure her body would burst into flames of volcanic proportions. No way would she be able to keep her distance after today. She was as good as enamored.

Jesus, dude, what the hell were you thinking? The words had left his mouth in a rush, as if trying to beat his brain to the punch. Because if his brain had won, he never would have told Harper that she was the most beautiful woman he'd ever laid eyes on. Or that he thought about her every night, counting down the minutes until morning.

But even though she didn't have a clue what he said, Galen knew his words had affected her. Her hazel eyes, large and sparkling, delved into his with an intensity that locked him into place. And her lips, parted and inviting, begged to be kissed. Harper's cheeks flushed red as she averted her gaze and Galen wondered what she was thinking. Because, right now, the only thing keeping him from vaulting the bar that separated them was the Internal Affairs investigation that would no doubt follow on the heels of today's episode with Davis. Too bad Galen's cock hadn't gotten the message about mixing business with pleasure. Christ, he was hard as a fucking brick, one more reason to stay firmly planted behind Harper's kitchen counter.

"That's beautiful," Harper breathed. "What did you say?"

For a goddamned year, Galen had shut himself off. No relationships, no entanglements. Not even a prospect. He could have passed the nights with a woman here or there. Hell, he'd been hit on occasionally, but they all paled in comparison to the woman who stood before him. And what did it say about him that he was willing to overlook her indiscretion, the fact that she'd deceived him and cheated on her boyfriend with him? Maybe he was more like his mom than he cared to admit, chasing after a dream. Great. Fucking wonderful.

"Oh, you know, just something about the weather." Nice. *The weather?* Maybe now was a good time to bang his head on the counter and knock himself the hell out.

"Well," Harper murmured, "you make the weather sound amazing."

Galen could definitely put his second language skills to good use. Spread Harper out on her bed, strip her until she lay bare, every inch of her exposed to his gaze. He'd whisper the words against her skin: *mollet* as he kissed her calf, *le ventre* as his tongue traced a path up her torso. *Les seins* before he cupped her full breast and drew her taut nipple into his mouth and *le cou* as he grazed his teeth across her throat just before he thrust into her.

Whoa. Well, that didn't do anything to cool him down. Nothing short of a dip in Arctic waters would quench the lust burning in his body.

"Heh." He choked out a laugh and cupped the back of his neck as though a quick massage would ease the tension that had settled there. "Yeah, well, everything sounds good in a foreign language, I guess."

Since day one of this assignment Galen had found it damned near impossible to deny his attraction to Harper. Rather than making excuses to put distance between them, he found himself looking for reasons to be close to her—like out in her hallway when he'd unlocked the door for her—even if it was nothing more than a whisper of contact. Did she have any idea of the effect she had on him? He was fairly certain that in the back of Harper's mind, he was still the asshole who'd picked her up in a bar and promptly forgotten her face the moment he'd come. And now, nothing more than property he was responsible for looking after. She did a damned good job of hiding her disgust if that was the case.

He'd killed any chance of a relationship with her, though, the day he'd decided that his job was more important than admitting to Monroe that he knew her. Now, only a couple of weeks after that decision he'd been so certain of making, he already regretted it. "What's on your work schedule for today?" he asked. No more French. No more details about his life spilled. Building intimacy between them would only lead to ruin. Galen needed to get his head back in the game. Distance. Detachment. Professionalism.

"Sam officially put me on paid leave," Harper said, her tone deflated, "since it's too hard to go out and do what I need to do. I'm used to leaving the office, going to meetings, press conferences, interviews. But since I'm not exactly low-key right now, showing up at a press event is probably not the best idea."

Galen hated that she was upset. If that stupid ass hat Davis would get off the paranoia train and actually *do his job*, then maybe they would have caught Ellis's murderer by now and Harper would be free. Then again, with Harper's safety in the clear, she'd no longer need him around. What would he do then? Just walk away? Again. Turn his back on what could be something amazing? Or take a chance and risk getting burned by Harper yet again?

"Sorry about work," he offered. "Maybe you should use the afternoon to get in touch with your friend about a lawyer?" He didn't want to thrust her back into reality so harshly, but after this morning's cluster fuck with Davis, he was pretty certain the scrutiny would only increase. For both of them.

Galen's phone rang and he didn't need to dig it out of his pocket to know who was calling. Let the scrutiny begin! He swiped his finger across the screen and brought the phone to his ear. "Kelly."

"So, you decided this detail wasn't quite exciting enough," Monroe said matter-of-factly. "That's why you pushed Davis into a wall. Because you wanted to bring the wrath of the FBI down on your head, right?"

Fantastic. Davis hadn't wasted a second before running off to tattle on him. Dick. "He said I pushed him? Completely overexaggerated."

Harper gave him a quizzical look. He shrugged and

brought the phone down. "I'm just gonna take this out on the balcony."

A hint of a smile tugged at Harper's lips and she nodded. "Tell Curt I said hi."

"Right." Sure, right after he tendered his resignation.

Galen stepped out onto the balcony and slid the door behind him. "Look, I don't know what Davis told you—"

"How about that you threatened him, for starters." Monroe's tone made it clear he wasn't in the mood for jokes. "And that you took Harper out of her interview before Davis had released her."

"Interview?" Galen damn near choked on the word. "It was a first-class interrogation, Curt. You should have heard the ridiculous bullshit he was throwing at her."

"Which," Monroe interrupted, "is his right as the agent in charge of the investigation."

"It's a load of crap and you know it. Harper had nothing to do with Ellis's death."

"Miss Allen," Monroe stressed, "is a witness under our protection. That does not, however absolve her from any wrongdoing." He sighed and added, "Look, Galen, I like her. She's a sweet kid. And you know that I don't believe she's involved. But that's not for us to say right now. Our job—*your* job—is to shadow her. Watch out for her. And make sure no one tries to take her out before Davis pulls his head out of his ass and decides to actually move on this investigation. Until then, you stay *out* of his way. Do not confront him, don't antagonize him, and for the love of God don't fucking lay a finger on him."

"For the record, I didn't shove him. I *crowded* him." He couldn't guarantee he'd stay out of Davis's hair. Especially if he put too much pressure on Harper.

"Well then, don't crowd the son of a bitch."

Galen scowled. "Fine."

"Peggy will be there in a few minutes to relieve you. I need you to come in and sign the complaint that Davis filed, and I want to go over a few non-related cases with you."

Galen checked his watch. He still had seven hours on his shift. But arguing with Monroe wasn't a good idea right now. Calling Peggy in to cover for him wasn't going to do much to endear him to her, either. "I'll head in to the office when she gets here."

"Galen." Monroe hesitated. Not a good sign. "Is there something going on between you and Ms. Allen? I don't want to take you off this detail."

"No, Curt." This was why Galen needed to keep his eyes forward and mind focused. It would be bad for both of them if Galen was compromised, and he refused to put Harper through that sort of embarrassment. "You have nothing to worry about."

"All right, then. See you in a half hour?"

"I'll be there."

Galen ended the call and leaned against the railing. He'd never been so torn between what he wanted and what he needed to do. What a completely fucked-up situation. Years spent building up his career. Weeks of SOG training and even more time to prove he was worthy of high-profile assignments. All undone by a snarky reporter with a thing for superheroes.

Would trying to balance his job with whatever this was building between him and Harper cause him to lose them both?

Chapter Fifteen

Is Landon still parked outside?

Harper smiled as she read Galen's text message. Four days ago, he'd taken her out for the best apple fritter of her life. Yesterday, he'd surprised her by sending a bacon maple bar from Voodoo Donut over with Peggy, and today he'd called and offered to pick up a couple of books for her at Powell's. He'd done a complete one-eighty from his initial hard-nosed U.S. deputy marshal routine, and unfortunately, it made the prospect of being with him every day harder and harder to bear. A little over two weeks had passed since they'd been thrown together in this crazy protector/protected relationship, and though she'd promised herself over and over that she would not get emotionally involved with him, the more time she spent with Galen, the harder that promise became to keep.

A smile curved Harper's lips as she typed, **Who is this?** and hit SEND.

Did Galen ever sleep? She looked over at her clock: almost eleven thirty. He'd texted her every night since day one. Checking, and then rechecking to make sure the marshals on the night shift hadn't abandoned their posts. As if.

Ha. Ha. You're hilarious.

She responded, I'm sure he's out there. It's his job. Where else is he going to go?

Go check. Now.

It was almost too easy to rattle his chain sometimes. But really, what did Galen expect? Everyone she'd met with the Marshals Service so far had been top notch, professional, and serious about their jobs. No way would one of them fall asleep at their post or run off for donuts. Mmmmm . . . donuts. Harper could really go for an apple fritter right about now.

Did you check?

Jeez. Someone was impatient tonight. She rolled off her bed and walked over to the window. Parked on the street in front of her building was the obviously nondescript SUV that belonged to Deputy McCabe.

I think he's down there, she typed. It's sort of hard to tell with the bonfire and crowd of gunmen storming the building, though.

She waited for a response, but when none came, Harper worried that she'd gone a little too far. Kidding! Just kidding. He's down there and everything's nice and quiet. She doubted Deputy McCabe would appreciate having his ass torn into by one freaked-out Galen Kelly. Hopefully, he hadn't called in the Marines or National Guard for backup yet.

That's not funny.

Harper smiled and flopped back down on her bed. Not true. You just said I was hilarious. I don't know what the big deal is. Peggy's in the living room camped out on the couch and there's another marshal down in the lobby. You need to learn to relax. The number of people watching over her was beginning to wear on Harper. Peggy spent almost every night in her apartment, and others had no choice but to sit all night positioned around her building. She knew it was for her safety, but honestly, it all felt like a huge waste of resources. No one had tried to mow her down with a machine gun yet.

I'll relax when I'm dead.

Harper's fingers hovered over her phone, her thumbs poised to type, though she had no idea how to respond. Up until a few days ago, Galen had shadowed her every move, his eyes tracking even the smallest movement. He was always hyper aware of his surroundings, and though they spent all of their time holed up in her condo, he never once let his guard down. Since her "interview" with the FBI, though, he'd been scarce, and she missed his constant presence.

Well, she typed, I don't want you dying on my account.

Minutes ticked by as Harper waited for a response. She checked her cell, checked it again, and still no conversation bubble popped up to notify her that he'd texted back. Had she hit a nerve? Maybe dying on the job wasn't something marshals joked about. After all, law enforcement wasn't exactly the safest profession you could choose.

I'm good at my job. I don't plan on dying any time soon. Concerned?

Harper leaned back against the pillows, brought her knees up to her chest and typed, You wish.

Hardly.

It was meant in jest, but the single word still bit into Harper's chest with razor-sharp teeth and wouldn't let go. That was the problem, wasn't it? She wanted him to care. To remember. To show even a hint that he'd taken something away from the night they'd shared other than a great orgasm. Then again, if he couldn't remember, maybe it hadn't been so great after all. Now, that was a boost to Harper's ego. Ugh.

Well, just between you and me, I don't plan on dying any time soon, either. No use continuing on the path of self-pity. It was time to end tonight's text-fest and get to bed.

Is Landon still out there?

Good Lord. Obsessive much? Mr. Control Freak needed to dial it down. Actually, I invited him over for a threesome with me and Peggy. He's on his way up right now. Good night!

Let's see how he responds to that one. A smile curved her lips as she set the phone beside her on the pillow and crawled beneath the covers. The sheets were cold, her condo silent. And despite the fact that there was a marshal camped out on her sofa, the loneliness Harper felt seeped into her pores and chilled her blood. She felt so isolated, and it wasn't simply being under house arrest. It was the thought of being so close to something she wanted and yet, still a million miles away. No matter how she forced herself to not think about that night with Galen, the memory of it burned through her like embers stoked by the wind.

Harper let her eyes drift shut. Her fingertips trailed a path down the column of her throat as she imagined his fingers on her skin. Across her collarbone and over the thin fabric of her tank top, she continued over the swell of her breast and brushed the tight point of one nipple. Her hips thrust forward as though no longer under her control and she went lower, past her belly button, to the elastic edge of her underwear.

A rush of warmth spread between her thighs as she recalled the wet heat of his tongue as it slid against her clit. The tremors that had shaken her body with each flick, sending her closer to abandon. She slipped her fingers beneath the fabric, seeking out that spot he'd teased so well. Her breasts tingled and grew heavy, and her nipples hardened when she imagined him rolling the peaks between her fingers, the barest sting to complement the pleasure.

The text message alert on her cell went off, but Harper ignored it. She didn't want to abandon her fantasy for the cold, hard truth of her reality. She was in the past, back in her old apartment, the barest sliver of light from the street lamps casting a harsh shadow on the ridges of Galen's body. Her fingers slid against her core and she imagined it was him touching her, bringing her close to release. Her own ragged breath was his, her fingers teasing the beaded pearl of her nipple, his. Eyes squeezed shut to block out reality; Harper continued to touch herself, her hips bucking into each stroke of her fingers.

Galen.

How she'd wanted his name on her lips that night at the moment she'd come.

Galen.

And, God, how she wanted him now. Just one night more with him.

Her body coiled tight, muscles taut, and Harper increased the pressure, her fingers sliding against her slippery flesh. His face loomed in her mind, as she imagined his body pumping into her, and she threw her head back against the pillow. "Galen." Her voice was a ragged whisper as she came, the waves of pleasure cresting and ebbing like a breaker rolling into the shore. A sob welled up in her chest, the ache so deep and so painful that she didn't know if she'd ever find anything to fill it up and make her whole. How much longer would she mourn the loss of something she'd never really had?

Tears stung at her eyes, but Harper willed them to stay right the hell where they were. No way would she shed a tear over him. No matter how much it hurt, she refused to cry. Her heavy breath was the only sound in the still bedroom, the traffic passing outside of her building nothing more than a low hum in the darkness. Her mind wandered as sleep began to take hold and she was only half aware of her phone ringing beside her. She let the call go to voice mail, but within a few seconds it started up again. One . . . two . . . three . . . On the fourth ring, Harper picked up, her voice already thick and tired. "Hello?"

"Harper," a man's voice said. "This is Deputy Landon McCabe with the U.S. Marshals Service. I was wondering if I could ask you to quit yanking Deputy Kelly's chain for the remainder of the night. Because, frankly, if he has to drive down here to see if I'm still stationed in my Chevy and not, in fact, up in your apartment, I doubt either of us will enjoy the visit."

"That's asking a lot," she responded with a yawn. "Yanking his chain is just too easy." She paused. "Okay, it's a little fun, too."

"You're my kind of people, Harper," Landon said. "But seriously, cut it out."

"I'm on my best behavior for the rest of the night. Promise."

"Good night, Harper," Landon said.

"'Night, Deputy McCabe," she said and ended the call.

She opened her text screen to find an unread message from Galen: I rescind my earlier opinion. You're not funny. Also, Deputy McCabe is getting reassigned in the morning.

A lazy smile tugged at Harper's lips as she reread his words. Concern? Jealousy? It was stupid to hope, but those words, no matter how she might have misinterpreted them, made her feel a little less lonely. She fired off one last response to Galen: Gotcha! ;-) She was pretty sure there'd be payback, but she'd worry about that tomorrow.

"How'd you sleep?"

Galen scowled at Landon as he slid into the passenger seat of his rig, two coffees in hand. "You're a dick."

"If Monroe finds out you're here, he's gonna have your ass in a sling. And since you bugged the shit out of me last night, I might be inclined to let him know."

True, Galen had been instructed to take a few days off from Harper's protective detail, but that didn't mean he couldn't stop by and check in. Which he had. Almost every day. He was still the deputy in charge, after all. "I'm just checking in. And I know you won't tell Monroe I'm here because if you do, I might have to mention the strip club incident."

Landon took one of the paper cups from Galen, pointedly ignoring his reference to a field trip they'd taken a few years back while looking for a stripper who'd blackmailed a congressman. "You know, I like Harper. Too bad you're jerking her around."

A twinge of guilt pulled at Galen's chest. He was growing more and more conflicted over pretending not to remember her. And Landon didn't miss an opportunity to rub salt in his open wounds. So, yeah, he was a dick.

"If I cop to having a previous . . ." The words died on Galen's tongue. What was it that had happened between them? Relationship? Not really. Hook-up? No, that was too cheap for what happened that night. Jesus, talk about confusing. "If I admit that I know Harper outside of this case, Monroe will pull me off the detail."

"Is this job worth what you might lose if you don't cop to it?" Landon asked.

"There's nothing to lose." Galen didn't bother trying to hide his disdainful tone. "She had a boyfriend, Landon. Hell, she might have one still. You know I don't play those kinds of games."

Landon fixed him with a dubious stare. "I haven't seen a boyfriend. Have you?"

No. But that didn't mean anything. No pictures of her and what's his name—Clark? Carlisle?—in her apartment. No phone calls, either. "She could have asked him to keep his distance until the investigation is over. You know, looking out for her boy."

"Whatever," Landon scoffed. "Sounds to me like you're making excuses."

"If I tell Monroe that I knew her before the investigation, it compromises me."

Landon rolled his eyes. "Which is just another way of saying the job means more to you than she does."

Galen took a long pull from his coffee. Of course the situation was black and white to Landon; it wasn't *his* situation. Yeah, the job did mean a lot to him. Aside from Michelle and Landon, the Marshals Service was the only family he had. Besides, no matter what he might feel for Harper—and he made no admissions—the fact remained that she'd cheated on her boyfriend with him. No cheating. His cardinal relationship rule. Broken. Inexcusable. "Sean Davis still has his sights set on her as suspect number one. If I'm not working this detail, no one's looking out for Harper. I don't have a choice."

If Landon's eyes bugged out of his head any further, he'd look like a cartoon character. "Are you fucking kidding me, dude? That hurts. One year as an SOG tool and you think all of your colleagues are completely incompetent?"

Galen pinched the bridge of his nose. The day had barely started and already he needed a do-over, not to mention he felt a massive headache coming on. Was it too late to call it a day and go back to bed? "That's not what I meant, Landon, and you know it."

"Really? You called me three times last night. One of them to make sure I wasn't upstairs having a threesome. Seriously, man, Peggy? Not. Even. And speaking of Peggy, how many times did you check in with her last night? Did you check up on Peterson too? Make sure he was still stationed in the lobby and not in the bathroom jerking off?"

"I called Peggy once," Galen begrudgingly admitted. "As far as Peterson goes, I do *not* want to think about what he does in the bathroom."

"How many times?" Landon prodded.

"Twice." Damn, when confronted with his OCD, it sounded bad.

Landon gave him a superior smirk. "Pretty damning evidence if you ask me."

"Whatever. I'm not allowed to be concerned?"

"Oh, no." Landon took a sip of his coffee. "That's not what I'm saying at all. Concern is okay. Emotional investment, not so much. Monroe mentioned you're trying to get witness security for her family?"

"What's wrong with that?" Landon was sure letting the accusations fly this morning. "It's standard procedure in high-profile cases."

"Yeah, when we're dealing with organized crime or the cartel," Landon remarked. "You're going overboard. We're not to that point yet."

"You sound like Davis."

"You're not yourself, so I'm going to forgive that slight to my character. All I'm saying is, try to get a grip. Or better yet, a little perspective. And for the love of all that is holy, think about coming clean to her. Your inability to communicate is going to bite you in the ass someday."

"What are you talking about? I communicate."

"Yeah. Okay. Keep telling yourself that and it'll be your lonely ass jerking off in the bathroom."

Yep, Landon was a total dick.

"Now, get the hell out of my vehicle and get your ass home. You're on suspension."

Galen cocked a brow. "I am not on suspension. I'm taking a break."

Landon's brow puckered and his eyes narrowed.

"Get the fuck out. My relief is here and I'm going to bed."

Galen climbed out of the SUV and jogged back to his truck. From the corner of his eye, he caught sight of Landon as he pulled out into traffic. He stuck his arm out the window and gave Galen a one-finger salute as he drove off. It was sort of their own fucked-up way of saying they cared.

There were days that Galen loved his job more than anything in the world. Today was not one of those days. Landon managed to remind him of why he had no business working this detail. He could only imagine the office gossip his behavior had managed to spawn. There would be those who attributed his over-the-top attitude to coming off of SOG duty in France. And then there would be others who would whisper that his intense interest in Harper Allen was anything but professional.

Phone calls, texts after hours, checking in with the other deputies until he finally passed out from exhaustion. He couldn't keep up like this. Concern for Harper's safety was one thing. Obsession was another. He'd even taken it upon himself to conduct an informal investigation into Senator Ellis's death, checking leads, asking a few questions here and there, digging where he had no business digging. All in an attempt to find something that Davis, in his arrogance, had overlooked. Something that would deflect his interest from Harper as a suspect and point him in the right direction.

If Monroe found out what he was up to, his ass would be in a serious sling. If Harper had any idea how often he checked up on her, she'd probably request a replacement. And if Galen didn't get his fucking head on straight and separate his personal life from the job, he was going to ruin a career he'd spent years building. This had to stop. No more phone calls. No more texts. No more toeing the line of professional indecency. Because the banter that he and Harper shared in their nightly texts had become something more than a simple professional conversation. Whenever he felt the urge to be playful, or witty, or whatever, Galen needed to remind himself why he'd walked out of her apartment without a word that morning.

And thanks to the disciplinary action spurred by Davis's tattling, he had one more day free to consider the benefits of practicing professionalism and detachment.

Chapter Sixteen

Harper stared at the flash drive in her palm. She slid her thumb across the smooth, metallic surface and ejected the USB connector. Peggy was stationed at the dining room table with a few files, her laptop, and a notebook spread out on the little square. Harper imagined that protective detail could be boring sometimes. If she were Peggy, she'd be ready for a nap right about now.

"Peggy, do you know anything about the SOG team?"

Peggy looked up from her work, a knowing smile plastered on her face. "Oh, sure, I know about it."

"What is it exactly?"

Peggy fluffed her perfectly coifed bob and turned in her chair to face Harper fully. She guessed the deputy's age somewhere in her late forties. Her hair was bottle blond, her makeup on the modest side, but always perfect. She struck Harper as the type of woman who lived by a routine and didn't like having that routine disrupted. "The SOG team is a little more highly trained than the rest of us. They get the higher-profile assignments and even though they're based in a certain city, they're on call and have to go wherever and whenever they're told twenty-four-seven."

Harper picked at her thumbnail as though it was marginally more interesting than the conversation. "So, if Galen got called, he'd have to drop everything and leave?"

"Pretty much. But don't worry, Harper. He'd have to wait for someone to relieve him first. He wouldn't just run out on you."

Heh. Don't be so sure, Peggy. Galen's pretty good at running off without a word. The phone call he'd gotten after Davis's interrogation had spurred him into action. He'd left her apartment with barely a "See ya later" when Peggy had shown up to take his place and she hadn't seen him in the few days since. "What does the SOG do?"

"Apprehend fugitives, provide security, transport high-profile and especially dangerous prisoners. Protect dignitaries and federal judges. Occasional undercover work. Pretty much all the high-risk stuff. They have to be ready to move out at a moment's notice. Last year, an SOG team staged a raid on a house in California owned by a heavy hitter in the cartel. They seized his assets, arrested his cronies. Cop stuff. On steroids."

"What sets them apart from the FBI?"

"Intelligence?" Peggy snickered.

Looked like disdain for the feds came standard issue with a marshal's badge. "I know an FBI agent or two who might not appreciate that statement."

"Probably not." Peggy shrugged as if she couldn't care less. "They say worse about us, believe me."

With that, Peggy turned her attention back to work, which was fine by Harper because she still had a mysterious flash drive to investigate. For days she'd been

waiting for an opportunity to crack into the little silver
nugget of information, but the ever present marshals
got in the way. She was constantly worried that someone might look over her shoulder, realize what she
was up to, and rat her out to Davis. A quick glance
over her shoulder confirmed that Peggy was finally
focused on work. Curiosity ate away at her and she was
tired of waiting.

Harper angled her laptop away from where Peggy
might catch a glimpse and slid the connector into the
port, anticipation shivering across her skin. She held
her breath as she double-clicked the drive's icon on
her desktop. The window popped open and she
scanned the folders: Budget, House Bill 23-072,
Photos, Agenda . . . fifty or more files stared back at
Harper, all of them indicating what she'd suspected:
That the flash drive belonged to Senator Ellis. He must
have dropped it in her bag right after he was shot.

Why? The stress, the speed at which everything had
happened muddled the events of that night in her
mind until it felt as though she were wading through
sludge for every tiny sliver of recollection. He'd been
about to confide in her. And his dying words about a
blue lake and hazard assessment—whatever the hell
that was—could have prompted Ellis to drop his flash
drive in Harper's bag. Hell, maybe Agent Davis wasn't
too far off in his assumption that Ellis had known his
number was up. Maybe Ellis had given her a trail of
bread crumbs to follow because he knew he wouldn't
have time to draw an actual map. The gunshot had
put a swift end to any confession he may or may not
have been about to make. And now, all she had to
unlock the senator's secrets were two words and a
bunch of meaningless files.

Well, maybe not completely meaningless.

Harper's eyes landed on a file named JOURNAL. Her journalistic Spidey sense tingled from each individual hair follicle down to the tips of her toenails. Her finger scrolled over the track pad on her laptop, the cursor hovering on the file. A weary sigh escaped her lips. Trashy gossip-mag-style reporting wasn't her thing and this was about so much more than landing a story. Her shoulders tensed as her mind filled with the deafening crack that had echoed in her ears, followed by Ellis gripping her as he fell, the hollow look in his eyes, the blood staining his shirt and bubbling from his mouth, and her own fear welling up inside of her and choking the air from her lungs as she crawled under his car. The realization that he was dead and that in a few short seconds, she was going to die right there beside him was as fresh in her mind now as it had been weeks ago. Her pulse jumped in her veins as she relived that night and it took all of the self-control she had not to shoot out of her chair and run.

No, this wasn't about landing the story of the year. Harper was interested in one thing: *Why did he have to die?* Why had someone resorted to murder to keep Ellis's mouth shut? He was a politician—and probably a slimy one at that—but his career wasn't the scope of his existence. He'd been someone's husband. Someone's father. And his family didn't give a shit about those secrets that died with him. The only thing that mattered to them now was the fact that he was gone and never coming back. And someone needed to be held accountable for their loss.

With a cleansing breath, she clicked the file and it revealed hundreds of individual Word documents, all listed by date. From the looks of it, Ellis had written an entry a week for a very long time. They began around the time Ellis had run for office three years

ago, and ended a week before his death. Harper
chose the first entry—more to find a baseline for subsequent entries—and skimmed the contents. The
senate campaign worried Ellis. His advisers didn't
want him to play the blame game with his opponent
and practice the time-honored political tradition of
deny first and apologize later. They had a new tactic
ready to roll, one that would encourage the public's
trust and buy him the election. Ellis wasn't interested
in drawing attention to himself, but he buckled to
peer pressure. With the help of his inner circle, he
became the Ellis the media had lauded. A straight
shooter who didn't try to hide his past or sugarcoat
the truth for the benefit of the voters.

Harper skipped forward six months. Though he
didn't seem to have much of an attack of conscience,
Ellis worried for his family, who had taken the brunt
of his honesty-first campaign. He'd admitted to an
affair early on in his marriage. Family counseling. A
bout with depression and anxiety. Questionable business dealings that teetered on the edge of what was
legal. His finances, tax returns, investments, even his
kids' report cards were made available to the media.
Harper had only been a sophomore in college at the
time, but she remembered reading the coverage of
Ellis's campaign and wondering if he ever felt guilty
over what his public admissions had done to his
family. Honestly, it was a wonder the guy had ever
been elected in the first place. Ellis was like the popu-
lar kid in high school who bragged about his misdeeds but was so charming no one seemed to care.

With each new entry, Ellis's outlook began to dete-
riorate as he became more and more jaded. Honesty
wasn't the best policy. He was alienated from his
peers, who refused to confide in him, the media and

his constituents began to doubt his intentions, and every bill, every vote was an uphill battle. His detractors were doing their damnedest to make sure he wouldn't serve a second term, and his family life had taken the brunt of his stress. With the recession in full swing, Ellis's investments had taken a hit, and his finances weren't what he needed them to be to keep his head above water.

Harper jumped forward in the journal entries to five months ago, around the time Ellis's staff had begun to dodge her interview requests. She skimmed the first half of the entry—mostly about how he and his wife were dealing with their daughter's formative teenage dramas—until something caught her eye.

January 3rd

Politicians lie. It's a fact. We don't represent the people. Our interests are our own. No one would have noticed or even cared about me if I was just another Washington asshole who didn't have a clue how the rest of the world lived. Now, I have to play the game, keep these secrets that I promised countless voters I'd never keep and hope that no one finds out. In hiding behind false honesty, I've guaranteed that when the shit finally hits the fan, I'll go down in history as the biggest hypocrite in national political history. No one will remember my environmental work. No one will acknowledge my education reform. Will anyone even care that my legislation helped to renew unemployment benefits for thousands and increase the base minimum wage for struggling families? No. The only thing they'll say about me is that I was worse than the rest of them. That I betrayed those who trusted me. And I deserve every ounce of their disdain.

*I'm starting to think the stress isn't worth it. I'm
one heart palpitation away from a heart attack. I
can't sleep. Forget about eating, the ulcer has pretty
much shut that down. I lived through the big reveal
of my secrets three years ago. Will this be any worse?
How could it be? I splashed my affair, the details of
my marriage, my shortcomings as a husband and
businessman throughout the media and plastered a
pleasant smile on my face while those greedy, nosy
bastards circled the sordid details of my personal life
like sharks scenting blood. Why not give one of them
the exclusive of a lifetime?*

As Harper read, her curiosity grew. Senator Ellis
had bared all during his campaign. What could he
have possibly done in office that was worse than recre-
ational drug use in college, a couple of extramarital
affairs, rage and depression issues, and troubled
teens? Did he kick puppies in his spare time? Sell
babies on the black market? Maybe Blue Lake was a
secret facility where they grew genetically engineered
wheat and prayed to the gods of GMO. Who the hell
knew?

*I guess the real problem here isn't me. I'm okay
with coming clean. But this time, the secrets aren't
mine alone. State-level heavy-hitters, and low-level
staffers alike will be at risk of exposure this time
around. And there's nothing to be done for it. In for
a penny, in for a pound. I can't come clean without
exposing everyone else who's involved and I'm
finally, completely okay with that. I have to do this.
There's no other choice anymore. If any of the
partners find out what I'm going to do, they'll try to
stop me. Honestly, I wouldn't put it past one of the*

*bastards to put a bullet in my head. They might be
okay with the secrets, the guilt, the underhandedness
of what we're doing. But I'm not okay with it. Not
anymore. And I'm going to do something about it
and suffer the consequences for my actions. Absolute
power corrupts absolutely. I never believed the truth
of that statement before now. No one should be above
the law, exempt from punishment. We've all got to be
held accountable for our actions and I'm going to
make sure that we are.*

Harper stared at the last entry. She scooted to the
edge of the couch, her head bent toward the screen
of her laptop as though she could crawl right inside of
Senator Ellis's memories. What? What was it he'd
done? And who the hell else was involved? How high
did this supposed scandal go? Questions burned
through Harper's brain and she was desperate to find
the answers. Not only because the investigative reporter in her demanded it, but because if this was as
bad as Ellis made it sound, the chances were pretty
good that Harper wouldn't be safe until his murderer
was behind bars. And at the rate Agent Davis was
moving, she'd be dead before that happened.

"Harper? Is everything okay?"

Peggy's voice jolted her and Harper jumped about
a foot in the air. She tried to laugh it off, but Peggy's
own marshal Spidey sense must have been tingling
because her expression was pure suspicion.

"I was just concentrating really hard," Harper said
with a shaky laugh. "You startled me."

Peggy's eyes narrowed. "Your mouth was hanging
open like your jaw had a couple of broken hinges.
And your eyes were pretty wide, too. To tell the truth,
Harper, you looked a little spooked."

"Heh." She tried to laugh it off, but Peggy wasn't buying the brush-off. Hell yeah, she was spooked. She might have inadvertently stumbled on the biggest political scandal of the year. That is, if she could figure out what in the hell Ellis's cryptic journal entries were all about. Until then, she was nothing more than a woman with a target on her back. "Just wrapped up in work. I sort of get that way when I've had an 'aha!' moment."

"Okay," Peggy said slowly. "But, Harper, we can't help you if you're not honest with us."

"I know." The answer came too quickly, almost defensively, and Harper wished she wasn't so damned jumpy. This was exactly why she'd waited so long to investigate the flash drive in the first place. It obviously didn't take much to rouse Peggy's suspicion. She needed something more concrete before she could share because right now, Ellis's journals were simply that. She had no motives, no suspects to offer up to Peggy or anyone else. The e-mail preview window popped up in the corner of the screen, and Harper turned her attention back to her laptop, closing Ellis's files and opening the new message. The sender was marked as "unknown," which wasn't half as disconcerting as the sound bite attached to the file. She turned the volume up and double-clicked the file. Her apartment suddenly filled with the sounds of her own voice, echoing in the distance, calling for help. "H-help! Someone help!" The sound of her own panic caused Harper's heart to jump up into her throat. "Senator Ellis has been shot!"

"Harper?" Peggy shot up off the couch and crossed the room. "What is that?"

Harper looked at the deputy marshal and balled her hands into fists to try to stop them from shaking.

"Peggy, I think we have a problem." *A problem? Way to make an epic understatement, Harp.* This wasn't a problem. This only confirmed that someone was trying to keep Harper's mouth shut. But about what? She couldn't remember Ellis telling her anything incriminating, and whoever had her digital recorder had all of the evidence of their conversation to prove it. Could Ellis's murderer know that he'd slipped her his flash drive before he died?

"Stay put, Harper." *Really, Peggy?* Where did she think she was going to go? "I'm going to call Monroe and get our forensics guys working on this e-mail to track down the IP address."

"Yeah, okay." The Marshals Service would bring in their guys, and probably the FBI as well. But Harper was going to take a page from Ellis's book—or journal—and watch out for herself, too. "I'm going to step into my bedroom for a second." She ejected the flash drive, which she slipped back into her bag. "I forgot I promised Galen that I'd call my friend about a lawyer today."

Peggy gave her a concerned glance as Harper left the room. She needed something concrete on Ellis if she was going to find out who'd killed him and get herself out of this mess. Right now, all she had was a bunch of cryptic journal entries and pictures from Ellis's family vacations and his daughter's dance recitals. Who knew if this new threat would be enough to keep Davis from throwing her in jail? It was pretty clear to Harper that he thought she was making the whole thing up; another clip from her voice recorder wasn't going to convince him. And revealing the flash drive now, with no clue what anything on it had to do with the murder, would only give Davis more reason to lock her up. She had to make sure that whatever she dug up on Ellis was indisputable.

"Well, at least you're not officially on suspension. Or fired. Or worse. It could be worse, right?"

Galen stared at Michelle for a second, a smart-ass remark on the tip of his tongue. He was still a little annoyed with her after the "isn't my brother the awesomest guy ever?" routine she'd laid down on Harper several days ago. But rather than follow through, he took a long pull on the straw sticking out of his iced tea.

Monroe had given him the equivalent of a slap on the wrist. A few days off and a strongly worded warning that Galen mind his p's and q's until this assignment was over. Not to mention a reminder on their policy regarding dating witnesses. Not that Galen had admitted to anything. *Way to rock the professional vibe, asshole.*

"It could be worse, though right now I'm not sure how." He'd been ready to cop to everything, including the fact that he'd met Harper and had something of a relationship—albeit a one-night relationship—with her a year ago. But when he'd opened his mouth to spill the beans to Monroe, nothing had come out. "I probably should have accepted the job offer in Paris. It would have kept my ass out of a sling."

"If you'd taken that job, I would have killed you." Michelle slid a plate with a huge cinnamon roll toward him. "So your boss doesn't know about what happened between you and Harper." She shrugged. "So what? If you asked Harper, she'd say you didn't know anything about it, either."

Galen cringed. When Michelle put it that way it sounded so much worse. "I fucked up."

"Yeah, you did." She grabbed a fork and dug into the cinnamon roll. "But, what's done is done, and worrying about it isn't going to change the way it went down. If you don't want your relationship with Harper to go beyond professional, I think you did the right thing. Her feelings are probably hurt, sure. I mean, come on, brother, that was a total dick move. But still, in the long run, it's probably for the best . . ." Michelle let the end of her sentence trail off. And how nice of her to remind him that he was a dick. He hadn't reminded himself of that fact enough in the past few weeks. "Unless . . ." Oh, great. There was an *unless.* "You want your relationship with Harper to be more than just professional?"

The silly, expectant smile plastered on Michelle's face made Galen roll his eyes. "I came in here for food and commiseration, not dating advice, Shel."

"Oh, bullshit. You absolutely came in here for dating advice. You think I'm stupid, Galen, but I know you. You brought her in here the other day to show her off and get my opinion."

"Not true." Yes, it was. It was totally true. "She has a thing for donuts, that's why I brought her here."

"Uh-huh. Sure. Then you should have taken her to Voodoo, not your sister's pastry place. You wanted to impress her and you wanted me to scope her out. This is sophomore year all over again."

In the tenth grade, Galen had lusted over Amy Renfro for months. It probably had something to do with the way her ass looked in her volleyball shorts. He'd flirted shamelessly, and when she'd finally agreed to go out with him, he'd invited her over to make chocolate croissants with him and Michelle. Later, Michelle had offered up the opinion that Amy had another guy on the side—some sort of women's intuition thing—and Galen's infatuation died shortly thereafter. Plus, he'd seen her making out with Todd Chamberlain in the gym the next week, which sort of sealed the deal. Michelle's opinion mattered, though. Galen wanted her to like whoever he dated. And yeah, maybe he'd brought Harper over for an impromptu inspection.

"Well?" he asked, feeling like that stupid tenth-grade kid again. "What'd you think?"

Michelle smiled. "I freaking love her. I swear to God, Galen. If you string her along and let her believe that you don't remember her, I'll kick your ass."

"If I admit it, I might lose my job."

"You can find another job. You won't find another Harper."

Galen took a bite of cinnamon roll and pushed the plate toward his sister. Goddamn it. Why did Michelle always have to be right?

Chapter Seventeen

Galen woke from a fitful sleep, his hips thrusting his hard-on into the mattress. A low groan of frustration worked its way up his throat as he buried his face in the pillow. Scraps of a dream lingered in his mind. One of full lips, voluptuous curves, and slick, wet flesh. His balls ached with the need for release, and his body was so goddamned tense it took a conscious effort to relax his muscles.

The swollen head of his erection brushed the sheets and Galen shuddered. As though he couldn't control the motion, he rolled his hips into the soft fabric, imagining Harper's body beneath him, her legs spread wide to receive him, her back arched up to meet him. He rolled onto his back, the motion abrupt as he gripped his cock and stroked himself. A shitty substitute for the real thing, but if he didn't find some kind of release, he doubted he'd sleep another minute for the rest of the night.

Galen's body jacked up off the bed as he worked his erection in his fist. Harper's face, her gorgeous body, and warm voice goaded every erotic thought. His thumb passed over the crown, slick with a bead of moisture, and Galen imagined Harper's tongue flicking out before she took him in her mouth. He'd wanted her mouth on him that night, but had been too impatient to bury himself inside of her. The way her body accepted him, so tight and warm, was a memory he couldn't banish no matter how hard he tried. The tight points of her nipples as he rolled them between his fingers and the sweet sensual sounds he coaxed from her had sent him into a frenzy the likes of which no other woman had managed before. He tightened his grip on his cock, almost desperate as he pumped into his hand, his mind full of Harper: her smooth skin, sweet mouth, intense hazel eyes, and her body, soft and curvy in all the right places and tight just where she ought to be. God he wanted her. Right now. So damned bad he couldn't stand it.

He gnashed his teeth together as he came, a low growl rumbling in his chest as the deep thrum in his body slowed to a warm pulse. The sound of his ragged breathing surrounded him, and his racing heart pulsed in his ears. After a moment, he rolled off the bed, and as he walked to the bathroom to retrieve a towel, he glared down at the still-stiff length bobbing with every step as though taunting him with failure. Galen cursed under his breath. Instead of calming him down, he only wanted more. But not from his own goddamned hand.

After he cleaned up, Galen flopped back down on the bed and checked the time, not even midnight. Fucking great. He had an entire night ahead of him with a raging hard-on, his own torturous fantasies, and not a minute of sleep in sight. Thank God this was the end of his mandatory time off. Another day alone with his thoughts and he wouldn't give a damn about his job, decorum, or anything else.

Against his better judgment, he grabbed his phone from the nightstand and opened up a text message. Closed the app. Opened it again. Stared at the empty conversation bubble casting a glow in his darkened bedroom.

Fuck it.

Are you up? He typed the words and hit SEND. It was a stupid question. Of course she wasn't up. And if his past experience with Harper was any indication of how soundly she slept, odds were he wouldn't be waking her, either.

He was about to chuck his phone somewhere by his closet when a response came in. Yup. Can't sleep. You?

Galen's fingers hovered over the touch screen. *Well, I was asleep until I had this a-ma-zing sex dream about you and woke up with a stiffy the size of a redwood. So I had to just take care of business and then*—Same. Insomnia.

He lay in bed, staring blindly at the ceiling. The time spent away from her had been worse than the seemingly endless days of being too near her. He wanted to call her. Hear her voice, low and warm in his ear. But the texts were safer. The soundless messages put a much-needed distance between them. Without it, he'd have no self-control whatsoever.

Are you coming over tomorrow?

As if she were asking if he was stopping by for a cup of coffee or some shit. Not because it was his job to be there, by her side, close enough to touch. Yeah. I'll be there. Why? Do you miss me?

Galen's body tensed with anticipation. Did her response even matter? For all he knew she was playing the game, keeping up with the banter for his benefit. The text came in and Galen smiled. **You wish.** No way would Harper give him an inch.

Who's working tonight? His gut had been in knots for days and Landon was on the verge of kicking his ass. He didn't trust anyone, not even his best friend, to keep Harper safe. Stupid. Because as of yet, no one had tried to gun Harper down in the street. But it was the calm that bothered Galen the most. Always a calm before the storm.

> **Peggy, of course. And a new guy on the street. Don't know his name, but OMG, he's great in the sack.**

Galen sucked in a breath through his teeth and fought the urge to throw his jeans on and drive straight to Harper's condo. His rational brain knew that she was pushing his buttons, but the irrational, primitive side of him wanted to pummel any man who gave Harper a second glance, let alone dared to get her into bed. He'd walk in, send Peggy packing, and fuck Harper until neither one of them could form a coherent thought. He'd make damn sure she never thought—or joked—about being with another man ever again.

His erection throbbed between his legs, and Galen scrubbed a hand over his face in frustration. He was obsessed. Consumed by even the simple thought of her. His blood burned, his body ached, his entire being craved her. He was worse than a junkie. Could he check himself into rehab? Detox from the memory of a one-night stand that haunted him?

You know I'm kidding, right? Harper's text lit up his screen. **Don't get anyone else kicked off their shift.**

You're not funny. He typed the words knowing what her response would be.

I'm hilarious.

He couldn't get enough of her dry sense of humor, her fiery disposition, her quick wit. He'd lie in bed all night, exchanging text messages like a fucking goofy teenager if he could. It was all he was going to have of her, wasn't it? Banter that skirted the edge of appropriate and nights of agony, as he dreamt about touching her, kissing her, tasting her, only to wake and find his arms empty.

You there?

Galen typed, **yep.**

I met with the lawyer today. She's really awesome. She said if Agent Davis doesn't let up, she's going to slap him with a harassment suit. I bet that'll make his day.

A ripple of anger vibrated through Galen. If anything, threats from an attorney would raise Davis's hackles. He wondered how many "days off" he'd get if he knocked the cocky FBI agent out. Probably more than a few. **Tell your attorney to tread on eggshells with Davis. I'm serious, Harper. You want him to lay off, don't give him any excuse to press harder.**

Galen didn't want Harper to press her luck with Davis, but that didn't mean Galen couldn't. Maybe not while he was on the clock, but he'd have an opportunity to get Davis alone. And when he did, it would be his word against Davis's. He'd make damn sure the agent got his shit together and left Harper alone.

Noted. Have you been scarce because of what happened the other day at his office?

Galen hadn't given Harper a reason for his absence, simply told her that another deputy would be spending days with her for a while. Yeah, Monroe thought I needed to calm down. Davis has always gotten on my nerves. He just hit one nerve too many the other day.

What happened out in the hall?

I kindly suggested he do his job and follow some new leads.

He could practically hear Harper's dubious laughter. Kindly?

Well, kindly for me.

I'm glad you're coming over tomorrow. I feel better when you're here.

During SOG training, a deputy trainee had smacked Galen in the windpipe during a hand-to-hand combat session. Just enough to knock the air out of him. Reading Harper's words had the same effect on him. A handful of responses jumped into his mind. Two or three of them bordered on lewd. But damn it, knowing she wanted him there was enough to make him want to throw all of his bullshit convictions out the window. I've got your back.

A long stretch of silence passed before the text message alert went off. Oh. Well, that's good. See you tomorrow, Galen. 'Night.

I've got your back? Seriously? Jesus fucking Christ. Galen knocked his head against the headboard a couple of times. He'd given her the text equivalent of a pat to the head.

Good night, Harper.

Maybe if he hit his cranium hard enough against the headboard, it would knock him the fuck out. No woman had ever managed to get in his head like Harper had. They came, they went. No big deal. Each entanglement was fun while it lasted and Galen never lost any sleep when it ended. Now, he was wide awake, his brain buzzing, his cock hard and annoying the shit out of him, and when she'd given him the opportunity to let her know she was more to him than some stupid job, Galen had brushed her off. Treated her once again as though she were nothing more than an accessory for him to lug around.

Wow. He was a real relationship pro.

I've got your back.

Harper poured a splash of cream into her coffee and stirred, her eyes locked onto Galen's text message from last night. Well, if that didn't clearly spell out how he felt about her, she didn't know what did. It had taken a lot of courage for her to admit that she was anxious for him to come back and resume his protective duty. And he'd basically given her a canned response.

I bet he says that to all the witnesses.

Peggy was gathering up her things, her expression weary. Of all the crap the U.S. Marshals Service dealt with, she assumed witness protection was the one duty they'd draw straws for. The displacement, the lack of routine—and, in some cases, comfortable bed—must be a huge pain in the ass. Could she really blame Galen for his detachment? He'd been off protecting dignitaries or busting international drug rings, or whatever else it was that the elite SOG team did. And he'd come home to mundane babysitting duty. She probably bored him to death.

"I'm off rotation for a couple of days," Peggy said as she slipped her arms into her jacket. "So I think Deputy Simpson will be staying with you while I'm off. You'll like her. She's super quiet."

As if Peggy were a laugh-a-minute chatterbox. "Okay. Thanks for letting me know. Anything on my secret admirer?"

"No, sorry, Harper. We checked the originating mail server and it was a known proxy in Morocco. The tech team said the place is a black hole for hacker activity and heavy e-mail spam. The original IP address of the sender could be from anywhere. We're working on it, though. Deputy Kelly was briefed on the situation this morning and he increased the number of deputies working your security detail for now."

Peggy sat down on the couch, packed up and ready to go. A knot formed in the pit of Harper's stomach. An adrenaline-fueled anxiety ball that made her feel like running a mile at full speed and throwing up at the same time. Though the added protection proved that Galen truly did have her back. Despite the sting of those impersonal words, she was glad he was good at his job.

She was taking a sip from her coffee and flipping

through the morning paper, more to see who was writing her feature while she was on leave than anything, when a text came in on her phone. She slid her finger across the lock screen and scanned a message from Liz.

Nothing on BL, but got Meader's number. Tell your marshal I like seafood.

BL? The British Library? *Ugh. No, Harp, you idiot.* Blue Lake. Was Blue Lake supposed to be one word or two? Harper wondered. Maybe that would affect her search results. Something to think about, anyway. She stared at the digits below Liz's message, her fingers itching to call Senator Ellis's former assistant. But with Peggy sitting in her living room and Galen about to arrive at any second, the best she could manage was yet another damned text message. Her last text conversation had been a disappointment. Hopefully, unlike Galen, Jason Meader would tell her what she wanted to hear.

This is Harper Allen, she typed. I'd like to meet with you regarding something Ellis mentioned to me. Off the record. Are you free?

A response came in a few minutes later. Two o'clock, at the art museum. I'll be in the impressionists' gallery. I'd rather keep a low profile. So no armed escort if that's all right.

Easier said than done. Harper peered over her phone at Peggy, who gave her a warm, commiserating smile. Sure, Peggy probably assumed they'd both rather be doing something else at the moment. But, whereas Peggy was probably thinking of the nap she'd be taking when she got home or what she'd do on her days off, Harper's brain was cranking at full speed as she tried to devise a way to ditch Galen and get to the art gallery.

Five hours to outsmart one specially trained, elite U.S. Marshal. Piece of cake.

First things first, Harper needed to get her shit together. Galen had been more than clear last night that protecting Harper was his job and nothing more. All of his flirtatious banter, the random texts at midnight, and jokes about coming over to check up on her had left her wound up and wanting more. Apparently, if she wanted to rattle Galen's chain enough to throw him off his game, she'd have to up the ante. A rattled Galen would be much easier to ditch. "Peggy, I need to shower. You can let Galen in, right?"

"No problem," Peggy said. "I'm sure he'll be here any minute."

Harper took her time in the shower. Usually, she tried to be up, showered, and ready to go—well, ready to go nowhere—by the time Galen showed up every morning. Today, though, she wanted him to see her disheveled. She'd never been much of a seductress, but she had to hope she still had enough sex appeal to at least catch his eye.

When the water ran cold, Harper figured she'd given Galen enough time to show up and relieve Peggy. She turned off the shower and threw on a fluffy white bathrobe. She arranged her wet, curling locks so that they looked just the right amount of messy. Then checked her bathrobe and adjusted it so the lapel hung open enough to reveal the upper swell of her breasts and a generous amount of cleavage. If she was simply another job to Galen, seeing her like this wouldn't bother him at all. Right? Then again, she could look like a total train wreck, which might turn him off for good. Damn it, if Sophie were here . . . *Shake it off, Harp. Focus. This isn't about getting him into bed. It's about throwing him off his game. Eye on the prize. Right? Right.*

Pep talk concluded, Harper walked out into the living room, pretending to towel-dry the ends of her hair. She forced herself to look up slowly, and feigned surprise when her eyes locked on Galen's.

"Oh, hey. I didn't realize it was so late already. Did Peggy leave?"

Galen waited a beat too long to answer and Harper gave herself a mental high-five. His eyes lingered on her chest before he dragged his gaze up to meet hers. "She left about ten minutes ago."

"So, how was your time off?" Harper plopped down on the couch like she was settling in to gossip with a girlfriend. She tucked her knees under her and didn't bother to do anything about the fact that her robe gaped open to reveal her upper thighs. "Did you do anything fun?"

Galen shifted his weight from one foot to the other like he wasn't quite sure what he should do. Or maybe, where he should sit. His gaze traveled the length of her body, and Harper suppressed a shiver. God, he could get to her with just a look. She wondered what he'd do if she loosened the tie and opened her robe. Would he reject her? Walk out on her like he had last year? Or would he strip down and take her right there on the couch? Oh, the possibilities . . .

When Galen's eyes finally met hers, she noticed an almost imperceptible hardening. "It was all right," he said as though she weren't sitting there, practically naked, in front of him. "I hung out with Michelle, slept in, watched *SportsCenter*. Nothing too exciting."

"The fast-paced life of a U.S. Marshal," Harper said as she feigned a yawn. "You want some coffee? I was just about to make some." Well, some more, anyway.

"Sure." Galen stayed planted to the spot on the floor where he stood. If Harper hadn't noticed the muscle twitch at his jaw, he would have painted quite the relaxed picture.

She pushed herself off the couch, careful to pretend that modesty was the last thing on her mind. God, she hoped her boob hadn't popped out of her robe. *Play it cool, Harp. Don't look.* A nip slip, whether intentional or not, was uncool. Wardrobe malfunctions: not sexy. She slung the towel over her shoulder and gathered her damp hair into a messy bun, tucking the ends in the twisted knot to keep it all in place. Galen pivoted on a heel, following her movement into the kitchen, though he didn't move to follow her.

"Crap. Peggy's taller than me and she put the coffee up too high yesterday. Do you think you can get it for me?"

Galen gave a long-suffering sigh as he followed her into the kitchen, and Harper pressed her lips together to keep from smiling. She didn't move, not an inch, forcing Galen to reach over her in order to get to the canister of coffee from the shelf. Her breath caught in her chest as his body brushed against hers, and she looked up to find him staring down at her, his blue eyes smoldering with an intensity that made her knees weak. Holy. Shit.

Had she ever met a more attractive man? She was certain she'd never met one who could make her body hum with desire just by standing close. That is, until now. Her thighs brushed together and Harper swallowed. Her core was slick, ready for him, and he hadn't even touched her. Likewise, her pulse jumped to a brisk thrum in her veins and she took a deep, steadying breath. Seductress? No, Harper was one-hundred-percent seduced.

Chapter Eighteen

Holy shit, was she trying to *kill* him?

After a night of no sleep, a thirty-minute cold shower this morning, and a twenty-minute drive's worth of the least erotic thoughts he could conjure—puppies, grandmas in swimsuits, compound leg fractures—he'd finally gotten his lust under control. And then, bam! Harper walks out of her bedroom damned near naked, damp tendrils of hair teasing her neck where they'd escaped the haphazard mess she'd piled atop her head, leaving enough skin exposed to send Galen's imagination running wild.

And now her body was touching his in more places than it had in a year, her hazel eyes soft and liquid, her mouth parted and inviting. Absolutely maddening. One tug on that belt and the robe would fall open to reveal her body to him. Six inches to close between them and his mouth could taste hers. He took a deep breath and inhaled her clean, floral scent. Screw the coffee. He wanted to lift her up on the counter and pound into her until neither one of them remembered their names.

Whoa, buddy. Put the brakes on. The last remaining

shred of logic in Galen's brain latched on and took hold. If he didn't cool his jets, he'd be pitching a tent in his slacks big enough for a carnival troupe to camp under. He'd just come off suspension and he'd managed to piss off the FBI's lead agent. Fucking a witness on her kitchen counter wasn't going to earn him any points with his boss or the FBI. Career suicide: not on his agenda for today. Besides, something was up. Harper wasn't the brazen type. Her behavior had thrown him for a loop, sure. But either she had no clue how damned desirable she was right now, or she was working an angle.

"Here you go." He shoved the canister into her hand and took a couple of steps back. Really, he'd need to be standing out on the street before he'd put enough distance between them and even then it might not be enough.

Harper's brow puckered and she worried her bottom lip between her teeth. Goddamn it, that was sexy. He wanted to suck her lip into his mouth and—

"Thanks." Harper set the canister down on the counter and gathered the folds of her robe tighter around her body before cinching the belt tight. She turned her back to him and grabbed a coffee filter out of the drawer. "Do you have any work to catch up on today?"

In the span of a couple of seconds, her tone had become more conversational. Formal. And a hell of a lot less breathy. Galen felt the distance grow between them, as though a cavern had opened up in the middle of the kitchen. He walked around to the other side of the counter and perched on one of the bar stools. "I'm caught up on paperwork for now. Are you still on vacation?"

Harper gave a derisive snort. "Vacation. That's one way to put it, I guess. But yeah, I am. So . . ." She hit the power button on the coffeemaker and turned to lean against the counter. "Since we're both going to be bored all day, why don't we break some rules and hit your sister's bakery for a couple of apple fritters?"

The suggestion was a little out of left field, but Harper was a pastry freak. And she'd raved about Michelle's apple fritters. It violated protocol, but maybe it was best if they left the confinement of her apartment behind today. Galen knew he could use the space. "Sure." Harper handed him a mug and set the sugar and cream on the bar countertop. "If we leave soon, they'll be fresh out of the oven."

"Um, no, not now," she replied too quickly as she poured coffee into his mug. "I have a phone call with my lawyer in about an hour, so maybe around noon? I don't mind if the fritters aren't fresh out of the oven."

"Okay." Galen took his cup and headed into the living room. He grabbed the remote and flipped on the TV. Her behavior was a little out of the ordinary, and though he wasn't complaining about her attire— maybe they could institute bathrobe Fridays—he was still suspicious of her motives. Harper was usually pretty up front, and Galen couldn't help but feel like he was being managed. In this case, he thought it best to err on the side of caution. Maybe she was trying to distract him with her body? For the record, it was totally working, but he had to at least try to beat her at her own game. "Go get dressed, though, will you? If Monroe stops by for a visit, I'll be hitting the unemployment line by the end of the day. Feel me?"

"Feel me?" Harper muttered under her breath in her best arrogant U.S. Marshal impersonation as she threw on a pair of jeans and a V-neck tee. She brushed out her hair and gathered it up into a ponytail. Okay, so using her seductive feminine wiles to turn Galen into a malleable lump of clay in her palm hadn't worked out like she'd planned. It might have helped to actually *know* how to be seductive, too. He'd looked at her like she had a third eye, or a horn growing out of her forehead. *Go, Harp! Way to rock your sex appeal.*

Had she misinterpreted the vibe he was throwing off? He'd gone from hot to ice cold in a minute flat. Like it mattered. Harper was stubborn, and she'd held out hope that Galen would remember her. Their night together. Why did she have to continue to remind herself that she was a notch on his bedpost, and now, nothing more than someone he was paid to look after? Her seduction tactics had been an epic fail, but at least she'd managed to get him to leave the condo today. Once they got to the bakery, she could give him the slip and take the light rail to the art museum. The suggestion to meet there had been pretty brilliant on Meader's part. No way would anyone look for her there.

When Harper emerged from her bedroom yet again, Galen had his feet propped up on the coffee table as he scrolled through channels. "Have you ever noticed how truly awful daytime TV is?"

She rolled her eyes at his attempt at small talk and took a seat in the recliner next to the couch. "It's not all awful. TNT shows reruns of *Supernatural.*"

"What's that about?"

Harper stared, mouth agape. How could she possibly be attracted to him? They didn't even like the same things. "*Supernatural* is pretty much the best show on TV. Dean and Sam Winchester are demon hunters and all-around badasses. You're missing out."

"They're probably Hollywood pretty boys, too, right? Too cute for words." Galen mocked a swoon.

Incensed, Harper jacked her chin up a notch. "Maybe. But that's not why the show is good."

Galen laughed and it caused her indignation to boil even hotter. "Right. That's like saying guys watch the Lingerie Football League for the sportsmanship."

Did he actually watch that crap? Harper could feel her eyes trying to pop out of her head. "No, you watch it for the fake boobs and ass cheeks hanging out of their booty shorts."

Galen shrugged as though he couldn't argue.

"At least what I'm watching displays a modicum of intelligence," she continued. Harper's face flushed and she knew her cheeks must be red as a beet. Why was she letting him get under her skin like this? "I mean, seriously, Galen. Is that what you like? Half-naked women slapping their teammates on the ass and tackling each other to the ground, pretending to be respectable athletes while they roll around on artificial turf in a bra and panties?"

"Maybe." His sardonic reply made Harper want to slap the smug grin off his face. "I'm a very dedicated sports fan."

Argh! It was moments like this that Harper wished she had laser vision. She glared at Galen, imagining him bursting into flames from the heat shooting from her eyes while she laughed maniacally in the background. Her stomach burned and clenched tight. Her entire body vibrated with . . . not rage, but something else. Ah, crap. Was she actually *jealous?* Totally, completely jealous of a bunch of good-looking women simply because he admired their bodies on some ridiculous television show? What was wrong with her?

"Yeah, well, at least the shows I watch aren't completely mindless." She should stop. Right now. Don't poke the bear. Oh, wait. She was the bear. So did that mean she was poking herself? "Yeah, the guys on *Supernatural* are smoking hot. Would I stop watching if Dean Winchester walked around in his tighty whities every episode? Hell, no. But he's not rolling around in the dirt with his equally sexy co-star, slapping him on the ass every five seconds, either. The show has actual substance."

"Oh, so it's like that?" Galen's brows came down sharply over his eyes, a crease digging into his forehead above the bridge of his nose. "You're harboring quite the double standard, there, don't you think?"

Harper rolled her eyes. Of course she was. It was obvious! "No. Not at all. I'm not objectifying anyone with the shows I watch."

"Really?" Galen leaned forward in his seat. Damn, when had their voices escalated? Harper only now realized they were both on the verge of shouting. She shot up out of her chair and Galen followed suit. Pent-up frustration boiled within her. She was so sick of all of this. Galen, her situation, her helplessness, her inability to control or change *anything*. He folded his arms across his chest and regarded her with narrowed eyes. "You don't watch that show and think about all of the ways you'd defile those *smoking hot* demon hunters?"

Harper took a step forward. Her breath heaved in her chest and angry tears stung at her eyes. Galen leaned in toward her, head bowed enough that they were almost nose to nose. Tension permeated the space between them, their bodies almost touching. Jesus, were they seriously fighting over a TV show? "I watch it for the world building."

Galen snorted. "You watch it for the hot piece of ass."

"Well, I've gotta do something," Harper spat. "I'm a prisoner in my own home and with you on my tail everywhere I go, it's not like I'll be getting laid anytime soon!" Oh, God. *OhGodohGodohGod.* As soon as the words left Harper's mouth she wished she could take them back.

"Don't let me stop you!" Galen shouted, his voice like acid, burning through Harper's rib cage straight into her chest. "You wanna go get laid? Be my guest, Harper."

He swept his arm toward the door, palm outstretched in invitation. Harper's heart plummeted to the soles of her feet and she bit her bottom lip to keep it from quivering.

"I've got a phone call to make," she said, fighting like hell to keep it together in front of him. She brushed past him, an immovable fixture planted in the middle of her living room, and when her shoulder brushed his arm, it sent her off balance. He didn't even try to steady her as she stumbled and kept going, down the hallway until she reached her bedroom and slammed the door behind her.

Harper took several deep breaths and swiped at the tears that ran in a rivulet down her cheeks. What a jackass! What a stubborn, opinionated, arrogant, smug pain in the ass. He'd just stood there, arms folded, face frozen in his best deputy marshal smirk. Why did she even bother with him? Especially when it was obvious he wanted nothing to do with her. If she didn't vent to someone, Harper's head was going to explode. She dug her phone out of her pocket and dialed Sophie.

"Hey, Harp. What's the word?"

"Do you think I'm sexy?"

"Of course you are, what are you talking about?"

Harper sniffed. "Do you think I'm Lingerie Football League sexy?"

"Somehow, I feel like this is a loaded question. What's going on?"

She flopped down on her bed and backed up against the headboard. "I don't know. I walked around in my bathrobe this morning. My boobs were practically hanging out. What's wrong with me that I'm so ignorable?"

Sophie sighed through the receiver. "I told you, you should have requested another deputy." Sophie's words weren't spoken in her usual boisterous, sarcastic tone. Thank God. Because right now, Harper needed her in best friend mode.

"I know. You're right. I just couldn't."

"You're awesome, Harp. Funny, smart, gorgeous. You don't have to be Lingerie Football League sexy to get a guy. But if you walked around in what they wear, I can guarantee you you'd turn more than a few heads."

A half laugh, half sob escaped Harper's mouth. "Thanks. I just hoped, you know, that he'd eventually remember. That maybe he'd want me."

"If he doesn't want you, then he's a fool. Don't sell yourself short."

No one gave a pep talk like Sophie. "You're right. I'm better than this."

"Damn straight. Screw him. So he's gorgeous. There are a lot of gorgeous guys out there and one of them is going to fall madly in love with you."

"Not while I'm under house arrest," Harper grumbled.

"Did you talk to my dad's friend yet?"

"Yeah, in fact, that's who I told Galen I was talking to right now." She'd covered everything during their initial meeting, but Harper wanted to stall Galen so they'd head to the bakery around the time she was supposed to meet Jason Meader. Hopefully their fight hadn't screwed up her plans. "I'm hoping this'll all be over soon. I'm tired of waiting on the FBI. So I'm going to do a little investigating on my own."

"Sans babysitter, I assume?" Sophie said with a hint of concern.

"That's the plan. If I can shake him. I'm meeting Senator Ellis's aide at the art museum today at two." Harper was secretive, but not stupid. "I just want you to know where I'll be in case you don't hear from me. I don't think the meeting will take more than an hour."

"And this is something you don't want Marshal Dickhead to know about, right?"

"Heh. Yeah. Unless you don't hear from me by three thirty, don't tell anyone where I am, okay?"

"Gotcha. But be careful, Harper. You still don't know what kind of danger you might be in. Make sure you're not being followed, okay?"

She was a reporter, not a character from a spy show. How would she even know if she was being followed? Still, she didn't want Sophie to worry. "I will. I'll check in with you around three."

"Sounds good. And really, don't let him get to you, Harper. You're amazing."

"Thanks, Sophie. Talk to you later."

"Bye."

Harper stared at the closed door, wondering what

Galen was doing out in her living room. Probably
calling Curt to request a transfer. She knew Sophie
was right. She shouldn't waste her time or energy
worrying about someone who didn't care about her.
Harper had too much self-esteem to let her worth be
determined by whether or not Galen wanted to see
her in lingerie running down a football field. The
problem was that she and Galen weren't on the same
page. She had this wonderful, well-rounded picture of
them that included their first meeting, the night
they'd spent together, and all of the subsequent days
and nights spent texting over the past couple of
weeks. But to Galen, they'd only just met in Curt's
office. She was simply some woman who had witnessed a crime and was his responsibility to watch and
keep calm until the dust settled.

His comments about sexy girls playing football in
their underwear shouldn't have bothered her. Harper
wasn't normally a jealous person. Girls used to hit on
Chris all the time. Sometimes right in front of her and
it hadn't even fazed her. But all it took for her to fly
into a jealous rage was Galen mentioning some hot
girls on TV. This was bad. So much worse than she ever
could have anticipated. The hurt of his rebuff this
morning, the butterflies she felt every time he showed
up or texted her, her nightly fantasies all led to the
simple fact that Harper was falling in love with him.

How had this happened? When? Where? One year
ago, at a bar, that's where. From the second he'd
grabbed that drink out of her hand and slammed it
down on the bar. Even though that night was so long
ago, the memory was so vivid that Harper could have
sworn it had happened just last night. She'd taken the
leap that night. Trusted him in an instant. Given
herself to him with total abandon. No one had ever

completely had her before Galen. Harper had always held a piece of herself back. And yet, she'd found her heart so easy to hand over to a virtual stranger.

If he'd never shown up again, she would have eventually healed. One night wouldn't have done permanent damage. But now, with the days melting into weeks, with the tension and the fights, and the text messages that helped her sleep at night. If she needed a year or more to get over one night with Galen Kelly, how many more years would it take to get over weeks—maybe even months—with him in her life? She'd met his sister. They talked about work, and life, and TV shows, and he indulged her superhero obsession. Oh, holy hell. She was done for.

Harper brought her knees up to her chest and hugged her body into a tight ball. The realization of her feelings didn't do anything to assuage the knot of fear and anxiety that solidified in her stomach with the weight of a boulder. Because she knew, without a doubt, that it was going to hurt like hell when he left her again.

Chapter Nineteen

For fuck's sake, he didn't even watch the Lingerie Football League!

Galen paced the confines of Harper's living room feeling goddamned suffocated. His shoulder holster was too tight, the weight of his Glock tugging his left side toward the floor. He took it off and set it on the counter and unbuttoned the sleeves of his shirt to roll them up to his elbows. It was hot as hell in this damn condo. Didn't she ever open a fucking window?

He tried to remember what had triggered their argument and came up empty-handed. Who cared what television shows she liked to watch? Hell, she could watch soap operas, infomercials, and talk shows all day, every day and he wouldn't have given a shit. He was reeling from the events of the day and he'd only been here a little over an hour. First she'd come out of her bedroom acting as though she was oblivious to the fact that she was practically naked. Then she'd turned off the flirt vibe so fast it had given him whiplash. *And let's not forget the way she all but called you a sexist pig when you didn't agree that* Supernatural *was the best show ever created in the history of television.*

Was she out of her mind? Why the manic bipolar act all of a sudden?

Because he treated her like she didn't matter. That's why. The proverbial cup, the one thing she didn't want to be. He'd been pushing her away since the day he was assigned to protect her, all the while knowing she thought he'd forgotten about what happened between them a year ago. Forgotten about *her*. Christ, how could he ever forget her? She was etched into his brain. Seared onto every inch of his goddamned skin. He had to force himself to leave this fucking condo every night. And then, he practically had to seal his cell phone in a safe buried thirty feet deep to keep from texting her until the sun rose and he could finally see her again.

Forget her? Galen was starting to think that he couldn't live without her.

She emerged from her bedroom almost an hour later, her puffy eyes rimmed with red. She'd tried to hide the fact that she'd been crying with makeup, but Galen noticed. Which made him feel like an even bigger asshole.

"Harper."

"Ready for some fritters?" She sounded upbeat, but it was forced. The smile plastered on her face was just as fake as her cheerfulness, and a feeling of foreboding settled into Galen's gut.

"We don't have to go," he said.

"Yes, we do. Come on."

"I think we should talk, don't you?"

Harper tilted her head to the side, her expression perplexed. "About what? TV? Don't worry about it, Galen. Let's just go so I can eat my weight in pastries, and then we'll come back and you can watch anything you want." She grabbed her keys and purse and headed for the door without giving him an opportunity to respond.

"I'm not leaving until we talk."

"Suit yourself," she said, pulling open the door. "I'll bring you back a fritter."

Galen stalked to the door, his ire as fierce as her nonchalance. He slammed the door closed and wrapped his hand around her wrist. "You're not going anywhere without me. Ignoring something doesn't make it go away, Harper."

"I have nothing to say to you, Galen."

Galen disregarded the warning in her eyes and pressed on, his hand still holding on to her. "You're obviously upset about something and it's not a fucking television show. We are going to have a conversation, Harper. Whether you like it or not."

She jerked her arm from his grasp. "You're not my therapist, Galen. Or my friend. You're nothing but a glorified babysitter. I don't have to talk to you about a damned thing."

Glorified babysitter? That stung. Still, Galen wasn't about to let her get away with it. "And you're nothing but a spoiled brat who doesn't appreciate that people are putting their own lives on *hold* to protect her. I don't know what's up with you, Harper, but I am not about to play your games."

"My games?" Her voice climbed to a shriek. "My games." Low laughter filled the room and Galen took a step back. Maybe they both needed to cool down a little. She was obviously on the verge of some kind of breakdown. "I think that's pretty hypocritical coming from you."

"Harper." Galen let out a slow breath and rubbed at his temples. Did she have to stand there, her cheeks flushed and parted, her chest rising and falling with each angry breath and looking so goddamned *desirable*? He forced his eyes to her face, anywhere but the curve of her hip, the swell of her breasts, barely concealed by the deep V-neck of her T-shirt. "All I said was that you needed to go put on some clothes before anyone saw you half naked. Do you realize what sort of trouble that could have caused if Peggy or Monroe had showed up?"

"Why should it matter? I'm nothing but a job assignment to you. You don't see me as anything other than cargo that has to get to a destination without a dent. It obviously doesn't matter to you what I do or don't wear."

Was she out of her mind? Did she think he was blind? Immune to her soft beauty, supple curves, and smooth skin? Seeing her in that state of undress had been sheer, unmitigated torture. "It wasn't unreasonable to ask you to get dressed."

"Piss off."

"Harper—"

"How could you forget me like that?" Her body shook with each word she shouted. "Was it seriously that meaningless to you? I thought about you, Galen. Every day for a freaking year! I really want to know, was I just another conquest for you? A girl you bragged about to your buddies at work the next day? Or was I wiped from your memory the second you walked out my door?"

Shit. He knew she'd throw it all back in his face sooner or later, and now he was paying the price for his deception. Galen despised liars, and right now he hated himself. He took a step toward her, palms up in surrender, and she held up a hand to stop him.

"Did you seriously not feel *anything* for me?" Tears glistened in her eyes, tearing Galen's heart to shreds. "Did that night mean absolutely nothing to you? Seriously, Galen, do you not have the slightest clue how humiliated I felt when I realized you had no idea who I was? How utterly used? How could you be such a dishonorable bastard?"

Dishonorable? "Me, dishonorable?" That was a good one. Galen shook his head, his eyes wide with disbelief. Talk about the pot calling the kettle black. "What about Cory or whatever the hell his name is? You failed to mention him during our so-called, no-bullshit, all-honesty conversation."

Her eyes grew wide with his admission. "Cory?" Harper replied, her tone perplexed. "What are you talking about, Galen?" She clutched her fists so tightly her knuckles turned white. "You walked out on me."

"Because you had a boyfriend!" he railed. "The text messages were piling up on your phone, Harper. 'Where are you?' 'Call me.' 'I'm coming over.' What the fuck did you expect me to do? Hang around until Curtis or whatever the hell his name is showed up? You wanna talk about humiliation? You played me. How could *I*?" he asked with incredulity. "How could you take me back to your apartment when you had a boyfriend waiting for you somewhere else?" A bitter laugh escaped Galen's throat. "How could I forget you?" he scoffed. "Jesus, Harper, you're all I've thought about for an entire fucking year! Who really used who that night?"

Galen took a deep breath and exhaled. His body was taut with frustration, his pulse racing in his veins. It was all out in the open now, and the worst part of all of this was that despite everything that happened, he'd do it again if he had the chance. All of it.

For just one night more with her.

Harper didn't know if she should be elated or crushed over the revelation that Galen hadn't forgotten their night together. Hadn't forgotten her. Was it worse that he'd deceived her? Pretended not to know her while she agonized for weeks over his casual dismissal. *I thought about you every fucking day.* Harper snorted. Yeah, right. Thought about how he'd managed to trick her into a one-nighter and gone on with his life while she'd been in a state of inertia, putting her life on hold for a memory.

"Yeah, well . . ." Crap. She'd reached the bottom of her cache of snarky comebacks. All she could think about was how much she wanted him to kiss her. Despite the fact that he'd lied. *You are such a loser, Harp.*

His tender expression made Harper's legs feel like cooked noodles. So much intensity. So much heat. So much *longing.* It only took Galen a few strides to cross the space between them and he took Harper in his arms before tilting her face up to meet his. "How could I forget this?" he said before touching his lips to hers.

Holy. Crap. Galen was the Jedi Master of kissing. As if some mystical force guided his actions, his lips caressed hers, slow, deliberate, an exacting torture that she gladly submitted to. When his tongue flicked out at the seam of her lips, she opened her mouth to him, deepening the kiss, and a low moan vibrated in his chest.

"I tried to forget you, Harper," he murmured against her mouth. Something inside of her cracked at his words, and she gripped his shirt in her fists, pulling him closer. "I couldn't get you out of my head, no matter how hard I tried." He reached up and gently pulled the elastic band from her hair, allowing the thick locks to cascade down her shoulders. His fingers wound through the curly length, sending pleasant shivers down Harper's spine. "Every day for a year I saw your face in my mind, heard your voice in my ears."

Galen eased her back, supporting her with his arm while his head dipped to the swell of her breasts. His heated breath seared her skin, quick pants that preceded a slow pass of his tongue and then, a light nip of his teeth. She had somewhere to be. Someone to meet. Oh, who the hell cared! She'd been waiting for this moment for an *eternity*. The rest of the world could wait.

"I don't care who you were with then or why you didn't tell me. I don't care if you're with him still. If that makes me a lousy son of a bitch, then so be it. I want you. And I'm tired of telling myself that I can't have you."

Harper couldn't talk. Couldn't form a coherent thought to save her life. Had the words she'd been dying to hear spilled from Galen's lips? If this was a dream, she wasn't even remotely interested in waking up. Her senses were awash with his clean, masculine scent, his skin on hers, the way his blue eyes burned with a passion that tied her stomach into knots. Galen seized her hips in his grasp and jerked her to him, his lips bruising, punishing as he slanted his mouth across hers. This was nothing like the playful, teasing way he'd kissed her their first time. This was hungry. Demanding. Desperate. And she gave as good as she got, nipping at his lip, thrusting her tongue in his mouth so she could revel in his taste. Her body burned with need, and her breasts tightened as they rubbed up against his shirt.

"I need to see you." His voice was ragged, strained. "I've wanted to see your body again for too god-damned long."

She wasn't generally self-conscious, but her few sexual escapades prior to Galen had usually begun with the lights off. Her first time with him had been such a sensory experience. In her darkened apartment, she'd forgone the full sight of him in exchange for the feel, scent, taste of him. Now, though, all bets were off. Like the last time they'd been together, he was in control and a rush of excitement cascaded over her. Submitting to Galen's desires was exactly what she wanted.

Harper hooked her finger in one of Galen's belt loops and began to walk backward, guiding him down the hall to her bedroom. She might have warmed up to him seeing her body in the light of day, but she wasn't quite ready to put it all on display in the middle of her living room. He followed willingly, his eyes glued to hers, a smile playing on his full lips. He could get to her with a look, and with each agonizing step she felt the proof of her arousal as a slick warmth pulsed between her thighs.

Once in the bedroom, she guided Galen to the side of the bed. She took a step back and, with her gaze still locked on his, dragged her T-shirt up the length of her body, discarding it beside her. She kicked off her shoes, and shucked her jeans. It took all of the courage she could muster to expose herself this way, and she moistened her suddenly dry lips with her tongue before slowly removing her bra and underwear and stretching out on the bed. Bare took on a new stark meaning as she lay before him, and Harper's heart hammered against her rib cage as he dragged his eyes slowly down the length of her body, pausing at the juncture between her thighs and back up to her face.

He scrubbed a hand across his mouth and drew in a ragged breath. "Jesus Christ," he said on an exhale.

Harper waited, her chest rising and falling with quick little pants of breath, as Galen stared. He stepped up to the bed and reached out, tracing his fingers from her throat, between her breasts, and down past her belly button. A shuddering breath escaped her lungs as he paused and his eyes met hers. "Open your legs so I can see all of you."

Harper let her knees fall open and an almost tortured groan escaped Galen's throat. He braced one arm to the side of her head and the pad of one finger resumed its path down the outside of her left thigh, around her knee, and back up the inside of her thigh. Harper arched into his touch, her body shaking with anticipation. His finger dipped into her slick heat and her entire body ignited with pleasure.

All of the pent-up frustration she'd felt over the past weeks melted away under Galen's touch. The heartache, the anguish, the utter embarrassment. So many miscommunications had formed a barrier between them, but with each touch, each heated gaze, that wall crumbled until there was nothing left but dust.

When he pulled away, Harper nearly cried out in frustration. "Look at me, Harper," he said as he unbuttoned his shirt and tossed it to the floor.

Was she supposed to say something? Pay him a compliment? Because the sight of his body as he quickly shucked his pants and boxer briefs left her absolutely speechless. How could a memory as vivid as the one she'd had of him be so pale in comparison to reality? Had his shoulders always been so broad?

The muscles curving his arms and torso so defined? His thighs so powerful and his erection so . . . *holy Christ.* The man was built like a freaking Greek god. "You're—" What? There weren't even words to describe his magnificence. "Amazing."

His answering smile turned Harper's bones to mush. It wasn't fair to the rest of mankind—or womankind for that matter—that there was only one of him. But even if she could clone him and share, she didn't think she would. Did that make her selfish? Absolutely. When her gaze lingered between his thighs, Galen grew harder, if that was even possible. A trickle of fear seeped into her bloodstream as Harper realized that once again, this one moment might be all she had with him. And if that was the case, she was going to be sure that it was something neither of them would ever forget. The world would come crashing down on them later, but this moment belonged to her and no one else. And damn it, she was going to make good use of her time. She'd always fantasized about what it would be like to take his hard length into her mouth. Harper reached out a hand to pull him close, but he seemed content to stare, taking in every inch of her as though he too believed these fleeting hours were all they'd be allowed.

A little shy and on the tame side, Harper had always stayed on the beaten path. Especially when it came to sex. It was always pretty cut and dry, him on top, her on top. Whatever. And how sad was it that she'd never felt the urge to test the boundaries of sexual logistics? Not now, though. Galen made her feel safe. She trusted him. And that safety and trust made her brazen.

He didn't want anything to interrupt his view of her body. Warmth suffused her skin and the thought that she could have that kind of power was truly a heady thing. If he wanted to stare, fine. She'd give him an unhampered view *and* live out her fantasy. Harper took a deep breath. Thinking she was brave and following through were two completely different things. Would he laugh at her? Think she was some sort of freak? Jesus, she hadn't really considered it, but the blood might rush to her head and she'd pass out. *Okay, calm down, Harp. Don't overthink it.* Worrying was just wasting time. She'd waited a year to be with him again. She wasn't waiting another minute.

Harper positioned herself on the bed so that she lay on her back, across the width of the mattress, her head tilting back over the edge. Galen looked down on her and quirked a brow. She allowed a slow smile to spread across her lips and she said, "Come closer."

Galen took a step toward her and Harper wrapped her hands around the backs of his thighs drawing him to the edge of the bed. She reached out and took the hard, velvet smooth length of his erection in her hand and guided it to her mouth.

As her tongue curled around the swollen head of his shaft, Galen drew in a sharp breath that hissed between his teeth. His thighs shook in her grasp as she closed her lips around him and gently sucked. Galen braced his arms on either side of her on the mattress and leaned over her body, his breath coming in rasping pants as he gave shallow thrusts of his hips. Harper took him deeper into her mouth and Galen's low moan sent a jolt of excitement through her. "Oh, God, Harper. That feels so good."

The vulnerable state of her position was an oxymoron to her intentions, but she wanted it that way. She'd given Galen ultimate control: the pace at which he thrust, how deeply he entered her mouth, whether or not he chose to be gentle or forceful. And she knew by his labored breath and the way his body trembled, that he was holding on to his own control by a thread. Harper traced the ridge of his shaft with her tongue as he withdrew to the tip of his glossy head before plunging into her mouth again. She reached back and cupped his ass in her palms, all but smug with the way she'd mastered him. Galen straightened and his hands came off the bed. She wasn't ready for this to end; she was drunk on the taste of him, the feel of his rigid length sliding between her lips. When he reached out and cupped her breasts before pinching her nipples between his fingers, Harper realized that their battle for power had just begun.

Oh, God, he had her. Trapped on her back, head dangling over the edge of the bed, her mouth wrapped around his hard length, she was at his mercy and he knew it. He began his slow assault on her body, never breaking rhythm as he thrust in and out of her mouth. Harper writhed beneath him as he plucked at her nipples, teasing them into diamond-hard peaks that ached for more of the pleasure spiked with the faintest sting.

When she didn't think she could take another maddening minute, he relented. But he was far from through with her. "You feel so good, Harper," he rasped as he bent over her, gripping her hips in his palms. "Spread your legs and let me see you."

Her knees fell to each side and Galen ran his hands up the insides of her thighs, stopping short of where she wanted most to feel his touch. "Oh, *mon coeur*, you're so wet." He circled her clitoris with the pad of one finger and she moaned around his length. It was a heady thing indeed to have rattled him to the point that he was mixing his languages. Such a turn-on. "I've wanted to taste you again. Dreamed about it."

Another sweep of his finger and Harper arched into his touch. "I don't know what I want more, to look at your body while I touch you or to feel you press against my mouth."

Holy shit, do both! Something! Anything! He was going to dirty-talk her right into an earth-shattering orgasm without having to lay a finger or his mouth to her. No man had ever said words like this to her before. And oh, God, it sparked something in Harper that set her ablaze with desire. She couldn't respond even if she wanted to, so she worked her mouth over his shaft, sucking deeply before pressing her tongue to the hood of his erection. Galen moaned and she dug her nails into his ass. She couldn't get enough.

"Maybe I'll do both," he said through pants of breath. Yes. Both. Both sounded good. The blunt tip of his thumb flicked over her sensitive bud before he bent fully over her and followed up with a pass of his tongue. When the heat of his mouth met her sex, Harper thought she'd lose consciousness, it felt so damned good.

If she'd thought cutting ties with Galen would help her get on with her life, Harper knew that after today, she'd never, ever get him out of her system. He was a drug she couldn't kick, an addiction she was willing to die for. And as he drew her clit into his mouth and sucked gently, Harper reasoned that there were much, much worse ways to die.

Chapter Twenty

Galen was a hypocrite for saying he didn't care whether or not there was another man in Harper's life. And a liar for keeping secrets from her. Not to mention a presumptuous asshole for storming in here and ordering her to strip down to nothing without even knowing for sure if she still wanted him or not. And right now, he was pretty okay with all of that. If he'd had any doubts before, they were gone now. Harper's body tempted him, her scent aroused him, her taste intoxicated him until he lost himself completely to her. He wanted her. End of story. Nothing—not his job, his morals, or his principles—was going to stand in the way of having her any longer.

Her position on the bed was precarious, but holy fuck was it ever amazing. With her head tilted back she could take him deeper into her mouth, and her tongue stroked the underside of his cock in a way that was downright maddening. It took all of the control he could muster, but he was careful not to thrust too hard or go any deeper than she accepted him.

Harper's adventurous nature turned him on almost

as much as the sight of her naked body. The way she positioned herself for him, took his erection in her hand, spread her legs to give him an unhindered view of her glistening sex. He leaned over her and fastened his mouth over her swollen bud, sucking it into his mouth. She moaned and the vibration shot down his shaft straight into his balls, tightening them with an almost painful need for release. No way was he going to go off yet, though. He refused to let it end so quickly. He slowed his pace to a shallow, easy rhythm, the warm, wet suction of Harper's mouth too good to be true.

She dug her fingers into his ass as Galen teased her opening with the pad of his finger. Her moans turned to whimpers as she continued to lap at him. His thighs trembled under the assault and he widened his stance to brace himself. He wanted her to come like this, with his mouth on her so he could taste her pleasure while he fucked her mouth. He'd make her come again and again until she screamed his name, forgot everyone else but him. Harper arched off the bed as he dipped his finger into her slick heat, and then another, slowly withdrawing before plunging in again, all the while working his tongue over her clit.

He'd waited a year for this. Three hundred and sixty-five days of celibacy, and he would have waited ten times that long for another chance with her. Harper writhed beneath him, her thighs twitching against his cheeks as he flicked his tongue over her sensitive flesh. He wrapped his arms around her torso, angling her hips up to his mouth. She tested the limits of what he could bear with her talented mouth, yet he couldn't bring himself to pull out. Instead, he buried his face between her legs, lapping at her as though he was starved for her.

Harper's moans became long and drawn out, her hips rolling in time with each of his thrusts. He circled her pink flesh with his tongue, applying a bit of pressure before latching his mouth over her and sucking deeply. She dug her nails into his skin, the bite spurring him on. A soft, languid lick. A long, drawn-out suck. Again and again until he felt Harper's body go rigid beneath him. He increased his pace as he thrust his fingers inside of her and she clenched around him, her core contracting as it built up for release.

Her legs opened wide and her body seemed to melt in his arms as she came. He withdrew from her mouth and she cried out, "Oh God, Galen!" His name on her lips drove him mad and he lapped at her unmercifully, until her voice was ragged from her impassioned sobs. Galen could have tasted her sweetness all day and into the night, lounging between her thighs, licking and sucking until she called his name again and again. But his own composure was hanging on by a thread and if he didn't sink his cock into that delicious heat soon, he'd lose his fucking mind.

As though she were made of glass, Galen scooped Harper into his arms and repositioned her on the bed so that she lay on her stomach. Her panting breaths and low whimpers stoked the flames of his desire until it was an out-of-control burn. He climbed up on the bed and planted kisses from her calf up her thigh and buttocks, across the small of her back to her left shoulder blade and then her right. Each kiss was like a brand, his mark on her, a declaration to her and anyone else who might want her: Harper belonged to *him*. And he'd be damned if another man touched her ever again.

He brushed the curling locks of her hair over her opposite shoulder as he kissed the curve of her neck below her ear. He rolled his hips against her, and when the sensitive head of his swollen cock brushed her ass, he gritted his teeth together on a groan. Her skin was satin caressing him.

"*Je veux te baiser. Fort. Toute la journée et toute la nuit.*" The words spilled from his lips, soft in her ear. Harper's head came up off the bed, her ear pressed close to his mouth.

"What did you say?" Her voice was smoky and lazy with desire, the rich sound rippling down Galen's spine as he rose above her, taking her hips in his hands as he kneaded her tender flesh. She fit perfectly in his grasp, as though her body were made for him alone.

"You don't need to know." He laughed. "It sounds less crude in French."

She thrust her tight, round ass in the air, and Galen brushed his cock against her skin once more, loving the way her soft flesh teased him.

"Tell me."

He'd tell her anything she wanted to hear as long as she kept rubbing her ass against his cock. "If you don't stop doing that, I'm going to be tempted to throw caution to the wind. I need to be inside of you now, Harper."

"Top drawer," she replied, without needing him to elaborate. "Now, tell me what you said."

Galen tried not to think about why she seemed to be so prepared. He meant what he said. He didn't give a shit about the boyfriend. Past or present. She rocked her hips against him once more, and he grabbed a condom from the drawer and ripped open the package. "I said I want to fuck you. Hard. All day and all night."

Harper moaned. "I think I like it just as much in English as I do French."

How was it possible for a woman to be so incredibly sexy? It wasn't only the curves of her body or her beautiful face, either. Galen was just as attracted to Harper's mind, her sharp wit, and her bravery. Maybe more so. She turned her head to the side, her expression curious as she looked up at him.

He bent over her and placed a kiss between her shoulder blades as he rolled the condom down over his erection. Pulling Harper up so that she was on her knees, ass up and arms stretched out on the bed in front of her, Galen slid his cock along the juncture of her thighs. She arched into him and reached her hand beneath them, cupping his sac in her palm. "Galen, I want you inside of me so badly," she all but purred. "Fuck me. Hard, like you want."

He entered her in a single stroke.

Galen paused, his body curved over Harper's as he panted through the intense sensation. She was so tight, so warm and slick and ready for him that he worried he'd come before he had a chance to move inside of her. He pulled out, slowly, and then plunged in again, seating himself as deep as he could go. Harper moaned low, and she tossed her head back. "God, yes."

Galen gently palmed her throat and drew her body against his. Turning her head to the side, he pressed his mouth to hers in a crushing kiss as he pulled out and thrust again. His tongue wound with hers, sliding in a silky wet tangle, and she moaned into his mouth, only stoking the raging flames of his desire. She was so blatantly wanton that it damned near made him crazy for her. Another deep thrust had her crying out, and with the next she screamed his name.

He would never, *ever* get enough of her. And it was his name she called out. His. Not Carl or Connor or whatever the fuck his name was. Each thrust was a claim Galen made on her body, each delicious cry of pleasure from her lips, an answer to a prayer. He pulled out completely and Harper reached back, clinging to him as though she couldn't bear for their bodies to be parted. Galen wrapped his arm around her waist and flipped her over on her back. She wrapped her legs around his torso, thrusting upward to meet him, her eyes glittering with passion and locked on his.

He buried himself to the root, seizing Harper's mouth in a frenzied kiss as he rolled his hips against hers. They moved in tandem, the rhythm of their thrusts an erotic dance as they parted and met, parted and met. Galen pulled back and searched her face, so in awe of the woman in his arms. "I want to watch you come."

Harper's tongue darted out and she licked her lips, red and swollen from the assault of his kisses. She ground her hips into his, and he reached beneath her to cup her ass as he rode her, his own breath ragged in his chest with each thrust.

"I'm close," she moaned as she arched into him. "Harder. Please, Galen."

He could deny her nothing when she was so willing, so soft in his arms. He thrust deep inside of her, pulling out to the tip before plunging in again. She threw her head back, and Galen grabbed the back of her neck, forcing her eyes to lock on his. "Don't close your eyes, Harper. Look at me."

He thrust harder, faster, grinding his body into hers, and her brow furrowed as her full lips parted in a silent *oh*. Just a few more strokes and she'd come for him.

"Oh, God. Galen!"

Harper's thighs locked around his waist, and her body trembled with the force of her orgasm. His balls tightened almost painfully, and as it had when his mouth greedily lapped at her, her body stilled, her sex clenching around his cock, and his own body went rigid as he came. He locked his eyes on hers, a low moan working its way up his throat as spasm after spasm rocked his body from the top of his head right down to his toes.

Fucking. *Amazing.*

Galen emerged from the bathroom and slid onto the bed tucking her body into his. He traced a careless pattern over her shoulder and down her arm and then back up the line of her throat, to the back of her neck, over her ear and then down again in a never-ending loop. A chill shook Harper's body. "I haven't been with anyone else for over a year." Her voice barely broke a whisper. "My relationship with Chris ended a few months before I met you. Why didn't you just ask me about him when you saw the texts that morning?"

Harper's eyes drifted shut and she was lulled by the

deep, even sounds of Galen's breath. Had he fallen asleep?

"I freaked out," he said after some time. He spoke close to her ear and his warm breath sent a shiver down Harper's spine. "I hadn't meant to look. The messages were all so intimate. It was obvious that they were from someone you were in a relationship with. I thought you'd played me. Picked me up for a good time. I don't like secrets, Harper."

"Me either," she replied. "I'm sorry you thought I lied to you."

He tightened his arms around her until their bodies molded together. "My dad's secrets destroyed my mom. She cried all the time. Took pills to battle the anxiety, depression, restlessness, you name it. And my dad made every problem in their lives seem like her fault, turned everything around on her until she actually felt guilty over his affairs. Like she'd pushed him to it. After he left, she just—" He took a deep breath. "Quit living. She slept all day, barely left her bedroom. She cut herself off from everyone including me and Michelle. Dad had been gone for about three months when she finally broke. I came home from school and found her on the bathroom floor. The coroner said I couldn't have saved her. She OD'd sometime in the afternoon and had been dead for at least a half hour before I found her. I tried, though. I did CPR on her until the EMTs showed up. It took me a long time to get over it. I haven't talked to my dad since the day she died. There's nothing worse than being betrayed by someone you love. It leaves a bone-deep scar that never fades."

Harper's heart broke for him. No wonder he'd walked out on her that morning. They'd made an agreement of total honesty and even though they were strangers, he'd put his trust in her. A trust he'd thought she'd betrayed. She wanted to say more. To offer him comfort. Condolences. Something. But she knew that he wouldn't accept her pity, so she lay in his arms, silent for a while.

"Chris had been trying to get back together with me for weeks," Harper murmured sleepily. "He showed up at my apartment after you left and I threw him out. I kept thinking you had a good reason for leaving and that maybe, we'd run into each other somewhere, sometime. But the days just got longer."

Galen kissed the hollow below her ear. "I left for Paris that morning," he replied. "I planned to postpone my flight, but when I saw the texts," he paused. "I had to get out of there."

Harper marveled at how a simple miscommunication had caused so much trouble. If it hadn't been for Chris's ridiculous text and stalkerish behavior, she might not have lost all of those months with Galen. They might be in a different place right now, their lives on a completely different path. "I feel cheated," she said.

"Of what?"

"Time. Experiences. Life. I can't stop thinking of all the days we've lost."

"You were with me." Galen turned her around to face him, and Harper stared into his deep blue eyes, losing herself in their depths. "Every second of every day."

How was it possible to have such a deep connection with someone you barely knew? They were only a few weeks into this whatevership and most people wouldn't consider that enough time to develop such strong feelings for another person. Harper reached out and brushed Galen's dark hair off his forehead. "A nameless face and one night. That's all I had of you, but I held on to that memory for an entire year. I refused to let you go."

"I can't believe I'm saying this." Galen gave a little laugh. "But, I'm glad you're so stubborn. I'm sorry I pretended not to know you." He smiled as he pulled her close enough that she could feel the warmth of his breath on her face.

"Yeah." Harper tilted her head and cocked a brow. "About that. Why the amnesia act?"

Galen's fingers did wonderful things to her body, gliding up and down her spine. Harper's stomach tightened and her breasts tingled as they brushed against the hard planes of his chest. "When I walked into Monroe's office and saw you standing there . . ." He hugged her close. "It killed me. First, I wanted to lay into you for the whole boyfriend thing. Then, I just wanted to strip you naked and lay you over Monroe's desk."

Harper swatted at his shoulder. "That's dirty."

Galen's eyes sparked with mischief. "Believe me, it was much dirtier in my imagination. But ultimately, I had to make a snap decision and I don't regret it, Harper. If Monroe realized that we knew each other, he would have taken me off your security detail. I already knew a little about your case and the danger you were in. There was no way in *hell* I was going to let someone else protect you. I didn't trust anyone else to keep you safe."

His rebuff had hurt at the time, but now that Harper knew the truth, she wouldn't have had it any other way. He didn't trust anyone else with her safety and neither did she. Only Galen made her feel truly protected. "Then we'll just have to keep our secret for a while longer."

"A while," Galen agreed. "I meant what I said, though. I don't like secrets. I'll have to come clean to Monroe soon."

"Soon," Harper said.

Chapter Twenty-One

Harper's phone chimed from somewhere in the living room, but she couldn't be bothered to move. She'd dozed off in Galen's arms and it was the first time since this whole ordeal had begun that she felt completely at peace. Another chime came on the heels of the first and reality rained all over Harper's parade as she remembered two very important things she'd chosen to ignore. One: meet Jason Meader at the museum. And two: call Sophie to let her know she hadn't met Jason Meader.

Crapballs.

Galen slept beside her, his breathing deep and even. A year's worth of pent-up longing and sexual frustration had just been released with the force of a hurricane. Anyone would need a nap after that. Her limbs were deliciously heavy and her body still hummed with the aftermath of her orgasms. It took an actual effort to roll onto her side and check the time on the alarm clock on her bedside table.

Two thirty. She really wasn't that late. She could still meet Meader and maybe even get back to the apartment for round two before Peggy showed up to relieve Galen for the night. Meader was pretty insistent on the whole "no marshals" thing and she didn't want to spook him by bringing Galen along. Still, she wasn't going to disrespect him by running off without a word, or ditch him at his sister's bakery like she'd originally planned. Not after everything that had just happened. And she'd much rather be reckless with Galen at her side than go it alone.

Harper slid out of the bed and padded to the living room, careful not to wake Galen. Midday love affairs weren't exactly common occurrences in Harper's life, but she planned on having many more in the future. And all of them with Galen. She released a contented sigh as a smile curved her lips. The possible days, weeks, and months ahead didn't seem quite as endless and depressing now. Especially if she was going to be holed up with Galen for all of them.

She grabbed her phone from the kitchen counter and swiped a finger across the screen. Nothing from Sophie, but Meader had fired off a couple of angry texts. Apparently the former aide didn't like being stood up. Well, he was self-important enough for a career in politics, that was for sure. Fingers flying, she tapped the screen with her thumbs, firing off a quick message that she was running late and for him to wait for her. The museum didn't close until five and if they left in a few minutes, she'd get there in less than twenty minutes. Meader's response wasn't exactly cordial: Fine. But at least she'd gotten him to wait.

Next she sent the same message to Sophie, letting her know that plans had changed and she wasn't going alone to meet Meader. Sophie responded with a simple: Thank God. I was worried I was going to have to smack some sense into you! *Heh.* Leave it to Sophie to know exactly what to say.

Two people squared away, one overprotective deputy marshal to go. "Galen, get up." Harper grabbed his slacks and underwear as she hurried into the room, tossing them on top of him while she searched for his shirt. "Get up! We have to leave." His shirt landed on top of his pants, followed by one sock and then another. "Now!"

Harper's resounding "now" had Galen shooting out of bed, eyes wide and reaching for his left side as though about to pull a gun. It was almost comical, but she had to appreciate his ability to spring into action. Especially now, when she needed him to get the show on the road. "What's going on? Are you okay?"

He was so cute, bleary-eyed and a little confused. She paused, a dreamy smile curving her lips. *No. Snap out of it, Harp! You can ogle the sexy marshal later.* "Yes, everything's fine, but we have to leave. We're going to the art museum and if you don't hurry up, you're going to make me late. Again."

"What in the hell are you talking about?" He scrubbed a hand over his face and disentangled himself from his clothes. "What museum?"

"The Portland Art Museum. Haven't you lived here for a while? You should get out more, which is why a field trip is exactly what you need. Get dressed. I'll explain everything in the car." His brow furrowed with confusion. "Galen, now!"

As he gathered up his clothes and pushed himself off the bed, Harper stopped to admire the view. Each individual muscle of his body rippled and flexed with his movement, like a living, breathing work of art. "Harper, the way you're looking at me isn't doing much to motivate me to leave."

Harper snapped to attention, her eyes meeting Galen's amused expression before venturing lower to see the evidence of his awakening arousal. She should have been embarrassed that he'd caught her staring, but she couldn't muster up an ounce of shame. He was the embodiment of masculine beauty. "Sorry." For the record, she totally wasn't sorry. "Just enjoying the view. But seriously, Galen, get your pants on and let's go."

By the time he finished dressing, Harper was ready to burst with impatience. Waiting for him to retrieve his shoulder holster, badge, and jacket was enough to give her heart palpitations. As it was, she was going to be late to meet Meader, *again*, and she still had to convince Galen to go along with her plan. This was definitely not how she'd planned the afternoon to go. But given the chance to do it all over again, she wouldn't have changed a thing.

"*No.* No way. It's not going to happen, Harper. Are you insane?"

The fact that she looked at him like she couldn't understand why he'd object was proof enough to Galen that Harper was, indeed, out of her mind.

"It's just an interview, Galen. In a public place. What could possibly happen to me in a crowded museum filled with people and priceless, irreplaceable artwork?"

Did she really want him to answer that? A million scenarios flashed in his mind, all of which resulted in him being shit-canned. "Give me one good reason why I should let you conduct an interview with someone who is involved in a federal investigation when—last time I checked—you have no reason to interview him? You're on leave from work and I'm pretty sure the FBI and Marshals Service haven't added you to their payrolls."

"I need to get to the bottom of Ellis's murder, Galen." You'd think she was talking about going to the grocery store as casual as she made solving a murder sound. "You know the FBI isn't going to let up on me as a suspect until they have someone else to look at."

True. Even with the latest threat, Davis still had his eye on Harper as a suspect. Which was completely asinine. Davis was reaching if he thought Harper was sending herself the sound clips from her interview with Ellis in order to throw them off her scent. Apparently her innocent, freckled face had diabolical criminal mind written all over it.

"It isn't your job to find Ellis's murderer, Harper. You're the witness. *Wit-ness.* Your job is to lay low and let me keep you safe while the trained investigators do their job. You are *not* Nancy Drew."

And yet, here he was, headed down NW Twenty-third toward the museum as though he had no choice but to chauffer Harper to her destination. The day had shifted gears so quickly Galen was experiencing a bit of whiplash. Harper tempting him with her near naked body, their fight, the intense, mind-blowing sex that had followed, and now, racing to the damned art museum so Harper could get a few minutes with the dead senator's aide before the museum closed for the day. The past twenty-four hours had his entire year in Paris beat. One thing was certain—life with Harper Allen wasn't boring.

"I could totally be Nancy Drew, but that's not the point." How could she be so calm about all of this? Galen was starting to think that he wouldn't level out until he had Harper locked up in protective custody somewhere. With him doing the protecting, of course. "I just want to talk to him, that's all. And it was tough enough getting him to agree to meet me. If I stand him up now, he might not agree to another interview."

Which was perfectly okay with Galen. "You should have told me sooner, Harper. I could have run this by Curt and we could have set something up at our offices. You know, where it's nice and secure."

Harper gave him a look from the corner of her eye. A sort of half grimace that made him nervous. "Well, that's sort of the thing. He requested that I come alone. No marshals."

What? "Harper, you don't think that's a little suspicious?" Requesting that she come alone without an escort threw up a red flag the size of Texas as far as Galen was concerned.

"It would be if he wasn't a politician," Harper remarked. "Meader is going to run for Ellis's seat and I think he's trying to put as much distance between himself and the investigation as possible. Meeting with the key witness and her protective detail is only going to invite attention. He chose the museum, not me. I would have been worried if he'd asked to meet somewhere secluded. You can wait for me outside."

"No."

She turned to face him, her expression full of that fierce determination that he admired so much. "It'll be okay. I promise."

Right. Then why was his instinct telling him to handcuff her to the steering wheel? "Sorry, Harper, but I can't agree to that. I will, though, let you go in ahead of me." The museum had decent security, and once inside the doors, Harper would be marginally safe. "I'll give you a five-minute head start while I check the outside of the building for anything unusual."

Maybe, together, they'd manage to dig something up
that would get Davis off her back. "Five minutes,
Harper. Got it?"

A smile lit her face and she leaned over to kiss his
cheek. "Deal."

Harper got out of the car and hoofed it across SW
Park. As she walked up the steps of the Portland Art
Museum, she regretted bringing her overstuffed hobo
bag. At the security checkpoint, she bounced impatiently on the balls of her feet, until a security guard
motioned her forward. He gave her a look and said,
"I'm sorry, but no large bags allowed inside the
museum. You're going to have to check this." *Argh.*
She didn't have the time or the patience for this, but
she handed her purse over with a tight smile, anyway.
It was for the best, she supposed. This meeting was off
the record. Jason would fly out of there like his high-
priced loafers were on fire if he thought for a second
Harper was recording him or taking notes.

The art museum wasn't too busy for a weekday, and
Harper wandered through the galleries toward the
Impressionists exhibit. She really didn't get out
enough. Portland was truly a well-cultured city, and it
had been a couple of years since she'd enjoyed what
it had to offer. Her senior year of college had been all
about work. And last year had been devoted to getting
her career off the ground. As she took a seat on a
bench in the center of the gallery, Harper had to
wonder: would being a witness to Ellis's murder help
or hurt her career? Would anyone take her seriously
after this or would she simply be the girl who made a
name for herself by being in the wrong place at the

wrong time? Harper tilted her head as she studied one of Monet's "Water Lilies" paintings on the far wall. The distinct thin brushstrokes, vibrant colors, illusion of light, and the texture and depth of the painting made Harper want to reach out and touch it. From a distance, the painting formed a complete picture, a pond filled with beautiful floating green pads and vibrant flowers. But up close, the image blurred and became nothing more than a chaotic splash of color. Harper's life was beginning to remind her of an impressionist painting: complete and smooth from a distance, but more riotous the closer you got.

Sam had been fielding calls from news outlets for the past couple of weeks. CNN, MSNBC, Fox News, *The Washington Post*, *The New York Times*. All of them wanting an exclusive interview with the witness to Senator Mark Ellis's murderer. Even TMZ had tried to horn in on the action. They probably studied at the Special Agent Sean Davis School of Assumptions and Wild Theories. They'd love a juicy exposé revealing Harper as Ellis's lover. When his killer was finally caught, then what? The Marshals Service—and Sam— had pulled considerable strings to keep her out of the spotlight, but when she no longer needed protection, who would she lean on when the media camped outside her condo and the tidal waves of requests became too much? Really, she was kidding herself. Harper had plenty of people in her life who loved and supported her. What had her bent out of shape was the thought that the one person she *wanted* to lean on wouldn't be there anymore.

"Did you know the term Impressionism came from a slur an art critic made about one of Monet's early works?"

Jason Meader stood beside Harper to the left of the narrow bench, looking as well-groomed and put together as he had for every one of his recent TV appearances. Whereas Harper had been shunning media attention, Jason had gobbled it up, using Ellis's death to kick his own political career into high gear.

He probably thought he was hot shit spewing little art factoids at her. Probably how he impressed the nineteen-year-old interns at the office. "He also drew caricatures when he was young."

Jason turned to face Harper. From the smug look on his face, he enjoyed making people feel small. She was pretty sure he was in his midforties, though he gave off a much younger vibe. He was the perfect cookie-cutter politician. Just the right amount of good-looking for television, with a smile that was both charming and self-assured. Straight nose, strong chin, and groomed eyebrows—even his nondescript brown hair was perfectly cut, not a hair out of place. Harper didn't have to look at his hands to know they'd been recently manicured. With his metrosexual style and Ken doll proportions, he was strong and masculine without looking too threatening. His gray wool suit probably cost more than a month of Harper's rent, and his light gray and blue striped silk tie accented his sky-blue eyes, which, in her opinion, were the only memorable thing about Senator Ellis's former aide.

Harper stood and led the way into the next gallery. No way was she going to let him take control. This was her meeting. "I hear you're running for Ellis's seat." It wasn't a question. Most of the major news outlets had hinted that Jason was after Ellis's Senate seat. "Are you ready to pick up where he left off?"

Jason smiled, his attention focused on the paintings

they walked past. He paused next to a Renoir and studied it for a moment. "This is sounding a lot like an interview." He gave her a million-watt smile. "I heard you were determined, Harper, but you could have just invited me out for coffee."

True enough. Harper was itching to dig in and get to the bottom of his story. He had his boy-next-door routine down pat. He'd be a shoo-in with voters. Damn. What she wouldn't give to be the first to report on his plans, platform, whether or not he planned to carry on Ellis's legacy of full disclosure. Well, sort-of full disclosure. But Jason was right, she wasn't there to talk about him or his ambitions. She was here to figure out how in the hell to get Agent Davis off her back and she had a feeling Blue Lake was the key. "Maybe when things settle down, you'll grant me an interview." Harper continued to walk and Jason followed. "I wanted to talk to you about something that Senator Ellis said to me before he was killed."

"From what I understand, you didn't glean much from Mark's last words. At least, that's what the newspapers are saying."

Harper didn't miss the sarcastic edge to his voice. Politicians and reporters got along about as well as chickens and foxes. He probably loved that her own kind had tried to cannibalize her. Jerk. "We talked for about five minutes. Maybe less. Enough for me to assume that he had a secret. A big one that would have brought a lot of bad press down on more than only him."

Jason stopped and pivoted toward Harper. He pinned her with a contemplative stare that made Harper think he was trying to exercise some sort of Jedi mind control over her. His eyes sparked with humor. "You know what happens when you assume, right?"

It makes as ASS out of U and ME. Jason Meader was a class-A funny man. He should take his act on the road. "My assumption has substance." Harper racked her brain, recalling as much of their conversation as she could. "He mentioned something about a hazard assessment. Mobile hazard assessment, I think. And Blue Lake. Do you know anything about that?"

Jason's face remained passive, but the barest thinning of his lips let Harper know that she might have touched a nerve. "It doesn't ring a bell. But, then, Mark was always dreaming about what he'd do when his term was up. I don't know anything about a hazard assessment, but isn't there a Blue Lake farm up by Eugene? Maybe he and Elaine were thinking about farming? He read this article about the University of Wisconsin's aquaponics project. Did you know they can grow a million pounds of food a year? I swear he wanted to go out and buy a fish tank to grow tomatoes over the next day."

For some reason, Harper doubted Ellis had been guilt ridden over his desire to leave politics and become a fish-slash-vegetable farmer. Jason had done his best to give both the hazard assessment and Blue Lake a casual brush-off, so Harper switched tactics. "He wanted to quit politics, then?"

Jason pursed his lips, put on a truly sad face. She wondered if he practiced his expressions in a mirror. "Mark was an idealist. He was one of the few men I believed when he said he wanted to change the world. But I don't think Mark realized what an uphill battle change could be. He planned to serve out his term and fade quietly into the background."

"But not before endorsing you, right?" Harper

didn't buy Meader's spiel for even a second. Ellis, an idealist? After peeking into his journal entries, Harper knew that Ellis was as much of an idealist as Superman was human. The only thing Ellis had strived for was the perfect distraction to snow the media with.

He gave her a wan smile. "That was the plan."

"He never confided in you about anything he might have felt guilty about? Aside from his disillusionment with politics, you don't know of any other reason he might have wanted to call it quits?"

Jason paused again. He gripped his hands behind his back and regarded Harper with a thoughtful expression. "Mark felt guilty about a lot of things. The reason he was so forthright in his campaign was because he was trying to absolve himself of some of that guilt. He wasn't a perfect man, but he was a good man, Harper. No matter how reporters like you want to spin his story, he was nothing more than a regular guy trying to do the right thing."

"I'm just trying to understand why this happened," Harper replied. "Why he had to die, and why I can't go anywhere without an escort because of it."

Jason looked around. "I don't see an escort now. Those marshals must be pretty good at the whole stealth thing." He leaned in close. "I think you should leave the investigating to the FBI. I'm sorry you got dragged into this, Harper. I really am. But you're not going to find any dark conspiracies or buried scandals. Mark was the real deal. Open. Honest. He was a gentleman and his death is a tragedy. Please don't try to sensationalize it."

Harper usually had a pretty good bead on people. But she couldn't tell if Jason was being sincere or not. "I just want answers."

"And I wish I could give them to you." He checked

his watch and pulled his cell from the inside pocket of his fancy two-button suit jacket. "Excuse me, Harper." Taking a few steps to the side, Jason conducted a quiet conversation with someone about his schedule. Harper imagined his life had gone through the wringer over the past few weeks. With a single gunshot, Jason Meader had gone from managing someone's schedule, to being managed. He ended the call and stepped back over toward Harper. "I have a meeting that I really can't be late for. Good luck, Harper. I hope this ordeal ends for you soon."

Jason turned, his face once again plastered to the screen of his phone, and he walked away leaving her staring after him. For all her hopefulness, Harper hadn't expected to risk Galen's anger only to have Jason Meader give the equivalent of an investigative cock block. It had been stupid, and optimistic, and damned risky, but damn it, she'd had to at least give it a try. Right?

Nothing soured her stomach like when a lead dead-ended. Right about now, she wanted to drown her sorrow and disappointment with a dozen donuts. Or better yet, a couple of apple fritters from A Slice of Heaven. Maybe she could get Galen to stop by his sister's bakery on the way home. They were already out—they might as well make the most of their field trip. There wouldn't be time for pastries or anything else, though, if she didn't hightail it back to the car. No doubt her five minutes were up. Hell, he might even be milling around, looking for her right now. Harper took off at a slow jog, toward a security guard in the next gallery. "Excuse me, do you happen to know what time it is?"

The guard glanced down at his watch. "Almost a quarter after four."

Shit. With a wave of thanks, Harper headed toward the exit. She was officially way past Galen's proffered five minutes.

Chapter Twenty-Two

He was *so* slapping a tracking bracelet on her after today. Maybe two. One for each ankle. And another on her wrist for backup. Galen waited impatiently at the bottom of the outside stairs while Harper retrieved her bag from the museum's security staff. Even though he was mere feet from where she stood, to Galen, it felt like miles. His protective instincts surged as he watched her, though he hadn't found any signs that might have suggested Meader wasn't on the up-and-up or that Harper had been trailed. She'd barely been out of his sight, but still he wouldn't be at ease until she was back in her damned apartment and far from the public eye. They were much too exposed for his peace of mind.

Monroe was going to have his ass for this if he found out Galen let Harper meet with Senator Ellis's aide. He'd never live it down, either. For a year he'd been the head of security for a U.S. ambassador and his entire family. He'd handled protective duties for witnesses to cartel hits and organized crime rings. Witnesses who begged, complained, and attempted to bribe him for a little bit of freedom. And he'd never given in to a single one until today. None of them had given him half as much trouble as Harper.

When she walked out of the doors and headed down the stairs, a wave of relief washed over Galen and he let out a slow breath. Harper scanned the area as though looking for him and he headed toward her. He couldn't get her out of there fast enough—

A resounding *pop! pop! pop!* echoed in his ears followed by a cacophony of terrified screams and shouts. Galen's heart jumped up into his throat and he pulled his Glock from the holster. He sprinted through the mass of terrified people and up the front steps of the museum, where all hell was breaking loose.

Harper scanned the crowd of people gathered outside of the museum as she looked for Galen. She shouldn't have rushed him into a decision that made him nervous. She'd asked him to neglect his duties and the guilt of that request settled on her with all of the weight of a boulder. *Stupid, Harp.* Not to mention selfish. Meader had done nothing but waste her time. And he'd offered up nothing in the way of information. She'd put her own safety and Galen's reputation on the back burner today, and that wasn't going to happen again. She simply had to hope that Davis and the FBI would find something, anything that would take her off their very short list of suspects. *So much for channeling Nancy Drew.*

A large chunk of concrete flew up from the step at Harper's feet a split second before a loud pop echoed in her ears. Every ounce of blood in her body seemed to rush into her head and she fought for coherent thought. *Pop! Pop! Pop!* What in the hell was happening? Frantic, Harper looked to each side and then behind her, her heart hammering in her chest as chaos spread like wildfire. Terrified screams rent the air and people pushed each other as they ran for cover. Earthquake? Zombie apocalypse? *Holy shit!* She stumbled backward and tripped on the step above her, landing square on her ass as another chunk of concrete went flying. The sounds assaulting her ears were gunshots. The bullets drilled into the steps near her feet. Someone was trying to shoot her!

The realization cleared Harper's mind in an instant. A lull in the successive shots meant one thing: the shooter was in the process of reloading. Cover. She needed to find cover right this freaking second. Standing out in the open was tantamount to volunteering to play the part of target and she wasn't about to get her ass shot today or any other day. She scrambled to her feet and assessed her situation. It was pretty safe to assume the only person in danger right now was her, and Harper wasn't about to hide in a crowd of people who might get caught in the cross fire. Sirens howled in the distance, but they weren't close enough to make her feel any modicum of safety. If she didn't get her butt in gear, she'd be dead before she had the opportunity to see the flashing red and blue lights of the PPB cruisers.

Why had she decided to exit through the main entrance? Stupid. She should have known better, damn it. She was out in the open, the nearest cover too far away for her to make a run for it. Her only option at this point was to go back into the building. Harper turned to retreat up the ten or so steps to the double glass doors when she felt a whisper of wind as another bullet zinged past her ear right before the report of the shot rang out. Her stomach clenched and her muscles all but seized up with fear. The next shot would surely hit her.

Before she could take another step, strong arms encircled her waist. In the next moment, Harper was jerked up in the air and spun to the right as another bullet dug into the concrete where she'd stood. She looked down at the arms clasping her, one hand clutching a gun. Oh. Shit. The contents of Harper's stomach threatened to revolt and her vision darkened at the periphery, but she refused to succumb to her fear. Or pass out. Apparently her would-be murderers were tired of missing. She kicked and fought against the arms holding her like an unyielding vise. A point-blank shot to the head. That's how she was going to die.

"Hang on, Harper. I've got you."

Harper let out a strangled sob and her muscles relaxed in a tidal wave of relief. Galen's voice in her ear was the sweetest sound she'd ever heard, and she gripped the arms wrapped around her waist like a lifeline. He took the steps three at a time, his pace quick despite the fact he was carrying her. As he hauled her back toward the museum, Harper's heart hammered against her rib cage. His body shielded hers, the expanse of his back a perfect target for the next bullet. The breath stalled in her chest as five steps felt like five thousand. Galen's path zigged and zagged up the steps, and the glass doors leading to the museum exploded into myriad crystalline pebbles as another shot rang out.

"Hang on!"

Galen dove through the entrance and spun in midair, crashing to the floor on his back while protecting Harper from the brunt of the impact. Her teeth rattled as her head knocked against his shoulder, but her discomfort couldn't have been half as bad as his. He rolled again, depositing Harper beside him, and she was vaguely aware of the sirens right out front, their wails a whisper in comparison to the sound of blood rushing in her ears.

He leaned over her, examining every inch of her body. Crimson smears stained his hands and she noticed several more near his left shoulder. Harper felt again like she might check out. Oh, God. Had he been shot?

"Harper, are you hit?" His words were clear, his voice, commanding. But for some reason, she had a hard time comprehending. "Are you hurt? Talk to me, Harper."

Concern etched every deep line in Galen's forehead, and his eyes were wide as he lifted her arms, then the hem of her shirt, and ran his palms down her legs. Harper continued to stare, her lungs aching, her vision darkening. What the hell?

"Breathe, Harper." Galen wrapped his arms around her shoulders as he brought her to a sitting position. He continued to search her body, his palm patting its way down her back. He checked her right thigh and arm, both shoulders, even her feet. "Come on, take a breath. It's okay. You need to calm down."

Calm? Wasn't she calm? Then again, maybe her lungs felt like they were on fire because she'd deprived them of oxygen for too long. She took a deep, shuddering breath, and then another. Ah, sweet, sweet air! But rather than calm down, her pulse rate jacked back up to frantic and the deep, even breaths she'd been hoping for turned into quick, desperate gasps.

Sweet Jesus. She'd almost been killed and Galen could have been killed trying to get her slow ass to safety. Angry tears blurred Harper's vision and she leaned forward, head bowed, as she tried to regain some shred of her composure. The earlier chaos was nothing compared to the onslaught of activity swarming around her now. FBI, Portland police, U.S. Marshals, and EMTs flooded the museum, which was already a mass of bodies as security guards and staff attempted to put the facility into lockdown. She buried her face in Galen's shoulder, hiccups of breath stuttering in and out of her lungs. If she didn't settle down, she'd hyperventilate and pass out.

"Harper, I need to know if you're hurt." Galen's voice vibrated against her temple and she wound her fists in his shirt to ground herself. "The paramedics are here and they need to check you out, okay?"

She couldn't formulate a response. Couldn't get her lips to move or mouth to form the words. Passing out wouldn't be so bad after all. At least she might stop shaking like a leaf. Galen shifted and scooped her up into his arms. Harper felt the sway of motion as he walked, but she didn't bother opening her eyes. In his embrace, she was safe. And when he bent to set her down, she clutched her arms around his neck, fighting the separation.

"I'm putting you down on a gurney," he explained as he guided her hands from around his neck. "Harper. Open your eyes and look at me."

Harper peeked through one eye and then opened her eyes to look at Galen. A flurry of activity swirled around her, and beside her, a woman in a white button-up shirt with a stethoscope was pulling on a pair of blue rubber gloves. "Hi, Harper," she said as she put the ear tips into her ears. "I'm Cynthia. Are you hurt?"

Harper shook her head. "Okay, well, we're going to check you out just in case." Two more paramedics joined her and began to wheel the gurney through the exit and down the ramp beside the stairs. Panic surged and Harper looked to Galen. She didn't want to be out there, in the open, where anyone could take a shot at her from anywhere.

"I'm here, Harper." Galen walked right behind the gurney, his expression fierce. "I'm not going anywhere."

If Galen's heart were beating any harder, it would explode right out of his fucking chest. Of all of the life-threatening situations he'd found himself in over the years, nothing could compare to the terror he'd felt as he watched Harper, standing there on the steps while bullets rained down around her.

Either the shooter was an amateur or simply interested in scaring Harper because by all rights, she should be dead. A skilled sniper could have taken her out with one shot. Whether intentional or not, Galen was damned thankful for the shooter's ineptitude. He wouldn't have made it in time to save her. And the thought of how close he'd come to losing her made him feel like slamming his fist through the nearest windshield.

When Harper had suggested going into the museum without him, he'd wanted to throttle her. But now all he wanted to do was hold her and promise her that he'd never let anyone get close enough to attempt to harm her ever again. Why had he so easily thrown his convictions to the wind, so eager to put his job in jeopardy just because she'd asked him to? When had he crossed the threshold of detachment?

The second he'd snatched that drink out of her hand a year ago.

"How's she holding up?" Landon stopped beside Galen on his way to the stairs. Monroe and several other deputies were already inside the museum, their badges affixed to black Kevlar vests with U.S. MARSHAL scrolled across the back in bright yellow to separate them from the other law enforcement agencies milling about.

"She's shaken up. Not super responsive. I think she might be in shock, so the paramedics are checking her out to see if she needs to be admitted." A hospital stay might be the best thing for her. Galen could keep a close eye on her and the security was tighter than at her condo. "Does the FBI know anything?"

Landon scoffed. "If anything, Davis might take Harper off his short list of suspects. It's not like she was shooting at herself, right?"

Galen cringed. God, the fear on her face as she'd scrambled up the steps . . . "As if she ever deserved the FBI's scrutiny." Fucking Davis. If he'd been doing his job, this might not have happened. He'd wasted precious time trying to build a case against Harper, making her feel like she had no choice but to take matters into her own hands to exonerate herself. Now that she wasn't a suspect anymore, the FBI would be back at square one, which meant it would be a good goddamned while before Harper was safe. "This investigation is total bullshit. Please tell me the U.S. attorney's office is stepping in."

"It's too soon to know for sure," Landon said with a shrug. "But I hope so. This should have been a multi-agency investigation to begin with. Monroe said he'd make a couple of calls, see if he could throw any weight around. I think he sort of likes Harper." Landon smiled. "He's taking this personally."

Monroe wasn't the only one. The threat of losing

his job—not to mention possible assault charges—was the only thing keeping him from laying Davis out on the art museum's marble floor. "Keep me posted, okay?"

Landon clapped him on the shoulder before heading off. "Will do. Take it easy."

Yeah. Right. Taking it easy was going to be impossible after today. The thing with security detail was, there was always a threat of violence. A possibility that you'd have to take a bullet for the person you were responsible for. Today was one of those rare occasions when the threat became a reality. And he had been more than willing to put his life on the line for Harper.

"Okay." The paramedic turned to Galen, her kind smile probably well-practiced for keeping trauma victims calm. "She's a little shaken up, but not in shock. No gunshot wounds, just a few cuts that won't need stitches and a couple of scrapes. We bandaged her up and I don't think we need to transport her. You can take her home if you want."

Galen looked over the paramedic's shoulder at Harper. She was wrapped up in a gray blanket despite the late-afternoon heat, clutching the ends in her fists below her chin. The once-neat ponytail at the crown of her head had become disheveled, strands of curling hair framing her face. Her hazel eyes glistened in the afternoon sun, though he hadn't seen her shed a single tear. Harper was strong. A weaker woman would have fallen to pieces by now. But, goddamn, even a little undone, she was beautiful.

She looked up and their gazes locked. The paramedic was still talking, about what he had no clue. The sound of her voice became white noise in the distance and everything melted away but Harper. "Thanks for checking her out," Galen said absently. He brushed past the paramedic, who apparently wasn't done talking to him. Whatever. The only thing he cared about right now was getting Harper the hell out of here.

"Deputy Kelly?"

With multiple local and federal law enforcement agencies on scene, the shooter was long gone. Still, Galen wasn't about to take any chances. He needed to get her someplace safe.

"Deputy?"

Jesus, was the paramedic still trying to talk to him? "What?" he barked, too distracted for any more small talk.

"You're bleeding pretty badly." She cocked a brow and pointed. Galen looked down at his shoulder, only now aware of the crimson stain on his shirt. "Maybe we should check *you* out."

There was so much adrenaline in his system right now, he hadn't felt a thing. Galen opened the three top buttons of his shirt—the fabric was ripped to mark the bullet's passage—but before he could peek inside, the paramedic had the shirt tugged halfway off his arm.

"I think it's just a scratch."

"It's a pretty deep graze," the paramedic countered. "You might want to get it stitched up."

No way was he wasting time at a hospital for a flesh wound while someone else looked after Harper. "Just slap a bandage on it and call it good," he said. "Because we're out of here."

Galen took a seat beside Harper in the back of the ambulance. He stripped off his shirt so the paramedic could properly bandage his arm and he winced as she swabbed the wound with something nasty and antiseptic. "I'm pretty sure she's trying to hurt me," he said as an aside to Harper.

A corner of her mouth hinted at a smile, but it didn't reach her eyes. "I think the blame for that falls on me."

She felt guilty. For the chaos, the museum's now shattered glass doors, the fear, and now his wounds. He didn't have to be a mind reader to know; her creased brow and the anguish in her eyes told him everything. "Once I'm bandaged up, I'm getting you out of here."

"Home sounds good right about now," Harper said on a sigh.

"Not home. Sorry, Harper, but you can't go back there." They wouldn't be going back to her apartment. Not after such a brazen attempt on her life.

Her expression changed and she sat up straighter. "I have to go home." She laced her fingers tightly together. "I-I need my laptop."

"I can send a deputy for your laptop." Jesus, someone had tried to make Swiss cheese out of her and all she could think about was her computer.

The anguish and stress that had softened her features hardened into determined stone. "No, Galen. We need to get it. Now. Then I'll go wherever you want."

Chapter Twenty-Three

"In and out, Harper. Okay?" He'd been running the drill for the past seven blocks, getting her ready to grab her shit and go. He wasn't going to take another chance with her safety. Full-on witness protection started now. "We need to get you away from anything that's familiar. Anything that can be connected to you. As soon as possible. Whoever shot at you? Not so interested in keeping a low profile. You get where I'm going with this?"

Harper folded her arms across her chest and stared out the window. "I know, Galen. I can do that. But I need a few clothes and my computer. We'll be in and out in five minutes. And for the record, I do realize that being shot at in a public place sends a pretty clear message. I'm through playing games."

Her defeated tone did little to quell Galen's anxiety. The steering wheel creaked under his grip as he took a left on Thirteenth Avenue. "You need to stay by my left shoulder at all times," he instructed. "Don't walk too fast or too slow. Got it?" As of now, it was safe to assume that whoever had shot at Harper would consider keeping his distance. For a while, at least.

Still, Galen couldn't help but feel on edge. This had quickly become the most important assignment of his life and he refused to be anything less than one hundred percent.

Galen wished she'd turn her head away from the window so he could see her expression. He didn't want to scare her any more than she already was, but she needed to understand the situation. From here on out, Harper would be confined to a hotel room and it was likely she'd soon be moved out of the Portland area entirely. If she thought being imprisoned in her condo had been bad, she hadn't seen anything yet. Total lockdown bothered witnesses the most. Half of them cracked before the first week was over. Harper, on the other hand, probably wouldn't last the first couple of hours. But maybe if he could drill into that stubborn head of hers just how fragile her situation had become, she'd settle down and be more cooperative.

She turned to look at him. "I want you to know that I'm not trying to make things difficult. I don't want to put anyone else in danger. We'll get what we need and get out of there. After that, I'll do whatever you tell me to from here on out."

"No one would be at risk in the first place if I'd done my job and kept you in your apartment where you belong. I'm the deputy in charge. And I made a bad call. I'm sorry, Harper."

"You have nothing to be sorry about." Her emphatic tone made his chest tighten with emotion. "I screwed up, not you. I didn't give you a choice and I pushed you into making a rash decision. I'm the one who should be sorry. Because I was in the wrong place at the wrong time, my entire life is someone else's responsibility to manage. Do you know how helpless that makes me feel, Galen? I'm the pet you take care of while your neighbor's on vacation. I can't even help myself out of this situation. I have to rely on the Marshals Service for protection, and the FBI for exoneration. And I have to sit tight with my fingers crossed and hope that nothing else happens. You want to protect me? Well, I want to protect you, too. I almost got you killed today."

Protect him? God, he wanted to pull the car over, take her in his arms and hold her until all of this bull-shit melted away and there was only the two of them. She didn't deserve the guilt she felt. This was his job, damn it, and she needed to quit being such a control freak and let him do it. When he pulled to a stop in front of her building, he threw the car into park with so much force it was a wonder the shifter was still intact. He cupped the back of his neck in an attempt to massage the king-sized knot of tension that felt like a metal vise clamped from shoulder to shoulder and took a few deep breaths. "Remember what I told you," he said on an exhale. "Stay to my left. Okay?"

"Okay." Harper opened the door and waited for Galen to come around to her side of the car. "But none of this covering my back, taking-a-bullet-for-me crap. Because I'm not going to let you do that."

Fucking hell. It was going to be a long night.

Harper strolled toward the building as though she didn't have a care in the world when in reality, she felt like sprinting for cover. Fear congealed as a cold knot in the pit of her stomach and she had to ball her hands into fists to keep them from shaking. She felt exposed, too vulnerable, and she questioned for the millionth time whether or not returning to her condo was a good idea.

She had most of what she needed in her purse. She'd kept Ellis's flash drive with her at all times, but her laptop contained months' worth of research that she'd accumulated on the senator while trying to ferret out any dirty dealings or questionable decisions during his term, not to mention new notes pertaining to Ellis's journals and his cryptic reference to Blue Lake. If her would-be murderer happened to find her computer, the information she'd stored on it might be the final nail in her coffin. She couldn't afford to sit around and wait for someone to take another shot at her. Or Galen. Or anyone else. Harper needed that information because it might help her make a connection to Ellis's secrets and his mysterious last words.

As they entered the building, Harper tried to control her breathing. Her head was spinning, her world reeling, and she'd treated her only support like he couldn't do his job instead of acknowledging that he was the only thing keeping her anchored to sanity. What had happened today had shaken her to her very core. Terrified her. And because of that, she couldn't risk anyone getting their hands on her laptop, and likewise, she couldn't bear putting anyone else in danger to retrieve it for her.

"Take the elevator, not the stairs."

Harper veered from their usual course and headed toward the elevator, wondering at his sudden change in tactics. "I thought the stairwell was always the safer choice."

"Not today. If someone's been watching your building, they might know that we usually take the stairs. It's best to change up our routine right now."

It scared the shit out of her to think that someone might have been spying on her for the past few weeks. She pushed the call button for the elevator and said a silent prayer of thanks that Galen was by her side. *You ruined the most perfect afternoon of your life, managed to get shot at, and all because you can't seem to quit micromanaging every aspect of your life. Way to go, Harp.* But right now, her control freak attitude had more to do with the fear that had rocked her to her very foundation as she watched the paramedic bandage Galen's shoulder.

Her stupid, childish antics had almost gotten *him* killed.

The elevator doors slid open and Harper stepped inside, steadying herself on the railing inside the compartment. Thinking of what might have happened made her light-headed, and dizzy, and sick to her stomach. The elevator shot upward and Harper thought she might yak right then and there. Losing Galen would have destroyed her and the realization of what he'd come to mean to her was more frightening than any attempt on her life. She was falling irrevocably in love with him. And the fact that she'd risked his life was like salt in an open wound.

"Harper? Let's get a move on."

She looked up to find Galen standing on the other side of the elevator, holding the doors open for her. *Great. Way to look like you've got your shit together, Harp.* She brushed past him without a word, but he wound his hand around her wrist in an iron grip and pulled her back.

"Stay at my left shoulder, understand?" His blue

eyes sparked with fire and Harper tried to pull away. He tightened his grip, and she relaxed at his side, knowing he wouldn't take another step until she did what he said.

Harper bit back the words she wanted to say. *Fine! Take the lead. Maybe this time you'll get a bullet to the head instead of a grazed shoulder. Just go and get yourself killed.* Bitter tears stung at Harper's eyes as she fell in step behind him. Why did he have to be so goddamned good at his job?

When they reached her apartment, Galen pulled a gun from the holster hanging under his left arm. He held a finger up to his lips and then stabbed it downward, indicating to Harper that she should stay put. Her heart jumped up into her throat and she couldn't take a breath to save her life. *God, please don't let there be anyone on the other side of the door.* She didn't think she could handle another shooting today.

He held his left hand out, palm up, and Harper handed him her keys. He slowly slid the key into the lock and turned it. Then, he chambered a round in the gun, gripped the doorknob, and turned. Galen took a deep breath, and his gaze locked with Harper's for a single moment before he pushed open the door and pressed his back to the wall. His gun drawn, expression fierce, he swung forward, and his large frame took up the entire doorway. Harper only knew something was wrong when a snarl tore from Galen's throat.

"U.S. Marshals," he called out.

Oh, shit. Someone was in her apartment. Adrenaline scorched through Harper's veins and her heart slammed against her rib cage. She fought the urge to grab Galen's arm and pull him back as she kept her body pressed tight against the wall, careful to keep out of sight. Damn it, what was going on?

Galen looked around, indecision warring with the determined expression on his face. "Do you know any of your neighbors?" he murmured. "Don't answer out loud."

Harper nodded.

"Go, quietly. Get someone to let you in. Lock the door and wait for me. Understand?"

Again, Harper nodded.

Galen jutted his chin in a silent *get out of here.* Harper tiptoed down the carpeted hallway, seven doors back to Mrs. Holloway's condo. Her elderly neighbor was the only person who'd be home this time of day, and right now, she was Harper's best bet.

After several successively louder raps at the door, Mrs. Holloway answered. "Well, hello, Harper. Did you misplace your keys again, dear?"

Okay, so maybe she occasionally locked herself out of her apartment. But Mrs. Holloway didn't seem to think it was quite as embarrassing as Harper did. She cast a furtive glance in Galen's direction and swallowed down the knot of fear that lodged in her throat as she watched him duck inside her apartment. *Please, please, please let him be safe.* "I'm sorry to bother you, Mrs. Holloway," she said as she went inside. No need to freak the poor old woman out. "My friend ran down to the lobby to get someone to let us in. I haven't talked to you for a while, so I thought I'd pop in and see how you were while I waited."

If she brought a gunfight to Mrs. Holloway's door, she'd never forgive herself.

A year seemed to pass in every minute spent in Mrs. Holloway's apartment. The small talk flowed, but to be honest, Harper wasn't tracking. She offered Harper a cookie, oatmeal maybe. It tasted like cardboard, and she had to remind herself to swallow.

When a knock came at the door, Harper jumped about a foot off Mrs. Holloway's couch. "That must be my friend," she said with a sheepish laugh. Mrs. Holloway started toward the door, but Harper stopped her. "Oh, no, it's fine. I'll get it." No freaking way would she let a sweet old woman take a bullet for her. It was bad enough Galen was risking his life. She peered through the peephole in the door and let out a sigh of relief when she saw Galen's face.

She tried not to cringe at the disapproving expression on his face when she opened the door. "The FBI and PPB are on their way. Let's get your laptop and get out of here."

Harper turned to an expectant Mrs. Holloway. "My keys are here," she said with a laugh. "Have a nice weekend, Mrs. Holloway. I'll stop by next week for a chat."

"Take a cookie for the road, and one for your friend, too."

Harper swiped a couple of oatmeal somethings off the plate and smiled. "Thanks."

"Cookie?" She held her hand out to Galen as she shut the door behind them. He scowled in response. "Gotcha. Not an oatmeal fan."

Her attempt at levity went without reward as Galen stalked down the hall to her apartment. Harper dumped the cookies in a waste bin at the end of the hall before she walked through her front door. And froze right where she stood.

The place was trashed. Furniture overturned, cushions scattered, drawers emptied. Harper walked through her apartment in a daze as she took stock of broken picture frames, her upended mattress and bed linens strewn from one end of her bedroom to the other. Her closet was wrecked. Clothes everywhere, shoes tossed—even the shower curtain in her bathroom had been torn down.

"We shouldn't have come here. I put us in danger and—"

"Get what you need. Quickly. Do you have any idea what they were looking for, Harper?" The accusation in his tone made Harper cringe. "Maybe your laptop?"

Harper had been a fool to think she could ever get one over on the savvy law enforcement pro. He had to have been suspicious of why she'd want her computer above anything else. "They didn't get it." Her own voice was nothing more than a murmur.

"How can you be sure?"

Harper sighed. She was tired as hell and just wanted to take a bath and go to bed. And now, she couldn't even do that in her own home. "I hid it, because I was afraid something like this might happen."

"Jesus fucking Christ, Harper." The expletive shot out of Galen's mouth, and Harper was pretty sure everyone on her floor could hear him. "Get it and let's go."

Okay, so she probably deserved his anger. She'd kept secrets and the result hadn't been great. She dug in her closet and moved the clothes and other crap away from the back left corner. "All of the units in this condo come with a jewelry safe." She pulled back the carpeting to expose a small lockbox built into the floor. "It just so happens to be big enough to hold a laptop. Do you have my keys?"

Galen tossed her keys and she caught them. She

unlocked the safe and pulled her laptop out, safe and sound, and tucked it under her arm. Hopefully, she'd find something in her notes to make this trip worthwhile. Otherwise, she may have pushed Galen away for good.

Harper wasn't ready to give him up yet.

"Let's go."

Chapter Twenty-Four

Galen sped down the freeway toward the Beaverton exit. He would have rather taken her somewhere farther away—say, Alaska or Siberia—but for now the suburb on the outskirts of Portland would have to do.

His temper hadn't cooled a single degree since they'd left Harper's condo. Monroe was there with the FBI now, dusting for prints and searching for any scrap of evidence. If the attempt on Harper's life hadn't been enough to exonerate her in Davis's eyes, Galen hoped that the state of her condo would seal the deal. Unless Davis thought Harper had shot at herself and then run home to trash her own place.

The silence pressed down on him, squeezing the air out of his lungs and settling on his shoulders with the weight of a boulder. The only sounds in the car were that of the tires as they rolled along the freeway and the occasional dramatic sigh from Harper. Awesome. Seriously, what did she expect? Over the course of the past few weeks, she'd broken her contract with the Marshals Service by ditching her security detail not once, but twice, almost gotten herself killed, and worst of all, she'd lied to him. She'd been lying to him. Or at the very least keeping things from him, which was still lying in his book. Damn it. Her stubborn independence was going to give him a fucking heart attack.

By the time he made it to the Comfort Inn where Monroe had made reservations, the sun had already sunk below the horizon, the sunset blazing a path across the western sky in a fiery burnt orange. He was exhausted and pissed off, and more goddamned worried than he'd been about anyone in a long time. Which pissed him off even more. Loving Harper wasn't going to get him anything but a whole hell of a lot of trouble and heartache.

Hold up. *Love?*

Nah. Galen didn't do love. He hooked up. He played the field. He *dated* more or less. He never stuck around long enough to get to that point of knowing someone well enough to want to stick around. But after a few weeks and one amazing afternoon with Harper, it was clear something had changed. He had changed. Harper was funny, sexy, intelligent—he actually enjoyed working her up for an argument—beautiful, strong, focused, and independent. Right about now he found that independence and focus a little exasperating, but he couldn't deny he admired it. Today, seeing her in danger, the soul-shaking fear he'd felt at the prospect of losing her, had nearly taken him to his knees. Damn it. Harper Allen had irrevocably changed him. And it rattled him to think that maybe love wasn't such a far-fetched notion.

Galen's phone interrupted his revelation and he retrieved it from the cubby on the dash. Harper sat in the passenger seat, staring out of her window at the hotel. Apparently, she was through with running off and taking the lead. He swiped his finger across the screen and answered, "Kelly."

"Hey," Landon said through the receiver. "Peggy's getting a bag together for Harper. Some of her clothes, toiletries, and other crap. She'll bring it over later tonight."

It might make Harper feel better to know she wouldn't have to wear the same clothes for weeks on end. "What about coverage? Are we lined up for the next few days?"

"Monroe has it taken care of on our end. FBI should have agents stationed around the hotel, too. Between the two agencies, no one will slip in unnoticed. We're running background checks on all of the hotel staff now. If we get a hit on any of them, I'll let you know, but so far, so good."

Galen wasn't too worried about the hotel staff. The occasional misdemeanor popped up when they did routine background checks, but for the most part, camping out at a hotel somewhere was pretty standard and they'd used this particular Comfort Inn before on other cases. "Did you find anything at Harper's condo?"

Landon gave a bitter laugh. "Nada. No prints, no trace evidence as far as we could tell. Davis's team took fiber and hair samples, but I'm willing to bet they'll connect to Harper or the handful of our people who've been in and out of her place. Whoever trashed her apartment was a professional. Covered his tracks well. But just a heads-up, Davis is suspicious. It's a no-brainer that whoever broke in was looking for something in Harper's condo. He thinks she knows what it was they were after."

For once, Galen and Special Agent Davis were on the same page. "Yeah. Me too."

"See if you can get it out of her," Landon said, all

playfulness gone from his tone. "Because if Davis finds out she was holding out on him, he'll charge her with obstruction. He's under heavy pressure from the White House now. The shooting at the museum was picked up by every national news outlet in the country. Things aren't going to cool down for Harper."

No, they were barely heating up. "I'll see what I can do. Keep me posted, okay?"

"Will do. Later."

Galen ended the call and turned to Harper. "Let's get checked in. Deputy Murphy is bringing you a bag with some clothes and toiletries and whatever else she can dig up in a couple of hours."

Harper gave an emotionless laugh but didn't turn to face him. "Well, at least I won't have to use hotel shampoo, right?"

If he thought things were strained between them now, Galen knew it was only going to get worse. Harper was obviously keeping something from him—namely what was on her laptop—and he needed to get to the bottom of her involvement in Senator Ellis's murder before Davis had a chance to grill her. The FBI agent was itching for an excuse to slap conspiracy or obstruction charges on her, and after the break-in at her apartment, Galen was fairly sure he'd get his chance.

Harper's silence was unsettling, in that it annoyed Galen to the point of spontaneous combustion. Passive-aggressive wasn't his favorite tactic. Truth be told, he'd rather have a knock-down, drag-out screaming match with her any day than this quiet, pensive bullshit. He checked in at the front desk and ushered Harper to the stairs that led to the second floor. The location was optimum: it didn't have ground-floor access, yet it wasn't high enough to hinder a speedy exit if need be. Logistically speaking, it was the best choice. Monroe had also arranged for the entire second floor to be shut down. The few guests in the rooms were moved and additional deputies would be stationed randomly throughout the floor. Total lockdown.

At Room 205, Galen slid the keycard into the lock and opened the door. A tiny, nondescript room with two queen-sized beds, a small desk, TV, and mini-fridge welcomed them. They hadn't chosen the location for its posh accommodations, and Galen couldn't help but notice the slump in Harper's shoulders as she closed the door behind her and swung the arm lock into place. She'd already been shot at, been the victim of a break-in, and had her ass handed to her about her reckless behavior. Now she was stuck in a tiny hotel room for God only knew how long. Galen figured now was as good a time as any to broach the subject of her involvement in this case. After all, it wasn't like her mood could get any worse. If she didn't want to spend any more time here than necessary, she needed to 'fess up. Now.

"Harper, we need to talk about what happened today."

"There's nothing more to talk about."

"Really? Because the bullets you dodged and your trashed apartment say differently."

Harper sighed. "Probably. But I'm not ready to talk about it yet." Her expression spoke of exhaustion as her jaw took on a stubborn set. "I'm taking a shower."

A shower? After everything that had happened, that was what she wanted to do? "You've got to be kidding me."

"No, I'm not." If her tone had been any more numb and lifeless, Galen might have been tempted to

check her pulse. Maybe the shock was finally setting
in. "I've got blood all over me. I need a few minutes to
myself, okay?"

She headed for the bathroom and shut the door
behind her. Galen heard the lock click into place and
he slumped down on one of the beds. Harper sure
knew how to take stubborn to the next level. Davis
wouldn't have to worry about arresting Harper, because before the night was over, Galen was pretty sure
he'd do it himself.

Locking herself in the bathroom probably wasn't
the most mature response to Galen's questions, but
right now it was her only option. It wasn't that she
needed to put distance between them; more to the
point, she couldn't stand to be apart from him. And
that scared the shit out of her. In Galen's presence,
she refused to show any sign of distress, but now that
she was alone, her limbs shook to the point that she
could barely strip off her shirt, or work the button
loose on her jeans. Once she managed to shuck her
bloodied clothes, she turned on the shower and let
the sound of running water drown out her thoughts.
While she waited for the water to get warm, she inspected herself in the mirror, taking stock of the cuts
and a couple of lovely bruises on her arm.

She shed her bra and underwear and stepped into
the tub. The stream of almost too warm water eased
the tightness in her muscles. She breathed in the
steam billowing up from the spray and held it deep in
her lungs before letting it all rush out in an exhale.
Harper was more than ready to come clean with
Galen, the FBI, and anyone else who asked. She'd
been stupid to think it was a good idea to keep the

information Ellis had given her a secret, no matter how cryptic. The need to control her situation down to the very last detail had kept her mouth shut. *Not the smartest move, Harp. You are so damned stubborn. Strike that. You are such an* idiot.

Harper slid down to the floor of the tub and pulled her knees up to her chest. Water sluiced down her body, the heat easing her stiff muscles. Nothing had been in her control since this whole mess started. She'd fooled herself into believing none of this was a big deal. That she hadn't inadvertently wound up in a very dangerous, life-threatening situation that went *way* beyond what she could handle. Her hardheadedness had almost gotten her killed today. *Way to fuck up your entire life, Harp.*

Harper washed the day's blood and grime from her skin, thankful for the minor cuts and bruises because she knew it could have been so much worse. She toweled off and sighed as she realized she had no choice but to put on her same dirty, bloody clothes.

"Did Peggy show up with my bag yet?" Harper called through the door.

"No. She's got to wrap up with the team at your condo first." Galen's response was about as dry and crusty as month-old bread.

With the towel wrapped around her body and tucked under her arm, she emerged from the bathroom to find Galen standing by the window, looking down at the parking lot. When he heard her approach, he turned to face her and folded his arms in front of his chest, his eyes focused squarely on her face. "I think it's time you told me what's on your laptop, Harper. You know how I feel about secrets. It's time to come clean."

"What in the hell is that supposed to mean? Come

clean. I haven't been lying to you, Galen. I just haven't had time to fill you in—"

"That's not true."

Harper felt the blood rush to her cheeks. A good ten feet of space separated them, but the tension building between them made it seem like they were nose to nose. "You were gone for days because of what happened between you and Agent Davis. After that, everything moved really fast. I haven't had time to take a deep breath, let alone fill you in on everything that's going on. You're so suspicious of people lying to you, you're not even going to give me a chance to talk to you before you start throwing around accusations? You have no idea what this has been like for me. You don't understand."

"Are you kidding me?" Galen's eyes widened, his jaw slack. "I don't *understand*?"

She took a deep breath and swallowed down the lump rising in her throat. "Forget it. I need some air."

Harper turned to leave. So what if she was only wearing a towel? They owned the entire second floor for the time being and there was no way in hell she was staying in this tiny jail cell of a room with Galen Kelly for one more second. Not when he was going to stand there and accuse her of being a liar.

He seized her arm before she could take another step and spun her around to face him. Anger boiled in her stomach and Harper's chest heaved with her labored breath. The ups and downs of the roller coaster of emotions she'd been riding all day had finally caught up to her and she didn't know if she wanted to hit Galen or kiss him as his angry gaze locked with hers.

He leaned in until she could feel his breath, warm in her ear. "You're not going anywhere."

* * *

Great. She was going to make this difficult. Her anger was way better than the broody silent treatment, though. "You don't get to walk out of here, Harper. You can't just leave whenever things get difficult. We are talking this out. No changing the subject, no walking out, no using your irrational anger to deflect me. I don't understand anything? This is my job. My life. I'm in this situation with witnesses exactly like you all the damned time. You're in the middle of a criminal investigation, Harper. I'm assuming that you're in possession of evidence that could aid that investigation. The only person making this situation harder than it needs to be is you."

She bucked her chin up a notch, but the indignant fire dimmed in her expression. Maybe he was finally getting through to her. He relaxed his grip and she folded her hands around the towel, holding it up.

"I was going to tell you, Galen. No lies. No bullshit. But when I *knew* I had something that was worth telling."

Galen cocked a brow. "And what makes you think you're the only one who can determine what's worth telling and what isn't? Did you think you could do my job—or hell, even Davis's job—better? You didn't trust me, Harper. Do you know how that makes me feel? Like I'm incapable of doing my job. Of helping you. Of *protecting* you. What's on your laptop? What do you know about Ellis's murder and why did someone ransack your condo today?"

"I don't know."

"You fucking told me you thought someone would break in for your laptop, Harper!" Galen's blood pressure spiked and he raked his fingers through his hair.

"Do you think this is a joke? That those bullets today weren't real? The stunt you pulled today was selfish, stupid, and immature."

"Don't you think I know that?" Harper shouted. "I don't know why someone wants what's on my laptop because none of it makes sense to me. I've been trying for days to figure it out and it's driving me crazy! Of course I think you're capable, Galen. It's me who isn't and that's the problem. I am so desperately dependent on you now, I'm no longer capable of helping myself!"

He took a step toward her and she backed away. Great. Just fucking great. Now who needed to cool down? She thought she was dependent? He'd laugh if he didn't think she'd take it the wrong way. Harper was one of the most independent, capable women he'd ever met. "You're not incapable, Harper, you're just not Superwoman. Why can't you trust me to help you?"

His cell rang in his pocket and for a minute, Galen considered letting it go to voice mail. But first and foremost, he was on the job and he couldn't let his personal life take precedence right now. He checked the caller ID—it was Simpson—and answered, "Kelly."

"I need you down in the lobby," the deputy said. "We've got an issue with a faulty exit alarm and the manager's worried about tangling with the fire marshal if we lock it."

Goddamn it. Of all the shitty timing. "Okay, I'll be right down." He ended the call and turned to Harper. "Don't leave this room—do you hear me, Harper?"

She stared, eyes wide, and Galen left her where she stood as he stormed through the door, slamming it behind him.

Chapter Twenty-Five

"Thanks, Peggy."

Harper took the duffel bag with her clothes and other necessities from the deputy's hand. She had shown up almost immediately after Galen left, though it hadn't really surprised Harper. He may have been mad, but Galen would never leave her unprotected.

"I'll be right outside if you need anything. Okay?"

Harper nodded and shut the door. Peggy must have sensed her need for a little alone time. For the past few weeks, she hadn't had a single moment to herself. And now that everything had finally boiled over, she needed solitude more than ever.

Harper peeked through the curtains and down at the parking lot. Back home, the night would be dark and impenetrable, the only light coming from the stars and the moon. But here, the artificial glow of the streetlights and the illuminated city beyond cast a permanent glow that blocked out nature's own soft glow. Harper swallowed down the knot that formed in her throat. A call to her parents to assure them that she was okay was all the Marshals Service had allowed. After that, she'd been instructed not to contact them.

It was for their safety, but it was still a bitter pill to swallow. Maybe, if she managed to get through this in one piece, she'd ask Sam for a little vacation time to go home and decompress.

The hotel was relatively unoccupied, but you'd never know it from the number of cars in the parking lot. Any idiot could tell that the black, unmarked vehicles were government issue. Apparently now that Harper had been shot at, they didn't give a shit about being blatant. It made her uncomfortable to think that so many people were giving up their time and resources to keep an eye on her. She wasn't anyone important, and despite what Ellis's murderer thought, she hadn't managed to uncover any of the senator's deep, dark secrets.

She tugged the curtains shut and dug through the duffel bag Peggy had brought, pulling out a pair of cotton sleep shorts and a tank top. Was Senator Ellis's wife getting the same level of protection that she was? Were his kids okay, or did they have trouble sleeping because they were afraid of what might happen to them? And by holding on to that damned flash drive for so long, was she prolonging their ordeal?

Harper flopped down on the bed, her stomach churning with anxiety. Galen was right. She'd been stupid, selfish, and immature, not to mention stubborn. She owed him, everyone else at the Marshals Service, and unfortunately Agent Davis several apologies. Galen had said she wasn't Superwoman and that was a fact that she needed to come to terms with. She couldn't do everything. Solve every puzzle. Unravel every mystery. It was okay to ask for help and it didn't mean she was weak, or lazy, or incapable. The FBI needed everything she had on Ellis if they were going to wrap this situation up once and for all, and she was going to hand it all over. This had to end, not only for her own sanity but for Mark Ellis's family, too.

She lay back on the bed and closed her eyes. Turning everything she had over to the FBI would lift a tremendous weight from her shoulders, but she knew it wouldn't really lighten her load. What pressed down on her, stole the breath from her lungs, was the knowledge that she'd risked Galen's life today. He could have died and she'd have never heard his voice again. They'd never again argue over who the best superhero was. Share another grilled cheese. She wouldn't feel the warmth of his smile. Be amused by his stern frown. She thought back to this afternoon and her body flushed as she recalled the heat of his mouth on her skin. His hands, cupping her breasts. The thrust of his hips and pleasure that had exploded within her as he'd claimed her.

Even now, her body ached for him.

A key card clicked in the lock. Harper's eyes flew open as the door to her room swung wide and she shot up off the bed as Galen stormed into the room, a small plastic bag clutched in his fist. He flung it to one of the bedside tables and Harper flinched, her heart hammering in her chest. "Galen, I—"

He rushed at her, cupping the back of her neck in his palm and his mouth descended on hers in a crushing kiss that left her breathless. Harper's head spun. She should stop this. There was still a lot they needed to hash out. She wanted to apologize but as his tongue flicked out at the seam of her lips, logic took a permanent vacation from Harper's mind. Her arms acted of their own accord, wrapping around Galen's neck, and she slanted her mouth across his, deepening the kiss as she pulled him closer.

"Damn it, Harper, I can't be away from you for even

an hour without going out of my fucking mind," he said against her mouth. "How am I supposed to do my job when all I can think about is getting back to you?"

Her head fell back as Galen's mouth wandered, from the corner of her lips, across her jaw, to her throat. His mouth was a brand on her skin and he nipped at her tender flesh, sending goose bumps chasing across her skin.

"I don't want to fight." His hands slid down her back, his fingertips pressing into her spine. Harper arched into him and he groaned against her throat. "We've lost too much time already, and I refuse to let one more minute go to waste." His tongue dipped to the hollow of her throat as he found the hem of her shirt. When his fingers brushed her bare skin, Harper shuddered. As though he'd reached the limit of his restraint, Galen dragged the tank up the length of her torso and over her head. Harper's heart skittered in her chest and she realized she might not take a deep breath ever again. Galen straightened and his eyes met hers. His gaze didn't waver, boring into her as he reached around and unhooked the clasp of her bra, yanking the straps over her shoulders. "I could have lost you today, Harper, and the thought of never seeing you again scares the shit out of me."

Was it desperation that had Harper tearing at Galen's clothes, her fingers flying over the buttons of his shirt? Absolutely. She was desperate to shed every last scrap of clothing from his body, possessed with a need to have him inside of her. God, she was going to explode right out of her skin. The urgency of their actions, the frenzied groping of hands as they stripped each other bare, and their greedy mouths seeking any inch of exposed flesh became all-consuming. There was no thought, no words. Just her and him and raw, primal desire.

A rush of slick heat spread between Harper's thighs and a low moan escaped her lips as Galen thrust his hand between them, capturing her sex in his palm as he worked his fingers over her swollen bud. His mouth wandered down her throat, over the swell of her breasts, and he caught one taut nipple between his teeth, nibbling lightly before taking it fully into his mouth.

Oh . . . God . . . remembering to take a breath was almost too much effort at this point. Harper threaded her fingers through Galen's hair and guided his mouth back to hers. He kissed her with a fierceness that had her clawing at his back, holding him as close to her as she could. They stumbled backward and the mattress caught their fall. Galen thrust his tongue into Harper's mouth, a sensual rhythmic motion that made her yearn to have him inside of her. She reached for his erection and his head bucked back as he sucked in a sharp breath. Harper closed her fist around his thick shaft and stroked. He was steel encased in satin, and she reveled in the feel of him, the way he rocked into her hand and the low near-growl that built up in his throat.

"I've got to have you, Harper. Right now."

"Yes." Her brain could barely push the one word past her lips. It was more like an incoherent hiss, need and desire manifested in a single sound.

He reached for the bedside table and pulled a box of condoms out of the plastic bag he'd brought in with him. She gave a little laugh. "Where did you get those?"

Galen ripped into the box and tore into one of the foil packets. "Hotel store," he said with an impatient smile that made her brain go fuzzy. "It goes against my training to be reckless."

Harper's throaty laughter rippled over him. "Thank God for training."

His expression grew heated once again and his eyes locked with hers as he entered her. Harper gasped as he filled her completely, each roll of his hips sending a jolt of pleasure through her body that had her panting and wanting more. This was a new side to Galen. He'd been gentle with her before, slow and tender. But now his passion was unrivaled to anything they'd shared yet. And Harper couldn't get enough.

Galen's entire body burned with want. It overtook him, clouded his thoughts, and drove him to a place that he'd never been before. Fighting with Harper stirred his blood, and walking out on her had only intensified his need, as though the brief separation was more than he could bear. All he could think about was getting back to her. Undressing her. And fucking her until he worked whatever this desperate feeling was out of his system.

She felt so damned good.

Galen couldn't take her hard enough. Couldn't thrust deep enough to satisfy the lust that ignited every last particle of his body. And Harper matched his fervor. Her fingernails dug deliciously into his ass as she urged him on, her hips rolling up to meet his as though she couldn't get enough. She arched into him, exposing the delicate lines of her throat, and he nipped at the flesh near the junction of her shoulder as he buried himself as far as he could go, her tight heat constricting against his shaft.

"Oh, shit, Harper," he murmured against her skin.

Her scent drove him mad, her sweet mewling sounds hardening his cock to the point of near pain. Galen pulled out, and stroked his shaft through the softness of her swollen lips, against Harper's clit and she bucked against him, a desperate cry exploding from her lips. He covered her mouth with his to keep her quiet—there were too many listening ears of law enforcement on their floor—and swallowed those sweet sounds as he thrust home and kissed her deeply.

Again he pulled out, teasing her, and her hands came up to grip his shoulders as she pulled herself up to meet him. "I'm close, Galen," she said next to his ear. "Don't stop."

Any restraint he might have thought he had dissolved under those five pleading words. His pace increased as he fucked into her and she dug her heels into the backs of his thighs, her back bowing off the mattress. "Come for me, Harper." His own voice was nothing more than a ragged growl. "Come for me."

Her arms flew back and she balled the tangle of sheets behind her in tight fists. Her inner walls clenched around his cock, so tight that it forced a deep, tortured moan from his throat. Harper's hips bucked into his and she bit down on her lip to keep from crying out.

Screw that.

Galen bent over her, driving deeper as her orgasm rocked through her body and into his. He cradled her head in his palm and kissed her as she came, every muffled, desperate moan vibrating through his body and stealing his breath. His own release was immediate and intense, and Galen threw his head back and gnashed his teeth together as he drove into Harper again and again until he had no more to give and collapsed on top of her.

There wasn't a single moment in his entire life that could rival what he felt right here, right now with her.

An emptiness opened up inside of Harper when Galen withdrew from her body. She wasn't ready to part from him. Not yet. That feeling of being whole, the connection that had fused them together, was the most powerful thing she'd ever felt in her life. She'd never made love to anyone with such a desperate intensity before. In fact, she'd never made *love* to anyone before Galen. Ever. Her chest swelled with emotion, and her mouth became much too dry. She loved Galen. God, she loved him so much it was a physical thing, grabbing hold of her body as it wound itself into her very DNA.

He gathered her up in his arms, and she rested her head on his chest, closing her eyes as she focused on the steady rhythm of his heart. Had they fought earlier? She could barely remember. The events of the afternoon paled and faded into the backdrop as her fingers circled one nipple, and moved down the swell of his pec, to the hard ridges of his abs and the crisp trail of hair that led from his belly button.

He sucked in a breath as her fingers teased his lower abdomen, and a sleepy smile curved her lips. "Galen, I'm so sorry about today." Her voice was thick and lazy as she continued to map his body with her fingertips. "I wasn't trying to keep secrets. From anyone. I just thought if I could—"

"Harper." Galen shifted so he lay on his side and guided her chin up to look at him. "You are so damned stubborn, it drives me crazy. But the thought of losing you today was so much worse than any anger I felt over what information you might or might not be withholding. There isn't anything that can't be fixed once you ask for help. Are you through going this alone? Are you ready for me to help you?"

She had been ready days ago.

"I want this to be over," she said. "I really don't have anything, though. Nothing helpful, anyway. Just a bunch of journal entries that the senator slipped into my bag before he died. I didn't even know I had the flash drive until Davis called me in for my second interview and so far, I haven't read anything that's incriminating. But"—and this was tough for her to admit—"maybe I'm not smart enough to know what to look for."

Galen's soft laughter rumbled in his chest. "You're plenty smart, Harper. We're just trained to look for things that you might think are inconsequential." She let his voice lull her and she felt comfort in the sense of partnership his words brought to her. "We'll get to the bottom of it. We'll find Ellis's killer and you'll be safe. I promise."

A quiet moment passed and Harper's eyes drifted shut once again as she reveled in the sensation of Galen's fingers dancing over her flesh. Their caresses were featherlight, their hands exploring one another's bodies, and the only sound in the room was their mingling breath. Galen rolled his hips into hers, and Harper flushed with warmth as his erection brushed between her thighs. She opened up to him, and he dipped his fingers where his cock had been and hissed in a breath when he met her slick center. She was just as ready to have him again as he was to have her.

"You're not running off to Paris any time soon, are you?" The sudden thought that he might leave her once this was all over filled Harper with dread. Would the SOG team call him away again once this was all over? Maybe he'd be gone for longer than a year next time. She couldn't lose him again. It would wreck her.

"You're in my blood, Harper." Galen lowered his head to hers and kissed her. The barest glance of lip to lip. "If I go anywhere ever again, I'll be taking you with me."

"I'm in your blood?" Harper teased his bottom lip with the tip of her tongue. "Like a disease?"

Galen flashed her a smile that made her bones go soft. "No. More like the spider venom that turned Peter Parker into Spider-Man. Powerful like that."

Harper rolled Galen onto his back and straddled his hips. He let out a low moan as she lifted her hips, brushing her core against the stiff length of his erection. "I think that might be the sexiest thing any man has ever said to me," she replied as she reached for the nightstand and the tiny cardboard box.

Galen reached up and cupped her breasts in his hands, and Harper's head lolled back on her shoulders as he said in a husky tone, "You haven't heard anything yet."

Chapter Twenty-Six

Harper stared up at the ceiling, the only sound in the room that of Galen's deep, even breaths. His arm was slung across her stomach, his palm wrapped around her waist as though afraid she might escape. She smiled into the darkness. In the past year, they'd both demonstrated they could be runners, but she wasn't going anywhere any time soon. Their second round of lovemaking had been better than the first, and she still couldn't believe such a feat was possible. Whereas the sex had been urgent before—the purging of need that built to a fervor—this last encounter reminded Harper of their first night together. He'd let her be in control at first, but then turned the tables on her, teasing and tempting Harper with his hands, lips, teeth, and tongue, driving her to the edge only to pull back until she begged him to take her. After tonight, she doubted she'd ever get enough of Galen.

He was in her blood, too.

The sun would be up in a few hours, and Harper thought of how they'd have to pretend that they were nothing more than acquaintances thrown together in this crazy situation. Would Galen sneak back into his adjoining room so Peggy or Curt or any of the other marshals wouldn't be suspicious? If any of them had ears on their heads, they would have heard her cries of passion. Galen had done his best to keep her quiet, but he'd driven her to the point that logical thought—not to mention discretion—meant very little to her. Harper Allen: keepin' it classy at the Comfort Inn.

Galen didn't like lying. Or liars. And by keeping secrets, she was helping him become something he despised. Harper wasn't okay with that. But maybe there was something she could do about it. Careful not to disturb him, she slid from under his embrace and out of bed, wrapping the coverlet around her body. On the small particleboard desk sat her purse and her laptop. She flipped on the desk lamp and turned on her computer while she dug through her purse for Senator Ellis's flash drive. As she waded through the junk, Harper considered the fact that she really ought to clean her bag out. Or downsize. Probably both.

By the time her computer booted up, she found the thin silver drive. She slid it into the USB port and opened the little folder icon on her desktop. The fact that someone had tried to turn her into Swiss cheese not twelve hours ago was all the reassurance she needed that something damning was hidden in the senator's files. And whoever had shot at her knew Ellis had given her all the ammunition she needed. Galen said they were trained to see things that she might find inconsequential. Maybe she simply needed to look for evidence in Ellis's files by starting with the least obvious choices.

She double-clicked on Ellis's journal entries and scrolled through the document to where she'd quit reading a couple of days ago. What she found was more of the same vague, guilt-ridden confessions without any clue as to what big secret was eating Ellis up inside. Would it have killed him to be a little more transparent? *Wow, stupid question, Harp.*

Skimming over the paragraphs and endless sentences, Harper looked out for any key words to jump out at her. Scandal. Crime. Jail. Secret. Lie. Hell, she'd settle for something small, like shoplifting at this point. A sentence caught her eye and Harper went back to the tiny entry standing alone on its own line:

> *I've decided to open Pandora's box. Let the chips fall where they may. My conscience is clear.*

Pandora . . .

Harper backed out of the senator's journals to the main file directory. There was an icon named Pandora, but Harper had overlooked it as a possible playlist or something. She hadn't really thought to venture past the senator's personal journals for information. *Way to flex those investigative muscles, Harp.* She double-clicked the file and a window popped up identifying the file as protected. Enter password. The cursor blinked at Harper and she stared at the screen, frustration roiling in her stomach.

Password? Crap. She typed in Mark Edward Ellis. No go. Elaine Ellis. Nope. His daughters, Blake and Jane, then Jane and Blake. Uh-uh. She Googled his bio and his obituary, entered his birthdate, hometown, and even his high-school mascot's name. Nothin'. Harper tapped her nails on the keyboard as she racked her brain. She typed **Jason**. Then **Meader**. **Jason Meader**. The year he was elected. The year he would've been up for reelection. Argh! Come on, Harp. Think.

She backed out of the file. *Start in the least obvious place.* She looked at the file icons and clicked on the one named FAMILY PICS. She scrolled through the list of pictures, looking over the thumbnail icons that depicted a pretty happy-looking family. Vacations, soccer games, birthdays, and holidays. Her stomach rolled as she thought of the upheaval Ellis's death must have caused for his wife and daughters. Her heart ached for them. A subfolder caught her eye, nestled between ARUBA VACATION and JANE'S DISTRICT SOCCER CHAMPIONSHIP. It was labeled BLAKE-SWAN LAKE. *Holy crap.* A lightbulb flashed in Harper's mind and she was possessed with the urge to knock her head against the desk. Duh. She'd thought Ellis's stuttering last words were blue lake. But that wasn't it at all. She backed out of the file and reopened the one named Pandora. The passwords screen popped up and she typed BlakeSwanLake. The document sprang to life on her screen.

Apparently she'd been barking up the wrong tree all along. She'd thought what Senator Ellis had given her was a lead to something she'd find in public records or title deeds. But what he'd given her was simply a password. The key to unlocking the door of his secrets and guilt. The amount of information contained in the protected files was totally overwhelming. It would take a week or longer to weed through it all as she made sense of the transactions that looped this way and that in an effort to cover Ellis's tracks.

Harper had been suspicious of Ellis's dealings with the firefighters' union for months, but seeing it in black-and-white didn't make it any less shocking.

She'd assumed there'd been some palm greasing, favors exchanged, weight thrown around for the benefit of the interested parties, but she never would have guessed the scandal was quite so big. Or so completely unrelated to the fire service.

The scandal had nothing to do with union corruption, though the state fire marshal had his hand in the cookie jar. From the looks of it, Ellis had helped the firefighters' union to arrange for a vote several months back that would allow them to opt out of Social Security in lieu of their own retirement programs. By doing so, the government would be required to pay back any and all Social Security payments for the past ten years to a ton of firefighters totaling close to five million dollars. As Harper read on, her jaw dropped. Half of the money recovered from the Social Security payments was supposed to go back to the individual fire districts for them to reinvest on behalf of the firefighters. But instead someone had found out a way to sneak off with almost two and a half million dollars of the firemen's money and Mark Ellis helped to set it up.

Holy. Shit.

Ellis had obviously gotten in way over his head. According to the documents, Ellis was using a state fire program called the Mobile Hazard Assessment to embezzle the money. A program funded through the state to provide top-of-the-line technology to help firefighters assess dangerous situations as they were happening and form a plan of attack before arriving on scene. The program was funded through grants managed by the state, and since the state was also managing the Social Security refunds, it was easy to shift the money from one account to another. But when the guilt became too much for him, he'd cracked.

His partners must not have appreciated the fact that he was going to blow the whistle on all of them. Harper scanned the documents. She recognized their names. Rick Kremer, Oregon's deputy fire marshal, Melissa Swinson, an employee at the state controller's office, and well, whaddya know. Jason Meader.

The four of them had managed to keep their secret until Ellis had cracked. But the thing about keeping a secret: once more than one person was in the loop, it wasn't a secret anymore. When Harper turned this over to Curt or Agent Davis, they'd investigate, continue to keep Ellis's dirty dealings on the down-low while they ferreted out all of the guilty parties and their associates, down the line until the last man or woman was arrested. It could take months, maybe even a year for the FBI to conclude their investigation. Nothing would change. Her life would still be in danger, she and Galen would have to sneak around and keep their involvement from everyone, and she'd be living out of a duffel bag at the Comfort Inn for months or until they decided to throw her fully into witness security. And if that happened, she'd lose everything: her family, friends, job, even her name. There'd be nothing left. Maybe not even Galen.

She refused to let a bunch of murdering, embezzling assholes dictate the course of her life. Harper had already gained national attention being caught up in this mess, and she was going to make good use of the spotlight while it was shining. By the time she was through, there'd be nothing to cover up. Everyone would know the truth. Obviously Meader and his cronies didn't read comic books. You should never, ever piss off Lois Lane.

* * *

Galen had never much thought about his sex life. He wanted it. He went out after it. He got laid and moved on. But with Harper . . . Holy. Fuck. Her mouth, her body, the tight, wet warmth that enveloped him, the sound of her passionate cries as she came. Even now, the memory of being with her made his cock as hard as stone. The memory of their night together a year ago paled in comparison to what they'd shared over the past couple of days.

Galen lifted his head off the pillow. The morning outside was gray and gloomy, but he figured they had another hour or so together before the world joined the weather outside to rain on his parade. It violated his sense of honor to lie to his superior. To keep secrets of any kind. Though Galen found that, when it came to Harper, he was more than willing to throw his convictions out the window and stomp all over the smashed remains. Was that what it felt like to love someone? After living through the drama of his parents' relationship, Galen had abandoned any notion of love. But the way he felt about Harper . . . the way he wanted to protect her and shelter her. To never be away from her for even a moment. Warmth blossomed in his chest when he thought of her brilliant smile, the softness of her skin, or her fiery personality. Did loving Harper mean that he could easily become a compromising man as long as the only thing he was *un*compromising about was her? Yes, he decided as he held her in his arms. That's exactly what it meant.

He was in love with Harper.

Harper rolled onto her back and Galen propped himself up on an elbow so he could look down at her. The sheet slid away from her body, revealing one supple breast. He itched to touch her, to take her dusky pink nipple into his mouth and tease it with his tongue and teeth. Instead, he blew lightly on her skin and her flesh puckered tight. The sight of it made his balls grow tight and he rolled his hips into her, swallowing down a moan when the engorged head of his cock brushed against her silky soft bare skin.

"Just what do you think you're doing, Deputy Kelly?" Harper asked sleepily. Her eyes remained closed and her face soft as though still asleep. But her hand wandered between his thighs and Galen sucked in a breath as she took him in her hand and stroked his length. "Doesn't it violate some code of honor to seduce a woman before she's fully awake?"

He bent down and kissed right above her collarbone and over the swell of her breast. Harper arched into his touch as she continued to stroke him. "You said yesterday that I had no honor." He took her pearled nipple into his mouth and sucked, eliciting a low moan from Harper. "I'm simply living up to your expectations of me."

She opened her eyes and put her palm to his chest, urging him back. "You know I didn't mean that, right?" Had it only been yesterday that they'd argued in her apartment? It felt like years. Her expression grew serious, her brow furrowed. "I was being stupid and immature."

Galen hushed her with a kiss. "Everything that happened yesterday before I got you naked is a little fuzzy in my memory," he murmured against her mouth. "And I want you naked as often as possible from here on out."

He rolled Harper onto her back and settled himself between her thighs. The ridge of his cock brushed up against her sex and her legs fell open as she thrust her hips up to rub her already wet and swollen sex against him. One more motion like that and Galen wouldn't be the honorable, prepared deputy he proclaimed himself to be. Before he could reach for the cardboard box on the nightstand, Harper turned the tables on him, wrapping her legs around his torso and rolling him on his back. She bent over him and placed a slow, soft kiss on his mouth before venturing farther down, across his jawline, down his neck and chest, over his abs, as she worked her way down his body.

"Are you always so pushy?" She bent over him and her tongue flicked out at the head of his erection. "You just want to mount up and get to it?"

"Yeah." The word drew out on a moan as she sealed her mouth over his shaft and sucked. "I'm impatient first thing in the morning." She swirled her tongue over the crown and his hips bucked. Hell, she was too damned good.

Harper sat up and gave him a wicked grin. "Well, that's too bad. Because it takes me *forever* to get going in the morning. I like to take my time."

Her lips sealed over him once again and Galen pressed his head back into the pillows. Thank God for thoroughness.

Harper hadn't been kidding when she'd told him she liked to take her time.

She took her time with him and then some. On the bed. The desk chair. In the shower.

Galen doubted he'd be able to get dressed on his own steam let alone walk anywhere ever again. His legs were shot. Arms weighted down. Muscles tight. But damn, did it feel good. Maybe they could move into the Comfort Inn. Live on the second floor like nudists, making love and lounging around all day. If only. He had to damn near force himself out of her room. And now that he was safely in his own adjoining room, all he wanted was to throw open the door that separated them and peel the layers of clothes from her body. He doubted the chief deputy would appreciate that, though. And it was only a matter of time before Peggy and a few other deputies showed up for their strategic planning session. After that, he'd be expected to hand Harper off to someone else's care while he met with Monroe. As if he were going anywhere.

The reality of the situation was like a gut punch. Things were going to get much worse for Harper before they got better. Ellis's murderer had escalated, going after Harper in public and ransacking her apartment. Which meant he was becoming more desperate to silence her. Even after they turned over everything she had to the FBI it could be weeks before the information in Ellis's flash drive provided them with a solid lead. And even though it felt so good to have everything out in the open with her, Galen knew that until she was safe from whoever had tried to kill her, he wouldn't truly be able to take a deep breath.

From the chair where he sat, Galen looked at the door that separated his room from hers. Leaving had been torture. Several yards, that's all that spanned between them, yet it felt like miles. Keeping up appearances would be harder than he thought when all he wanted was to be near her, touch her, reside in her orbit, hovering like the moon as he watched over her and kept her safe. Surely his colleagues would notice, if they hadn't already. Honestly, it was a wonder Landon hadn't filled everyone in, if only for his own entertainment rather than any sense of responsibility.

A steady knock interrupted any theories on whether or not he was the subject of office gossip. He crossed the room and answered the door to find his friend standing in the doorway holding a pink box with fluffy white clouds and tied with a black ribbon. Speak of the devil and he appears . . .

"I'm wondering, since when does room service fall under the duties of a highly decorated deputy U.S. marshal? This is twice I've been your food delivery boy. I'm not sure I like it."

"Highly decorated?" Galen scoffed. "If you're talking about your designer jeans and overpriced shirt, then, yeah, I guess I'd consider you pretty highly decorated."

"It's sad, Galen, that you're such a hater." Landon brushed past him and entered the hotel room, his neck craning toward the bathroom before he settled in at the desk. "And that you have to bribe women with your sister's fancy pastries to get them to like you."

Galen knew he never should have told Landon about Amy Renfro. "Harper had a rough day yesterday and she likes Michelle's apple fritters."

"Right. Like you're not totally laying these fritters at her feet as a token of your love. Dude, if you don't watch it, you are so gonna lose your job."

Galen flopped down on the bed and stared up at the ceiling. He'd known Landon for years, and he hoped his transparency was more because Landon knew about his and Harper's history, rather than the fact that he was walking around like some lovesick teenager. "I won't be taken off this detail," Galen said, turning to face Landon. "I know the deep shit I'll be in if Monroe finds out before I tell him. But until

I know Harper's safe, I'm not letting anyone else protect her."

"I'm not telling you what to do, man." Landon pushed himself out of the chair and headed for the door. "It's not like I'm squeaky clean. Play it cool, that's all I'm sayin'. Did you get Harper to spill anything about what's on her laptop? Because I overheard Monroe on the phone this morning and it sounds like Davis is ready to move with obstruction charges. Which means he'll be sending agents over soon to arrest her and seize her laptop. Just a heads-up."

If Davis laid a finger on Harper, he'd break the bastard's arm. "She's ready to talk. If anyone gets to take custody of Harper or her computer, it's going to be our agency, not the fucking FBI."

"If I can, I'll give you a heads-up on Davis before they head out. Maybe you can get her to our office before they show up. In the meantime, I'm getting ready to head out on assignment."

Galen sat up on the bed. "Where?"

"You remember Ruiz?"

"The federal judge who extorted all that money from Mendleson Corp.?"

"The one and only. He escaped during a routine transfer. Can you believe that shit? The guy's got to be in his sixties *and* he has cancer. Totally badass. That's what they get for using undertrained pussies for something like that. Ruiz took out the guards somewhere between Sheridan and his oncologist's office in Salem. They think he'll try to contact his daughter. I get the ass-numbingly dull task of staking her out. Yay."

Galen pushed himself off the bed and crossed over to where Landon stood with one hand on the doorknob. Emma Ruiz and Landon had history. During their first investigation into Ruiz, the judge's daughter had been a major pain in Landon's ass. He could only imagine what a reunion between the two would be like. And he almost hoped she gave him hell.

He clapped his friend on the shoulder. "Be careful, man."

Landon snorted. "Right. The worst that could happen is I get a fucking hangnail or sprain my finger playing *Temple Run* on my phone. Your girlfriend got shot at and you took a bullet. I swear to God, you are the luckiest son of a bitch on the planet. Later."

"She's not my girlfriend," Galen said as Landon walked out the door. Was she?

"*Right*," Landon replied. "Galen, you're such a loser."

Galen laughed. "Hater."

"Damn right," Landon called as he headed down the hallway. "You suck."

Chapter Twenty-Seven

Harper alternated between eating her apple fritter and typing. She did both with gusto. Her fingers flew on the laptop's keyboard, and Galen marveled at the focus she exhibited, both in eating and working.

"Are you going to tell me what you're typing?" Galen asked from his perch on the bed. Channel surfing was losing its luster as he'd much rather watch Harper. The only thing that would make the view better was if she were in that desk chair, naked. With her legs propped up on the desktop. And him pumping into her. *Focus on the job, Galen. The job.* Not *the beautiful woman you want to fuck until neither of you can walk straight.* God, he was hopeless.

"I'll tell you when I'm done," Harper said, apparently oblivious to the raging hard-on he was sporting. "But trust me, once this story is finished and I get Sam to upload it to the paper's website, all of our problems will be solved and we can finally put this bullshit behind us."

"Oh, you think so, huh?" Galen couldn't be quite as optimistic as long as he was in the dark. "And when did you come to that great revelation, may I ask?"

Harper looked up from her laptop and gave him a wicked grin. "Between orgasms three and four," she said in a husky tone that did nothing to cool Galen's lust. "Seriously, though, around three in the morning."

"And what was I doing while you were solving the world's problems?"

"Sleeping," she said. "You make the cutest little snuffling sounds at night. Did you know that?"

"I don't know if you realize this or not, but guys don't really appreciate being told anything they do is cute."

"Oh." She laughed. "Sorry. Did you know you make the most badass, manly, snuffling sounds when you sleep?"

"That's better. So, while I was sleeping, you were up doing what exactly?" For some reason, he could totally picture Harper dangling off the second-story balcony, dressed in black and ready for some covert ops.

"I was reading this." Harper brandished a tiny silver flash drive. "And it's full of all sorts of juicy little tidbits."

"Such as?"

"Such as what had Ellis in hot water and who was sitting right there in the pot with him."

Galen didn't like Harper's triumphant expression. It was that cavalier attitude of hers that sent her running off toward danger instead of away from it like she should. "Okay." Galen sat up on the bed and faced her. "Don't you think this is something you should be turning over to Monroe rather than writing a story about? There's still someone out there looking to put a bullet in you."

"Exactly. Which is why turning this stuff over to Curt isn't the best idea. Yet."

Harper continued to type away, the *clicky-clack* of

the keys driving into Galen's skull like tiny swords. He rubbed his temples and took a deep, calming breath that turned out to be neither deep nor calming. The thought of Harper in danger was too fucking stressful. "Explain to me why that's not a good idea, Harper, because I'm really trying to understand why you think obstruction of justice is the most logical option."

"Silly mortal," Harper said with a grin. "You have no idea of the scope of my powers."

"Hmmm." Her humor was lost on him. He couldn't help but think of the additional trouble she was about to cause. "That sounds more like a super villain proclamation than hero."

"Heroine," she corrected without breaking her stride. *Clicky-clack, clicky-clack.* "Galen, trust me. I know what I'm doing, and turning this information over to the FBI or even Curt isn't going to make anything easier for us. This is the best way. Wait, strike that. This is the only way."

Galen sighed. Her tenacity was one of the things he loved most about Harper. But right now, it was one of the things that drove him bat-shit crazy. "So, what's your next move?"

Harper paused to dig into the last of her apple fritter. She washed it down with a gulp from a plastic cup with COMFORT INN printed across the front. "Next, we're going to the paper and I'm going to sweet-talk Sam into posting this ASAP. Once it's live, it'll go viral. Blogs, news outlets, everyone will want to report on it. Boom!" She made an explosive motion with her hands. "No more secrets. News reporter level: Boss."

Great. She was so excited she was mixing her comic book and video game analogies. If she didn't settle down, she'd be reciting Mel Gibson's monologue from *Braveheart* soon.

"If I agree to stop at the newspaper first, will you go with me to the office after that? So we can turn everything you have over to Monroe?" His phone rang beside him and Galen checked the caller ID to see Landon's cheesy face pop up on the screen.

"Scout's honor," Harper replied, holding up two fingers.

Galen swiped his finger across the screen as he flashed Harper a stern look. "Hey, Landon. What's up?"

"Just an FYI, Special Agent Dickhead is on his way over to arrest your honey," Landon said. "Better get while the gettin's good."

Shit. "Thanks, man. You headed out?"

"In the morning. Meeting up with prison officials this afternoon and the lead investigator tomorrow morning. God, I hope someone gets shot."

Landon was the biggest adrenaline junkie Galen had ever met. But just because he enjoyed the rush didn't mean he seriously wanted someone to get shot. "Yeah, well, if anything, someone will shoot you for running off at the mouth. So be sure to wear a vest."

"Hater," Landon said before he disconnected the call.

"Harper, how far are you on that article?"

Harper shot him a dirty look. "This is not an article— it's an exposé."

Good Lord. Now was not the time for her to get cheeky. "Whatever. Is it almost done?"

"Yeah. Just putting on the finishing touches. Why?"

"Because if we're gonna go, we need to get out of here now. Davis is on his way over to arrest you."

"Are you kidding me?" Harper had the nerve to sound outraged. He smiled. Tenacity. "I can finish up at the paper." She shut the lid on her laptop and stuffed it into a case along with Senator Ellis's flash drive. "Let's go."

Galen peeked his head out the door to see if any of the other deputies were patrolling the hallway. Coast was clear. "Okay, take the stairs and the back exit. I don't want anyone to know we're gone until we're in the car and heading out of the parking lot."

As he followed Harper out the door into the hallway, Galen couldn't help but think that she and Landon would get along just fine.

Harper was antsy as hell for her story to go live and it wasn't helping that Sam was being all responsible and professional in his consideration of it. It was the kind of anticipation a kid feels on Christmas Eve, or on your birthday when you know you're going to get something awesome. This story would make her career. She wouldn't have to daydream about getting a job offer from *The Washington Post* because after the Ellis scandal broke; she was pretty sure her dreams would come true. *Suck it,* Washington Post*! Cuz I'm staying in Oregon.*

Galen had been quiet for most of the drive and she figured it might be best to give him some space. Again, as a deputy U.S. marshal, it probably didn't look good for him to be helping someone hide from the FBI, let alone conspiring with that person. And by asking for his help, Harper had definitely made Galen her coconspirator. Truth be told, there was no one she'd rather conspire with. But she hoped this would be the first and last time either one of them would be sneaking around.

"You've gotta help me out here, Sam." Harper sat in front of her editor's desk while Galen stood like a sentinel at the closed office door. She tried to ignore how amazing he looked: arms crossed at his chest, legs braced apart, muscles bunching in all the right places. His blue eyes were alert and narrowed, his jaw set. He looked like a freaking god keeping watch over her, and it turned Harper's insides to Jell-O. *Focus on the story, Harp. Not the sexy marshal.*

"You know I want to jump all over this," Sam said, leaning forward to get his point across. "But it's irresponsible to throw something up on the Web like that. Once your story's live, we can't simply delete it, or edit the content, or filter anything." He sighed. "I can't believe I'm saying this, but, if you're going to post this online you might as well chisel it into stone and fill in the words with your own blood, Harp. The Internet is permanent. The original story will never go away. And if any part of it doesn't hold water, the media will *crucify* you."

"I've thought about that, Sam, but I was very careful in the write-up. Until we can dig a little deeper—and trust me, it won't be hard with what I've got—the way the story stands is liability-free."

Sam scanned the document on Harper's laptop. "So basically, this is your story. Not Ellis's. You start off recounting the night he was shot and go from there."

"Yep."

"But you do claim to have evidence that proves Ellis was in league with union and state officials to defraud the Social Security Administration as well as the state's firefighters. That's not small potatoes, kiddo. The first accusation is borderline treasonous. The second . . ." Sam scrubbed his palm over his balding head. "Ellis might as well be guilty of kicking puppies and old ladies or abusing nuns. I mean, you rip off the unsung heroes of the country and you're in for it."

"Exactly!" Jeez, had Sam been listening to her *at all* the past half hour? "That's why he's dead, Sam! Ellis felt guilty over the fact that he'd become a puppy kicker and was ready to clear his conscience."

"Here's the deal, Harper. Ellis isn't here to corroborate your story. You're about to expose the most forthright senator in recent political history. The guy might as well have been a freaking saint. And you're not only implicating Ellis. If you're wrong, you can kiss your career good-bye."

She'd thought of that. But her career was a small sacrifice for her freedom. What good would all of her hard work be if she was spending the next year or longer living someone else's life? She could see it now: she'd be Becky Farmer, grocery store cashier in Nowhereville, Tennessee. Or something like that. And yeah, there were worse things to be than Becky Farmer, cashier. But she wanted to be Harper Allen, political beat reporter for *The Oregonian*. She deserved the life she'd worked for, the education she'd paid for with her own blood, sweat, tears, and student loans. And nothing—no one—was going to take that from her.

"You're right, Sam. Ellis isn't here to corroborate. And I'm pretty sure the people I accuse will turn around and try to discredit me. But that's not the point."

Sam leaned his elbows on his desk and fixed Harper with a serious stare. "Then what is the point? Because if I publish this story, it'll be my ass on the line, too."

"I want my life back, Sam." Harper couldn't help the desperation that leaked into her voice. This was her last and only shot to do something about her situation. This time tomorrow, she'd be in FBI custody and Davis would be off somewhere laughing his evil federal agent laugh. "Here's the thing. I didn't exactly name names in the article—"

"That's stretching it a bit, Harp," Sam interrupted.

True. It's not like it would be hard to match a name to the description since Harper reported an alleged conspiracy to commit fraud involving someone in the state controller's office, one of Ellis's aides, and a state deputy fire marshal. Anyone in the know could connect the dots. "I was careful with my wordage, I didn't outright accuse anyone. I know the legalese. Here's the deal, Sam. Whoever killed Ellis and tried to kill me wants the information on Ellis's flash drive kept a secret. If there isn't a secret to keep, there's no need to kill me. Unless the murderer is nothing more than a vindictive ass, and I'd be willing to bet he isn't. Once the story breaks, everyone involved will forget about me because they'll be racing to cover their own assess before the FBI comes knocking on their doors."

"And if you're wrong?" Galen piped in from the back of the room, his tone as dark as his expression.

Harper turned to face him. "If I'm wrong, I'm no worse off than I am now. Davis will still arrest me for obstruction. I'll still be under witness protection. And my life won't belong to me until the feds conclude their investigation and make arrests. By which time, Ellis's coconspirators will have a chance to take the money and run. I'll be Becky Farmer forever."

"Becky Farmer?" Galen asked. "What in the hell are you talking about?"

"Never mind." Maybe they'd let her be a Suzette or Pria. Something exotic. *Focus, Harp.* "Sam, how often do we get a chance like this?"

Sam's eyes lit up and a smile tugged at his mouth. "Well, it would be the scoop of the century."

"It has to go live today, Sam. Now." There wasn't time to run this by the editor-in-chief. Every second wasted was another second closer to a stay in a federal prison. And truth be told, Harper was too short and pale to pull off an orange jumpsuit. "The window of opportunity is only going to get smaller and smaller. Come on. Will you post it?"

"Is it ready to roll?"

Harper smiled. She knew she could count on Sam to have her back. "Almost. A few finishing touches and one more read-through and it'll be ready."

"Use the conference room," Sam suggested. "I don't want anyone reading over your shoulder. You've already got everyone's tongues wagging with the way you barged in here this morning with that I-just-hit-the-journalistic-jackpot grin on your face."

"You have to admit, I totally did."

"Yeah," Sam agreed begrudgingly. "Let's hope you don't get us all fired because of it."

"Oh, ye of little faith!" Harper tried to sound hurt, but she was too excited. "Go have a cup of coffee and relax. This is going to turn out great."

"Coffee," Sam snorted as Harper grabbed her laptop and headed for the door. "I'm gonna need a fifth of whiskey to get me through working with you."

Chapter Twenty-Eight

Galen paced around the conference room, right hand resting on the butt of his gun, his stomach twisted into an anxious knot. His phone had been vibrating in his pocket for the past hour and he had a feeling that he wouldn't be able to dodge Monroe's phone calls for much longer. And the text messages coming in from Landon weren't much better:

I can't believe I'm leaving on assignment right as you're about to get your ass in a sling. They'll probably put the flag at half-mast. Ha!

Is there a US Ambassador to Tasmania? Because I'm pretty sure that's where your next job will be. Did you know the spiders there are as big as small dogs? And don't even get me started on the snakes.

Is Harper good in bed? It's not relevant to anything. I'm just curious.

He thought about pulling out his Glock and putting a bullet hole through his phone, but that probably wouldn't earn him any points with Monroe. Then, he thought about doing the same to Landon. Nothing too severe, maybe his foot or the fleshy part of his calf. But he figured Landon was getting what he deserved, chasing after a sixty-year-old fugitive and living out of his car while he staked out the daughter's house. With any luck, the assignment would suck the sarcasm right out of him.

Galen's gut was usually spot-on, and something about what Harper was about to pull left him feeling less than confident everything would play out the way she wanted it to. If this were any other case, Galen would have slapped the cuffs on the witness before the FBI even had a chance. Obstruction of justice was a serious charge, and by helping Harper post her story behind Davis's back, Galen had probably secured a conspiracy charge for himself. It could be that the roiling knot in his stomach had more to do with his own concerns over losing his job. Because one thing was certain: Davis wasn't going to take this lightly. He'd be after Galen's badge for this, and if it didn't get him kicked out of the Marshals Service entirely, it might get him axed from the SOG.

He looked over at Harper, her forehead creased in concentration, eyes trained on her computer screen. She worried her bottom lip between her teeth, clicked away on the keyboard for a moment before she continued to read. When she paused and looked up from her work to give him a brilliant smile, he knew that he'd do it all over again. Risk his career and his reputation for one of her smiles. His chest ached as he took her in. He loved her so damned much it hurt.

"Excuse me, Deputy Kelly?" A man peeked his head in the conference room door. "There's a phone call for you at reception. Would you like me to transfer it here?"

Well, shit. Apparently Monroe had tracked him down. Maybe he should have turned his phone off. He was willing to bet they'd tracked the GPS. Rookie mistake. Of course, it could be Davis, but did it really matter at this point? As Landon had so helpfully pointed out, Galen's ass was in a sling and there was no use trying to get out of it now.

"I'll take it at your reception desk if that's all right." He didn't exactly want Harper to overhear his conversation. She'd only worry if she knew what kind of trouble they were in. And he needed her focused and her story finished. They had no choice now but to see this through to the end. He'd stall his superior and the FBI for as long as possible. He just hoped it was long enough.

"Sure. There's a public phone on the reception counter. Jess can transfer the call to that phone for you."

"Thanks." Now came the hard part. Leaving Harper unprotected. It was going to take a real physical effort to pry himself away from her and walk the hundred or so feet to the reception desk. She was like the sun and he was caught in orbit, circling around her, held in place by her gravitational pull.

"I can keep an eye on her if you want." The guy standing there like a squirrel poking its head out of a hole jutted his chin toward Harper. Jesus, was his reluctance to leave that obvious? Awesome. "I'm sure she'll be fine." Squirrel Guy laughed. "She's totally oblivious to anything going on around her anyway. I doubt she'll even realize you're gone."

Galen noticed that she hadn't even broken stride, eyes still scanning her screen, interrupted by the occasional tap of her keyboard. "All right." After all, how long could it possibly take for Monroe to say, "You're fired."

"No worries. I'll hang out until you get back."

Galen relaxed a little and headed for the door. "Thanks. I shouldn't be more than a couple of minutes." As he walked toward the reception desk, Galen smiled to himself over his own overprotectiveness. How much trouble could she possibly get into in the conference room? His step faltered. Then again, this was Harper Allen. He quickened his pace and picked up the phone at the reception desk. Damn it, he shouldn't have ignored Monroe's phone calls.

He showed his badge to the receptionist and said, "I'm Deputy Kelly with the Marshals Service. I was told I have a phone call."

"Just hit line three," the receptionist said with a smile.

He pressed the corresponding button on the enormous phone base. "This is Deputy Kelly."

"I'm going to assume that you're ignoring my phone calls because *The Oregonian* is under siege and your phone was taken by assailants. Is that correct?"

Sarcasm. Probably not a good sign. Monroe didn't sound happy and Galen couldn't blame him. No one liked a rogue deputy and sneaking Harper out of the hotel had been about as cowboy as you could get. "Actually, no. I'd consider this a pit stop before I turn custody of Harper over to our office. She's going to turn herself in."

"You don't say?" Monroe didn't sound any more at ease with the revelation. Huh. Go figure. "This pit stop wouldn't have anything to do with the alleged evidence Harper is withholding from the feds, does it?"

"Curt—"

"That's Chief Deputy Monroe. You're in a shitload

of trouble, Galen. If Harper isn't delivered to our office in thirty minutes, I'm gonna help the FBI arrest your ass. Understand?"

Oh, yeah. He was so fired. "Yes, sir. We'll be there."

"And Galen," Monroe added. "Cuff her. If the feds see her walk in as anything less than a suspect in custody you'll be turning in your badge when you hand her over."

Great. Davis had to be responsible for Monroe's nasty attitude. He liked Harper. No way would he want her cuffed. "She's in my custody now. We're wrapping up a few loose ends."

"Get the kid a donut on the way over," Monroe said in a low voice. "We'll get her out of this."

"Will do."

Galen hung up feeling a little better than he had a moment ago. Despite the fact that Monroe was pissed at him, he knew that his boss was ultimately in his corner. There was no love lost between any of them and Davis. Hopefully, Harper wouldn't put up too much of a fight when it came to cuffing her. To be honest, Galen was more afraid it would turn him on than anything—they couldn't afford another pit stop.

As he made his way back to the conference room, Galen was hopeful that Harper had put the finishing touches on her story. He pushed open the conference room door, prepared to give her an update, but the words died on his lips. Harper's chair was empty, her laptop gone, and lying on the floor, unconscious, was one *Oregonian* employee. Galen reached for his gun as his heart jumped up into this throat. How could he have been such an idiot to think that Harper would be safe anywhere?

A low moan issued from the guy on the floor and Galen rolled him over onto his back and gave his cheek a light slap. He blinked a few times and stared up at Galen as if he might be seeing more than one of him. Great. "What happened? Where's Harper?"

"I tried to stop him, but the guy slammed my head with the butt of a gun." He sat up and rubbed the back of his head. "After he hit me, I think he told Harper to head for the roof, but I'm not sure. It's all sort of fuzzy. He said if any of us made a sound, he was going to put a bullet in her head."

Fuck. Panic swirled in Galen's chest and his brain buzzed with anger so intense he was seeing red. He pushed himself off the floor and said over his shoulder as he flew toward the door, "Call 911, Special Agent Davis at the FBI, and Curt Monroe at the U.S. Marshals Service. Tell them to get down here, now."

Being held at gunpoint wasn't much of a shock to Harper's system at this point. The fact that it was Jason Meader on the other end of that gun, however, was a different matter altogether. She'd always figured him to be more of the brains of the operation. His pricey suits and manicured hands didn't shout, "I'm the muscle here!" She was going to have to rethink that assumption now, though. Because the way he hauled her around like she weighed nothing at all gave her a glimpse into a side of Jason that she hadn't known existed.

"The first thing they teach you in special ops is that mercy is for the weak. In a combat situation, it's kill or be killed. Sorry, Harper, but you stepped right onto the battlefield."

Ugh. If he really wanted to get rid of her, he should try talking her to death. She didn't think she'd be

able to stand much more of his arrogant banter. It
wasn't like he was talking to her, really. Just at her.
Either way, he liked the sound of his own voice. That
much was obvious. She hadn't realized he had a military background. Another failure in the investigative
department. *Way to go, Harp.*

"You must be some kind of magician, Jason. Either
that or you have an eviler twin I don't know about. I'm
assuming your alibi was checked, yet there's no way
you could have gone back to the office to get Ellis's
phone *and* stuck around to shoot him."

Jason graced her with a self-congratulatory smirk.
Arrogant jerk. "Always the nosy reporter, aren't you,
Harper? I was almost around the corner when I heard
you grilling Ellis. He'd been hard enough to contain;
I wasn't going to risk him running off at the mouth.
So, I doubled back, took care of business, and when
those idiot security guards chased me off, I headed for
the office. Lucky for me Ellis's secretary was a flaky air
head who couldn't remember the exact time I'd come
in. Davis was already hot for you as a suspect so it
wasn't tough to placate the FBI. Besides, with my military record, I was above reproach as far as Davis was
concerned."

Davis. Ugh! Harper was going to smack him in the
face if she lived through this. "You know, killing me
isn't going to do much for your campaign, Jason."

He gave her a rough shake as he ushered her up
the last flight of stairs to the door that opened up to
the roof. He might not like what she had to say, but
hey, it was still the truth. In a few minutes he'd be on
everyone's most wanted list and he could kiss his
future political career good-bye. She'd published her
story the moment he'd come through the conference

room door, gun pointed straight at her face with a threat to unload the clip into her head if she made a sound. Meader was a real tough guy picking on a girl. Asshole.

"You called me, Harper." Jason spoke as though trying to rationalize with her. "You were feeling guilty about all of the problems you've caused in my life. Throwing accusations around in an effort to further your career." He shook his head solemnly. "The stress was simply too much for you."

His fingers bit into Harper's arm and the cold metal of the gun barrel jammed into her ribs with enough force to cause her to cry out. She'd have a nasty bruise from that one, no doubt. "No one is going to believe that."

"Women like you sometimes do stupid things to get attention," Jason replied. "It won't be much of a stretch."

Harper didn't know what offended her more. The *women like you* bit or the fact that he thought she was some attention whore out to snag the spotlight at any cost. What a jerk. Harper looked away from Jason's smug expression and her stomach took a dive to the soles of her feet. The edge of the building was only thirty or so feet away now and it appeared that they weren't going to stop for an in-depth chat any time soon. "The guy you hit in the conference room can identify you, and my boss has Ellis's flash drive," Harper blurted in an effort to buy some time. "I told him everything. About the money, the embezzlement, the Mobile Hazard Assessment. Whatever you do to me will be a waste of your time. You can't kill everyone here."

"I'm a problem solver, Harper." Jason said. "The SEALs used me to clean up messes for them and so did Ellis. The man was a serial sinner. He thought admitting to a couple of affairs would clear his conscience, but the thing is, he never really stopped with any of it. He slept around, drank like a fucking fish. Who do you think cleaned him up and kept the media far enough away that they couldn't smell the liquor seeping from his pores? I managed to keep that ex-Ranger FBI idiot off my back, too. You wouldn't believe how easy it is to lull someone into a sense of comfort when you have similar backgrounds. All I had to do was share a few combat tales with good ol' Agent Davis and he looked the other way. I spent two years cleaning up after Ellis, and that money was supposed to be my bonus for a job well done. And just when we were close to a payday, that asshole has a change of heart?" Harper dug her heels into the asphalt roof, desperate to slow their progress. The edge was only ten feet away now, and she didn't like where this was going. "I knew when you ambushed us in that parking garage that he was going to spill it all to you. The timing couldn't have been worse. So I shot him. Kremer should have taken care of you at the museum. The guy can't shoot for shit, though. I guess if you want a job done right, you have to do it yourself. And once I get rid of you, I can get back on track to getting my goddamned money."

Harper guessed she could be thankful the fire marshal was a terrible shot, but it didn't do much to put her at ease right now.

"You don't think someone's going to hear the gunshot?" Harper's heart beat wildly in her chest and her vision darkened at the periphery. *Please, oh please don't let me pass out before he kills me.* "This isn't a very stealthy move, Jason."

"Like I said. The stress got to you. You felt guilty about the trouble you stirred up in an attempt to further your career. I tried to talk you out of it, but . . ." He paused and brought his face down to hers, his expression that of contrived concern "You jumped before I could stop you."

Oh, God. He was going to push her off the roof and watch as she fell to her death. Harper's chest constricted and she fought for a deep breath. She couldn't die like this, pitched off the roof by some crazy asshole after a few bucks.

"You'll be nothing more than another sad, sorry girl who threw herself off a roof. The media buzz will die down after a week or so. No one will care. No one will miss you. And my secrets will be safe and sound."

"My boss has Ellis's flash drive." Did Jason miss that tidbit? Was he even listening to her?

"That'll be easy enough to recover. I know some pretty powerful people, Harper, who'll be more than happy to lean on your boss and that idiot I clocked in your office for me. I'm not worried."

"I uploaded the story on the Ellis scandal to our website right before you walked into the conference room." The words spilled from Harper's mouth in a rush. "Your secrets will be national news by the end of the day."

Jason paused with mere feet separating Harper from a five-story drop to unyielding pavement. She was going to die. Her family would see her death sensationalized on every news channel in the country. The public would be convinced that she was some sort of fame-crazed lunatic who lied and concocted stories to get ahead. The fact that she'd been acting like a secretive fool, withholding evidence from the FBI, would only lend credence to Meader's interpretation of events. And Galen. Oh God. The thought of leaving him left a dark, gaping hole in her heart. She'd waited for him. Hoped and prayed for an entire year that she'd see him again. And now that they'd found each other, she'd never see him again. Never feel the heat of his skin against hers or shiver at the warm timbre of his voice in her ear.

She couldn't let her life end like this.

"You're lying," Jason said, his eyes searching hers for some hint of truth. "Ellis's files were password protected."

Harper took a shuddering breath. "Blake. Swan. Lake."

Jason brought his arm up, the gun clenched tightly in his fist. He swung at her and a white-hot pain exploded in Harper's skull as the back of his fist made contact with her face. She fell to her knees and stars swirled in her vision as her surroundings grew dark. Her cheek throbbed and she wanted to swipe at the warm trickle of blood that tickled her face. But she couldn't raise her arm higher than her waist. Dizzy and weak, she listed to one side and then the other. Two Jason Meaders hovered over her. *Gah.* As if one weren't bad enough. She'd pass out and he'd throw her off the roof while she was unconscious.

Good-bye, *Washington Post.* Good-bye, career. Good-bye, life she'd worked so hard for, family, friends, colleagues. Good-bye, delicious apple fritters and Voodoo Donut.

Good-bye, Galen.

The two Jasons leaned down and, as Harper's vision cleared, became one. He wrapped his left hand around her throat and hauled her up to stand, and then jabbed her in the ribs again with the gun. *Ouch.*

"You're a pain in my ass," he snarled as he forced her to the edge of the building. Harper fought as hard as she could, but she was still a little dazed and had a hard time holding her ground. Her feet slipped on the asphalt roof and she leaned in toward Jason, winding her fists into his shirt. If she was going over, she was taking him with her. "I can still discredit you, though. Once I get Ellis's flash drive back, your so-called story will be nothing but libel. Maybe I'll sue your paper and make a little extra cash on the side."

"Jason." Harper's voice was nothing more than a ragged whisper with his palm squeezing her throat. Air. She needed more air. He wouldn't really suffocate her before he threw her off the building, would he? What a sadistic son of a bitch. "Please. Don't."

"You shouldn't beg, Harper," Jason said as he released his grip on her throat to pry her fists from his shirt. She wasn't strong enough to fight him. "It's beneath you."

He pushed at her and she felt herself lean back. Harper peered over the edge of the building at the street below. Should she pray? Send one last positive burst of energy out into the universe before she died? Harper closed her eyes as she fought for a deep breath.

Please, God, don't let it hurt.

Chapter Twenty-Nine

Galen took the last set of stairs three at a time and burst through the door to the roof like a man possessed. Each second that passed was a second closer to Harper's death. Whoever had snatched her out of the conference room wasn't bringing her up here for a friendly chat, and he prayed that he could get to her before anything happened.

The haze of panicked rage that clouded Galen's vision cleared the instant he saw Harper leaning over the edge of the building. He recognized the asshole holding her by the throat as Senator Ellis's aide. His goddamned smug face had been plastered all over the news for weeks. Harper's right cheek was swollen, the skin split and bleeding, and Galen promised himself that this man would feel, tenfold, every injury he'd inflicted upon the woman he loved.

But he wouldn't get retribution without a clear head.

He'd been conditioned to keep his shit together in high-stress situations like this one. His SOG training hadn't mentioned anything about keeping it together when you were emotionally attached to the person you were supposed to protect, though. Logic warred with irrationality. Years of training dictated that he play it cool. Keep his distance. Do nothing to rile the suspect. The other part of him, the man who couldn't lose her, wanted to charge at the gunman and put a bullet through his chest.

"U.S. Marshals Service," Galen announced loud enough for the people down on the street to hear him. "Put the gun down and step away from Miss Allen."

The asshole had the nerve to chuckle. He turned to face Galen and wrapped his fist around Harper's throat. "You guys are the laughingstock of federal law enforcement, you know that? Special Agent Davis and I had a good laugh at your expense this morning. I mean, seriously, you practically let Harper parade herself around town with a target on her back. Not exactly the kind of spectacle you want from a high-profile witness. And bringing her here?" He shook his head. "Sorry, Marshal. But that was a bad call on your part."

Galen clamped his jaw shut so it wouldn't fall to his feet. If Monroe had known he and Harper were here, it wasn't a far stretch to think that Davis had known as well. And that dumb son of a bitch had let it slip to Ellis's murderer right where he could find Harper. The Marshals Service was a laughingstock? The FBI had them beat by miles.

"This place will be surrounded by police, FBI, and marshals in a matter of minutes. I suggest you opt for the easy way out and jump. But since I don't take you for a coward, you should give yourself up now and make this easier on everyone."

The guy had the nerve to smile at Galen. "You're right. I'm not a coward. And I'm not giving myself up, either. I've gotten out of worse scrapes than this before.

She'll be dead by the time anyone else shows up. You can join her if you want."

He had the sharp expression and calm demeanor of someone with a lot of experience in the field. If Galen had to guess, his money was on special forces. Trying to talk him out of whatever it was he had planned was out of the question. Guys like that didn't bargain. They picked a course of action and saw it through to the end, no matter what. Which made Harper's predicament that much worse. At least fifty feet separated them. He'd never make it to her before this asshole pushed her off the roof. And likewise, he could take a shot, but doing so put Harper at even greater risk. He could take them both over the edge or his finger might slip on the trigger and he'd shoot Harper anyway.

Fuck.

Galen felt Harper's eyes on him, but he refused to look at her. If he gave any indication that he was overly concerned for her—felt *anything* for her—the guy would only exploit their situation and expedite her death.

"I think we need to take a breather and reason this out, don't you?" Talking might buy him some time and every second was precious. "You might think you have the FBI in your back pocket, but they aren't the only game in town. Whether you kill Harper or not, you're going to be under a lot of scrutiny, and an investigation, no matter how small, is going to ruin any plans you have. Don't heap a murder charge onto your already very full plate."

"You know dick about my plate, so maybe you should lose your sidearm and shut the fuck up before I introduce Harper to the sidewalk."

True. Galen had told Harper that desperate men

had nothing to lose. This guy was different, though. He wanted her out of the picture because he was holding on to something, not because he'd let it all go. "I'm putting down my weapon." It went against every instinct to leave himself vulnerable, but he had to play to his opponent's arrogance. He set his Glock down beside his right foot.

"Kick it toward me."

Damn it. Galen extended his leg and nudged the gun several feet away. "I don't think I got your name. I'm Deputy Galen Kelly."

He smirked. "Jason Meader. Soon to be Senator Jason Meader. They really ought to keep you deputies up on current events, you know." Oh, yeah, this guy thought he was a big freaking deal.

Galen shrugged. "I've been in France."

Meader gave him a caustic look. "Charming."

Monroe couldn't be more than eight blocks away, and the Portland police and FBI wouldn't be much farther behind. Galen needed just a moment of distraction to redirect his attention. If he could get Harper clear of the danger, Meader would be easy to take down. This time he took a chance and let his eyes find Harper's. She'd been staring at him the entire time, and the fear reflected in the hazel orbs set off an explosion of rage inside of him. A tiny distraction. That's all he needed. Just a second or two. *Come on, Harper. You can do it.*

"I made a copy of Ellis's files." She spoke as if she'd read his mind. Her voice was a raspy whisper thanks to the grip Meader had on her throat. Galen was going to show him exactly how that felt soon enough. "If you kill me, you'll never find it."

Meader pressed the barrel of his gun into Harper's temple and a tear trailed down her cheek.

Her precarious position at the edge of the roof was the only thing keeping Galen from plowing into that son of a bitch. "Where is it?" Meader snarled next to Harper's ear.

Galen took a step forward and Meader swung the gun around and leveled it at his face. "Take another step, Deputy, and Harper's going to try her hand at flying."

Gun still trained on Galen, Meader turned his attention back to Harper. "Where. Is. It."

He squeezed her throat and between rasping breaths she squeaked, "In the mail. On its way to CNN." She twisted in his grip and brought her knee up and connected squarely with Meader's groin. He spun away, releasing Harper as he clutched at his nuts.

Galen focused his attention on Harper. She rubbed her neck and gasped for air. There was no time to take a break. She'd have to catch her breath later. "Harper, take cover!"

Harper stumbled as she ran toward a large air vent, because to be honest, she wasn't even trying to pay attention to where she was going. The sight of Galen charging toward Jason Meader made her heart catapult up into her throat. The sound of Meader's gun discharging echoed in her ears as he took a wild shot. Harper held her breath, relief cascading over her as she realized he'd missed his target. On the heels of relief came an undeniable sense of awe at the sheer maleness of Galen as he took Jason down in a football tackle that was so reminiscent of that first night they'd met. Galen Kelly was a freaking *god*.

They rolled around on the rooftop, a tangle of limbs as Galen threw several punches that connected bodily with Meader, while he fought to keep hold of the gun that had swung too close to Galen's head for comfort. All it would take was one wild shot and she'd lose him forever.

In the distance, the sound of sirens grew closer, and Harper breathed a sigh of relief through her raw and ragged throat. She didn't even try to swallow. A simple flick of her tongue was painful at this point. A scream built up in her chest, but it had nowhere to go. She wanted to call for help. To make sure that someone—anyone—knew they were up here. If anything happened to Galen, Meader wouldn't have to pitch her off the roof. She'd gladly jump because Harper knew she'd never be able to live with the guilt of knowing that her irresponsibility had caused the death of the man she loved.

The man she couldn't live without.

She'd underestimated Jason. Sized him up as nothing more than an overprivileged snake in the grass with more ambition than actual common sense. God, had she ever been wrong. He fought like he'd been conditioned and trained for it. Deflected Galen's punches as though he instinctively knew where each one would land. Got his own jabs in at the right moment, using the butt of his gun for leverage. And despite the fact that Jason could have given an MMA champion a run for his money, Galen held his ground and was actually gaining the upper hand.

From the corner of her eye, Harper noticed Galen's discarded gun. She rushed to where he'd kicked it away and picked it up, the heavy metal weighing down her hand. Was the safety off? Was it loaded? Could she even shoot it if she wanted to? She'd never used a handgun before. What if she screwed something up and managed to blow her own face off! To hell with it. She could bluff with the best of them. Whether or not she was a sharpshooter didn't matter.

"Stop!" Her vocal cords were on fire as the word tore from her throat. The two men didn't even break their stride, rolling and throwing punches as though she hadn't just shouted. Well, sort of shouted. Fine. She could do better than that. She pointed the gun away from anywhere that a stray bullet might hurt someone, closed her eyes tight, and squeezed the trigger. The report was instant, her arm flew backward with the recoil, and she lost her grip on the gun sending it soaring toward Galen and Jason. Her ears rang and she wondered if maybe she'd blown her eardrums. It didn't matter. She got the response she wanted.

The gunshot was enough of a distraction to break up the fight. Unfortunately, Jason still had possession of his weapon while Harper had foolishly sent hers flying. *Way to save the day, Harp.* Her breath stilled in her chest as Jason aimed his gun at Galen's chest. Time stopped. Her heart quit beating. Oh, God. She hadn't helped at all. She'd done nothing more than give Jason an opportunity to empty his gun into Galen's chest.

I killed him.

Jason pulled up to aim his weapon right as Galen rolled away in a maneuver that sent Harper's head to spinning. He looked like a character out of her favorite superhero movie as he positioned himself to land where Harper had dropped his gun. He scooped the weapon into his fist and fired off a shot without even taking the time to aim.

Like it mattered.

Galen was totally a superhero as far as Harper was concerned. The shot cracked in the silence, and

Jason's right arm went limp. A crimson stain spread over his shoulder and down his arm, blooming over his fancy white dress shirt like a rose under the summer sun. He looked down at the wound, disbelief marring his usually controlled expression. Galen kicked his discarded gun away and shoved him down on his face, not bothering to take care with his wounded shoulder as he produced a pair of handcuffs from his belt.

"You're under arrest for murder and conspiracy, asshole," Galen growled. "Oh, and for assaulting a federal officer. You have the right to remain silent . . ."

His voice faded to the back of Harper's mind as sensation returned to her limbs. She felt as though all the blood were rushing back to her brain in a single tidal wave and she became light-headed, the world tipping on its axis while she tried to hold her footing. The roof seemed to slip out from underneath her and she crumpled to her knees. Her pulse raced in her ears, a baseline to accompany the high-pitched ringing. She'd almost lost him today. Hell, she'd almost lost herself today.

"Harper?"

She looked up from what she assumed was a super attractive position—bent over with her head between her knees—to see Galen standing over her, his brow pinched with concern. His eyes searched hers and he cupped her elbow in his palm as though afraid to make too much contact. "How bad are you hurt? Harper? Talk to me."

The words came to her as though she was submerged underwater and Galen was on dry land shouting at her, but at least she wasn't deaf so she was counting it as a win. "I'm fine." Ugh. She hoped she wasn't shouting. "I'm just freaked out. *Really* freaked out."

His expression transformed from worry to relief in a second flat. He took her in his arms and held her so close that she wasn't sure where her body ended and his began. She pressed her palms into his chest, taking comfort in the strength of his presence, the steady thrum of his heartbeat. Her own personal hero had swooped in to save her butt. Not once, but three times. "I bet you're tired of getting me out of trouble," she murmured against his shirt. She inhaled deeply and held his scent in her lungs. She'd never get enough of that spicy, masculine smell.

"Never." He planted a kiss to the top of her head and squeezed her tight. "I can handle whatever you dish out, Harper. Bring it."

Laughter mingled with tears and she sniffed. "Believe me, I'm going the low-profile route from here on out. No more excitement for a while."

Galen led her toward the edge of the building, and she stole a glance at Jason, handcuffed to a metal rod near one of the roof vents. The bloody stain had spread down his arm, and his head was slumped, but it looked like he was going to live long enough to face the consequences of his actions. Good. He didn't deserve the easy way out. Maybe now that everything was out in the open, Ellis could, in death, have the clear conscience he'd wanted.

She peered over the building to see why Galen had brought her over. Below, the street was crowded with police cars, unmarked government vehicles, two ambulances, and several news vans. The scramble of activity was dizzying and Harper leaned against Galen for support.

"What were you saying about no excitement?" he said with a small laugh.

"Oh man, all of the local news stations are here!" She peered farther over the edge. "*Holy crap.* CNN is here!" Harper stifled a groan. "And MSNBC, and Fox News."

The door to the roof burst open, and a wave of federal and local law enforcement spilled out onto the roof. Curt Monroe led the charge, gun drawn and hyperalert. "You're going back to that hotel," he said, pointing an accusing finger at Harper. "And you"—he jabbed a finger at Galen—"aren't letting her out of your sight. Do you understand me? I'll get your statement later tonight."

Harper exchanged a look with Galen. It would be tough to endure, but they'd get through their time at the hotel somehow. "Yes, sir," Galen answered.

"We'll finish up with your suspect and get him into custody. There's a media circus forming down there all waiting to get a piece of Harper. I think you'd better go." If she didn't know better, Harper would have thought Curt was trying to keep them away from Agent Davis, who was fighting the crowd of cops as he made his way toward them. But of course, Curt would never do anything to thwart an FBI agent. She smiled at him and he gave her an exasperated look. "Well, get out of here!"

Harper didn't need to be told twice. She let Galen lead the way. She'd follow him anywhere.

Gladly.

Harper lay next to Galen, her body entwined with his. One hot shower and a full-body massage—followed by some erotic play—later and Harper was almost at one hundred percent. It was a wonder either of them had the energy for anything more than a sponge bath and a nap after what they'd been through. But Harper was learning very quickly that she'd have to be dead and buried before she ever got enough of Galen Kelly. Maybe not even then. His breath stirred the hairs at her temple and goose bumps sprung up on her skin. "That tickles."

He nuzzled below her ear, careful not to touch her bruised face. A paramedic had checked them both out when they got back to the hotel. She didn't need stitches for the cut on her cheek. She'd be sore for a few days, but thankfully nothing was broken.

"I'll go with you into the interview room tomorrow. I won't let Davis bully you again."

She wasn't exactly looking forward to another round with the arrogant FBI agent, but she wouldn't get Galen involved in it, either. "It's okay. Remember the attorney I spoke with a few days ago? She's going to go with me. Agent Davis won't get too lippy with a lawsuit hanging over his head."

"Either way, I'm here for you."

"I know you are," Harper replied through a yawn. "And I'm glad. Thank you." She wiggled in closer until her back was flush with the hard planes of his chest. The heat of his body was a soothing balm. One that Harper craved like a drug. He reached around and cupped her breast in his palm, his thumb feathering over her nipple, and Harper sucked in a sharp breath.

"I love you, Harper," he whispered in her ear. "I think I loved you from the second I laid eyes on you."

She reached around and cupped the back of his thigh as his hand left her breast and wandered down her body to the juncture between her legs. Her throat was still raw, but it didn't stop the low moan that escaped when he stroked her slick center. "I love you too," she said. "I love you more than I ever thought I could."

He rolled her over on her back and settled himself between her thighs. Their eyes met and the emotion that passed between them didn't need words to be expressed. He was her friend, her lover, her hero. Everything she ever wanted and more.

"*Je t'aime.*" The words slipped from Galen's lips as he entered her and Harper cried out, arching into him.

"What does that mean?" she breathed.

"It sounds better in French." He pulled out and thrust slowly in again. Teasing her, the way she liked.

"Tell me."

"It means, I love you."

She wrapped her legs around his waist as he thrust deep inside of her. Tomorrow they'd have to face reality once again. But tonight it was just her and him, and she wasn't about to waste a single second.

"It is pretty in French." She ground her hips against him. "But if you learn to say it in Klingon, that'll really be something."

He laughed before his mouth claimed hers in a hungry kiss. "I'll get on that first thing in the morning," he said as he pulled away.

"Or better yet," Harper teased, "Elvish. Like Tolkien."

"Harper," Galen murmured against her throat. "Be quiet."

She used her ankles to pull him deep inside of her. "I'm a reporter. It's in my nature to be wordy."

He rolled her on top of him and bucked his hips to thrust deeper. God, he was too good for words. "Did I ever tell you I have a thing for journalism majors?"

"I do recall something about that. But tell me again. And be thorough."

He rose up and flicked his tongue across her nipple. "Oh, if there's one thing I am," he murmured against her skin, "it's thorough."

Oh, man, did she ever love his attention to detail.

Keep reading for
an excerpt from the next book in
the U.S. Marshals series,

ONE KISS MORE,

coming in Winter, 2015
from
Mandy Baxter
and
Kensington Books!

Landon could think of a thousand things he'd rather be doing right now. Skydiving, BASE jumping, climbing to the top of Mount Hood would be nice. When did the running of the bulls begin, anyway? Law enforcement was supposed to be an exciting, adrenaline-infused career. Maybe he should have applied for the SOG program when he'd had a chance. Of course, knowing his luck, he'd get an assignment like his friend Galen had snagged: babysitter to some foreign dignitary for a year. Prestigious? Maybe. But Landon wasn't interested in recognition or prestige. He was in it for the action. Which was why, as he pulled up to the swanky Aspira building in downtown Seattle, he wished he was jumping out of a plane, thousands of feet from the ground. He hadn't felt an exhilarating rush of any kind for a long goddamned time. And just like any addict, he was itching for a fix.

He pulled his phone out of his pocket and dialed. After a few rings, Galen answered and the fucker had the nerve to sound upbeat. "Hey, man. Did you see me on *Piers Morgan* last night?"

Galen had recently come off a case that had landed

him not only in the media spotlight, but in bed with the woman he'd been assigned to protect. Lucky bastard. "Yeah. And you know what? It's true what they say about the camera adding ten pounds. You might want to think about hitting the gym."

"Jealous much?"

"Please," Landon scoffed. "I've got nothing to be jealous about. You go ahead and be the poster boy for the Marshals Service while the rest of us go out and get shit done."

Galen's laughter rumbled through the receiver. Playful hostility was what Landon appreciated most about their friendship. Galen deserved his accolades, though. He was damn good at his job. "Have you questioned Ruiz's daughter yet?"

The consummate professional, Galen would forgo the banter for work talk any day of the week and as always, Landon was on the same page. "On my way up to her condo now," he said as he flashed his badge to the parking attendant at the underground garage. He pulled the phone away from his ear long enough to get directions to the public parking and pulled through the levered gate. "I doubt she's going to be cooperative, though."

"Who's your contact there?"

Technically, the Ruiz case was in the Portland division's jurisdiction, but since Ruiz's daughter lived in Seattle, the investigation had become an inter-regional effort. "Ethan Morgan," Landon replied as he hit the key fob with his thumb and locked his black Chevy Tahoe. He pivoted on a heel as he searched out the elevators and found a bank of silver doors on the far left wall. "I'm meeting him at the office later, but I thought I'd get a jump on Emma first."

Galen was silent for a moment and Landon could

almost picture the shit-eating grin on his face. "Get a jump on her, huh?"

"Unlike you, I'm a professional," Landon remarked, as he stepped inside the elevator and hit the button for the fifteenth floor.

"Touché," Galen replied.

"Dude, the French," Landon said with a snort. "So not manly. Later."

Galen's answering laughter was the last thing Landon heard as he ended the call. For the past few days, he'd been staking out Emma Ruiz's building and tracking her every move in the hopes that she'd lead them to her father. But the only thing he'd learned so far in his time on this assignment was that the more things changed, the more they stayed the same. Emma was still a hardcore party girl. She still hung out with pro athletes and rich playboys and lived her life as publicly as she dared, as though she invited the media attention and gossipmongers while simultaneously not giving a shit about any of it.

The Ruiz case had been high profile six years ago when they'd conducted their investigation into the federal judge's dealings with Mendleson Corp. Once one of the country's shrewdest and most successful attorneys, Ruiz, the consummate legal hero who defended the little guy, had landed a federal judgeship in Oregon after retiring from a firm that dealt primarily in environmental safety and wrongful death suits. His judgeship had taken a nosedive when his dealings with Mendleson had been scrutinized. The U.S. Marshals had gotten involved after he'd dismissed what should have been an open-and-shut FTC trade violation case against the multinational corporation. Through an anonymous tip, the feds had been alerted that Ruiz was extorting money from Mendleson, and the CEO had admitted to paying the judge in exchange for a favorable ruling in their case.

Emma had been a staunch supporter of her father, declaring his innocence on several national news programs as well as *E! News* and *US Weekly*. A first-class celebutante, Emma was often categorized as famous for being famous, or whatever it was the gossip rags said about overprivileged daddy's girls like her. She had often been whispered about in the Portland office when they'd investigated Javier six years ago. At eighteen, she had already been on the road to stop-your-heart gorgeous and had a reputation for playing fast and loose with several pro athletes. She'd had a mouth on her, not to mention a penchant for fucking with anyone who fucked with her dad. During the course of the Marshals Service's investigation, she'd made it her life's ambition to cause any deputy involved in bringing dear old daddy down a world of hurt. Landon's team had been on the receiving end of several of her malicious pranks, including the old potato-in-the-tailpipe routine. That shit wasn't urban legend, and the blowback from the exhaust had damned near asphyxiated him. Not the best experience for a rookie on his first case.

Watching her over the past couple of weeks had stirred up all sorts of memories. One of those being the euphoric rush he experienced every time he laid eyes on her. Landon couldn't explain it. He wasn't usually the sort of guy who got twisted up at the sight of a pretty girl. But Emma was different. Her presence triggered something primal in his subconscious. And that instant, gut-clenching reaction bothered the shit out of him. So, yeah, he wasn't exactly enthused about paying a visit to the now twenty-four-year-old Emma, and grilling her about daddy's whereabouts while he tried not to fall under her spell yet again. Landon was certain that no matter what, Emma was going to give him a run for his money. Paybacks were a bitch.

Emma Ruiz hung up the phone and stared off into space as she tried to collect her thoughts. One of the benefits of living in a building with top-notch security was getting a heads-up from the front desk that a deputy U.S. Marshal was about to pay her a visit. Not that she hadn't been expecting it.

She cast a furtive glance toward her closed bedroom door as a riot of butterflies took flight in her stomach and fluttered toward her throat. Everything was happening so fast and she needed to play her A-game right now. The key to a good offense was a strong defense. Any sports fan worth her salt realized that. And Emma knew that if she wanted the ball to be in her court with the Marshals Service, she needed to make sure they were off their game. She looked down the length of her purple tank top, black yoga pants, and bare feet. Not exactly an outfit that screamed *I'm in charge!* And whereas she'd hoped never to go toe to toe with those self-righteous do-gooders again, she guessed she'd just have to suck it up and face the music. At least the next few weeks wouldn't be boring.

When the doorbell rang a few minutes later, Emma took a deep breath and held it in her lungs before expelling it all in a rush. The cops weren't as scary as they liked to come off. Emma wasn't easily intimidated, and besides, she'd done this dance with them six years ago. If she could handle their pushy bullshit then, she could certainly handle it now. She could do this.

A round of obnoxious knocks followed on the

heels of the bell, and Emma rolled her eyes as she walked to the door. God forbid she keeps the U.S. Marshals waiting. After all, they had a dangerous criminal to find and apprehend. She snorted. They were all a bunch of idiots if they thought that Javier Ruiz was a criminal mastermind. They were all so ready to believe he'd orchestrated the perfect escape and were itching to get one up on him. And of course, none of them knew how far off base they were.

Emma plastered what she hoped was a pleasant smile on her face to mask the apprehension creeping up on her and swung the door open. The smile faded in an instant and her stomach did a twisting backflip that kicked out at her lungs on the dismount, leaving her breathless and a little stunned. *Great.* They would send the guy who'd arrested her dad in the first place, wouldn't they? The one guy who'd get under her skin. Emma clenched her fists at her sides as she wondered how much time she'd get for socking a U.S. Marshal in the jaw.

"Deputy McCabe," she said, infusing her voice with innocence. "What a surprise. By all means, *don't* come in."

The bastard had the nerve to smirk.

"Obviously you know why I'm here," McCabe said. "So tell me where Javier is and I'll be on my way."

Emma relaxed against the doorknob, shifting her weight so that her braced arm supported her. It took a lot of effort to look so calm while her knuckles turned white as her fingers clenched the knob. Coming face-to-face with Landon McCabe again was like stepping back into time. He was technically the enemy, but even after all this time Emma couldn't deny his appeal. His voice tumbled over her like a cascade of warm water, relaxing the tight knot that had settled in her chest. His blond hair was almost too short, but Emma was willing to bet she could still tangle her fingers in its length. And his eyes . . . keen and bright blue with a warm spark that ignited something low in her stomach. Her brow puckered as she realized his presence had become even more commanding, his face even more handsome with the passage of years. Totally not fair.

"Why ask me?" She made sure her voice was devoid of any emotion. "When Dad was remanded into the *care* of the U.S. government, I was sort of under the impression that you'd be keeping an eye on him. It's not my fault you guys suck at your jobs."

"Come on, Emma. I'm not in the mood to play games."

Emma saw an opportunity not only to intercept Deputy McCabe's innuendo, but to deflect his questioning with her own distraction while she ran in for the touchdown. "That's too bad, Deputy. I love to play. Maybe later? You can be shirts and I'll be skins."

McCabe's jaw tensed, and it gave Emma a perverse sense of satisfaction to have rattled the cocky deputy's chain. The quicker she could get him out of here, the better.

"Don't say I didn't try to make this easy on you." His voice hardened and lowered an octave, causing a pleasant chill to race down Emma's spine. "You'd better clear your schedule for the rest of the day, *Miss* Ruiz. A pair of deputies will be along in an hour or so to escort you to the federal building for questioning."

Yeah, well, Emma could be hard, too. "What's the matter, McCabe? Not man enough to cuff me yourself?"

He took a step back from her doorway as though tempted to do just that. He looked down the length of her body, and though she assumed it was meant to be disdainful, a thrill rushed through Emma's veins. "Just be ready to cooperate," he said. "Otherwise, I won't hesitate to issue a warrant for your arrest."

Without allowing her to respond, McCabe turned on a heel and sauntered down the hallway toward the elevator. Emma couldn't help it, she leaned out of the doorway to watch him leave, appreciative of the way his designer jeans hugged his ass. Boy was tight. His shoulders rolled as he walked, the precision and grace of every placed step a thing of beauty. Deputy U.S. Marshal Landon McCabe was still the enemy. He was the one who'd arrested her father and the man who was looking to do it again. But, damn, was he ever something to look at.

"That wasn't so hard, was it?"

Emma bristled at the sound of the voice behind her. A chill that was nothing like what she felt in Landon's presence chased over her skin and she rubbed at her arms to banish the goose bumps that rose up there. "I told you, you have nothing to worry about."

"Oh, I know, *chica*. I only wanted to be sure you could play your part. Now that I know you can, I'll leave you alone. For now."

Emma tried to slow the racing of her heart with a few deep breaths. All of this was her fault. If she'd stayed out of trouble like her dad asked her to, he'd be okay and getting the care he needed right now. "I know what's expected of me," Emma said, still refusing to turn and face the man speaking to her. She just wanted him to get the hell out of her condo.

"Good. That's good." His low voice snaked around her, dark and dangerous, squeezing the air from her lungs. "I'll be in touch."

Emma closed her eyes as he walked past her through the door. His body brushed against hers and she cringed as she inched away. She waited until the sounds of his footsteps disappeared down the hallway before she closed the door with shaking hands. Her mind raced as adrenaline seeped into her bloodstream, making it difficult to focus. Landon McCabe's appearance in Seattle was going to be a problem. And she hoped that his interference in her life wouldn't get him killed.